I0618963

RIJEL 12

THE RISE OF NEW AUSTRALIA

King Everett Medlin

chandra

ISBN: 9781949964042
www.chandrapress.com
www.facebook.com/officialchandrapress

King Everett Medlin

CONTENTS

ACKNOWLEDGEMENTS

First off, my wife Caroline, who inspires me every day to pursue this crazy dream of being a writer.

The team at Chandra Press, specifically Erik Evans. Thank you for giving me my big break after years of rejection.

My stepfather Herb Whittall for taking the time to critique the scientific aspects of the book, such as long-distance space travel.

Miguel Alcubierre, scientist and Star Trek fan, who developed the theory of ADM technology, also known as Alcubierre Warp Drive.

My daughter Candace for patiently listening to me reading sample chapters to her while sitting with me at a diner in Denver.

My son King Avery for always introducing me to his friends saying, "This is my Dad... he's an author."

And most of all, my mother Nancy for hearing my weekly updates over the phone the past few years; always believing in me whether I did or not.

King Everett Medlin

CHAPTER 1: INTERGALACTIC PENAL COLONY

The President of the Assembly, an aged and respected Suidonji named Abrafrilric, suddenly stood up and cleared his throat. The murmuring inside the gigantic hall swelled into that kind of roar that comes as a result of hundreds of people making discreet and not so discreet comments to the neighbors seated next to them.

Pig-like, rotund, and gruff just like most full-grown Suidonji, Abrafrilric's throat-clearing was like a snarling, snorting, gurgling growl, but even this had little effect on the mass of beings crowded inside the convention hall. It was a gigantic building, spanning a quarter mile square, located near the supreme government building in the planetary capital of Suidonj. The interior was a cavernous facility made of stone walls, stone floor, and a remarkably high ceiling. It was lit only by lamps and chandeliers suspended from the vast wood-beamed ceiling above. Suidonji didn't really need or even like bright lights. Their extremely sensitive snouts directed their movements more than their eyesight; their floppy ears carried out the rest. But their buildings and rooms were extremely large. Large beings as they were, they liked having lots of space to move around.

There would still be a few moments of tense murmuring within the crowd before he'd be able to regain control. Abrafrilric could already tell this would take a while. It usually did. So, he stood and waited patiently for the tumult to subside. No use in trying to regain order—that would be like interrupting ancient earth pigs at a feeding trough, back in more barbaric times when swine were bred for slaughter. But on Suidonj, the evolutionary process that led from tiny rodents to wild boars and then on to pigs continued to advance that life form into a bipedal sophisticated being, which grew to dominate other species on its planet. Suidonji learned to stand, to walk, to communicate, and to develop higher technologies over the millennia.

Abrafrilric was the duly-elected leader of this year's meeting, honoring a tradition that had gone back over seventy galactic years, the equivalent of three hundred one earth years. The Interplanetary Convention had been held every galactic year since the Peace Treaty of Slartigifij, which ended the war between planets Zorgolong and Enosh. This first convention was conducted by the very wise and gentle Slartigifijian planet elders and was held to establish terms for peace between those two bitter long-time rivals. After that, the event was moved annually from one planet to another, to promote fairness and balance in decision-making. Tradition held that the host planet would choose its own President for the annual convention. This particular galactic year, comprising four point three earth years, the convention was held on planet Suidonj.

Abrafrilric gripped and lifted his gavel, but the murmuring still rose. No one heeded his gesture – determined gavel-grabbing somehow didn't seem to draw their attention. He even thought for a moment about raising his hoof to calm them. Suidonji had hoof-like claws that could grip much like a human's thumb and fingers. The difference was that their grip was incredibly strong, as were their bodies.

The audience was made up of ministers and delegations from all six planets of the Interplanetary Authority, as well as their colonies and their satellites. This throng of advanced beings dealt with issues affecting free and open trade, as well as threats to the health and welfare of the galaxy's billions of citizens. Today, the proposal being presented to the thousand-odd life forms in attendance was very nearly as controversial as it was ingenious: the creation of an Intergalactic Penal Colony for violent criminals.

It all started with a proposal that originated from the Earth delegation regarding prison over-crowding and the "practical treatment of inmates." Murmuring had begun just a few minutes before, after Abrafrilric had announced that debate would soon begin on the measure. Behind him a giant screen, the size of a soccer field, was activated and switched from its usual static image of the Interplanetary Authority logo, to an electronic banner which read: NEW AUSTRALIA PLANETARY PRISON. Then it began scrolling down and detailing in Galactic exactly what the proposal included. On smaller computer screens located inside each planet delegation box, the same information was being conveyed in that species' native language as well. However, most of the creatures in the audience were highly educated, preferring to read and speak in Galactic. As the audience read along, the murmuring rose higher and higher as more details were revealed.

What the Earthmen suggested was to develop a global penal colony on a barren planet located inside a distant star system. As the Earthmen explained it, the twelfth planet in the Rijel system already had a small mining operation, located far below the surface. What they desperately needed was labor, and below the forbidding planet surface, it would be easy to support a population of forced labor with the planet's already available supply of subterranean aquifers. Less than a mile below the surface it was quite easy to dig wells inside the planet's infinite cavern system, they claimed.

The commercial mine could simply be purchased, it was further proposed. The current staff and administration of the mine could be retained, and all the Interplanetary Authority needed to do was create a prison to supply the mine with workers. Existing labor there could continue to be employed as supervisors and foremen. "The whole thing will come together quite easily," they boldly professed. That's when the derisive comments began to fly, then grow in intensity.

"*Sss-simple!*" scoffed one of the members of the Zorgolongian delegation, causing the others in his section to emit hissing snickers. It was just like everything else proposed by those slippery Earthmen, and therein lay the irony: almost nothing about Earthers and their so-called "ethics" or basic "logic" was in any way simple.

The underlying issue lay in Earth's long-standing reputation for deception and ulterior motives when it came to intergalactic politics. They always seemed to be justifying their policies or actions by claiming it was necessary for the greater good; oblivious to how it might negatively affect other planets or the natural order of things. Other delegations could readily assume those crafty devils were trying to devise some scheme to either rid their own planet of a problem, or perhaps to make a lot of money. Then again, it might be a combination of both. It was always like that with those shifty Earthmen. Their "logic" as they called it, always seemed to rationalize away most anything resembling morality or common sense much like a fresh coat of paint being used to cover up rusted metal.

As the famously wise Slartigifijian planet elder Sektarpuldifleej once put it, "They aspire to greatness which they cannot truly achieve, so they espouse noble ideals which are quite beyond their capacity." Another way of putting it might have been that Earthers, "humans" as they called themselves, were compelled to accomplish more than their natural abilities could accommodate. So, they would typically embellish, boast, and exaggerate. They would very often portray an image of what something could be, rather than what it would become. They would make unrealistic projections, then decry and chastise the failure of those involved in its implementation. The human way of developing and managing an operation was typically to set goals which were technically unachievable, then blame everyone but the planners themselves for not reaching them.

Certainly, all planets had the occasional violent criminal who was beyond reform. But most had a more black and white view of the treatment of antisocial behavior. On Enosh for instance, they followed a very simple code when it came to errant acts. These cat-like creatures believed that an offender should have the capability of repeating the offense removed from their person, so they could continue their contribution to the greater good of society without being able to commit the same offence. A rapist? Castrated, no questions asked. A thief? Severed paw or paws, depending on what was stolen. A liar or blasphemer? Tongue removed. All Enoshi grew up knowing the consequences of their actions, so it was also known that if an adult committed the act, it could only mean they'd made the choice to violate the law and deserved punishment.

The difference with humans was that they could lie – and do so quite skillfully. That was what made them so confusing to other beings in the galaxy. Just what were they up to this time? An intergalactic penal colony where the galaxy's violent criminals could be disposed of? The different species in attendance hastily weighed in with their opinions.

"That is immoral," stated the Slartigifijians. "If Earth needs to house and reform its criminal element, then they should do so with better prison systems and larger facilities which might reeducate their inmates and reintroduce them into peaceful, law-abiding society."

By way of comparison, the short and lizard-like Zorgolongians assumed that the Earthmen were merely looking to capitalize on the untapped potential of the twelfth planet's mineral resources by using "free labor." Of course, they should have thought of it themselves, frankly, but it was far too late now, and that frustrated them more than anything else. Hence, the sarcastic sniggering and sniping barbs being hurled from their section of the convention hall. "Don't be naïve, my friend," remarked the Zorg delegation leader, "I'm sure they know exactly what they're doing."

As for the diminutive rodent-like Schpleefti delegation, they simply sat in confusion. For them it was difficult to understand the concept of institutionalizing the processing of criminals. Polyamorous by nature, this rodent-like species functioned on the sheer whim of emotional inspiration, for the most part. Violent criminals were merely banished from their communities. Nevertheless, they thought the Earthmen's proposal was a refreshing idea. What's more, they wanted to make sure they got an even cut of the profits. A global mining operation, like the Earthmen were suggesting? That could be quite lucrative, and the leaders within their delegation fully realized the implications.

Such was the hullabaloo over the Earth delegation's proposal, that Abrafrilric needed to just stand there and let everyone argue from their delegate boxes until all had spoken their minds. It always worked out better that way, letting the delegates fight it out for hours on end, occasionally summarizing points repeatedly made until everyone had heard all angles and every side of the issue. It was important that delegations understood potential consequences of Interplanetary Authority policy, and that they avoid rushing into hasty acts or decisions which might adversely affect one another in the future. That's partly why these conventions were only held every galactic year, because the debate sessions could last for hours, sometimes days.

Yet, Abrafrilric could let this debate last for only so long before he had to step in and get back in control of things. That was also his job as president. Eventually, it would become time to vote; to pass this measure would require only a simple majority. Four delegation votes and the Earthmen would have their prison, plus the full cooperation and financial backing of the Interplanetary Authority. There were only six planets, so the likelihood of requiring a deciding vote from Abrafrilric was minimal at best.

Debate raged on of course, but those sly Earthmen knew exactly how to sell it. As the Earth delegation minister put it, "Prisoners will only be sent there to serve their sentences, work hard to achieve production goals, in exchange for housing and food. Hard work and the removal of opportunities for criminal behavior will give errant beings the best chance for reform. They can be returned to their societies renewed, cured of their criminal urges once and for all." It wasn't long before that bold statement drew a reaction as well.

"Typical Earthmen," scoffed the Zorgolongian minister, standing up from his delegation box, "always exaggerating things." This drew an indignant snort from Convention President Abrafrilric; nevertheless, he chose not to interrupt. The delegation leader continued, "Cured once and for all? My good Earthman, that's preposterous-sss! The reason they're criminals in the first place is that they cannot control their urges! Do you think we're idiots-sss?"

But the Earth delegation minister, one Robert Gunton from the province of North America, was unflappable. He rebutted, "My dear fellow, I hasten to point out that the natural deterrent to further criminal behavior shall be the planet itself. You must understand that. No one will want to be sentenced there, and absolutely no one would wish to be sent back there either." The Earth minister glanced at his Zorgolongian counterpart to see if he had any further comments, but the little fellow—at least for the moment—did not. Thus, he continued, "They shall repay their debt to society for committing crimes, return home, and live out the rest of their lives on their home planets as good citizens." That's all the minister from Earth was proposing and this served to quell any further interruptions for a while. He knew he held all the cards and what he started hearing from other delegates only served to support this belief.

"My fellow delegates," remarked the minister from the Schpleefti delegation, "let's not miss out on this wondrous opportunity. If the Interplanetary Authority does not approve of this scheme, then we must consider what might happen next. Earth will simply develop the mine on Rijel 12 by herself and cut us out of the deal completely." This made sense, even to the brooding, warrior-like Enoshi who due to their imposing size always seemed to garner cautious respect from other species at these gatherings – even if they weren't particularly bright.

What's more, he was quite right, the furry little creature from far away Schpleefti. Earth would make a veritable fortune and hold a virtual monopoly on mineral distribution throughout the galaxy. Minister Gunton from Earth sensed it was time to close the sale.

The Earth minister's message, once it was his turn to speak again, was simply this: "If all planets participate this, my friends, will become a global operation with the funding to build Rijel 12's mining network into an economic success. And do it rather quickly according to our projections." He then feigned a bit of well-timed humility in order to suck them in further. But it really wasn't necessary; it went without saying.

"Of course, Earth could do this all by herself, but the Rijel system is many light years away from us. Several planets, as you may note, are closer. Much closer."

The Suidonji and Zorgolongian delegations immediately reacted to that obvious fact. So much nearer to the Rijel star system, they could easily reach Rijel 12 and develop it. But alas, it was Earth's idea and they'd be wiser to participate in the new plan. Earth, as everyone knew, had all the best technology for deep shaft mining.

Only the wise and sedate Slartigifijians held fast to their argument against this shameful idea of forcing prisoners into what they deemed to be slave labor for the sake of profit. Their contention was that it would only lead to abuse and oppression over time. Nevertheless, when Abrafrilric held the final vote on the measure it was approved five to one. And with that, the intergalactic penal colony of New Australia was created.

CHAPTER 2: LIFE ON RIJEL 12

Over the years, the penal colony expanded. Certainly, in the early days it was slow going. The planet's surface was impossibly forbidding. Nevertheless, within a half century, the population grew and grew, from a couple hundred to over a hundred thousand. The different planets in the galaxy, even cultures which were hesitant about it at first, found they could send convicted felons of all kinds. Murderers, rapists, thieves, political agitators, and other social undesirables could be delivered to this facility and thereby rid their home planets of the dangers they posed. But it didn't take long for things to degenerate into something far more sinister.

At first the sentences were reasonable, spanning three to twenty years, with only extremely violent offenders sentenced there for life. The planet itself was completely barren and devoid of any flora and fauna, covered on the surface by global deserts, volcanic mountains, and extremely forbidding temperatures during the day. At night, temperatures often plunged into the teens, but during the day it could reach one hundred fifty degrees Fahrenheit. It was certainly unrealistic to live on the surface, but far underground, the planet had massive caverns that extended for miles and miles in every direction.

On Rijel 12, there was just enough atmosphere to provide

breathable oxygen for most creatures, but the Interplanetary Authority chose to expand the already existing system for manufacturing purer oxygen for the caverns, so that workers could maintain better stamina. The planet's oxygen was too thin and could lead to light-headedness and fatigue during prolonged exposure. Therefore, the mining operation was sealed off from the surface and the oxygen production system could be added onto in phases. Blowers moved manufactured air around the caverns and tunnels to keep workers healthier and more alert.

The Rijel 12 planet interior had hundreds of underground glaciers located miles below the rocky barren surface, protected from the incredibly hot daytime sun. Subterranean aquifers closer to the surface provided water to the new inhabitants, but it had to be filtered. The original miners, years before, didn't actually drink the water from the aquifers. They imported purified water from nearby planets, and it was very expensive to do so. However, scientists believed the water on Rijel 12 could be made safe for prisoners to drink. Earth advisors devised an elaborate filtration system that extracted water into great reservoirs then filtered it into drinking water at hundreds of stations throughout the mining network.

Technically it was fine, but not surprisingly, those human engineers designed a system that needed to be maintained at a hefty cost, a cost that less ethical prison operators didn't prefer to continue paying as time went on. Systems deteriorated over time and needed repair. Mine operators looked the other way, and gradually prisoners suffered from consuming bad drinking water.

They had no choice. Besides, these same prison managers were making money for their employers. Profitability was being reviewed constantly, and no one felt inclined to speak out about the deteriorating conditions for prisoners. Better water could be imported for the guards and operation managers, so why worry about those hapless prisoners being slowly poisoned below? More prisoners arrived all the time to replace the ill and dying. It didn't really matter to those cynical, over-worked, profit-driven mining operators, always under pressure from their superiors to achieve lofty goals.

In only a few earth years, the prison complex was constructed a mile below the treacherous surface, and then expanded over the decades to where it housed thousands of prisoners. Earth ships arrived regularly, and construction workers in the early years worked feverishly to create more barracks below ground.

New facilities were built to house the ever-expanding prison labor supply. When a new cavern was opened up, these laborers would build a prefabricated barracks and live in it while they built the infrastructure around it. The air system would be connected to new parts of the mine, and new water filtration systems would be installed then tapped into underground aquifers. When each new section was complete, the construction teams would leave; the barracks they lived in would then be occupied by new prisoners sent there to work the newly opened section. For years it went on like that, ever-expanding the mining network as more and more convicts arrived.

However, these barracks would soon become overcrowded as more prisoners were sent to work there, and over the years they became dilapidated. As the decades passed, prisoners eventually resorted to carving out homes inside caves.

Additional mineral deposits were discovered. Veins of gemstones were found too. It seemed the opportunities for wealth being extracted from Rijel 12 were boundless; this only served to fuel the machine. Mine expansion required additional labor, and every planet was soon being urged to keep sending more convicted criminals. It became all too easy for abuses to occur. New prisoners being brought in meant even more barracks and even more supplies. Expanding the mines required more equipment, which led to more expenses and even more aggressive production goals. This would have been the case for any rapidly growing labor-intensive industry. But in the case of New Australia Planetary Prison, the difference was that labor was free.

Things eventually got overlooked, neglected, or downright ignored. Greed replaced compassion or even any semblance of justice, and everyone gave in just a little, if not completely. The greater good became nothing more than the motivation of greater profit, and from the top down, no one wanted to admit it. When existing veins of minerals were expanded and dug out further, even more workers were needed to fill the workload, as well as replace the dying and ruined laborers below. New Australia Planetary Prison became a death sentence to most all prisoners sent there, and within fifty earth years, few expected to return.

"So, how long you boys in for?" asked a rather portly guard assigned to oversee prisoners being led into the dusty hold of a large ship orbiting the Earth's moon. Francois had spent three weeks inside a stinking pit, a lunar prison ward designed to temporarily house a thousand men awaiting transportation to Rijel 12. However, the weeks of waiting as well as the ongoing flow of convicts into the facility had led to overcrowding of epic proportions. There were easily ten times that many crammed inside. Beds stacked six high required ladders to reach the top bunk and were arranged in rows so narrow even a submariner would find them cramped. Sewage backup and sickness from poor food made the untenable situation impossible to stand, yet they had no alternative. That's why arrival of the prison transport felt like a godsend.

The size of the ship dwarfed even tall buildings, and it was outfitted with advanced warp drive technology, which enabled it to travel at twenty times the speed of light via the creation of a warp bubble in space that allowed the craft to ride the wave to its intended destination. This theoretical phenomenon had been proposed centuries before back on Earth by a bright young scientist from Mexico City.

With a target programmed into the ship's computer, the now-perfected mechanism simply propelled it across the warp bubble, allowing passengers to move through time and experience very little in the way of aging. The ship could not be steered, didn't have to be maneuvered or even controlled for that matter. Using the warp drive, the ship simply appeared in its desired location months later with the onboard computer having calculated the entire journey and executed it systematically.

For security reasons, prisoners were placed in lidded compartments where they'd be put to sleep until the time of arrival. The mines needed healthy strong bodies, and the limited staff on board could not be tasked with supervising them during the months they'd spend in space. That was far too dangerous.

"Three years," replied one of the prisoners, and in response the guard snickered. "Three years, huh? Well, that's not so bad I guess. You can make it three years I'm sure." Then he chuckled cryptically. Others within the crowd of prisoners weren't so tactful.

"Oh, don't bet on it, pal," remarked an older fellow among the mass of men being herded into the ship's hold. "You might make it through," quipped the burly man. "Might not. Hard to say. But don't go fooling yourself about no getting home to your momma. Ain't nobody coming back to get you when you're done with your stint."

The guard shot an icy glare toward the fellow, then shook his head. Yes, he'd heard the same things, and yes, he'd experienced similar realities during his last three junkets to Rijel 12. For only half the ship's hold was filled with prisoner compartments. The rest was full of supplies, food for the prison staff mainly. And the entire hold was destined to be refilled with tons and tons of extracted mineral ore, such as platinum, nickel, copper, or iron.

Even the prisoner compartments themselves, those not covered up under mountains of raw material during the return voyage, would be occupied largely by the crew. He himself would occupy one of them for the long flight back to Earth, only to reload more doomed souls for the next trip across the galaxy. New Australia Planetary Prison and its thriving mining operation had by now expanded into a diabolically efficient, decades-old, going concern.

Prisoner processing and assignment to work details were handled below the surface. Rijel 12's original mining operation was established on the site of a canyon formed from the collapse of an ancient cavern. A surface facility was built next to it; the canyon was eventually converted into a loading bay for supply ships. It used a landing pad lift which elevated to the surface to receive arriving spacecraft. Once landed, the elevator descended several hundred feet to be processed. Then a retractable roof closed over the canyon to seal it off from the forbidding elements of Rijel 12.

New prisoners would be unloaded and assigned to some part of the mines that required more workers, randomly at first, then gradually based on species. There were always new job openings, and there were always more prisoner ships landing. When transport ships were emptied of prisoners, the other side of the bay would open, and vehicles would haul in loads of mineral ore to be loaded onto the craft. Upon completion, the retractable roof would open, the elevator platform would ascend back to the surface, and the craft could take off once again.

By the fiftieth Earth year of operation, there was a freighter landing every few weeks, and usually there was another in orbit around Rijel 12 waiting to land and offload new prisoners. Pilots and crew were never allowed to leave their ships, and most didn't wish to. This was a prison after all, and security was air-tight at all times. But what did these pilots and crew see when they landed? It was enough to send the message back to their home planets that this was a truly hellish place. They didn't need to see what was going on below. Construction workers finishing their projects could shed even more light on the realities of New Australia Planetary Prison, but even they didn't care about inmates in a prison. They just wanted to leave Rijel 12 and get back home as quickly as possible.

With all the financial backing of the Interplanetary Authority, those enterprising Earthmen were brutally efficient in devising a prison system that continued to feed the mining operation, and production goal-setting became increasingly aggressive as the years passed. Government officials began to see dollar signs. Profitability increased, and the operation was a success within only a few galactic years. Everyone was thrilled with the results.

Well, most everyone was, anyway. Prisoners in the early years were immediately pressed into service working in the mines until they completed their sentences, and just like the Earthmen had promised, these prisoners who'd paid their debt to society were able to crawl or limp onto freighters and eventually returned to their home planets. They'd be aged and broken down by then, but at least they could finally go home. Go home and die at a very young age and in terribly poor health, that is. It was hard to feel sorry for them. After all, most had certainly deserved to be sent there. Law-abiding citizens could rationalize it that way. But it was nevertheless shameful, treating other intelligent beings in such a manner. And it was a reflection on the societies themselves who allowed it to go on like that.

Then it got even worse. Eventually the planets stopped going back to get their prisoners. It became an embarrassment really, seeing a released prisoner all haggard and crippled, withered and squinting from daylight which they hadn't seen in many years. They'd return to their home planets almost unrecognizable to their loved ones.

The Slartigifijians were the first of the six planets to stop sending prisoners to New Australia Planetary Prison, protesting that conditions there would have to improve before they'd resume. After nine earth years, they ceased transports of criminals entirely, but they left thousands behind to finish out their miserable lives and chose to forget about the whole nasty experiment.

Enosh threatened to do the same, but eventually relented. Enoshi were very strong and capable of bearing up to the rigors of the workload. Plus, the Enosh government couldn't bear to miss out on their share of the profits from the mine. The other planets, by way of comparison, kept right on going. They began seeing it the way Earthmen portrayed it from the very start.

"Violent criminals and repeat offenders need to be removed from a society for the greater good of their communities, and once they've repaid their debt, only then may they return to their home planets," is how the Earth delegation put it each galactic year at the Convention. Yet this commitment to "reforming" criminals gradually faded into a distant memory when governments felt the backlash of social revulsion over the results of even a three-year sentence. Frankly it was the lure of incredible wealth and the expansion of their planetary economies that caused them to temper their protests. Soon they stopped protesting completely.

Most grew to look at it the same way as the Earthmen. At the conventions, the Earth delegation would delight in reporting production numbers and exaggerate the vast improvement in social order: "We're shipping out mineral ore, and shipping in our criminals and ne'er-do-wells to work the mines. It's still a win-win."

Crime didn't stop, nor did crime rates fall. Beings still murdered, stole, raped, or conspired against the government. Yet it didn't matter. It only fed the machine. The justice systems didn't have to worry about prisoner reform. Murder another being on your planet, and you got sent away for life. It made perfect sense at first. But eventually even first-time offenders were being dragged onto transport vessels headed for Rijel 12 to serve "minor sentences." Within fifty Earth years, even they would never return. No one went back to get them.

Initially, much like any poorly thought-out social experiment, the stated intent turned out to be unachievable. From the start, the promise was to respect the concept of a set prison sentence and to return the convict to society upon its completion. Greed got in the way of that. But, so did the fear of political repercussions at home when freed prisoners returned and spoke of the conditions at New Australia Planetary Prison. Earth and Zorgolong were the first two planets to stop returning their prisoners. Schpleefti never did in the first place. In their world, a Schpleefti who'd severely broken the law was banished from their community. For them it was just plain common sense. Threaten the peace and tranquility of society, and you lose the privilege of living within it.

The Enoshi followed suit. Given time, they began to see how it fit in with the philosophy of their culture. Removing the capability of repeating the crime by severing a paw, castrating, or removing a tongue meant that the example was set for all those tempted to duplicate the act. But this was even easier. Just send them away to Rijel 12 and the problem was solved.

For Slartigifijian prisoners it was different though. Most couldn't handle the conditions in New Australia and perished within a few years. However, not all of them died. Their innate intelligence and wisdom became highly valuable to other prisoners and some lived on to serve vital roles in prison society. Besides, Slartifigians had much longer life-spans than humans. This became very important later on, for the sake of the other inmates' survival.

The hard life of mining killed off thousands of prisoners every year, and there was no predictable pattern to it. Stronger prisoners died in the mines just as easily as weaker prisoners. Determination to survive, or resentment at having been sent to this subterranean hell, could certainly sustain a being for a while, but accidents were quite common. Death could come easily, and at most any time. Prison administrators didn't care. They didn't have to. In another few weeks, there'd be a ship arriving with more prisoners anyway. Life deteriorated into a matter of brutal survival for the desperate beings on Rijel 12.

After half an Earth century of dumping unfortunate prisoners on the planet, the place had become a death sentence, and everyone knew it. Inmates would tell newly arrived prisoners, and even prison officials communicated the same message. As one infamously cruel guard used to put it to arriving convicts as they were processed in the receiving bay, "You have been sent here to die, and that is likely what you'll do. Accept it, and your miserable existence here may end peacefully. Who knows? You may die tomorrow. We don't know, and we don't care. Work and you eat. Eat and you live. That's all you need to know for now."

And yet fifty Earth years after its creation, even when faced with such an impossible existence, amazingly, some beings learned how to survive. They adapted, and they overcame by creating a society of their own. Leaders arose, structure developed, and the situation stabilized, partly driven by necessity and partly due to the sheer determination of intelligent creatures seeking to exist, no matter what the circumstances. They figured out ways to live on.

Chapter 3: Crystal Discovery

"Nebelung? Hey, Nebelung! Break is over, brother. We must get back to work now." yelled one of the other prisoners. In a daze, Golan Nebelung snapped out of his temporary solace. He had been dreaming of his wife and little ones back home, and in the twenty minutes it had taken for equipment to be moved in for his crew to continue work on the new tunnel, he'd fallen into a deep sleep.

Exhaustion was a foregone conclusion, as he'd come to learn. Covered in fur from head to toe, he, just like his fellow Enoshi, didn't need nor wear any form of clothing, and in the cool, damp confines of the mine, his thick gray coat was perpetually soggy and speckled with dust.

His workmates were all Enoshi in this section of the mine and suffered the same deprivations. It did no good to try and clean their fur. Every last one of them stayed filthy every hour of the day, until their colors and stripes were all but indiscernible. It proved virtually impossible to tell one breed from another, which was vitally important in their culture. Breed denoted status. But then again, status was yet another of the many luxuries abandoned or forgotten once they set foot inside the mines of Rijel 12.

"You take the front, Nebelung!" shouted another one of his

crewmates. "We'll work in behind you. That delay has set us back a bit, and we still have to make quota if we're to be fed today, brother." That perked him right up. Nothing was more important than fulfilling their load requirements by the end of their work shift. To fail meant going hungry. Going hungry meant a long night curled up in his cave trying to sleep through hunger pangs.

It had gone on like that for weeks, months, years. Golan didn't know just how long he'd been down here. The same was true for most anyone on his crew. And it would go on for as long as he could muster the wherewithal to get up from his pallet and go back to work. Only death would deliver him from this nightmare. Dreaming of home was about all he had to cling to, and even those pleasant memories of his family back on Enosh were already beginning to fade.

"Right," muttered Golan instinctively. "It's my turn, I know," he then added with a yawn. There was no use arguing and for that matter why would he? His team of miners took turns at the more dangerous duties they faced, including burrowing into a freshly dug tunnel and hoping against hope there'd be no cave-in. If that happened, they could suffocate under tons and tons of rocks and berm, and the lead worker? He faced the worst of the danger. Rescuing crewmembers was something Golan had experienced before, and it didn't always work out very well for the victims.

"Had yourself a little nap, did you?" joked his neighbor on the work line. The big Enoshi, a member of the Angora clan and quite large for his breed, patted Golan on the shoulder with a monstrous paw. His once-beautiful white coat had been stained and matted with so many years of grime that his color was a matching shade of gray compared to Golan's once shimmering hide. Now practically no one from back home could have told the difference between them.

"Yes, brother," replied Golan with a grunt as he bent to pick up his tool set – a long pick which would have required both hands if he'd been a human, along with a bucket and trowel the size of a spade. "I was dreaming of home. Trying to remember my wife's face and eyes again. It's getting harder and harder to recall her beautiful face and the smell of her fur. Every day it gets a little fuzzier," smirked Golan with a defeated sadness in his tone. "I miss her so much."

"We all miss our loved ones back home, brother," remarked the hulking Enoshi. "Like it or not, the sooner you try and forget her, the better. I'm sorry to say it, I really am. You know as well as I, there's no chance of seeing them again. No one's getting out of here. We must accept it. Have to get our job done and if we do we get food. Fond memories of home are useless to us. Understand?"

Golan knew his crewmate was correct. This had become reality for the doomed souls in his section of the mine. As far as he knew no one was being released anywhere in the infinite networks of tunnels and shafts. The dead were discarded and replaced. New workers fell right into line with the living. Day after miserable day, week after miserable week. Never a day off, or even the faintest hope of getting off this rock one day. After many years, inmates realized no one was ever coming back to get them once they got sent to New Australia Planetary Prison.

Governments spun lies about it publicly. In news conferences they denied a cover-up. Otherwise they ignored it or claimed they had no knowledge of what had happened to prisoners who'd finished their sentences. When family members inquired as to the fate of their incarcerated loved ones they got nowhere. No information was forthcoming. Moreover, there was no record-keeping at NAPP after a while either. Files on prisoners were created in the early days, of course, but then in later years, these files were simply "misplaced."

Families of inmates never fully grasped this. Rijel 12 was simply too far away to have to pay a freighter to transport home one, five, or even twenty convicts and NAPP was not in the business of tracking down a prisoner once they'd been sent into the mines. Meanwhile, prison wardens and their managers were making quite a good living for themselves under the table. There were port fees, docking fees, and loading fees. Ships landed to offload supplies, then took on as much ore and raw gemstones as they could. Neither the ship captains nor the warden bore any concern for fulfilling promises made by other planets regarding completed sentences.

But then something happened that made conditions even worse. A new discovery deep within the mines of Rijel 12 caused quite a stir. Discovery of large veins of perovskite on Rijel 12 occurred in the thirty-fifth Earth year of operation. At that time copper, lead, and zinc could already be mined in abundance and refined into silver to make silver wire, a commodity in high demand.

Perovskite could be mined from Rijel 12 in great abundance. Quartz was also discovered, and when crystals the size of an office building were found within the planet's depths, it was merely a matter of burrowing down and extracting them. This required many hours of labor for the already hard-pressed inmates because they had to dig around the massive crystals with hand tools to finally free the giant crystals for extraction. This eventually meant that space craft could be powered by crystals mined from Rijel 12.

Immense power could be drawn from these crystals, enough to get ships across vast reaches of space. The key was piezoelectricity. Certain crystals could become electrically polarized when the crystal was subjected to mechanical pressure, thereby generating voltage. Compression and stretching generated voltages of opposite polarity. The piezoelectric effect merely needed to be amplified and then channeled along silver wire, preferably, to create a vast amount of energy. Rijel 12 had all these raw materials in one convenient place.

Once scientists announced that the crystals could now be used to power generational spacecraft, the stock markets went wild and demand for the crystals skyrocketed. Now ships the size of cities could explore and colonize the universe. Suddenly Rijel 12 had a brand-new income source. And the new warden, an unscrupulous Zorgolongian named Ggggaaah, began to see how he could become extremely wealthy. The only problem was figuring out how to most effectively capitalize on this incredible opportunity.

"Good day Warden," said a young assistant to the general staff and effectively the warden's lackey. His job as scullion was to see to the warden's basic needs and comfort, as well as relay messages from him to other prison staffers. Most importantly, he had to screen calls from overly stressed operators trying to elevate issues and complaints to the front office. "And how did we sleep sir? Are we refreshed and ready to tackle the day?" asked the assistant timidly. Warden Ggggaaah hissed in response.

Now for a Zorgolongian, hissing could mean most anything – from joyful acknowledgment to dismissive sarcasm. It depended upon the intonation and the circumstances. In this case it was the latter.

"Not really," sighed Ggggaaah. He'd gone back to his quarters the night before worried about production goals and had endured a fitful sleep thinking about his plight. This new opportunity, mining perovskite crystals for generation ships now being designed by all six planets in the coalition, meant trillions in profit, if he could only convert portions of his operation to their extraction. It also meant redirecting the work efforts of thousands upon thousands of convicts below. It was a daunting task, and one quite worthy of keeping him up late. He'd hardly slept a wink. "But we'll rise to the occasion my young friend. That we will do, whatever it requires of us," continued the pot-bellied little warden.

Zorgolongians were prized for their ruthlessness when managing things, especially other intelligent beings unfortunate enough to be in their charge. Merciless, they were. Well known for it too. Ggggaaah sat in his high back chair and paused for a few moments to tap on the glass of a small terrarium located on his desk. Inside, small creatures, unevolved rodents imported from his home planet Zorgolong, cowered in fear seeing what was to them a giant lizard glaring at them from outside their container. Soon, one of them would be the beast's breakfast.

"Give me the reports, please," quipped the warden, and the young scullion quickly produced an electronic notepad from on top of his little desk in the outside reception area. "Let's hear the good news, if there is any," Ggggaaah added smugly. "How are we doing getting those loathsome devils to stay on task?" he asked coldly. "Do we need to transfer more convicts to the new sector?" His assistant hesitated to tell him the latest. It wasn't all bad, but it certainly wasn't likely to please his cold-hearted commander.

Lately there hadn't been much to celebrate in terms of production successes. Freeing giant crystals and transporting them to the surface had proved to be phenomenally difficult. Highly profitable once accomplished, sure, and when a freighter had loaded them up for transport? When that was finished, it meant a huge payday. Plenty to keep him employed and able to present his superiors with glad tidings whenever they saw money transferred into their operating accounts. But those successes were long in coming, and in between would be endless messages and inquiries from management about what progress was being made.

The problem, it seemed, was the prisoners themselves. He could work them to death, and true, he often did. Yet the challenge was in supervising their efforts in the many hundreds of locations surrounding those gigantic crystals during extraction. Managing that process had been the most difficult task he'd yet faced in his long, rather shady career. "Well you see sir," replied the scullion. "It seems the prisoners in that sector... well, the crew leaders I mean... they've been making demands." The young assistant braced himself for an angry response.

Warden Ggggaaah was a Zorgolongian with a past full of piracy, who had taken over after the third prison warden had retired. By that time, the realities of New Australia Planetary Prison were accepted at face value. They were only there to make money for the Interplanetary Authority, and as long as production goals were met or exceeded, there was plenty of *lucre* available for Ggggaaah and his managers to enrich themselves. He got rich quickly. So did his cronies. Warden Ggggaaah also instituted new reforms which changed the way things were done on Rijel 12. For as far as Ggggaaah was concerned, the whole concept of work performance could be managed by the control of food.

Guards were difficult to recruit from other planetary systems, especially as the years went by, so the quality of beings willing to work there had declined markedly. But it also became a wonderful place to go disappear for a while if a being needed a fresh start: if he was running from the law, business associates with a score to settle, an angry spouse, or family obligations. Ggggaaah seized upon this to recruit guards who would carry out his orders without question – or be sent back home to face justice. It was an approach that worked well in fostering loyalty among his staff.

These new guards, recruited by Ggggaaah or by his administrators, rapidly replaced the original staff, and their function eventually became distributing food and achieving production quotas. To do so, they learned to manage their sections of the prison by delegating work detail to the prisoners themselves—then allocating food based on performance.

That was how Ggggaaah envisioned it, much like in the way pirate ships operated in his youth. Work and you eat. Mutiny and you die. The system worked quite well that way, and guards became nothing more than well-armed proprietors for the food depots. Meanwhile, these depots became fortified underground military outposts.

Then a remarkable thing happened. A social structure developed among the prison population where crews established themselves to protect the flow of supplies, making sure everyone got to eat as well as providing protection to its membership from other crews. Some crews developed more quickly than others and benefited from stronger leadership, so over time prison officials found they could refer more and more of the supervision duties to crew leadership. Crews gradually took over almost everything involving prisoner management. They would train and manage their own work shift supervisors, order materials, tools, and supplies. Guards developed into mere go-betweens, commanding sections of the ever-expanding mining network, and dealing with crew leaders exclusively.

Though requiring filtration, water was plentiful. Slartigifijian prisoners were excellent engineers and because they often lived very long lives, many crews prized them. However, food was not, so the planet imported most all its food stuffs, sending supplies down into the mines to be provided to well-performing teams meeting their quotas. Enforcing discipline was otherwise relatively simple: work hard and your teammates ate well. Thus, crew chieftains were incentivized to keep their crews on task. Amazingly this system worked quite well, and death or disease from malnutrition began to stabilize or even decline. At least for a while, anyway.

"Demands? Is that what you're telling me, scullion? Preposterous-sss!" blurted the warden with yet another hiss. "They have the temerity to make demands … on us-sss?" He flew into a rage at this unwelcome news, even if he shouldn't have been so surprised. His method of organization – his strategy of letting crews control their own work details – had led indirectly to this conundrum. Nevertheless, he couldn't comprehend what he was hearing. Prisoner laborers banding together and sending their elected leader to try and negotiate terms of servitude? Given his pirate background such a notion was absurd. It simply would not be tolerated. Ggggaaah reacted immediately.

"Shut down everything in their sector! Shut off the lights – shut off their electricity! Cut off all food rations! Let them starve in the dark, the bastards. Then we'll wait … wait until they submit."

The nervous young scullion nodded in obedience, though indicating a measure of hesitancy in his eyes. After all, he knew Warden Ggggaaah had spent nearly an hour on a video conference call with his superiors the evening before. They'd been reviewing his production numbers and asking difficult questions. The kind of difficult questions upper management always asks of middle managers, really. They did it because they could – and because it was going to be their own necks on the chopping block when it came time to face shareholders. The minion was only concerned that a shutdown of one sector of the mine might lead to further delays in reaching their production requirements for the quarter. What's more, the demands reported from the guard station several miles below? They were actually quite reasonable. Regardless, the warden was adamant.

"Tell them! Tell those cowardly guards down there. Call the power plant and tell them too. You hear me? We'll put a stop to this right now!"

Unfortunately, Warden Ggggaaah in his hubris was underestimating the determination of his adversaries – the very prisoners he sought to control with his vast resources and "limitless" power. If only he'd known what was truly going on in the infinite caverns and tunnels of Rijel 12.

The evolution of crews into hierarchical communities, based on specialties and exhibited service to the crew, had led to prisoners identifying themselves with their new crew identity rather than with their previous lives. As prisoners, they gained a level of respect for each other: in spite of whatever they'd done to get sent to prison, they had indeed endured this hellish place together. That was something they all shared in common.

But even with this amazing effort to find a way to survive the un-survivable and create a meaningful existence, the beings of New Australia Planetary Prison still faced the failings of character and ethics that inevitably accompanied the evils of absolute power. The last straw occurred when prisoners would meet quotas, only to find supplies being held back by corrupt guards who cruelly demanded higher yields in order to further their careers. Many post commanders did that, and when they felt they could get away with it, they'd try and starve prisoners into submission. Warden Ggggaaah had never been informed of that handy little piece of information.

Prisoners would naturally be compelled to step up production, boosting the numbers of those unethical guards engaging in this practice. But prisoners would often die from malnutrition as a result. It required so many calories to work a full shift. Malnutrition led to exhaustion. Exhaustion led to illness. Illness led to death.

Air and water systems needed maintenance, tools needed repair, and food quality was often quite lacking even when plentiful. Sanitation was downright abhorrent. Risking disaster, the crew leaders began finding ways to organize and call a strike to damage production. It did little, except for repeatedly proving the immorality of prison administration. Warden Ggggaaah made things far worse whenever prisoners decided enough was enough and went on strike to demand better living or working conditions.

In order to quickly bust strikes he would suspend food deliveries in order to starve the malcontents. Warden Ggggaaah simply cut off all food distribution to that sector, including electricity to the fans, lighting, and water filtration systems. Days later, work would inevitably resume. A hasty meeting would be called with striking crew leaders and a settlement would be reached. But little would change, and a few more prisoners would die from malnutrition each time it was attempted. Nevertheless, crew leaders had to at least try and force change. Their very position as leader of the crew demanded it. Failure to defy the guards could be construed as complicity, and crew leaders could and did get deposed on occasion.

Malnutrition wasn't the only major problem. There was a lack of medical supplies for injured or ill workers. Not being able to secure these supplies could lead to resentment toward crew leadership. After all, the crew leader had promised strong leadership, safety, and had taken responsibility for their well-being. Crew leaders often argued during these negotiations that the warden should consider the potential threat of losing this crew leaders and subsequently lose control of the entire prison if there were to be a wide-scale riot. Crew leaders really were the key to maintaining order. There were over one hundred thousand prisoners in those mines now, and only about thirty-five thousand guards. In their view, Warden Ggggaaah needed their help in preventing a rebellion.

"That's far enough, Leptailurus. Stop where you are. We can smell you from where you're standing," sneered the Zorgolongian commander. In a clearing, there was a no-man's land out front of a blockhouse occupied by armed guards with automatic weapons trained on the Enoshi chieftain's torso. The large feline had approached, illuminated by spotlights run off reserve batteries during the blackout imposed by the warden. He stopped and stood still; paws outstretched to show he was unarmed. He raised his voice until it echoed throughout the cavern.

"You know what we want! We've asked and asked. You've agreed that our demands are acceptable, Commander. Now we must have them! We need medicine! Antibiotics especially. You know what will happen if we don't get them. My brothers who will continue to die. And if they rise up, my friend, it might be a new chieftain you'll be dealing with next time. One far less reasonable I'm sure. If you can't help us, then let us present our demands to the warden so he might understand our situation."

The Zorgolongian post commander had no doubt that was a plausible threat. If Leptailurus returned to his brother Enoshi empty-handed, he'd likely be assassinated, and the next day there'd be a brand-new leader presenting demands. The strike would continue, and production deadlines would be missed. There was little choice but to give in and provide the hulking beast with a crate full of medical supplies, including enrofloxacin for respiratory, skin, and urinary tract infections. Those were common ailments for Enoshi working in the mines.

The post commander thought long and hard about the potential consequences, then he directed several of his comrades to carry out a large box containing the drugs. Syringes, vials of medicine, and bottle of pills were included. This scene was repeated throughout the mines of Rijel 12 on numerous occasions as of late. The warden rarely heard of these secret arrangements. The less he knew, the better. Leptailurus quietly walked over and picked up the massive crate, returning to his crew with their much-needed medicine. The strike ended an hour later and the prisoners in his section returned to work without any further delay.

No, Ggggaaah never knew what was going on way down in the mines. For example, he didn't know what kept provoking the strikes. He never found out how deliveries of antibiotics might be withheld in order to force prisoners to achieve higher output. Given that he was the only one who could control the food supply, electricity, and, the guards themselves, he didn't need to worry himself with the workaday issues down in the mines. He simply couldn't conceive of the prisoners rioting. How could they expect to succeed? Food depots were armed fortresses. Prisoners possessed little more than mining tools. They'd stand no chance against modern weapons. And attacking a guard station? Well, that was suicide.

He didn't know that negotiations were ongoing below the surface. Once they were concluded, peace would temporarily be restored in that section of the mine, and production would return to acceptable levels. For a while. Each strike would lead to some mild concessions or promises of reform, but nothing would be done to deal with the actual issues.

"Brothers!" bellowed Leptailurus triumphantly. "They agreed! I got the antibiotics we demanded." The large crate he was gripping with his paws was unwieldy and difficult to carry through the tunnel leading to his crew's cave network. Their housing facility had collapsed years ago. Now, parts of it had been pulled off the original structure to fashion walls and doorways for makeshift homes hewn from the rock. A crowd formed as several more crew members emerged from their caves, some of them too weak to stand. Some limped toward their brave leader with the aid of a friend.

"You did it! All hail our brave chieftain!" cried one of them with a triumphant growl. Soon others chimed in. "Great work," yelled another. "We sure needed this." And that was quite correct. Enrofloxacin was more valuable than a bag full of diamonds right now, and Leptailurus had been wise in calling the strike to try and obtain it. Only problem was, they couldn't have held out for even one more day before his brothers would start dying from starvation. The difference was, and the guards would have had no way of knowing this, Leptailurus had an ace in the hole.

Years before, the crew had taken in two injured and exhausted Slartigifijians. They were in no way capable of handling the rigors of working in a mine. Their bodies dried out quickly from the dust. Their health had declined to the point of withering away like rose petals on a hot asphalt street. But some clever Enoshi working alongside of them had taken an opportunity to spirit them away from the worksites and nurse them back to health. With their immense life-spans, those same two Slartigifijians had not only recovered, but had gone on to serve the next three chieftains.

Now they worked for Leptailurus, and what little they could harvest from a secret farm, located nearly a mile further down the tunnel, was barely enough to sustain their fellow crew members during this latest work stoppage. This top-secret farm had been concealed from the warden's guards since long before Lepatilurus had become chieftain. Without this they could never have survived a work stoppage.

By stockpiling task lighting left over from construction teams, sifting through food rations and droppings for seedlings, and using filtered water from a nearby aquifer, the Slarts had managed to develop a hydroponic farming operation. They grew vegetables and citrus fruits which supplemented the crew members' diets. What's more, the they had meticulously calculated the precise caloric requirements of the crew down to the last minute when the strike would have to end. Leptailurus had barely made their deadline, even if those selfish guards had no inkling just how close he'd come to capitulating.

"Have some food, Chief!" yelled yet another among the brethren as they formed up into work details. Some were munching on dried spinach leaves trying to fortify themselves for a long day of digging. They'd have to scramble to make their quota, then they could dine on prison rations and replenish themselves. "You really came through for us this time," added the dust-covered Enoshi with matted fur. He smiled, revealing dark green flecks lodged in his fangs. In response, Leptailurus grabbed a piece of spinach and bit into it with a grin. Crisis averted. He was still in charge, for now.

Long term, it was known that a successful hydroponic farm network, one which could be connected globally to all other crews, was the key to surviving a planetwide general strike. A farm network capable of feeding the entire population of miners for some reasonable period of time to gain an advantage over their heartless jailers was needed. With this in place, greater concessions could be achieved.

But that dream, shared by crew leaders as well as the Slartigifijian scientists and engineers, was taking too long. They still had to rely on their captors for food and medicine, and there was little they could do about corrupt individuals raising production quotas in isolated sections of the mine. The guards would behave for a while, but eventually they'd slip back into their old habits.

Over time it became apparent to the prisoners of New Australia: open rebellion was the only answer. Even the cautious Schpleeftii were compelled to admit it. The naturally warlike Zorgolongians, Sudonji, Enoshi, and humans downright demanded it. The only thing left to do was organize. Planet-wide. Come together as one. It was time for action.

CHAPTER 4: OPEN REBELLION

Riots are an ugly thing. Prison riots especially. They aren't organized. A singular act sparks an explosion of violence and then things escalate. Destruction, bloodshed, and tragedy follow. But rebellions can take many forms. An armed rebellion usually centers around a charismatic leader who steps forward to state very eloquently what everyone else is already thinking. People rally around that leader to go out and fight the forces of oppression. Rebellions need that: a catalyst to organize and direct their anger. That's all the prisoners on Rijel 12 needed, and one day such a creature came forward. His name was Architeuthis.

Early in the harsh days of New Australia Planetary Prison, a Slartigifijian named Architeuthis was sentenced to permanent banishment. His crime back on Slartigifij was not known. That was often the way it was with prisoners from that planet. Their culture was built around the maintenance of one's image, and embarrassment or humiliation were the only strong emotions for a Slartigifijian which might elicit a detectable reaction. Architeuthis came to work in the mines and struggled to survive just like everyone else did, laboring away for many years. No one asked questions about his past.

Life on Slartigifij was an advanced form of what Earthmen might describe as a feudal society. From top to bottom, all "Slarts," as beings from other planets referred to them, had a role which they must serve in society, and they were expected to be satisfied with their station in life, regardless of what it was. Every farmer was expected to be happy with his function as a farmer. Every mother, father, craftsman, builder, manager, driver, pilot, bureaucrat, doctor, or college professor knew what their role was and accepted it. Early in life, a Slart was identified as having an aptitude for either higher education or apprenticeship to a trade, and they were brought up in that trade or educated to run or manage things according to this early evaluation. Slarts simply could not lie, guess, or exaggerate. They countered with sober evaluations of what they estimated was the truth and said only what they deemed to be irrefutable fact.

Though a Human might speculate, theorize, claim, postulate, accuse, or outright lie, a Slart had neither the ability nor the inclination to do so. They were squid-like in appearance, and their head was conical-shaped, with eight little tentacles extending from around the base of their face. These little appendages performed no known major functions but would flutter comically when a Slart spoke. Their speech was soothing and musical, much like the sound of an oboe or a baritone saxophone. Their lifespan was twice that of most species including humans. They had two long tentacles which formed from what humans would call shoulders. These tentacles were quite adept at grabbing and manipulating objects of any kind, and their grip was quite strong. A Slart stood erect on a set of eight shorter tentacles which served as feet and enabled him to scurry about. Compared to most humans they were shorter, averaging five feet tall.

Architeuthis, by way of comparison, was a giant by Slart standards, towering over six feet in height. Nevertheless, he struggled just like everyone else to live in the hellish mines of New Australia Planetary Prison those first few Earth years, and there was little else that might distinguish him from any other prisoner, except for his size.

Well, that and the fact that he spoke out. He spoke out often, too, and in early times when other beings were becoming demoralized or being abused by guards, Architeuthis was often the only voice of reason. Guards appreciated his cool head and prisoners respected his wisdom. He had an aura about him. Incredibly wise and honest, he could explain things in a way that everyone, regardless of their mentality or their underlying intelligence, understood his advice or counsel. He didn't convince or persuade, he patiently simplified things in a way that all could understand, making clear what the correct course of action should be.

Architeuthis believed that all intelligent beings, deep within their souls, knew the true path they should follow which would benefit both themselves and the society around them. All beings desired balance. They only feared taking the right steps toward achieving it. It was fear that was stopping them: fear of failure, fear of losing face, or fear of humiliation. He believed that fear led to a lack of confidence. And the lack of confidence was the root of every conflict between intelligent beings.

Architeuthis was instrumental in persuading other Slarts to aid in the development of prison society. This effort was vital to the welfare of those realizing they'd been sentenced to die on Rijel 12. Architeuthis inspired prisoners of all species to persevere despite the immense hardship they faced. Most Slartigifijian inmates were humiliated at having been sent to New Australia Planetary Prison. Many had resigned themselves to dying of starvation and disease. They gave up, and since suicide was not acceptable in their culture, most would remain in a depressed state, slogging through their daily work detail, hoping for death. Inviting it and longing for it even.

Architeuthis explained to them how their devotion to the betterment of the beings around them, and their aid in supporting other prisoners' survival, would heal their "radula," meaning their tongue, but it was a Slartigifijian metaphor for one's ego. This would eventually return to them their sense of dignity. Best of all, it would free their hearts to love one another and themselves once again. Slarts incarcerated in Rijel 12 slowly began to accept his wisdom, and when they applied their intellect to matters of repair, maintenance, sanitation, farming, and medical care, the woeful state of affairs on Rijel 12 began to stabilize. Architeuthis' legend soon grew.

He became a sort of spiritual leader for the struggling beings on Rijel 12. And though he was not a member of any particular crew, the crew concept was inspired by him. The Schpleeftkorkii were his main protectors, but he professed no allegiance to them. This crew, which was a hodge-podge of several species including humans, Schpleeftiis, Enoshi, Zorgolongians, and some Suidonji, had been one of the first formed at New Australia Planetary Prison, and had absorbed other crews over the years.

But when the corruption of the guards proved to be a threat to survival, Architeuthis again spoke out. Up until then, his philosophy had been for his fellow prisoners to accept the fact that their home planets had discarded them. Now, they must embrace their new life and identity as a member of their associated crew. Their crew would care for them, benefit from their labor, protect them, and see to their needs.

"All of us must work together to achieve production goals and earn our food rations, so we might survive and flourish. Your crew is your family now. And they will protect you while you serve them … for the rest of your lives," Architeuthis explained. His philosophy was communicated throughout the growing convict population, giving beings of all species some form of hope. Yet the prisoners were reaching their breaking point, and Architeuthis recognized this. The policies of the new warden, Ggggaaah, had led to new levels of suffering.

The discovery of quartz and perovskite meant wide-scale tunneling throughout the planet's interior, and the creation of giant shafts for moving these humungous crystals. In so doing, the entire planet was slowly being connected. Crews, once isolated, were now able to communicate with each other. This meant the spread of information was much wider, and communication meant sharing of ideas. Everyone was talking about it. A rebellion was now possible to coordinate planet-wide. The planet's spiritual leader Architeuthis needed only to say the word.

After another series of embargos on medicine were reported through the new network, Architeuthis had finally had enough. He knew it was time to speak out against the regime of Warden Ggggaaah. What he actually said was something quite unusual for a Slartigifijian. A Slart didn't say things like that in normal circumstances. But these were far from normal circumstances, and when Architeuthis spoke these words to a gathering of prisoners at a meeting held deep inside the caverns of Rijel 12, it set in motion a series of events that Warden Ggggaaah could not have foreseen.

In his baritone voice, Architeuthis addressed an assembly of leaders from the farthest reaches of the planet. It had been planned a month in advance, and carefully concealed from the prying eyes and ears of guards and post commanders in such a way that only a handful knew of it. These chieftains had snuck through the infinite network of tunnels and caverns to a top-secret location. The meeting was conducted within the borders of the Schpleeftkorkii territory.

The event had been kept necessarily hush-hush during the planning process, with emissaries relaying the message from one mining sector to the next. All participants had been sworn to secrecy, upon pain of death. They were only allowed to bring a bodyguard troop of up to five trusted members from their home territory. No weapons were permitted. Attendance required them to leave old rivalries and historic resentments at the door. Everyone invited heeded the call. Only Architeuthis could draw such solemn dedication from otherwise violent individuals.

"Beings of New Australia," began Architeuthis in a soothing voice. "It is time to rise up and face evil, for evil is facing us." The reaction in the crowd of chieftains and their loyal cohorts was to be expected. They fell silent as a church when hearing a Slart speak that way. Most had never seen him in person, however they all respected his reputation.

"It is an evil which is facing down upon us," continued the tall figure, "oppressing us and threatening societies that we have struggled and strived to create in this, our new home… far from our original planets. The enemy is stronger than us, has more technology than us, and controls our very livelihood. But there is one thing our enemy has never been able to take from us, not the whole time we've been here. The enemy cannot and never will take away our spirit."

Eyes moistened, even among those crew leaders who'd risen up from among the ranks to become undisputed chief. Strong, brave Suidonji. Quick, nimble Schpleeftii. Clever, ruthless Zorgolongians. Smart, fierce humans. Ferocious, warrior-like Enoshi. All of them. Heartrates rose. Murmurs and even a few shouts emitted from the audience. Hardened beings who'd survived years of deprivation were standing with mouths agape, hanging on the very words Architeuthis spoke – wanting him to say those things they'd longed to hear. This was the day, and this was the moment they'd all been waiting for. But would he really say it? Would he call upon them to make *war*?

After a calming sigh which fluttered his facial tentacles, Architeuthis went on to satisfy their yearnings for inspiration and provide the impetus to organize their efforts. Didn't take long to get what they came for.

"And so, we will challenge this evil which threatens us, and we will overcome it. We will use the resources of our minds and the cooperation and skills of the over one hundred thousand of our brethren struggling to survive throughout New Australia. We will declare war on our oppressors. Yes, there will be bloodshed. But we will succeed, and we will survive, like we always have. And when we have achieved our freedom, we will once again see the Rijel sun shining upon the surface of this very planet, this world which now belongs to us."

At the moment he concluded his speech, Architeuthis bowed his conical head and closed his enormous eyes as if in prayer. The crowd erupted. They cheered wildly, all those crew leaders and their bodyguards who'd risked detection traveling across the globe for this clandestine meeting. Soon a chant arose among them which became the nickname for the revolt, and eventually the new moniker for the beings of Rijel 12. For upon hearing their leader refer to their home as "New Australia" instead of Rijel 12, they became wildly inspired. They boldly screamed "NEW AUSTRALIA," repeatedly and with several different accents, until it gradually started sounding like something else.

The chanting and screaming continued for several minutes, until the audience kept hearing something run together that sounded like "Nah-sty" or "Nah-stees". It was an historic moment. One, or perhaps a few, eventually started shouting "NAUSTIES! NAUSTIES! NAUSTIES!" And within a few moments, the whole chamber was screaming their new title.

From that point on the name stuck. From then on, the revolt and the rebels on Rijel 12 became known to each other by that name. From that day forward, they were prisoners no longer. They were now "Nausties". The Naustie Rebellion had begun.

Mobilization for the uprising took nearly a year to put together. This was not a prison escape. This was an armed rebellion against vastly superior technology. Prison security troops, which numbered only about thirty-five thousand, carried electrical impulse cannons, or EIC's. These weapons were hand-held, much like an old Earth machine pistol or Thompson submachine gun. They used an electrical charge from a crystal powered generator and could fire a .30 caliber projectile into targets at rates of five thousand feet per second, without using gunpowder. The target of an EIC would often become mortally wounded by the impact, devastated internally by shrapnel, because the projectile was designed to disintegrate upon striking organic tissue.

EIC's were automatic weapons which fired up to three hundred rounds per minute. They could be sprayed at a crowd of protesters or a wave of attacking troops, rendering appalling casualties in a matter of seconds. Larger fifty caliber versions were installed in kill slots on the outside walls of every guard outpost, and they could mow down beings of any species that came within range.

Guard outposts were formidable, constructed of steel, and safely secured along major access tunnels throughout the planet. One was attached to every food depot. Each outpost was garrisoned with at least 300 guards and located next to elevator shafts or output collection sites, where prisoners would bring in their daily production to earn rations.

Slart mechanics, repairmen, farmers, scientists, engineers, and physicians embedded in all the crews now began nominating the best and brightest among their kind to come together and become a planning team for the revolt. A headquarters was established and protected by the Schpleeftkorkii crew, so that the planning team could go live and work directly with Architeuthis in devising the initial planet-wide attack. This group of geniuses assembled immediately and began assessing what the Nausties had to work with in terms of developing battle solutions for enemy defenses. Despite the challenges, within a few weeks they had many working theories.

"Let us begin," intoned Architeuthis. That was his usual way of beginning sessions with his staff. They were Slarts, most of them, mixed with a Suidonji, a Zorg, an Enoshi bodyguard or two, and a couple of Humans. These beings were not necessarily part of the think tank itself but would occasionally be called upon for input. Mainly, they were there as military escorts for the Slarts who'd been volunteered from their home crews.

One Schpleefti was in attendance as well, occasionally eyeing his Zorgolongian counterpart across the room whenever he thought Architeuthis wasn't looking. Their two factions had a rivalrous past that went back several decades, due to their homelands neighboring each other. Didn't help matters much knowing that Zorgs during olden times used to hunt rodents, but no conflict was to be tolerated this day – not when there was serious business to be discussed.

This was the thirty-third consecutive day of meetings, oftentimes stretching for ten hours at a clip. Architeuthis would broach a topic, present a challenge that had to be considered, and then wisely fall silent while his brilliant planners hashed it out and argued, at least by Slart standards, over their proposals. Their subtle style and patient dispositions, even when disagreeing with one another, were quite amusing to their escorts; yet after days and days of this, it was more likely to lull them to sleep. Probably would have, if it weren't for the vital issues being raised. Chances were just as good that Architeuthis might call upon one of them to weigh in with their opinions.

They knew things. Architeuthis needed this knowledge, and so did those brainy Slarts. They had abilities – every species did – which exceeded those of Slartigifijians. Strength, endurance, agility, plus years and years of bottled up resentment. Loads of it. When it was their turn to address the planning session, their commitment was both assumed and expected. The Great Leader, as he was now being referred to, had to count on every last one of them.

"We left off yesterday discussing our initial assault phase," continued Architeuthis, calmly. "Coordination of this is crucial, as we agreed, and it has been established that we need lightning-quick attacks which will subdue at least a handful of the outposts within a short period of time, lest the enemy alert the entire network and stage a counterattack. Shall we begin?" He then as always grew quiet, encouraging his panel of advisors to respond.

One of the planners spoke up immediately, a Slart named Megalocyathus. His crew was made up primarily of Suidonji who were known for their durability and strength. Diggers and burrowers by nature, they developed into fabulous tunnelers. The elder Megalocyathus already had a brilliant idea in mind and was anxious to provide details on it to the others.

"If I may, Great Leader, I'd like to start by proposing we consider a prolonged period of tunneling leading up to the day of the assault. A clandestine operation is what I envision, intended to surprise the enemy and limit casualties during our frontal attacks. This would hasten the capture of outposts if successful." Architeuthis nodded and gestured with a long tentacle for him to elaborate.

"What I envision is sending units up under the outposts as well as through the roofs … dropping through ceilings and emerging from floors. Our brethren from among the Enoshi, assuming the breach is large enough of course, can then crawl through and provide our hosts with a nasty surprise. This could happen during the frontal assault, when the guards are otherwise occupied fending off the main attack."

Architeuthis was intrigued. If he was hearing him correctly, this would mean any frontal assault would thereby become a mere diversion. If successful, it might also imply that those troops committed to the main attack would not have to suffer heavy casualties. Simply keep the occupants of the outposts busy long enough for shock troops to break in and slaughter their opponents, right about the time the enemy were sensing victory. It sounded magnificent.

"Outstanding," proclaimed Architeuthis. "I like your thinking, Megalocyathus. Please go on. We've got a possible solution to one of our problems, would everyone agree?" Consensus was, for once, almost immediate. The other Slarts nodded politely in agreement. Reactions from the Enoshi, humans, Suidonji, Zorgolongian, and Schpleefti were far more pronounced, however.

"Yes." snorted the Suidonji proudly. He went by the name Scrofa. "My crew could pull this off quite easily, given enough time. Quietly too. Those bastards won't even know we're there until it's too late!" He shot a glance over to his Enoshi counterparts and grinned widely. "If the tunnels can be dug big enough and wide enough, perhaps even an Eno could squeeze through. If not, we can always get Zorgs to do it. That is, if they don't mind killing their own kind."

The lone Zorg in attendance shot a look of profound annoyance toward Scrofa. Then he smiled and gave out a "Hmmmph." If called upon, he knew his crew of cutthroats would have no qualms about murdering every last one of the guards they faced. Years of oppression had affected them just as much as any other being living under the heel of Warden Ggggaaah. No matter what species they found inside, death would come swiftly once they broke through – no question about it. "You can count on us, pinky," retorted the defiant Zorgolongian ....

What happened in the meetings was never discussed outside of the meetings, not with anyone. Battle strategy for the upcoming attack had to be kept top secret until everything else was in place otherwise the entire enterprise could be compromised. Secrecy was an absolute priority and attendees were sworn to keep their mouths shut, even with their crews. The beings of New Australia knew something was going on but had no idea what was being discussed or when they might be called upon to act. It was frustrating, and the members of the meeting knew it, but it simply had to be this way.

There were pressing matters that had to be addressed: for one thing, infrastructure. To conduct a large-scale military operation, the Naustie Army would need ways to move supplies and information quickly. Global tunneling meant they could set up a communication network with runners relaying messages throughout to organize coordinated attacks. It took months for Suidonji diggers to improve it, but when the network of tunnels was eventually connected, Zorg runners were soon sprinting in relay teams, keeping all the crews updated on progress and deadlines. Zorgolongians were quite well-suited to that function. Spectacular runners, they could cover a mile or two of open ground much faster than a human.

The planning team also knew they needed scouts to work with the Suidonji and Zorgs, shielding them from detection. For that task, the Schpleeftii, or Spleefs as they were nicknamed, made perfect candidates. Spleefs had sensitive snouts which could sniff out gases, salt, sulfur, and body odors quicker than any other being. Next, the Slart planning team ordered the crafting of carbide lamps.

Calcium carbide would need to be acquired from the guards for this. Longer term, it could be manufactured by heating coke and lime into making acetylene, but there were already large stocks of it for cutting torches used in the mines. In the short term, they'd have to stockpile their own carbide lamps to create lighting for the communication tunnels. Stockpiling them was an easy solution for supplying the tunnels with lighting; however, the planners knew they'd need a lot more. Once Warden Ggggaaah shut down electricity in the mines, which he would, they'd be in complete darkness, and those lamps would be their only means of light.

The biggest issue was food. The planning team meticulously calculated just how many calories a warrior would burn during a prolonged attack on a guard station. Next, they calculated just how long the whole planet could survive once the revolt began and the network of food depots was shut down by Warden Ggggaaah. A carefully devised a time table for this, down to the very last hour when their fellow convicts would begin to starve, was developed.

"Five days, Great Leader," said one of the more mathematically-inclined Slarts on the team. They all were excellent at math, really, but Dofleini was exceptionally gifted. It was now the one-hundred and ninety-eighth consecutive day of meetings, and he'd determined they'd have precisely five Earth days to capture at least thirty food depots before the entire planet would run out of food.

"Five days?" asked Architeuthis. The two Enoshi growled apprehensively. Scrofa the Suidonji snorted nervously. The Zorgolongian hissed. It had been nearly seven Earth months, and the target date for the initial assault was fast-approaching.

The topic of discussion on this particular day was consequential effects following the initiation of hostilities. Architeuthis felt it was important that they consider all conceivable outcomes. "Failure is not an option" was a Human saying, and typical of their reputation for hubris. Slarts didn't think like that. Failure was a very real option and had to be planned for as a possible outcome. If not, there'd be no contingency in place for it.

Architeuthis had no doubt Dofleini was correct. However, he had to fulfill his role as facilitator: engage his staff in discussion, foster debate, get everyone involved in picking apart every idea, proposal, or factual observation, take all the time necessary to address any relevant factors. The stakes were the highest they could be, lives were on the line. For every mistaken assumption, hundreds if not thousands of lives might be lost. What's more, the rebellion could fail quite easily if his staff were not precise in every aspect of their determinations. Therefore, Architeuthis put a question to the floor, "Are you absolutely certain five days is all we have?"

"Yes, Great Leader," Dofleini responded solemnly. "We have five days, no more no less, according to my calculations based on our projected food supply as of the date we're planning to attack. We have to be in control of thirty food depots within five days and be able to distribute their contents globally before that period ends. I've run the numbers repeatedly the figures are correct."

Architeuthis did not argue. The other members at the meeting table certainly pressed Dofleini for details, as well as the sources of his information and their reliability, but few doubted his accuracy. The elder mathematician, pushing one-hundred and thirty in Earth years, patiently answered them.

"To calculate this, I took into consideration the amounts of food stored in a typical depot. They receive a shipment every seven earth days via a massive elevator system. Each day, the freight elevator will send up ore output in the same shaft. Guards travel in the same manner, but they only refresh their staff every Earth week when food shipments arrive. Each depot has a one-month reserve, just as a precaution in case of cave-ins or mechanical breakdown. But to control prisoners, the guards give out daily rations only, as we all know, and those distributions are based on production from the previous twenty-four hour period. You see, the system was originally designed by Earthmen, so they tended to observe Earth-like time tables in its creation." Dofleini continued as the others patiently listened.

"Subsequently, food rations are calculated precisely to feed a specific number of beings of every species with enough calories to sustain them for twenty-four hours. Based on statistics I've compiled from crews as to their membership and numbers of each species, I was able to work backward and project how much food would be stored in each depot and how many depots we need to capture to make this operation a success. As I said, we only have a limited amount of time to achieve this goal and distribute food throughout our network."

Architeuthis was impressed as always, but he wouldn't be doing his job if he didn't make sure they'd thought of everything that could go wrong. He decided to play devil's advocate and spark further debate.

"Very well then," he stated, now addressing everyone. "And how can we ensure this works out properly, my friends? Assuming we capture thirty depots of course – which we must. I hasten to point out we can only estimate the amount of food we'll capture. Might be more. Might be less. What if we're wrong?" Dofleini's fellow planners were quick with ideas.

"The best option, I believe, is to step up production for at least six months to earn ration bonuses and stockpile food," suggested Sepiolida. He knew such an idea would not be well-received but decided to mention it anyway. "It will be difficult, but it will buy time for our hydroponic farmers to increase crop yields deep inside the mines."

This was a potential solution. The problem was in convincing already hard-pressed crew leaders to place such a heavy burden on their membership. They agreed on it though, eventually, and Zorg runners were subsequently sent out to relay directives throughout the global network. It was one of many issues decided upon that day, only to be followed by other ingenious solutions in the days and weeks following. Information was pouring into headquarters all the time, and edicts were being sent to outlying sectors regularly.

The only major item left to accomplish was for an initial battle plan to be devised and implemented. That was something Architeuthis knew he needed help with. Slarts couldn't do it. He most certainly couldn't do it himself. For this he needed a strategic mastermind, a general.

In front of each food depot was a receiving area for bringing in production output on electric dump trucks which were the size of a house. This was the only approach to a food depot, so attacking en masse across this killing ground could very well be disastrous. Because of this, the planning council proposed that a more thoughtful approach would be necessary to reduce casualties until warriors could get close enough to employ spears or javelins, which human prisoners were already designing and crafting back in their homelands.

This became their specialty. Earthmen, with their more dexterous fingers and hand/eye coordination, had superior ability for craftsmanship in designing weapons for close order combat, so many of the stronger but less agile Earthers, as they were often called, became blacksmiths for the Naustie Army.

Naturally, Enoshi arose as the most fearsome and fearless warriors. They were larger for one thing, standing an average of six and a half feet tall; whereas human males averaged about five feet ten. Plus Enos, as they were sometimes called, were highly skilled at hand-to-hand combat. Thus, it was they who initially became military commanders and trainers for the assault forces.

Yet surprisingly enough, Earthers proved to be the next best fighters, and quickly dispelled any myths others might have held about their ferocity. Earthers could dish it out and they most certainly could take it, as everyone soon discovered. Enoshi drill sergeants were delighted with how fast they learned, and how ruthless Earthers were in physical combat. They weren't just brave; they were downright cruel. But they were also smart …

"By the gods!" exclaimed the giant, a burly sergeant named Chase Burmilla. He'd just witnessed something he thought he'd never see in nine lifetimes. A Human had bested his clan's champion in a grappling match. A big pit had been dug after a long night of training, and two champions chosen from each crew had jumped in to battle it out. No weapons; the combatants had to fight hand to hand, and as the dust settled a clear winner had just been determined.

Ecstatic cheering arose from the crowd gathered around. It was almost deafening. It was like seeing a thirty-point underdog in an old Earth college football game pull off a stunning upset of some highly favored opponent. Yet, this hardly looked like an upset, thought the fearsome feline. It looked more like an ambush.

"By the gods," he observed once again, shaking his head. Sgt. Burmilla was directing a series of war games with a human prison crew which occupied a neighboring cavern. Many years before, mining sections had been organized according to species, to prevent conflict and further enable standardized labor practices. Now, most crews within the prison's network, with the exception of the Schpleeftkorkii of course, were made up exclusively of either Suidonji or humans – Enoshi or Schpleeftii. There were also eleven crews made up primarily of Zorgolongians.

"Don't say I didn't warn ya' Sergeant. 'Cause I did, diddun I?" laughed the beefy Irishman standing next to him. 'Ole Daniel there … he's a beast. Hell, I wouldn't a' wanted to go up against that monster o' yours either, but that Danny Craft … he sure took down that big cat." He then screamed, "Good on ya' Boy-o!" as he joined in with the celebrations and jeers from the exhausted convicts watching the match.

The Earther now speaking to Sergeant Burmilla was also a soldier of sorts. His name was Edward McGrath, and, in his past, he'd murdered a man back in the tiny region of Ireland, now part of the Province of Western Europe. His current role in the "Whyos" was primarily enforcer. But now, given the newly established Naustie Army was about to be initiating hostilities, his function had changed.

Tough as a coffin nail, Eddie McGrath was put in charge of training his troops to be fearless when faced with certain death, and to acquire the necessary skills to achieve victory in combat. That's what tonight's wargames session was all about. Burmilla was flabbergasted. What's more he was quite humbled.

"Yes, he did!" roared the beast. "I mean, I would have thought that – well – I would have imagined – I mean, by crumb, this was not what I expected." Eddie McGrath slapped him on the back, causing a cloud of dust to rise off the beast's dingy white fur.

"Yep. And you wouldn't take the odds I offered ya'. Wouldn't take the bet. Too bad. I woulda cleaned up tonight." laughed Eddie. Sergeant Burmilla was still getting over the shock of seeing an Earther practically dismantle one of his strongest warriors.

"It was amazing," Burmilla said stroking his dirt encrusted beard. "For every move, there was a counter-move. For every punch or swipe of my champion's paw there was a block, a kick, or a jab. Your Earthman, you say he is called Dahn-yahl?" To this McGrath nodded as Burmilla continued. "Wasn't much more than half his size. Yet he moved quickly. Seemed to me he observed our champion's moves and devised defenses for them while he fought. What's more, he used his opponent's own force of motion against him. Incredible. Practically threw our guy into the wall whenever he lunged at him."

To this McGrath chuckled even more. Truth was Daniel Craft had weaved and bobbed and dodged so well that the Enoshi was repeatedly off balance during the contest. Threw him over his shoulders. Blocked punches. Sent the monstrous creature sprawling.

"More than once, Boy-o. Tossed your big fella' at least a couple o' times by my count." Then McGrath sighed and collected himself. There was no point rubbing it in. Years and years of surviving in this God-forsaken hellhole had transformed him. He still talked like an Irish mobster, yet he was by now a changed man.

"But why quibble, eh? Let's get the boys together and have 'em call it a night, eh? Maybe in a few days, you know – maybe we can do some more trainin'. Whaddya say to that? I'll bring a different crew with me next time. Let you 'n yer crew show 'em how to be better fighters. That be alright, *a chara*?" Sergeant Burmilla was more than happy to oblige. Today had changed everything he'd ever thought about Earthers and their abilities.

"Certainly, brother. You do that, yes. Bring more. We'll get them ready for battle. And let me say this, my friend," he then added, turning to face the former gangster, "When it comes time for us to charge the enemy, I'd be honored to have you and your Earthmen protecting us with your javelins and charging alongside of us into the fray." Burmilla held out a humungous paw for Eddie to grasp, which he did in the Enoshi style, by grasping the forearm above the wrist.

"Bang on, Boy-o!" exclaimed Eddie McGrath. He knew full well how serious of a compliment this was. Enoshi didn't do that sort of thing unless they sincerely and truly meant what they were saying.

The truth was, Earthers possessed better instincts during a fight, they used their minds and their bodies, and over time Slart planners took notice. Soon, they began choosing Earthers over Enos to become officers, and once they did, some very fresh and creative ideas emerged from newly-selected Earther captains and lieutenants. Enoshi were indeed very brave and fearless, but humans were crafty and deceptive. Members of the planning council were amazed at their innate ability to complicate matters for a defender and create an isolated advantage or window of opportunity that might only exist for a few minutes yet yield a chance for overall victory. Thus, when it came time to select a supreme commander, it was not an Enoshi. It was a human.

In fact, it was Archibald Hicks of the Templar Knights who was eventually promoted to General of the Army. Bald and razor-shaved from head to toe, Hicks had tattoos up the sides of his neck, as well as his arms and legs. He, like most prisoners, had abandoned clothing by now, and merely wore a loin cloth. The Knights were Caucasian humans from various parts of Earth, and one of the most feared crews on New Australia. Hicks also displayed an eight-inch Templar cross tattooed on the back of his shaved head, from the nape of his neck all the way up to the top of his cranium. At his first major strategy planning meeting with the council, he explained his ideas for assaulting a fortified guard station. When he showed up at headquarters the members of the council were both shocked and amazed at his audacity, right along with his terrifying appearance.

"Welcome everyone," stated Architeuthis pleasantly. The Great Leader then gestured with one of his tentacles toward an imposing-looking figure standing at the entrance to the secret cave where the council had been meeting daily for a year. He was beckoning for the man to come join them.

"My friends, after careful consideration, it is with great pleasure that I present to you our new General of the Army, Archibald Hicks. Please join me in welcoming him." As Architeuthis said the words, Hicks walked in like he owned the place, followed by his second in command, a slender but wiry human with noticeably fewer tattoos on his body. There was no doubting who was in charge now. Hicks acted as though choosing him to lead the army was a forgone conclusion.

General Hicks leaned forward over the planning table and glared for a moment, nodding subtly toward the other Slarts seated at the slab of polished stone which had become their conference table. Then he said in a gravelly, emotionless voice, "Alright, gentlemen, let's get started." He established authority easily with both his confidence and his stature. The room grew quiet as the new supreme commander began presenting his plans. Even Architeuthis settled in to let the man speak.

"I'll get right to the point if you don't mind," continued the General. He had little patience for formalities. Heads nodded. "My men and I have come up with a multi-step process for eliminating those damn blockhouses we're goin' up against next month. With your permission, I'm now going to detail exactly what we're gonna do."

He then looked around the room at the other members in attendance. Two Enoshi. Another human. A Suidonji. A Spleef and a Zorg. He didn't know these creatures, and it made him pause for a moment. "Are we uh – is this a secured room?" he asked with a raised eyebrow. Architeuthis acknowledged his concerns by nodding, then gestured with his tentacle for the scary-looking fellow to proceed. Hicks snorted, then launched right in with his presentation.

"Very well then, first we draw out the commander of the enemy garrison and assassinate him. Simple as that: cut him down right where he stands. You follow?" Several heads nodded, more eyes blinking with apprehension. Clearly, Architeuthis had picked someone who was not inclined to mince words when it came to the subject of killing.

"Food deliveries and changing of guard staffs occur every seven earth days, as I'm sure you all know by now. The plan is to catch them off balance during one of their personnel changes. Kill as many as possible while they're moving in and out of the station. That's how we create chaos. And, gentlemen, in this engagement, chaos is our friend," Architeuthis nodded. Yes, that's exactly why the Great Leader wanted a human formulating battle tactics in the first place. This was the sort of thing they excelled at. Archibald Hicks was only getting started.

"Now the guards that survive this initial attack will flee inside the station if they can and lock down the place, thinking they can fend off the assault. Meanwhile, our Zorg friends will do the job of convincing them it really is a frontal attack. That's what they'll expect. But it's not." General Hicks then cleared his throat, still glaring at the creatures watching him. He was blunt, but most liked that he didn't take long to get to the point. Hicks then reached around and pulled out a three-foot-long, two-foot-wide diagram of a food depot. Those seated at the table slid back on their stools to give him room.

The diagram, which displayed arrows and directions of attack, had been drawn onto an actual cutaway picture of a food depot and its accompanying guard station barracks. It had been part of a blueprint at one time. How he'd acquired it was anyone's guess. It was probably lost somewhere years before by work crews constructing one of the depots, left behind once the project was complete and later discovered by miners. Hicks's adjutant had affixed the diagram to a large metal plate, and it included an overhead, as well as profile view of one of the facilities. These depots had been constructed in exactly the same way in factories back on Earth, then shipped in components to Rijel 12 to be assembled. Therefore, the Nausties could use the same attack plan on every food depot on the planet.

"Zorgs are quick and small," continued General Hicks. "We'll use them as light infantry to draw fire from the guards while our heavy infantry moves up – protected by boulders and transport vehicles is what I'm planning on. Now, these boulders I'm speaking of will be discreetly placed, and transports will be parked in a random fashion so as to create narrow kill zones. Meanwhile, our heavy infantry will move from protective cover to protective cover while taking fire, slowly working their way toward the guard station. Casualties will be high, but this is necessary while we get our infantry close enough to fire salvos of javelins and eliminate guard positions."

Of course, the meticulous Slarts were not terribly impressed with the battle plan so far, but they nodded politely anyway as Hicks stopped, gave a big long humorous glance over at his handsome assistant, then looked back at his audience with an icy cold look on his face. He spoke again.

"But it's only a feint." All the emotion drained from his face. At that, he turned back to the diagram. It was lying on the large stone conference table, so everyone could see what he was pointing to. Hicks gestured with his hands as he described the rest. "You see, gentlemen, by drawing fire from the guards posted in those kill slots, we'll be able to burst through the floor of the station and come right up between their legs and right up their asses."

He grinned while he gestured in an underhand motion with his thumb. Then he reached over the top of the diagram and pointed downward, saying "Our Suidonji will also drill through the ceiling of the tunnel. Break in through the roof. By the time those guards realize they're being crushed like a grape, our infantry will be able to cut through the gate of the depot with acetylene torches and eliminate the entire garrison."

All eyes immediately shifted to Architeuthis. This was precisely the idea devised months before by the planning council. And yet Hicks had arrived at the same conclusion, on his own. *How? Those discussions had been kept top secret.* There was no way the General could have heard about them, not from the council anyway. He was presenting the same concept, as though it were fresh from his mind. The Slarts who'd come up with it a year earlier started to react, however Architeuthis raised a tentacle cautioning them to remain silent. By now, he was far more interested in what the human would say next. It turned out that he was not alone.

Hicks continued. The plan would require a thousand soldiers for each food depot, with teams of Suidonji drilling and tunneling carefully above the roofs of each structure and below the floors simultaneously without being detected in the hours leading up to the attacks. The tunneling would need to be completed before the actual assault could begin. Finally, each attack would commence once the shift change was happening. This would require coordination on a global scale, but that is what the tunnel networks were for. It was a brilliant plan. And it proved once and for all that given a little bit of freedom to think up solutions, those Earth men were nearly as bright as the Slarts themselves.

Architeuthis chuckled, causing his facial tentacles to flutter. "Excellent. Go on General," he said calmly, deciding against revealing that his staff had thought up the same thing months ago. General Hicks nodded impassively and proceeded with his presentation.

"Casualties in the diversionary assault will be heavy," he stated coldly. "But, those Suidonji tunneling in will face a mauling when they break through the floor and the ceiling." Hicks was very blunt about that part; nevertheless, the Slarts liked the new General's boldness, nodding toward each other, as well as toward Architeuthis.

"General Hicks, we appreciate your thoroughness," said Architeuthis. "Your ingenuity and cunning have served you well in this endeavor, and we are grateful for your efforts. We also thank you, Perry, for assisting in the presentation." Perry was the name of Hicks' right-hand man.

The General's adjutant smiled proudly. He wasn't looking for kudos that day. He was only there to make his partner look smart. But Perry wasn't just an assistant: Perry was also the man's devoted companion, and actually the brains in that power couple. Emboldened, Perry politely asked if he could add something to the meeting, and to everyone's amazement the rough-edged general suddenly became quite apologetic when he realized he'd skipped over something terribly important: smoke bombs.

"Oh yes, I almost forgot," snickered the grizzled warrior, "My partner here has something more to add. Something that'll make things a little easier on us." Perry snickered and winked subtly at Hicks, then composed himself hastily as he spoke.

"Thanks, General. We've determined that smoke bombs can be made, to use as a screen to disguise our movements within the guard station as we try to climb through the holes. To break inside the roof and floor of the guard station, our Suidonji friends will use acetylene cutting torches. The noise outside should be sufficient to keep the guards distracted on one end of the station, while they cut through the steel. Once through the hole they can hurl smoke bombs inside, and confuse the occupants for long enough to climb in." Perry smirked humbly at his audience, appreciating how vastly intelligent they were.

"Now I'm no scientist, but anyone with a working knowledge of chemistry knows potassium nitrate and brown sugar is about all you need: three quarts of potassium nitrate and two quarts of raw sugar, to be exact." The Slarts blinked patiently. They understood what he was talking about, but not exactly how he intended to use such a compound. What Perry proposed was to boil the mixture in a cast iron vessel until liquefied, then pour it into metal boxes lined with aluminum foil wrappers, which came out of the food ration packets. Before the mixture had set, a fuse could be embedded in it. Before tossing the bomb inside, it could be lit with acetylene torches to ignite the smoke. What's more, barium salt could be added to the mixture, so that the smoke would have a green color and be more terrifying to the trapped defenders.

Perry enjoyed his moment in the spotlight, talking through his clever idea, concluding with, "Our Suidonji tunnelers, supported by lightning quick Zorgs, can then climb through ceilings and floors to get safely inside, before attacking and eliminating the last of the guards."

Casualties would be heavy, but this attack plan was innovative and had a good chance of success, if all went to plan. What's more, if conducted in several parts of the mining network, against several different guard stations simultaneously, there'd be no time to send a relief force to quell the uprising – not before the Nausties would have captured enough food to supply the rebellion for a full week if things turned out well. They'd also have a very large cache of captured weapons for their assault on Warden Ggggaaah's headquarters.

"Very impressive," said Architeuthis. He sat forward on his stool and addressed the Human. "But General, if I may, how do you propose we get all the way up to the main terminal to attack and overwhelm the security forces protecting it?" General Hicks smiled. Clearly, he had done his homework. He again cleared his throat.

"Well sir, that's where it gets really interesting." He gestured toward the table that the Slarts were sitting around and pulled out a grease pencil that would usually be used for drawing a target for a power drill or cutting torch.

"With your permission, gentlemen?" he asked. The Slarts moved back from the table while the half-naked man leaned over to begin drawing a rough sketch of the planet's inner network of shafts and tunnels. As he wheezed and murmured to himself, the tattooed fellow meticulously created a detailed picture from rote memory. It took several moments for him to draw it, while the Slarts fluttered their facial tentacles, fascinated with the General's thoroughness.

What Hicks had remarkably memorized over the years, was a blueprint diagram of the elevator network and maintenance ladders used in case of a breakdown. This was because the same diagram was posted on the inside wall of the guard commander substation near the Templar Knights' section of the mine. When entering guard stations to negotiate better conditions for his men, Hicks had learned how ore and crystals were being shipped from the planet's depths, as well as what happened to them afterward. Now, he was showing the Slarts just how his troops could get back to the surface, along with what they'd find when they got there. Hicks spoke in a low voice, while he drew a cutaway view of this elaborate system.

"Long ago, these freight elevators were constructed in deep shafts drilled into the planet. We've all figured that's what they did, anyway. But what I learned is they connect to one main tunnel system that spreads around the planet like a giant city grid. Up there, massive dump trucks ferry the materials back to the loading bay here, where the main terminal is located." He drew a large oval to indicate the bay. "We can ascend several of these shafts simultaneously, using emergency ladders attached to the walls, if necessary. Better that we capture a working elevator or two, but from this tunnel we'll form a bridgehead to supply the final assault on the main terminal."

Architeuthis was impressed. "Yes, I see." he exclaimed. He remembered vaguely, from years before when he was brought to the planet, how the transport ship had descended below the surface several hundred feet to a distribution center where he was off-loaded with the other prisoners. This must be what Hicks was referring to. He asked politely, "General, how do you propose we fight the security forces defending the terminal and the transport tunnel?"

Hicks looked right at him and grinned. Once again, he was not about to mince words. "Bloody carnage, sir. We'll use weapons we've captured off dead guards to fight them, but I'm expecting ten-if not twenty-thousand dead and wounded by the time we're through with this operation. I'm sorry, but that's what it looks like."

The other Slarts from the planning committee gasped and murmured to each other in their native Slartigifij, mixed with some Galactic. It didn't matter. Hicks could understand them just fine.

"I know, I know gentlemen," he said in a raised voice which quieted the cacophony. "It's a tall order, but we've thought this through and it's the only way. We've got explosive charges we've used for years to blast open cavities and cut away rock to free crystals. We'll get in eventually. They can't stop us forever. The sacrifice will be great, I'm not pretending otherwise. But, if we want to win this war, it is required." He did not break eye contact with the group while he replaced the cap on his grease pencil. Perry, standing nearby, crossed his arms and stared at the Slarts right along with his partner.

The gravity of the situation was finally hitting Architeuthis and sank in, lodging deep in his soul. Was he really willing to sacrifice so much? Could he order such an attack and endure the devastating loss of life that was bound to occur? General Hicks was fully prepared to go forward. Clearly, he was willing to risk the lives of his crew members, his lover Perry, and for that matter even his own. *These humans… these Earthers… do they really have no fear*? he thought. Was it brilliant and likely to work? Or was Hicks just brash and foolhardy, like Earthmen were often said to be? Architeuthis was convinced it was the former not the latter.

The leader of the rebellion looked around the room and saw the sad, emotion-filled eyes of his fellow Slarts. He looked back at the determined face of General Hicks, and the confident expression of his partner Perry. The Suidonji would fight. The Zorgs and Spleefs would fight. The Enos? They'd rush into battle headlong with the fearlessness of jungle cats. All Nausties would sacrifice everything they had to support their brethren in this epic battle.

Architeuthis thought for a moment. He needed to decide right now. What's more, only he could make the decision to send thousands of fellow Nausties to their deaths. Only he could take responsibility for this, come what may. With a deep sigh, Architeuthis calmly said, "General Hicks ... you may proceed. Inform the planning committee of all your supply and manpower needs as well as your timetables. Communicate with no one outside of this room about what we've discussed tonight. We will convene again in thirty Earth days."

CHAPTER 5: THE NAUSTIE REVOLT

Maintaining the utmost in secrecy, General Hicks of the new Naustie Planetary Command established battle groups throughout the planet in order to coordinate attacks on key guard posts. As was agreed, Suidonji did the tunneling, and work crews carefully moved large boulders or vehicles into place in a tactical grid pattern in front of their objectives. After that, they went right back to work and awaited word on when to mobilize.

As the time for the assault approached, unit commanders were told of the plan: on the day of attack, a unit of Zorgs was to assassinate the captain of the guard as they conducted their shift change and new guards were arriving from the surface. The goal was to kill as many of these miserable cretins as possible, while only a few of their comrades were still inside manning their guns.

The Zorgs would use deadly slingshots, with which they'd demonstrated proficiency during training. Their weapons were simple devices, thick rubber tubes around a metal brace which locked over the wrist and fired a stone projectile the size of a golf ball. At thirty yards they were fairly accurate and were deadly if they hit the head of a victim. Even closer in, these "slingers" hardly ever missed. Earthers were better at using javelins, so they were to move up and occupy forward positions and attempt to impale as many guards as possible after the Zorgs knocked off the commander.

Yet, despite the presentation to the planning commission months earlier, Hicks and his partner Perry had decided to attack only three guard posts for the initial assault. These first three guard posts selected were located nearest to elevator shafts leading up to the main terminal. General Hicks calculated that by securing these simultaneously all remaining guard posts would be abandoned planet-wide, once Warden Ggggaaah believed his stronghold was threatened. With the objective secure, they could assemble assault troops for the ascent. The entire offensive could then be directed on the main terminal. It was ambitious, to say the least, and a hard sell. Hicks had to convince Architeuthis and the others to sign off on it.

"Good day Gentlemen," began General Hicks. This was the last full meeting of the council before the big day. Everyone in attendance, from the Great Leader on down, was exhausted from months of planning and issuing deadlines to already-overworked crew leaders, farmers, blacksmiths, and soldiers, training for battle. The general was to give them a run-down of his objectives for the attack, which would be commencing within a few days.

"I'm adding a few more wrinkles," he admitted. As usual, he got right to the point without wasting time on formalities. "With your permission, I'd like to focus our efforts on these three food depots that I believe will yield the best results." As he said this, he pointed to a detailed diagram that Perry had drawn for him on a piece of prefab taken off a collapsed housing facility. For the past seven Earth years, it had been used to wall up the entrance to his and Archibald's cave back in the Templar Knights' homeland. Today, it was serving as a drawing board.

By now, Architeuthis knew that Hicks always came prepared, always had an answer for their objections. The Great Leader had chosen this general for good reason, and there was no doubt the man appreciated that he had the authority to carry out his duties however he saw fit. He wasn't stubborn – just supremely confident in his own judgment. That's what made him difficult to disagree with.

"Having determined the enemy's vulnerabilities, I've selected three strongholds to attack simultaneously. These three outposts are located next to main elevator shafts and what's more, are closer to the surface. We'll hit these first and use them as a bridgehead. Things should fall into place rather quickly after that." He then paused to allow for the inevitable reaction and debate to follow. Hicks, too, had learned something about his counterparts on the council. They liked details and they were diametrically opposed to bold assumptions.

"Three?" retorted Megalocyathus. "But General, three outposts won't provide us enough food to sustain ourselves. The offensive, that is. According to our calculations, this will never suffice. We need many times that number. Otherwise, within a week we'll start running out of supplies." As usual, Hicks and his partner Perry had anticipated their questions and were ready to respond. Perry had a way with the Slarts, due to his patience, so the grizzled General typically let him field their initial questions. Afterward, he'd summarize what Perry said, speaking directly to Architeuthis. This formula had worked repeatedly in extinguishing prolonged debate.

"We're aware of that, Megalocyathus." Perry stated respectfully, without waiting for Hicks to attempt a response. They'd been together so many years they knew each other's cues, just like an old married couple. "But there are greater issues here to deal with. Let's look at the bigger picture, shall we?" Hicks raised up, stood back from the table, and let his adjutant wear them down for a while.

"We know what these folks are like." continued Perry. "They're thugs, and to beat them we have to take them out, one by one, as rapidly as possible. It's not simply about just the food depots, either. I mean the guards themselves. We need to capture the entire service tunnel network within days. On the first day, preferably. Cut them off. Cut off any potential counterattack. Do that, and we can mop up the remaining depots in short order. With no central command, and finding themselves isolated miles below the surface, they'll be easy to handle." After that, General Hicks was quick on the draw to close the deal. He turned to a wide-eyed Architeuthis and gave his summary with typical bluntness.

"You see, it's better to go for the jugular instead of trying to secure numerous food depots in hopes of consolidating our forces for a prolonged engagement. That won't do shit for us when it comes to dealing with that bastard Ggggaaah. It'll never work, and we all know better. But let me tell you, what'll most certainly happen if we fart around too long is organized retaliation. Within weeks, if not days, those guards up there'll invade our caverns and kill everyone who resists. I can guarantee you that." He then paused as he turned to the council members. "That's how it is, gentlemen. Like it or not. The only way to win out is to go all out. We only get one chance to pull this off. And we'll never get a better one than right now, when we have the element of surprise."

Architeuthis fluttered his facial tentacles, as did the other Slarts sitting around the conference table. Most were taken aback. This was not what they'd anticipated at all. A gradual, systematic elimination of enemy strongholds was what they'd thought the plan was, with the primary objective being to capture supplies and sustain the offensive. Accomplishing that, they'd hold all the cards. Then they could make their move on Ggggaaah's headquarters with their full army and win the war.

Hicks was already way past that, and it was obvious. He wanted to aim right for the very heart of his opponent and overwhelm him while he was off-balance, before he could organize, before he could consolidate. The idea had merit.

The only problem was how dangerous this could be if the attack fizzled out only a few days into the campaign. *And what of this so-called service tunnel?* Architeuthis wondered. No one had ever seen it. Didn't know what they'd find there, even if they made it all the way up. It could turn into an ambush.

Nevertheless, Architeuthis was out of his element when it came to military tactics. Hicks knew what he was doing. *Or perhaps he is a madman*, speculated the large Slart. That, too, had to be considered. Architeuthis sighed and thought for a moment, raising his tentacle to placate his outraged planning staff. It was his decision now. Not theirs. But what should he do?

If he overruled his general, he'd be setting back the clock on an operation that was ready to move forward within a day or two. He could shut this down right now and in so doing save thousands of lives. But what if he was wrong? What if this was their one big chance to go for the jugular? He weighed the alternatives as best he could, but he had to decide.

He only knew what he'd always known. Humans were ruthless, and his enemy was the same if not worse. Hicks had the advantage in terms of numbers, there was no question of that. He also had the element of surprise, as the general had so eloquently put it. Besides that, his troops were totally committed. Committed to achieving their freedom and inspired to make sacrifices. What's more, if Hicks was right and thousands of Nausties made it into that service tunnel, what could stop them? Who could stop them? With no time to organize, would prison security forces even stand a chance?

Architeuthis stood. This he never did during meetings. And when he raised himself up, he stood eye-to-eye with his glowering, fiercely-determined commander – the one he'd bet all his fortunes on to deliver his fellow Nausties from tyranny. He fluttered his facial tentacles and spoke directly to the man, to convey his answer and let there be no doubt he'd approved the general's audacious plan. He'd take full responsibility, come what may. History would record it as such, regardless of the outcome.

"Very well, General," the Great Leader said. "I approve. Proceed." He then placed a dusty tentacle on Hicks' shoulder before adding one more thing. "And may the gods protect us in all our brave endeavors."

Thus, using Earth time measurements, the worldwide attack was slated to occur at 05:00, two days later. Architeuthis and his Slart planners sent out the message to the rest of the planet's crew leaders, ordering Zorg runners to spread the news. When the big day came, all of New Australia braced itself for the Great Naustie Revolt. They were about to go to war.

The planning, training, and preparation paid off, for as luck would have it, all three stations fell within a few hours. It wasn't even a fair fight. By burning sulfur combined with potassium nitrate, Slart scientists had developed a corrosive incendiary they called Vitriol. They contained the substance inside clay vessels which were hurled against fortified guard positions. As planned, Zorg slingers took out the post commanders at each station with a single salvo of stones, then hurled these sulfur bombs at kill slots located on the outside. The burning liquid corroded and burned the eyes and flesh of the surprised defenders.

Earthers who had trained at the javelin then stood up from behind boulders and fired salvos of throwing spears, while heavy infantry units made up mostly of Enoshi warriors moved up behind mobile steel blocking shields attached to a wheeled chassis. In the final phase of the outer assault, Earthers using acetylene cutting torches sliced through the security gates and made it into the stations to exterminate the last of the guards.

Eventually, the defenders were demoralized and fighting

desperately for their lives. In the case of one guard station, they were reduced to huddling terrified in the center, tending to their wounded, only to find their floor being cut away, and the ceiling being sliced open by Suidonji diggers. The smoke bombs Perry had designed were tossed through the openings and in the confusion, light infantry hopped through and butchered several guards with daggers fashioned from hand tools. When Enoshi warriors finally burst in through the sliced-open security gates, it was all over. In close combat, Enos could easily overwhelm the most formidable fighters quite easily. Most of these meagerly-trained prison guards didn't stand a chance.

Zorg runners circulated news of the victories using the communication tunnel created for them months earlier. And when word got out, troops assigned to the second phase of the attack amassed at all three locations for the long climb to the surface. The easy part had been accomplished. Now came the hard part.

Architeuthis, upon hearing of these tactical successes, heaved a deep, resonating, almost burbling sound, like Slarts commonly did when acknowledging something joyful. He then sat down with a relieved sigh, collapsing and curling his legs into a sort of bed, as Slartigifijians often did when at rest. It had all happened so fast, and as reports got back to the Great Leader of the victories, he so completely wanted to share in the jubilation of the other Slarts and staff members at headquarters. Unfortunately, there was still too much weighing heavily on his mind.

"Great Leader! We are winning." the Zorg messenger exclaimed. He was breathless from excitement, combined with the exertion from his run. Information had been relayed all the way down to Naustie headquarters deep below the surface; ten different Zorgs had been involved in the process. Skeeesh, as he was called, was the last runner charged with delivering the message. Architeuthis could only nod feebly in acknowledgment. All that ran through his three hearts was an icy feeling of dread.

"Yes, that is wonderful news, Skeeesh, thank you," was about all he could muster. His enormous head was adrift in a sea of worries. The poor young Zorgolongian, sentenced to this penal colony for aggravated assault five long years before, couldn't imagine what was afflicting the Great Leader so.

"Architeuthis? Are you alright?" he asked timidly, still wheezing trying to catch his breath. The large Slart calmly gestured with a big tentacle that he was fine. "Yes, I'm okay. Go on, Private. Give me the news. I'll be alright," he said. The youthful Zorg was only too happy to oblige.

"Well, Great Goddess of the sss-Sea!" he proclaimed. That was a common expression among Zorgolongians, who believed life on their planet had been created at the bottom of the ocean by divine beings which separated fish from amphibian – from whence all Zorgs had evolved. "Warden Ggggaaah has sounded a general alarm and shut down the elevators," he went on to say. "He has cut off his guard stations, abandoning them to fight to the death!"

The rest of the news was outstanding, however. One, then two, then three depots, one by one, had fallen like dominoes to the Naustie Army. The ecstatic Zorgolongian hissed with excitement, flicking his reptilian tongue. "Yes-sss, all three depots in a matter of a few hours. The guards are now trapped below with us. Ggggaaah has cut them off!" It was just as predicted. The heartless Warden had left his hapless security forces to battle it out on their own. Shut off the elevators. Pull back into a defensible position. Make it harder to get to him.

Architeuthis had prepared for that, yes, but these early reports were not completely accurate. Messengers arrived later and clarified: one elevator that had been captured was able to send up a unit of Enoshi and human shock troops, armed with captured EIC's taken off the dead bodies of the guards. This unit had made it to the service tunnel several miles above, right before Ggggaaah's staff had gone into lockdown. It turned out the evil Warden's only plan for defense was to hole up in his fortified headquarters and let his guards below fight it out until the whole planet below starved to death.

Now to be fair, Ggggaaah had every reason to assume such a strategy would succeed. The depots below the planet surface had only enough food to supply the rebelling prisoners for one month. Moreover, they'd have to capture all of these depots and defeat the garrisons, just to get to it. Even if they could accomplish this, the rebels were doomed to failure, and once they began to starve, thought Ggggaaah, they'd fear disaster. Then they'd surely surrender. Besides, even if they didn't they'd wither away eventually. Just like any pirate captain, Ggggaaah merely planned on bringing in thousands more prisoners once the mutiny fizzled out. In a few months, he'd be right back in business.

This did not concern Architeuthis, because General Hicks' plan already took that into account. Hicks had assumed that Ggggaaah would shut off power to the elevators as a security measure. In desperation, any trapped commander would encircle himself with his best troops and just let the enemy come to him. But Ggggaaah didn't yet consider himself to be trapped; that was the difference. He had underestimated his opponents and presumed he could defeat them by starving them into submission, just like he'd always done. Sadly – for Ggggaaah anyway – he was dead wrong.

True, General Hicks didn't know which of the three food depots would fall the easiest, so he had a thousand Enoshi shock troops in reserve, at the ready, at each location, to try and board freight elevators before power was cut off. It would be a twenty-minute ride to the surface in those gigantic cargo lifts. If all three captured elevators worked, that would make things easier, but if none of the elevators worked or didn't carry the warriors all the way to the surface, then the next few days would be very rough going for the rebels.

Luckily, however, one elevator was still serviceable all the way to the surface before Ggggaaah shut off power to it. While the other two food depots were being secured by the rebels, a thousand brave Enos scrambled into the first captured freight elevator, along with a platoon of Earther fire teams accompanying them. Each fire team used captured weapons from dead prison guards and set up barricades to protect themselves for when the elevator door opened at the service tunnel above.

"Prepare yourselves, brothers," growled Sergeant Burmilla. It was his unit now packed into the lone elevator which had been captured intact and still operable. "It's a long ride, we've been told. You Earthers up there … get ready with your weapons. When that gate opens, unleash hell, you hear me?" This command elicited more than a few determined grunts from the mass of sweating, anxious soldiers crowded in around him. They'd waited weeks for this day – and had been held back from the initial assault. Now, they were spoiling for a fight.

Not sure what they'd find when it opened – an ambush or a lone sentry, the Earthers at the front prepared for a deadly battle. The elevator hummed, whined, and groaned, then lifted the comparatively light load of grime- and dust-covered bodies for twenty terrifying minutes as it ascended from the bloody scene below. Packed in shoulder to shoulder, it was going to be an agonizingly long journey. Would the elevator complete its ascent? Or would it stop somewhere along the way, and leave them with another thousand feet to have to climb using service ladders? No one knew for sure.

"Well, you heard him, private," remarked Corporal Martinez. "When those doors open – the gate I mean – we'll blast them all to hell. Everyone we see – no matter who they are. You know that, right?" He was standing next to Hans Offmier, a German and former chef from the Earth province of Central Europe. Offmier had poisoned his unfaithful girlfriend and been convicted of murder. Now, he was intensely focused on the wall of the shaft in front of them. As long as he could see the car was moving, he knew things were going to work out fine. Still he struggled with the wait.

"And don't you worry about this here elevator. If we get stopped, we can climb out and go up that ladder over there," Martinez said, indicating with a subtle head gesture. He was still gripping his EIC and feeling around the buttons trying to remember all their functions: blast, scatter, etc. It reminded him of better times, when he was a cop back in New Los Angeles … before the shooting, before the trial, before he'd been stripped of his badge and sentenced to this awful place. He was soon interrupted by the platoon's resident cynic, Private Drummond.

"Yeah, just be sure if that happens you hold on real tight," he drawled. "Probably don't wanna mess up and let go. Long fall to the bottom if that happens, you know? Give you time to think about things before you splatter, eh Hans?" The burly Nebraskan then chuckled derisively. Corporal Martinez turned his head to glare at him, but it was too crowded to make eye contact. Instead he hissed at him to be quiet. This was no time for wry humor.

"Don't listen to that asshole. You stick with me, Private," Martinez assured the nervous German. "Focus on the mission. We gotta clear out that service tunnel in every direction." Private Offmier nodded as his eyes continued blinking from the dust inside the compartment. *Bitte beweg dich schneller!* he thought, *if only this damn elevator would move more quickly!* He continued to watch the wall of the elevator shaft as the massive lift crept ever so slowly upward.

Thankfully for the heavily armed Enoshi and Earthers holding carbide lamps in case of a power shutdown, the elevator completed the ascent. Then, to their relief, the doors opened and only about a hundred Zorgolongian security troops were awaiting its arrival. Only this was no ambush. The poor guards were still expecting an empty elevator to open up for them to ride down and suppress the rebellion. Remarkably, their Lieutenant had called the elevator right about the time the Enoshi and their Earther allies had boarded it, so the entire band of Zorgs were anticipating an empty chamber. Most hadn't even activated their weapons yet.

As the lift crept over the edge of the service tunnel floor, Earthers holding EIC's and manning larger EIC machine guns on tripods opened fire, decimating the surprised security force, and scattering those not immediately killed. That's when the massacre began.

"No quarter!" cried Sergeant Burmilla. "No prisoners!" he then roared. Corporal Martinez, by way of comparison, was blunter. "Kill 'em all boys!" he yelled, as they rushed out into the tunnel, stepping on dead Zorgs as they did so. It was, as General Hicks predicted, bloody carnage.

As the last of the prison response team fell or tried to flee in terror, Enoshi warriors went wild and rushed forward to slaughter them, as well as more than five hundred mining engineers, truck haulers, and unarmed personnel working in the tunnel. These terrified civilians employed by the mine had been working in relative safety for years, never expecting anything quite like this. Their screams and cries for help filled the tunnel for miles in every direction, as bloodthirsty killers chased them down to butcher them mercilessly.

"Get that one!" yelled Martinez. He was screaming at Private Drummond to shoot down a fleeing Zorg who'd panicked and dropped his EIC before sprinting away. Drummond was quick to comply. "Hell yeah!" he called out, as he aimed his weapon and fired. He paused for a brief moment, only to set it on spray. The Zorg was nearly cut in half. "Got him, Corporal!" he responded with a hearty laugh. And with that, the platoon of Earthers moved into a tight formation and began trotting forward in a mass of combined firepower. They advanced as one, shooting anything that moved.

So many years of oppression and humiliation came to an end for these brave warriors. Left on the doorstep of an eternal hell by their home planets – abandoned to serve out the rest of their lives in near-darkness – occasionally starved into submission – abused and over-worked by heartless prison guards. Enraged Enoshi and their Earther allies became overcome with bloodlust. They killed anyone they saw, maimed and mutilated everyone they could catch. Soon an orgy of violence was engulfing the service tunnel in both directions, as Earther Nausties blasted round after round from captured EIC's until they ran out of ammunition. Then, they picked up unused weapons from dead security troops and started all over again. Everyone was an enemy. Everyone was a target. There would be no prisoners taken today, and as Sergeant Burmilla commanded, no quarter given. Those who tried to surrender were shot or bludgeoned to death. Those who tried to escape were heartlessly mowed down.

"You can run but you'll die tired!" screamed a human from the Earth province of North America. A Texan, he'd been dreaming of this moment almost every night for nearly a year. "You like that?" he yelled tauntingly. "How about that?" he then added, as he clipped off twenty more rounds into the face of a surrendering Suidonji tunnel driver. The poor fellow's head spattered like a crushed watermelon.

The slaughter continued for hours, until the main terminal was only a mile or so away. Victory was within their grasp. Yet, they would need reinforcements to try and tackle Ggggaaah's headquarters. Inside the terminal on the planet surface, located under a large tinted glass dome the size of a small city, was a military base that housed thousands of security troops and personnel from several different planets. This was their goal, and it would be one tough nut to crack.

But General Hicks had prepared for this. Below the service tunnel, nearly a mile underground, Schpleefti light infantry were already scrambling up service ladders inside the two deactivated elevator shafts. Spleefs were rodent-like beings that had evolved from rats and mice on their home planet, to eventually become the dominant species. Yet, they were just as brave as they were cunning, standing about four-and-a-half feet tall on average. They were fast and nimble, able to scramble using claw-like hands with strong fingers, perfect for the task. Possessing daggers, their job was to burst into the massive tunnel through maintenance hatches, using explosive charges if necessary. Then, they were to fan out to slaughter anyone and everyone they could find. If possible, their orders were to reactivate the elevators and send up Enoshi, Suidonji, and Earther reinforcements.

Zorg units followed, and their task was to reinforce any

bridgehead established by the Spleefs. Not quite as nimble at climbing, Zorgs were nevertheless bigger and more powerful. They were far crueler and more cold-blooded in combat, too, so if the Spleefs faltered or scattered in the face of enemy fire, their Zorg allies were quite capable of sustaining the attack until help arrived.

Eventually, word got back to Warden Ggggaaah that prisoners had broken out and were threatening the main terminal bay with a small force of infantry. Still not fully grasping the seriousness of the threat, Ggggaaah merely ordered electricity shut off to the mine. Planet-wide, the convicts below found themselves in total darkness, and had to rely on carbide lamps to move about. However, that left another major problem to contend with: how to capture all the remaining well-defended food depots, in the dark, and feed those tens of thousands of Nausties below.

Architeuthis and his planners had prepared for this as well, actually. Springing into action on the day of the attack, Earthers, Suidonji, and Zorgs commandeered captured mining vehicles and transport trucks, while Spleefs hurried to collect the hydroponically farmed crops, then raced through miles of mining tunnels to distribute food. Abandoned guard stations and food depots were also assumed to be available once the guard stations below were vacated. That's what Hicks had predicted would happen, once Nausties made it into the service tunnel, yet now, trapped inside, were thousands of terrified guards, left behind to fight it out on their own. It seemed the Nausties would have to conquer each one.

Architeuthis and his planners didn't panic, though. They merely hoped, now that the first three depots had fallen, the same tactical plan could be used over and over again to secure these remaining strongholds. It would be at the expense of thousands more killed or wounded yes, but eventually, they could be taken. Hicks and his staff went right to work mobilizing units for assaults on the remaining depots, and within hours, he had battle plans for the next fifty.

"Well, gentlemen," began Hicks at his next meeting with Architeuthis and his team. As his army was busy mopping up in the service tunnel up near the surface, he had made one last trip down to headquarters to meet with his superior. Things were coming together, and he was brimming with confidence. He entered the secret cave as though he were a conquering hero.

"The good news is, it's gonna be a lot easier hittin' these 'ole guard stations in the dark." Then he grinned. Perry chuckled darkly. If Slarts were capable of laughing derisively they would have as well. Instead, they merely nodded and fluttered their facial tentacles. "We're gonna take 'em out one by one though," Hicks continued. He proceeded to detail for them his strategy for accomplishing this.

But then an amazing thing happened. Guards at the remaining food depots actually began surrendering. Sure enough, after a day or so, seeing the futility of their situation, and cut off from any communication with headquarters, guard posts began negotiating terms for surrender. When large forces of Nausties appeared outside, most simply gave up and tossed out their weapons.

General Hicks ordered all their lives to be spared, of course – they'd be vital sources of information later in the war. Thus within a few days, the Nausties had secured nearly the entire planet's interior. Soon they were massing inside the service tunnel itself. The tide was turning; however, this was still going to be a desperate battle.

CHAPTER 6: THE RAMP

"Alright boys, how do we crack this walnut with our butt cheeks?" asked General Hicks with a sarcastic grin. In the dimness his men chuckled and snickered quietly. It was still a very serious situation, but the general's surprising levity was nevertheless appreciated. Hicks had gathered his military advisors inside the giant loading bay to plan the final attack, and the first expectation he wanted to set was this: no idea was too far-fetched. Nothing was too crazy. Time was running out. By now, Ggggaaah surely must have put out a distress call. The only bad idea anyone could have suggested was to wait it out for a few days. They didn't have a few days.

Emergency lights were all that shone inside the service tunnel now, and as far as anyone could tell, the entire area for miles in every direction had been secured. This was their bridgehead, and supplies were beginning to pour in from below.

They'd been fortunate so far: as it turned out, freight elevators could run on emergency backup power, connected to their own auxiliary systems in case of a planet-wide blackout. True, elevators were equipped with a shut-off switch that could be engaged at the top in case of a riot. But, they still had their own individual power systems, which could run the elevator separately from the main electrical grid until they'd need to be recharged.

The discovery that they could operate elevators was indeed a relief, especially after those poor Spleefs and Zorgs had climbed all the way up and realized just how difficult it turned out to be. No one wanted to have to do it again – not to mention repeatedly. Carrying up supplies in that way would have required thousands of Nausties wearing backpacks filled with water vessels or food rations. It would have taken days to perform this, and to continually supply forward units in this manner would have been a monumental task. Yet, amazingly enough, the leader of the Schpleeftkorkii crew had devised a system for just such an operation.

His concept, which fortunately never ended up having to be implemented, was to use two captured elevator shafts and create a gigantic circuit of Spleefs, Earthers, and Zorgs working in supply brigades of fifteen hundred to two thousand troops. They would, if necessary, wear sacks tied to their backs filled with several pounds of supplies and climb all the way up to the service tunnel on ladders three feet wide. Then, when they'd completed the ascent, they'd use captured transport vehicles to travel across the service tunnel to another empty elevator shaft and climb all the way back down. Service vehicles below would transport them back to the other shaft to reload with supplies, then they'd climb back to the surface once more. The Schpleeftkorkii crew leader, one Solomon Mwanga, was an Earther, and he'd allied with several other crews to create three brigades for this ingenious scheme.

Schpleeftkorkii crew members were able to ferry up supplies on enormous platforms. What a lucky break that was. And this rebel army was in dire need of lucky breaks too, because the air below the surface was getting thinner and thinner every day they fought on against security forces defending Ggggaaah's stronghold.

In the meeting between Hicks and his aides, the General urged the men in his unit to think outside the box as he put it, using an old Earth expression. Standing on the cavern floor, looking up at the ceiling, Hicks and his men had to contemplate the monumental task of getting all the way up to the command center above them. And, no doubt, up in that command center, 250 feet above the cavern floor, Ggggaaah and his own aides were looking right back down at them, trying to guess their next move.

All access to and from the loading bay had been cut off when the riot alarm had sounded, so Hicks and his men were going to have to figure out a way up to the planet surface, where the main terminal facility was located. Otherwise, they'd have to find a way of breaking into the terminal office complex, up near the top of the canyon. That's what was to be discussed today.

Hicks folded his arms and glared. "We've got about three days of good air before it starts thinning out in here, boys. We've got to find a way up there and we've got to hurry up too," he said, gesturing toward the sliding roof above them, now sealed tight. Nausties had discovered the emergency controls for it, located at the base of the loading bay, and had disabled them already. At least for the time being, Ggggaaah couldn't control it from his headquarters. That would have been disastrous. "Nothing's too crazy, like I said. Give me any idea you can come up with." There was a long pause. No one wanted to be the first to suggest something stupid.

"Anything at all, come on boys." he added, hands on his hips and glaring at them with a smirk. Finally, several long moments later, ideas began to flow in from members of the group. Some were creative, some were unrealistic, and some were downright apocalyptic: from spot-welding components of equipment together and creating a giant scaffolding, to detonating the thermonuclear warheads inside the captured spacecraft, still sitting down in the loading bay with them. This idea involved blowing up the entire terminal, leaving nothing but a giant crater. The premise behind this desperate approach was simple: if the Nausties could not survive much longer on thin air and dwindling rations, they'd take out Ggggaaah's staff and security forces, right along with the whole terminal. Then, they'd find a way to survive on the planet, further developing their hydroponic farms below.

Perry dismissed that idea immediately, saying with an annoyed sigh, "No, no, no. We're not desperate enough to blow up the terminal … not yet, anyway." After all, Perry reasoned that capturing the terminal intact was still the best solution, regardless of casualties. His greatest fear, after the fall of the Warden's headquarters, was for the planet to descend into chaos, murder, and perhaps even civil war.

But that one crazy idea about blowing up the entire terminal eventually led to less crazy ones. Eventually, an extremely ambitious idea was proposed, one that only someone like Perry could grasp and be inspired by. In fact, when it was first mentioned, everyone balked at the sheer audacity of it – except for Perry. It just needed a little tweaking, that's all, because someone in the group suggested they build a giant hill – out of mineral ore. It took a madman to come up with an insane concept such as this, and the Templar Knights certainly had plenty of those.

The man's name was Vladimir "the Impaler" Vyebyvatsya, and he was from the Earth province of Russia. Back on his home planet, he'd been leader of a Russian mafia cartel, and responsible for over a hundred different murders. Some, he'd participated in himself, or been the triggerman. Now pushing fifty, he was tattooed from head to toe, just like a lot of Russian gangsters, and though long in the tooth, he was still quite terrifying. His strong accent made him all the more intimidating.

"I have idea, General," he suddenly said, after all the other proposals had been rejected. "What if we were to dump truckloads of dirt all over that large space craft still parked over there? Build a large mountain out of it. One that could reach top of cavern." Hicks gave him a confused look, then glanced over at his assistant's reaction. Perry was expressionless at first, then the slender fellow began stroking his chin. That was a sure sign Perry was mulling things over. General Hicks instinctively remained silent as the others on his staff did the same. Sensing no one was shooting him down quite yet, Vladimir continued.

"Then we construct a spiraling roadway," making a swirling motion with his index finger around an imaginary mountain of berm. "One we could ascend, you see? And once we reach the summit, our men could use explosive charges to take out command center. From that breach, we enter facility and kill defenders." The other aides at first scoffed at such an idea, believing that it would take too long, even if it were feasible. After all, the base would have to be quite enormous to create a road wide enough for vehicles to drive to the top. Perry however immediately saw how the concept made sense, given the resources they had available. It only needed a slight alteration.

"You know what, General? I think The Impaler may have something there," he interjected. Suddenly all eyes were upon him, especially those of the scary Russian who'd thought it up. The rest of the aides looked at Perry with surprise. He continued, though, gesturing at the space craft, and then up at the walls of the cavern above, while the General and his staff watched curiously.

"Let's think about this a moment. Say we take this idea of a large dirt mound but make it into a ramp. We use the spacecraft underneath to support its weight, like the Impaler is saying, then we simply back a dump truck up it to speed up the process. Before long. Bingo! We've got an incline leading up to the command center. Walk right up it and dynamite our way through."

The Impaler nodded in approval then added, "Right. See General? Or maybe we drive tractor up that dirt ramp to the wall of space terminal offices and use like battering ram. They're right over there, you see?"

Hicks looked across the massive loading bay which was the size of a sports stadium and nodded. He immediately grasped what the Russian was speaking of: an array of windows, several levels high, reinforced glass extending floor to ceiling. He could even see desks and furniture. Now it was all coming together. Perry took over from that point.

"He's right, General. Captured guards have told us that on the other side of that wall are hundreds of offices and barracks for soldiers, even a mess hall. You can see them through the windows up there. Look."

There were indeed many windows, and if the assault ramp were wide enough, there could be a constant convoy of dump trucks driving up with full loads to put down additional layers – allowing plenty of room for a tunnel driller to drive up and break through. Hicks was sold. Those brainy Slarts could figure out the engineering. He had thousands of experienced mine workers to help create it. He already liked the way it sounded, probably because it reminded him of something from his youth …

Archibald Hicks loved reading about ancient warfare when he was a student in college, and he could recognize immediately how they were taking a page right out of Earth's ancient history: much like Alexander's ingenious mole, which he had constructed to attack the city of Tyre in 332 BC, or the Assyrian King Sennacherib's siege of Lachish in 701 BC. More specifically, this sounded much like the way the Romans did it during the Siege of Masada in 73 AD. This plan that Perry and the Impaler proposed would be almost exactly like that of General Lucius and the Tenth Legion. In the assault on Masada, the same strategy was employed: an earthen ramp was built, leading up to an otherwise impregnable mountain fortress, perched on a mesa overlooking a valley.

It was brilliant what the Romans devised, using ten thousand legionnaires, auxiliaries, and slaves, to build an earthen causeway, in the desert heat no less, by hand. But, somehow, they did it. Soldiers dumped basket after basket of soil onto a narrow path that gradually led up to the gate of the fortress. It took three months to create the ramp and make it wide enough and strong enough for their army to attack up it. They knew they'd be pelted with arrows and stones by the defenders as soon as they got within range; however, that failed to deter them.

The Romans were successful in finishing the ramp, which is still there to this day, taking thousands of casualties in the process. They built it with bedrock and soil from the nearby desert, broiling under the sun as they worked, day after day. Yet, they kept on dragging dirt up that ramp, until it was solid enough to hold horses with wagons. After that, wagons carried even more dirt for them to pile up and smooth out, to create a solid roadway. They used wooden beams to add stability. Then, they dragged a metal-clad battering ram up to the gate to punch a hole.

Of course, when they finally got there, the Romans found only horror and death. Almost all nine hundred sixty-one rebels had killed themselves in the night. It seemed none of them wanted to live out the rest of their lives as Roman slaves. Preferring death, they'd committed mass suicide. When they secured the fortress, the Romans found only a few women and children left alive, hiding in an empty cistern. These they spared, selling them to slave traders who'd no doubt been anticipating a much bigger haul.

This concept would be similar. They'd build a giant ramp by using thousands of already experienced miners to pile up millions of tons of soil and ore, then form a road on top to drive a tractor across. The tractor could have a drill mounted to the front, which could punch a giant hole in the wall hundreds of feet above them. And just like the doomed defenders of Masada thousands of years ago, the Warden and his staff would get to watch this amazing feat going on below them, with nothing to do but wait and see if the rebels could make it all the way.

In antiquity, it took the Romans about three months to finally take the fortress of Masada; could the Nausties pull off the same thing? And could they do it before the thin air exhausted them? Before their food supplies ran out? Moreover, before help arrived to rescue the besieged Warden and his staff?

Perry looked around at the other aides from the war council. Hicks was grinning and nodding, so was The Impaler. A few others grunted and rubbed their bald heads. Looking up at the challenge before them, it struck them with a sense of awe, as well as apprehension. This was going to be a monumental task, yet they had all the resources to do it. Historically, the Romans had much more time to build theirs; however, the Nausties had mechanized vehicles and mining equipment. Plus, they had thousands of workers. It could most certainly be done.

The General and his men were standing right next to the enormous landing pad and their newly captured spacecraft, *The Unity* which had been docked and readied for loading when the rebels burst in. Perry had renamed her *The Anarchy*. Everyone looked up one more time at the command bubble suspended from the ceiling of the cavern. It seemed so far away, so very high above them. It made them pause and think about how this would factor into their plans. That became the next topic of discussion.

"Okay then. You sold me," replied Hicks. "Now what about that big thing up there? That big glass bubble commanding a view of the loading bay. What're we going to do about it once we get close? You boys got any solutions for that?"

He imagined his fellow Nausties working hastily around the clock, only to come under deadly fire from defenders occupying it. At some point, this ramp they were speaking of would close well within a hundred feet. "You know, sooner or later those security forces are going to figure out they can pick us off like flies on a screen door from up there," he observed.

The command bubble was a glassed-in traffic control building, suspended from the top of the cavern like a chandelier in a giant ballroom. It was enormous and oval shaped, about the size of a townhouse with two levels of offices and desks manned by mostly Zorgs and a few other beings, who observed and coordinated the loading and unloading of ships in the cargo bay below. From the command bubble, terminal traffic controllers could see everything going on, and this idea of a dirt ramp? They'd see everything the Nausties were doing from start to finish.

"No deceiving those bastards this time, P." muttered General

Hicks to Perry. But Perry was still thinking deeply, arms crossed and with one hand still stroking his three-day beard. He thought about the captured freighter and the nuclear warheads inside. He pictured the enormous ramp leading up to the offices above and imagined a long line of dump haulers moving up and down the earthen causeway. Perry looked over at his General with a mischievous grin. He was forming yet another brilliant idea.

Within hours, Slart planners were brought up from Naustie headquarters. A new field headquarters was established, in full view of the command bubble. That was Perry's idea, and though Hicks questioned him on it, Perry assured his partner that it was better the Warden and his staff think they knew everything that was going on at all times. As Perry put it, "Let them see what we're doing, for a while at least. We want them to plan for their defense according to what they think they see. Trust me. I've thought this one through, General." He then winked subtly.

The General raised his hands, shook his head slightly, and chuckled playfully. No use questioning his long-time companion. Hicks and Perry had been together for ten years, and by now, Hicks knew full well that when his right-hand man was onto something just to let him be. Hicks was the brawn, Perry was the brains. Doubtless, his adjutant had taken everything into consideration.

Meanwhile, the Slarts estimated that the height to reach would be two hundred feet, with a feasible grade for a fully-laden dump hauler. This would put them right up next to the wall of the canyon, and level with the employee mess hall looking out at the loading bay. The command bubble was about fifty feet higher and suspended from the ceiling about three hundred feet from the cavern wall. The plan Perry initially hatched was to drill through the thick glass wall, create a breach, then rush through with shock troops eliminating any defenders. That's the way Perry wanted the Warden to see things that is. Most importantly that's what he wanted his enemy to prepare for.

The Slarts then estimated how long the ramp would need to be. They calculated necessary labor and equipment needs and assigned work teams. Thousands of Nausties were called up from the mines below, and for three long weeks they worked in shifts, dumping and then packing, piling and spreading millions of tons of soil, rocks, and mineral extract. Crews followed dump trucks with water buckets to douse the ramp, and packed it firmly with shovels, so it would bear the weight of the tractor drill. Thousands more worked in teams, loading full-size haulers with ore from the nearby crushing plant. Drills were used, and in some cases, explosives were employed to blow up walls and doors to warehouses storing food supplies or tools. Warden Ggggaaah's aides watched with amazement at the frenzied activity below ....

"Sss-sir, the prisoners... they are building a ramp!" exclaimed the nervous messenger. He was a browbeat on the Warden's security team – the equivalent of a Sergeant Major in most armies. A Zorg just like Ggggaaah, and much older than the young scullion who ran the front desk in the Warden's executive offices, he'd raced from the command bubble to notify his commander. Prison security forces had been monitoring the rebels in the terminal bay ever since they'd flooded into the area. Watched them overwhelm personnel still trapped there. Saw them storm the humongous transport vessel parked on the pad, killing the crew onboard. In only a few days of observing, he was now able to report back to the boss about the rebels' progress. Now the picture was becoming clearer. This was no longer a containment operation. It was a siege.

"A what?" asked the headstrong commander. Warden Ggggaaah couldn't believe his tiny reptilian ears. "A ramp, you said. Out of what?" This made no sense, and for the life of him he couldn't imagine why they'd do such a thing.

"Yes, Warden. A ramp. I'm certain of it," the officer replied. "They've been piling dirt onto that big freighter on the pad, the one they captured a few days ago. They've covered it and have started driving dump haulers onto it. They're making a road, sir."

Ggggaaah suddenly came unglued. "Preposterous-sss!" he hissed. "This I've got to see." He went down to the command bubble to see for himself; and to his dismay thousands upon thousands of convicts were now hard at work. Enoshi, Zorgolongians like himself, Earthers, Schpleeftii, Suidonji, and amazingly over in one area of the cavern, Slartigifijians. Among them was one very tall figure standing in the center, clearly in charge of the operation. The excited browbeat pointed him out with a long scaly claw.

"That's got to be Architeuthis, Warden," he indicated. "I've heard of him, sir. Troublemaker. Been here for years. That's him I'd wager." The browbeat's name was Yeeeeeeek. Warden Ggggaaah hissed angrily for a moment then muttered cynically.

"Hmmm. Oh yes-sss, I see… Architeuthis. I thought that pathetic old Slart would be dead by now." He then chuckled nervously. As ridiculous as things looked from up in the command bubble, Ggggaaah couldn't help an icy chill running up and down his spinal column, which protruded from the skin on his back. On older Zorgs this was much more pronounced.

"They must be insane, Warden," commented Yeeeeeeek, trying to placate his superior. Ggggaaah chuckled evilly, only it wasn't very convincing. The browbeat could sense growing apprehension within his normally cool-headed commandant.

There were other things Yeeeeeeek and his comrades would see happening during their 'round-the-clock shifts in the command bubble over the next few weeks: organization for one thing. The more they watched the more they noticed. Those rebel prisoners exhibited military-like precision in practically everything they did regardless of their shoddy appearances. Browbeat Yeeeeeeek got an increasingly sinking feeling with each passing day.

Sealed off rooms and chambers the Nausties burst through with explosives let manufactured air in from the air processing plant on the surface, replenishing supply within the service tunnel. This was a pleasant surprise to the suffering workers, and one they hadn't anticipated. Yet despite that bit of good fortune, precautions were carefully adhered to. Slart planners had calculated for each species just how long they could work on the ramp before having to take a break, and other crewmen rotated in. Crewmen taken off the hill for mandatory breaks were sent to recovery rooms to replenish their oxygen levels. These ventilated chambers and warehouses made for excellent facilities to rest workers who'd exhausted themselves. Therefore, plundered food warehouses became a splendid place to set up a barracks. It allowed crews time to convalesce between work shifts.

However, it also gave General Hicks an idea. If those rooms and warehouses were ventilated, then they had to have air ducts, and if there were industrial-size air ducts pumping fresh air into those rooms, then perhaps smaller beings could move through them. Schpleeftii were tiny enough for the job, so Spleef night raiders were sent through the air shafts with the goal of capturing the air processing facility itself. They got quite far, but eventually their surprise attack was blunted by far superior security forces when they tried to secure the pumping plant. In this bloody five-day battle, nearly a hundred engineers working for the enemy were slaughtered, and Nausties were able to override the air system controls to pump fresh air back into the mines.

Their hold on the oxygen pumping plant was temporary though, and afterward, the Spleefs had to retreat through tubes which only they were small enough to fit inside. Their daggers and throwing knives were no match for electrical impulse cannons. Yet, for several days, the air system blasted freshly oxygenated air into the caverns and caves below. Workers were revitalized.

It came right on time, too, because by the third week, work crews found themselves having to be rotated every few hours to stave off exhaustion. Food from plundered warehouses and drinkable water were plentiful, manpower was plentiful, and so was raw determination. But healthy air still remained as the only thing in short supply. Yeeeeeeek and his comrades could see how they struggled down below, slaving away day after day. He wondered what drove them. He also marveled at their ingenuity. If only he could have seen what was really going on behind the scenes.

During this period, far below in the planet depths, the Slarts and their new Zorg assistants, former guards who'd surrendered and joined the Nausties, had been working feverishly for days in developing solutions for the challenges going on above. Each Food Depot and Guard Station had its own generator which had been provided in case of a riot or electrical outage. Hundreds of these were cannibalized and eventually combined to form a make-shift power plant. This gave electrical power for running water filtration systems and for charging electrical vehicles, both of which were vital to the operation. Best of all, these generators were powered by piezoelectricity, and the planet had plenty of crystals that could be used to power them.

Aquifers continued to supply water for their filtration systems. Crews of Nausties were recruited for the purpose of transporting water and food to the service tunnel above. Soon, over half the planet's former prison population were up in the service tunnel, serving in any capacity they could. Meanwhile, nearly ten thousand Nausties worked feverishly loading dump trucks full of soil and mineral deposits to form the ramp. It would take several million tons to create it, and as long as no relief force arrived in time Slart engineers were certain they could complete a ramp long enough, as well as high enough, to reach the Mess Hall windows above.

Again, none or at least very little of this activity remained secret to the Warden and his forces for very long. That's what Perry was hoping for. He intended for it to be seen and prepared for by his enemy. Security troops as well as Warden Ggggaaah could view practically everything going on from above. They even calculated the exact location for an eventual breach, based on the trajectory of the ramp. To be sure, for the first week they did scramble a bit – and panic – realizing the rebels controlled the loading bay. Worse, the only ship on the whole planet, their only means of escape, was now sitting right in the middle of it, firmly in rebel hands.

This giant cargo ship was an Earth Cruiser, capable of defending itself in a fire fight. It was armed with thermonuclear missiles. It was able to hold a payload of many tons of processed mineral ore. Captured early in the uprising, it now served as the central support for the rebels' attack ramp. The crew had been dispatched, butchered right where they sat when rebels burst in. It was about the size of a five-story Earth office building lying on its side, and carried a complement of 200 crewmembers, engineers, and support personnel when fully outfitted.

Yet, to the amazement of the Warden and his besieged security forces, the rebels had buried it in mineral ore – enough ore to fill two or three transport ships. Warden Ggggaaah still refused to believe they'd succeed however. Others shared in his sentiments – and for good reason. He noticed it almost immediately. There seemed to be a flaw in the ramp's design ....

"They'll never make it. You know that don't you, browbeat?" queried the Warden. He was visiting the command bubble one day and mocking those silly fools laboring diligently below. Yeeeeeeek nodded in agreement, even if he was still impressed at the rebels' determination as of late.

Only days before, his forces had driven back hordes of Schpleeftii in an attempt to capture the planet's air processing plant. They'd barely fought them off; there were so many. What's more, they were courageous, those Spleefs – fast-moving, strong, and deadly with their daggers. He'd lost 50 of his comrades on the first day of the battle. Another 200 perished trying to secure the facility four days later. It was a bloodbath.

"No sir," replied Yeeeeeek. "I mean, yes sir. They won't. I'm sure of it. I've been watching the past few days, and noticed they've been sending out Slarts to examine the construction site. Seems like they're in a quandary, eh Boss?" Warden Ggggaaah began to snicker.

"Oh yes. The fools are at an impasse I can tell. But they finally noticed the problem, I'll give them that. I'm surprised it took so long. A hatchling could see it. Their ramp has nothing stable holding it up on the other side of that freighter. Idiots. They'll march up that path thinking they're ready, thinking they'll get to us, only to have the ground collapse below their feet."

Ggggaaah turned to leave the command bubble and return to his office. "No, I wouldn't worry about our unwelcome guests bothering us much longer down in the loading bay. Another month or two and they'll be out of food. When that happens, I'll make them clean up their own mess once they surrender. If not, I'll let them starve. Oh, you'll see, browbeat," he quipped. "They'll never make it. Mark my words." Then he stalked off. He'd made a good point, Yeeeeeek had to admit. With nothing supporting the backside of the ramp, it would never support the weight of an assault force. Only Ggggaaah had once again underestimated his enemy's capabilities. The Nausties had already determined a solution.

As the earthen causeway reached, then cleared the captured Cruiser, it was determined the ramp would need further support. So, while dump haulers carried material up one side, Suidonji welders rigged together scaffolding out of inoperable vehicles, mine train cars, guard outposts, and cannibalized equipment from the rock crushing plant to provide stability on the other side. These would be driven or dragged up to the base of the spillway and buried as the dump haulers progressed with their loads. Massive stalagmites at the base of the ancient cavern would form much of the remaining support as the ramp got closer and closer to the canyon wall, it was determined.

But this created a host of new problems. The first of these was just how close trucks could get to dump their contents, and secondly, how much support was needed at the very top for the tractor drill. Objections arose repeatedly from those meticulous, ever-calculating Slarts. To hear their side of it, it would have seemed like every day there was yet another crisis that had to be addressed. Yet Perry was undeterred. Privately he would tell Hicks to simply brush them off. Instead of addressing their concerns he kept assuring the General he had it all figured out ....

"Not to worry, Hickey," Perry would say whenever they were alone. He was always doing that sort of thing even before the rebellion and Hicks being made Supreme Commander of the Naustie Army. He'd try and calm his partner whenever he was faced with a challenge. Whenever they'd run out of food, water, or medical supplies. When they were low on acetylene for their welding torches and needed to repair equipment. Within days or hours, he'd have a solution. Never failed. What's more his solutions typically worked out perfectly. Archibald grew to rely on it. But this time? This time it was far more important to be accurate. Guessing or assuming could be disastrous. In a way, the General was becoming more and more like his annoying Slart advisors.

"Well, goddammit, of course I'm worried, P!" retorted General Hicks one night as they settled into their pallet for a four-hour nap. The Slarts were complaining, yet again, about engineering problems with the ramp.

"You keep saying you've got things all figured out. Slarts keep saying we don't. They say spillage on the other side of the Earth Cruiser has to be much wider and cover the whole width of the tunnel leading out of the canyon. They say as the ramp widens, it creates more instability toward the top. It'll never support our tunnel drill is what they're telling me. I mean, shit. I got a lot of folks counting on this to work out. Lives are at stake. The whole rebellion is too." Perry was unfazed. He smiled and put an arm around Archibald's shoulder, embraced him with the other as they lay there in bed. They were practically nose to nose.

"It's like I told you, Hickey. I got this all worked out. You'll see." Hicks was growing impatient. *What could he be planning?* he thought. *The lunatic! He couldn't possibly be out-thinking those damn Slarts, so why is he so confident?* That's what General Hicks wanted to know.

Progress was being made, he had to admit. Dump haulers were climbing ever higher with each passing hour, backing up the long path to the top and slowing as they neared the summit, poised precariously at the edge and emptying their payload. It went on and on like that around the clock. Maybe Perry was smarter than them. It was far too much for Hicks to understand, anyway. He was exhausted, for one thing. Had a job to do, and, like any good general, that's all he cared about.

"I got this," Perry whispered, caressing his stomach. "Leave it to me, okay?" Perry then kissed him sweetly. "We're getting closer and closer every day," he added softly. General Hicks sighed and soon drifted off to sleep.

In a way Perry had a point. With so many Nausties working together, and with such excellent crew organization, the massive undertaking had started coming together in only a few weeks. By then, Spleef night raiders had explored more of the air system network and opened up air shafts with explosive charges to feed cleaner air into the cavern where thousands of their comrades labored.

Then, yet another setback. The ramp by now had reached a height that was unfortunately within firing range of security forces inside the command bubble. That presented an even deadlier challenge. Sure enough, just as Hicks had feared, defenders tried blowing out glass walls with dynamite to fire their EIC's at the rebels below, and in a quarter of an hour they killed off several hundred who had no choice but to try running down the ramp in terror.

Perry's genius continued to shine, as he'd prepared for just that very thing. His approach was dangerous, but it worked. Zorg slingers were sent up behind rolling shields pushed by Enos. Armed with acid-filled clay pots, they flung these incendiaries through open windows and burned the flesh of security forces manning gun positions inside. Concealed behind metal shields, Enos then hurled grappling hooks with ropes in giant salvos into now-vacated openings.

Next, brave Spleefs climbed up those ropes with directional charges slung over their backs. These they attached to the lower part of the structure, while the defenders desperately tried braving expert javelin fire—from Earthers supporting the attack—to try and cut the ropes. Some succeeded at the cost of their lives, but only a few lines were cut. Sadly, a handful of Spleefs fell to their deaths. It was too late, however; the damage was done. Charges were set all around the base of the now-doomed command bubble as its defenders fought on.

The charges were set for only thirty seconds, and with one massive roar from their unit commander, the entire ramp full of warriors fled, down the incline to the cavern floor to take cover, with Spleefs repelling from above onto their comrades' shoulders. Soon the blasts went off, and debris was flying in all directions, crashing down on the cheering Nausties below. Bodies fell from the command bubble too.

It was a smashing success, literally.

The explosions were not enough to destroy the whole structure, but the entire base of it did collapse and fall, letting even more freshly manufactured oxygen into the canyon. Best of all, it was right where they needed it – near the top of the ramp. Casualties in that battle were horrendous, but the thrill of seeing so many guards being eliminated lifted the spirits of those tired Nausties observing from the base. Bodies of around 165 guards littered the ramp, with mangled body parts and looks of terror frozen on their faces.

Now, Warden Ggggaaah would have no other option. No relief force was coming, and everyone sensed it. No ship would dare land on that planet, now that it was under attack. What's more, they had no place to retreat to. No other means for defense. They could only wait helplessly for the invaders to break into their mess hall and try fighting it out to the death.

Perry's genius had shone brightly that day. Hicks would never doubt his partner's judgment again. It was only at that very moment that Architeuthis and the rest of the Nausties began to realize: they might just win this war.

Chapter 7: For the Honor

While the tide had turned in their favor, there was still much further to go. So many Nausties had already died. So much had been sacrificed. Yet even more was going to be asked of them. Much, much more perhaps. Oh, they'd bear up to it, of course. These Nausties possessed hardy souls. Still, just how far would they be willing to go to win their independence? Could they sacrifice all they had? It might very well come to that, General Hicks feared.

On the twenty-fifth night of the rebellion, General Hicks finally called it a day, and staggered over to his and Perry's bed pallet inside one of the captured food warehouses. The air was better in there, so he'd finally be able to breathe deeply and perhaps finally get over the pounding in his head. That's what the thin air was doing to workers outside in the canyon. Thin oxygen was giving many of them splitting headaches.

The General would be trying to get a few hours of sleep, while crews worked frantically to form the last part of the ramp. So much was still on his mind. Had he considered everything? Every potential danger? Lying next to him, as always, when he sat down on the bed was his long-time companion, Perry. They'd been together for a decade now, and Perry had always been his confidant. Hicks was the warrior-leader type, who had that rare ability to see inside men's hearts and stir them into action. Perry, by way of comparison, was the analytical type who could help a man with such abilities come up with a viable plan to succeed. Always the man behind the man – always the man behind the scenes, Perry was. Now Perry's brilliance was under the spotlight, and General Hicks was thrilled to let his partner's star shine bright.

"What am I not thinking of 'P'?" asked Hicks with a snarling sigh. His throat had been badly damaged in a fight many years earlier by an Enoshi's razor-sharp claws and had never healed completely. His neck still bore the terrible scar. He began to digress. "This ramp. It's insane. The Romans built one at Masada, just like the one we're trying to build. 'Ole General Lucius had about ten thousand men working on it just like we do, give or take a thousand. And like us, those tough sons of bitches built one out of dirt and rocks in the middle of a goddamn desert." Hicks lay back onto the mattress next to Perry and continued. "Theirs was three hundred seventy feet high. Did you know that?" Perry nodded with a grin. He had heard his partner tell the story several times.

Perry rolled up on his side, so that Archibald could curl in next to him. The tired General gave out a long sigh and continued in a low mumble. "Yep, they did all that just to assault a damned fort full of rebels. Ironic, huh? But they did it somehow. They made it all the way up." Hicks took in a long breath of air, then let it out. "And I guess so can we. But I just don't know, P. So many things could go wrong. At the top, I mean. You know. With the attack?"

Perry snuggled up and caressed his chest to calm him down. Of course, he knew. He knew very well what would happen if they tried a frontal assault with nothing but light infantry. They only had around a thousand captured EIC's to use, and half of those were low on ammunition. Therefore, they'd be using mostly spears and javelins against advanced weaponry. He further assumed they'd be going up against a well-fortified barricade inside that mess hall, once they broke through, and they'd be facing a hellish barrage of weapons fire once they tried exploiting the breach. Nevertheless, Perry wasn't worried in the least. Not even a bit, really. The man lying next to him was quite worried, however.

"So, let's go over this again, P," said the General. "What really happens when we get near the top? You got some kind of trick up your sleeve or somethin'?"

Perry heaved a big sigh. He said soothingly, "Forget about it for now. You just get some rest. Tomorrow I'll show you exactly what I have in mind. I promise. This time I really will. First thing in the morning. But for now, you need to sleep." Again, Hicks relented. He needed to put everything on ice for a little while and breathe in the better oxygen circulating inside the converted warehouse. His head needed to stop pounding for one thing, and his body needed recuperating.

Gradually Hicks drifted off, despite the cacophony of noise going on outside: the constant whirring of electric motors from dump haulers positioning themselves at the base for the long descent, overseers roaring instructions at impatient drivers awaiting their turn, shift teams being called off the ramp for mandatory breaks.

Four hours of sleep. That's what he kept telling himself. That's all he required. Just sleep for four hours and try not to think. Come out swinging the next day. Tomorrow was going to be a really big day once again, Hicks knew, and people would be counting on him. And no, he wasn't going to bother Perry anymore about his plans for the final assault. His partner probably had it all worked out anyway. He always had before, after all.

Archibald Hicks took yet another deep breath and exhaled slowly, recalling that heroic day when they'd blown up the terminal traffic control bubble. He could remember embracing Perry around the shoulders and hugging his neck proudly. Around them, a crowd of at least 10,000 screaming Nausties went wild with delight. It made him smile faintly as he felt the weight of mental and physical exhaustion washing over him. The pounding in his head was already subsiding. Sleep was only moments away, he could tell. He'd be unconscious in no time.

General Hicks was quite correct of course. Perry had things all worked out in his mind. In the final phase of ramp construction, dump trucks welded onto tractor chassis would continue to back slowly up to the edge of the ramp and expel their contents, then drive down the ramp as quickly as possible. Each dump hauler would continue to be followed by yet another, backing up the long causeway to the top. They'd proceed one at a time though, just in case security troops tried detonating the mess hall window and opened fire on them. No need to lose another three hundred Nausties in a surprise attack.

Each tractor would release its payload, repeating this process hour after hour, until the ramp was nearly complete, slowly but surely rising those last few feet to the window of the mess hall. However, there was a twist: when the ramp was finally within about ten feet of its objective, and hopefully before enemy soldiers inside started to react, Perry had a very, very nasty surprise waiting in store for them. Something they would have never suspected nor could have prepared for.

Perry never planned on using a tunnel drill to bash through that thick wall of reinforced glass. Ram through with a spinning drill bit, followed by thousands of screaming fanatics pouring through the breach? Nonsense. They'd be slaughtered. The first wave would get mowed down and wave after wave following would suffer appalling casualties. Even if they established a bridgehead, which was questionable, they'd have a hard time holding off enemy counterattacks. They'd likely never advance further; and once driven off? Forced back down that quarter mile-long dirt ramp to the base? The Naustie Revolt would be over and done with. Perry had no intention of that happening. Absolutely not. He'd been planning something else since the very beginning.

Back at that first war council when the idea of blowing up the terminal first came up, Perry was already considering those nuclear devices inside the captured Earth Cruiser *The Unity*. But he had no designs on obliterating the entire canyon in a nuclear holocaust. This is what Perry actually had in mind for the battle at the very top of the ramp, and he'd been keeping it secret from everyone all along. Even from Archibald. He had never told his long-time companion a thing about it. Kept it totally to himself.

The next day he would venture inside the now-buried Earth Cruiser to retrieve the detonators from those thermonuclear missiles. Just the detonators off the top of the three warheads and nothing more. Perry would have them mounted in the back of a dump hauler. Then, just like hundreds of times before, they'd back that vehicle all the way up the ramp to the top. The way Perry imagined it, those detonators could be welded into a rack and placed in the open bin of the tractor. Then they could be covered in dirt, concealing them from view. Because of this it would look just like any other load, and the security troops inside the mess hall would have no inkling what was about to happen.

Perry merely needed General Hicks to have the entire army assembled in formation for the final assault in full view of the Warden's forces above. The large tractor with a huge drill mounted in front would be positioned at the base of the ramp, while the last fifty dump haulers took turns ascending the ramp, one after another. The unsuspecting defenders would wait patiently for them to spill their loads, thinking the real battle was yet to come. But they'd be wrong. Death would come swiftly to them all.

As Perry envisioned it, security troops would assume all along that when the tractor drill was mounting the ramp for the final assault and troops were queuing up behind it for the attack, that's when they'd need to prepare themselves. Thus, they'd pay little attention to the last few trucks hauling up more dirt. They'd be waiting for the drill. And they'd be waiting for the masses of warriors forming up behind it. That's how Perry would catch them totally off guard.

They'd brace themselves for the final attack and arm themselves expecting to gun down thousands of half-naked, oxygen-depleted, riot-crazed lunatics until the bloody uprising was suppressed. After all, why should they worry? They had every reason to be confident. They had advanced technology. The rebels had nothing but some captured EIC's to complement their spears and javelins – and of course the false bravado that so often comes from achieving a few minor victories in the early part of a rebellion.

And these security troops? Oh, they had tear gas and concussion grenades to eliminate whole platoons of attackers as they approached. Perry was no fool. That mess hall up there probably held an arsenal of weapons by now and ammunition stockpiled for its defense. The enemy must be thinking it would be nothing more than bloody murder, once that drill rolled up the ramp and broke through. However, they were sadly mistaken. Instead, those unwitting souls would be blown to bits by what they would have thought was just another load from a dump hauler. A dump hauler which actually contained three thermonuclear detonators concealed under a mound of innocent looking iron ore.

Detonators from a nuclear warhead would create a charge big enough to demolish several floors of the mess hall and even the offices above it. If all three went off at the same time, the explosion would be devastating enough that General Hicks' forces would have plenty of time to rush right up the ramp unopposed. The hole would be so large, the Nausties could easily hop across, and into the building. Thousands and thousands of them. They'd only need to carry up long steel planks to lay down over the gap created by the explosion. Then they could rampage through the terminal and overwhelm its defenders quite easily.

Perry knew all about nuclear weapons because of his background. Years before, he'd been recruited by a large military contractor right out of college, where he'd been a top-flight physics student. Eventually, the young fellow found himself on the fast-track to a stellar career in the defense industry, developing advanced weapons technology. Soon he was on the inside and learned of all tactical uses for them. But that's when he got into a romantic relationship with one of his older mentors at the company.

The man Perry fell in love with was a colleague who was clearly going places in the corporation, and Perry had every reason to believe he could ride the man's coat-tails to the top. However, the relationship soured over time. To begin with, the older gentleman was already married, and after a year or so, his wife had become suspicious of their affair, or so the man claimed. He sought to end it, he told his lover, and though it broke the young man's heart, Perry accepted his decision honorably enough.

Within less than a year, that same colleague was right back in the saddle and quite openly dating another man. This new lover was from a different department and fresh out of college. They'd be seen everywhere together, not even trying to conceal their exploits, frequenting the hottest gay nightclubs. Perry was devastated.

Then one day that older colleague was found dead inside of a men's room, brutally murdered as it would turn out. The perpetrator could have been most anyone really, what with all the jilted lovers the man must have had, but suspicions pointed to Perry as the killer. He denied it of course, even though he didn't have an air-tight alibi, yet whether he did it or not, Perry was eventually convicted of the crime and sentenced to twenty years hard labor.

One day, a high-flying, young up-and-comer employed with an intergalactic military contractor. The next day, hauled off to stand trial in a bright orange jump suit with shackles on both his ankles and wrists. Six months later, he found himself exiting a large space cruiser along with six hundred new prisoners to work in the mines of Rijel 12, knowing he'd never see home again.

That had been almost eleven years ago, and yet somehow that bright young man had survived. He'd developed into a hardened, tattooed, and rather muscular, head-shaven member of the Templar Knights prison crew. He'd been ritualistically partnered, according to Templar Knights tradition, with the slightly older crew leader Archibald Hicks right after joining. Perry had been his partner and companion ever since.

It was because of his physics background that Perry knew the detonators would create a massive hole in the building, easily eliminating troops poised to slaughter the Naustie assault force. The concussion from the blast and the flying debris would wipe out reinforcements positioned behind the initial defense line too. In the confusion, the enemy would be uncoordinated in mounting any form of counterattack for several minutes at the least.

Perry knew something else, too. These were proximity detonators on those warheads, so the vehicle transporting the load would merely need to get near enough to the windows and the three devices would explode. One driver and one spotter would be all that was needed. The spotter might have to activate the detonators right before they got to the top of the ramp, allowing them enough time to exit the vehicle to safety, then the detonators would be triggered by their proximity to the walls. Within thirty seconds, it would all be over. Chaos and carnage would follow. Thousands of Naustie warriors would pour into the breach. In a matter of hours, the entire terminal would be overrun by bloodthirsty killers …

"Wait, am I getting this right, P?" queried General Hicks. "You mean we're gonna use those nukes after all?" As the ramp neared completion, the day before the assault, Perry and the other War Council members were meeting with their superior. Perry had finally begun to reveal his plan for the final phase of the attack, and Hicks for the first time in several years was actually a bit skeptical of his partner's logic.

Of course, he understood the basic premise: create a large explosion that the enemy would not possibly expect and wipe out a large section of their defensive position. Pour troops into the breach before the enemy recovered and overwhelm the entire stronghold. It was much like the Battle of the Crater in 1864. Archibald couldn't help but draw similarities between the two.

In this deadly battle during the American Civil War, Union troops secretly tunneled underneath Confederate Army positions while they laid siege to the city of Petersburg, Virginia. On July 30th, they set off a large amount of gunpowder right before dawn, killing two hundred seventy-eight enemy soldiers and creating a crater thirty feet deep. Nearby Confederate reinforcements were paralyzed for several minutes, while Union troops rushed into the pit full of mangled bodies. The follow-on attack by Federal forces was unsuccessful. In the aftermath, the Union general was relieved of command. He was suspected of being drunk during the battle.

Hicks snarled and shook his head. "I see what you mean Perry, but this idea of using nukes. Do we really know what we're doing? I know YOU do. You were a physicist. But how? I mean who is going to be able to activate the timing mechanism when the dump hauler gets to the top?" he asked. He gave Perry a suspicious look, which began to melt into raw concern. It was one of the few times anyone had seen the man nervous. Perry grinned, and folded his arms nonchalantly.

"Not to worry General," he replied. "The detonators can be activated long before the vehicle gets to the window. We just need about ten feet." Then Perry pointed up the ramp to the mess hall window. He continued, "Get that ramp within ten feet of the glass, leave the hauler in reverse, hop out, then run like hell! The detonators will do the rest." This was enough to satisfy the group, but Hicks still had an eerie feeling deep within his soul.

Who could Perry trust with such a task? The Slarts couldn't go. Enoshi were too big to ride in the vehicles. Spleefs were not incredibly bright when it came to technology and they'd never be able to handle activating the timing switch if there were any technical difficulties. Zorgs were unreliable, and they'd likely jump out of the vehicle before they got close. Suidonji were plenty brave enough, but quite uncoordinated at manipulating small devices. Only an Earther could do the job, and the smartest Earther anyone knew of was Perry.

Hicks tried to not think about it, but fear was growing within him and he couldn't shake it. Could it be that Perry was planning on driving that last tractor himself? *God forbid, no!* raced through his mind. Yet Perry was never the type to trust anyone with complicated details or instructions. Plus, Perry was a much braver man than most anyone knew. He'd never ask anyone else to drive that last hauler. Not with thermonuclear detonators concealed in the bed. Still, and

Hicks tried not imagining such a thing, if Perry was gone from his life, the aging crew leader simply couldn't go on without him. His love for Perry was just as devoted as it was pure.

"P... uh, seriously 'ole buddy. This all sounds way too dangerous. You sure you got your head around this one?" asked the General. "I mean, we got this mapped out already. Got the drill lined up. Those Slarts got the battery checked out and all. Suidonji are going to drive it up there and bash through. Been gearing up for it for weeks. Got units ready to make the big push once we get things opened up for them. Why are we wanting to take a chance on sketchy stuff like nuclear warheads?" He was revealing far too much to his military aides about his worries for his partner. It was making them uncomfortable. Many were fidgeting or looking down at the ground embarrassed. Perry replied, calmly as ever.

"Detonators, just the detonators. We're not going to nuke the bastards. Just give them a big surprise. I've calculated the force of the blast, even thought about using only one just to give us a big enough hole to rush through. But I decided we needed an enormous explosion. Big enough that it'll throw them back. Wipe out all their forward units in one fell swoop. Make it so devastating that they can't recover from it in time. It'll work, trust me."

Hicks was getting a sick feeling in his stomach. He was certainly no coward. He'd led his men into battle during crew wars against neighboring Enoshi dozens of times. Wars to establish boundaries between homelands. Wars over access to water supplies. Wars to decide who got tasked with choice mining assignments. Battling for jobs that offered the most rations or yielded the best potential for food bonuses. Feuds between individual crew members which had escalated into open conflict. He'd never considered his own personal safety. Would lay down his life for his men anytime, any day. Nevertheless, this was different. Perry was the love of his life, and the growing apprehension in his gut told him he needed to protect the object of his affection from danger. "I don't know, P. I just don't know," was all he could say.

By way of comparison the rest of his aides were all for it. "General, if I may," interjected one of them. He was a Templar Knight who'd killed forty Enoshi during his time in prison. Tattoos on his chest documented his exploits, though only members of his crew would have known what they meant, of course. "I think Perry's got this one all sewn up. Hell, I don't want to send my boys up that ramp into a damned turkey shoot. That's what it'll be like if we stick with the original format. We've known it for weeks and so do the troops. Half of them are expecting to die already. I hear them talking about it and it breaks my heart, sir." He made eye contact with the general, but Hicks uncharacteristically looked away. This was happening way too fast. How could he explain? Perry might be killed.

"I agree with Billy Clyde, mon Générale," added another; a Frenchman who'd once commanded a battalion of Legionnaires in a massacre down in Africa. He'd been sentenced to death, only to have it commuted to life imprisonment. "He, I mean Perry. Perry's been coming up with wondrous ideas this whole campaign. You have seen. We've all seen. Now he wants to try something that might save thousands of lives. Why should we doubt him?"

Soon everyone was hopping onto the bandwagon. "Let him try, General." several of them exclaimed. Hicks eventually had to yield. There was no denying it. They loved Perry, almost as much as he did, and their confidence in his judgment was unshakeable. Archibald eventually gave in.

Finally, it was the day of the main assault, the day everyone had been waiting for and diligently working toward. Slart planners were now estimating that less than fifty truck-loads of dirt would be necessary to complete the ramp, and word had spread to the thousands of Nausties now camped inside the cavern or nearby service tunnel. Practically no one was left below in the mines besides supply divisions under the command of the Schpleeftkorkii.

Excited Nausties gathered, surrounding the dirt-covered Earth Cruiser, and cheering each dump hauler as it came back down from the summit as if it were a parade. Only there was a problem. One that none of them could have known about. No one but Perry and his cohort Megalothyacus, that is. The two had been preparing the detonators and examining the timing mechanisms since early that morning. The news, unfortunately, was bleak.

"Damaged? How?" asked Perry. "When?" Megalocyathus fluttered his facial tentacles in apparent frustration. Somehow, some way, the timing mechanisms on the three detonators had been "fouled" as he put it. Perry's reaction was quite unsettling. "When could that have happened?" he asked again in desperation.

"That has not been determined," the Slart replied nervously, which meant he had no idea what could have gone wrong. This was a Slart's way of saying 'Damn if I know'. However, Perry was certain that his colleague had no doubts about his findings. He could rest assured of that.

"You mean they won't work?" asked Perry with increasing alarm. It seemed the timers had been installed incorrectly, or the wiring was faulty, or they'd been mishandled during installation. Megalocyathus could not determine which. Perry tried rationalizing what this meant. Suddenly his clever plan of activating the timers, then hopping out of the moving dump hauler, was disintegrating like a sugar cube in a cup of hot coffee. The whole idea had been to link them together into one single switch ahead of time, allowing Perry to ride up with a driver and simply press a button. A death-defying run down the ramp would follow, trying desperately to avoid being trampled by a galloping Suidonji. He'd pictured it in his mind so many times.

"It's none of our own doing, my friend. We removed the warheads together. You saw. We were very careful handling them," observed Megalocyathus. "But I've tested the mechanisms repeatedly. Occasionally they operate smoothly. Sometimes they continue for a few seconds only to cease functioning. Other times they do not respond. There's no logic to it. They might work perfectly if I tinker with them some more; however, I can make no guarantees. Based on my calculations thus far, we have a one in five chance they'll work."

Perry was floored. "And if they don't? You mean the detonators might not go off at all?" The full weight of the situation was pressing down on him like an elephant sitting on his chest. His heart raced. A cold rush went through his body as he began to realize what this implied. *A one in five chance?* He couldn't risk that. What if they didn't explode? He'd be left on top of that hill looking back at his dump hauler sitting there idling, pressed up against the wall and blocking access to the drill.

Then? Well he couldn't begin to think of what would happen after that. The element of surprise would be lost. Thousands of warriors would have to assault that fortified stronghold with the enemy knowing full-well what he'd just attempted. His brethren would have to storm the ramp like American soldiers had done on Omaha Beach back in 1944. They'd lose half their force in the initial wave and likely lose the war. What's more, there'd be no artillery barrage, like the Americans had relied upon from their naval flotilla. They had no grenades, no Bangalore torpedoes like Army Engineers had used against German positions. It would be an unmitigated disaster.

"Shall I keep trying, my friend?" asked Megalocyathus patiently. Perry could only nod pensively. He was already picturing what would likely have to happen and it made his blood run cold. What if General Hicks found out about this? He'd cancel the mission and return to his original plan. Worries swirled in his mind. Perry began fishing for alternatives.

"What about an override?" he proposed. "The captain of the vessel. Maybe he had some form of override mechanism. To deactivate the detonators on his warheads. You know, on the command bridge. In case he wanted the missiles to explode before impact. Abort an attack. He could do that, couldn't he?"

Megalocyathus was perplexed. Why would a ship captain fire a missile at a target then change his mind? That was illogical. "And why would he wish to do that?" asked the old Slart, now realizing Perry was becoming irrational. Perry was no longer thinking clearly, he surmised. Missiles fired from a spacecraft would arm themselves immediately and when launched there was otherwise no method of controlling them. They'd seek their target, a target programmed into the computer with an associated firing solution, then streak through space to deliver their deadly ordinance. Megalocyathus suddenly felt concerned for Perry's emotional state. His questions were not making sense.

"My friend, what is troubling you so?" he asked. "We can only do what we can with what we have to work with. You know this. You are a scientist. The facts are what they are and cannot be refuted. The timers cannot be relied upon. That's all we've established." He then raised a tentacle and placed it on Perry's grimy shoulder. The poor man had not bathed in years. His skin was covered in dust and filth from a decade of surviving in the subterranean hell of New Australia. Nonetheless, the Slart tried to comfort him.

"This we have to accept. Go tell your General. He'll understand. He loves you and he trusts you. We all trust you."

Perry couldn't bear the thought. What's more he knew he had to try and keep this matter secret. That was paramount. He knew what he'd have to do now, and the thought was terribly unpleasant. However, there was simply no choice. He'd have to change his plans yes; however, *only slightly*. He was still going up in that dump hauler.

No question of that. Everyone was expecting him to. Only now he'd be going alone – and there'd be no timing devices attached to those three detonators. He wasn't coming back either. He'd set them off himself when the vehicle reached the wall.

The former nuclear physicist relaxed his shoulders under the weight of the long tentacle wrapped around them. He then drew in a deep breath while he tried to speak calmly. The clean air inside the empty tool shed revitalized him. Megalocyathus would understand. He could count on that. Slarts more than any other creature understood personal sacrifice for the good of the community. It was engrained in their very culture. But a suicide mission? No, they had no way of comprehending something like that. Slartigifijians were peaceful creatures – steeped in tradition. Given the circumstances, Perry believed he could rely on Megalocyathus to accept his deadly logic.

"Thanks, brother," Perry replied. "You know I appreciate all you've done. You've been a friend to me from the start, even when we didn't see eye to eye. I'll always appreciate that about you." This caused Megalocyathus to recoil slightly. His tentacle released from Perry's shoulders then gripped his bicep firmly. Perry's words now seemed dark and cynical. Final was what they sounded like, as if he were saying goodbye.

"You can take a break now, old buddy," Perry continued. "I'll see if I can mess with this a while on my own. It's okay. I just need a little peace and quiet for a while, so I can think." Megalocyathus shot him a concerned look.

"What is the meaning of these words you're speaking? And why are you acting this way?" he worriedly asked. No explanation was necessary. Megalocyathus knew full well what Perry was indicating. The brainy Slartigifijian was already deducing the answer long before Perry attempted one.

"Oh, I'm okay. Don't worry about me," said Perry. "You just scamper off and go check on things up at the ramp. I've taken enough of your time already." Megalocyathus felt a tug on his three hearts. He hesitated to comply.

"But my friend, I'm quite sure I am not needed out there. Everything is going to plan. Besides, I've been assigned to this project with you," he pleaded. "I have orders." He knew not to leave Perry there alone. Something wasn't right. The old Slart feared he was going to rig those three detonators to go off with a single flick of a switch, exploding them and himself simultaneously. Sadly, that was correct; however, Perry couldn't bring himself to form the words to say so. Not that it was needed. His loyal colleague could see it in his eyes.

Megalocyathus slumped his narrow shoulders and dropped his tentacle. Then he reached out and grasped Perry by the wrists. "Please let me stay and help," he implored. "I sense what you're considering doing my good fellow. Let's not be hasty. It may not be the only option. Maybe –"

But Perry was already shaking his head. A strange smile formed on his face. Perhaps it was that kind of insanity which accompanies the decision to lay down one's life to save others. It rose within him like a torrent. His extremities tingled. His eyes burned with intensity. Then it passed. He realized he had to compose himself. What's more he'd have to ask the impossible of his brilliant associate. He'd have to swear him to secrecy. Somehow, he'd have to convince a Slartigifijian to lie.

"No, Megalocyathus. I don't need your help now. I can handle it. Go. Find some way to help with the troops. They're nervous. Everyone's stressed. It's going to be a big day for them, you know?" Then Perry paused as he tried thinking of how he should phrase the next part. All he could do was make a sincere request and hope for the best. Yet, he knew within hours everyone would know, regardless. Someone would ask just the right question, and kindly old Megalocyathus would spill the beans.

"And if you don't mind terribly, let's uh, let's keep this matter secret okay? Just between us, eh? No need to worry the others. Fair enough?" Megalocyathus fluttered his facial tentacles again, creating an audible gurgling sound. It would have been comical in normal circumstances.

"I'll do my best, Perry," was all he could offer. Perry grasped his tentacle and squeezed. That would have to suffice for now.

The rest of the day went much like they'd planned it. The trip up the ramp for each of the last few dump haulers took less than five minutes, but the trip down was accomplished in less than sixty seconds. Suidonji drivers had become quite skilled at backing uphill by now. Yet the drive back down was certainly—more than anything else—a big relief when completed. There was always the threat of a counter-attack from security troops positioned behind that thick glass wall. Thus, after dumping their load those wily creatures only wanted to high-tail it back down.

Each loader full of dirt would be cheered as it carefully backed up the ramp. These Suidonji were now the bravest of heroes. Each returning vehicle's driver, or his spotter would announce how much farther they had to go before the ramp would not only touch the glass wall but bear the weight of the tractor drill. Anticipation grew with every truck load, and relief followed with each driver's safe return. Truth was, it was becoming a very treacherous climb.

As the last of the fifty trucks came down from the ramp, the driver gave a triumphant signal, announcing that the distance now was within ten feet. News spread throughout the throng of excited miners, diggers, supply workers, and thousands of warriors waiting to rush up the ramp to glory. A deafening cheer rose up from the crowd. Almost everyone in that enormous mass of bodies was ecstatic. Excitement. Anticipation. The thrill of combat. Plus, the thought of bloody revenge for five long decades of oppression and cruelty. These feelings seemed to stir within their souls. It was payback time. They now realized that in less than an hour, they'd be battling their way inside that main terminal, fighting through hails of bullets, and slaughtering everyone they found.

There would be no quarter, no prisoners taken, no mercy either offered or expected, and no surrender possible. This was not just a takeover, or a coup d'état. This was an eradication. A cleansing, one might say. Architeuthis stood in the back of the crowd, near a large table with all his Slartigifijian planners. This was his vision, and he was there to bear witness. Now it was finally about to happen.

Every Naustie in that crowd was spoiling for revenge. They'd make Ggggaaah and his troops pay dearly for all they'd done. The souls of tens of thousands of their comrades who'd died in those mines over the years, all would be avenged. Beings in the crowd sporadically called out vows of determination, as the last vehicle finished its journey up the ramp and returned empty. Some who'd lost a lover or a friend in recent battles sang songs or chanted the names of their fallen comrades. Many joined in with those songs too. It was an historic moment for New Australia.

Oh yes, everyone was excited, from Enoshi to Slarts, from Spleefs to Zorgs. Humans and Suidonji cheered together, and almost everyone shared in the celebration. Everyone, that is, except one single Earthman in the crowd.

Indeed, only one among them failed to share in all the revelry and saber rattling. For this lone human, that last tractor returning from the ramp meant something far more terrifying. Perry's face went completely cold. It was time for him to perform the mission he'd been planning all along. One last mission. One that he'd been saving for himself since the first load of berm was dumped at the base of that massive freighter still parked on the terminal pad.

All along, he'd been revealing only bits and pieces of his plan, which had begun forming the very day the Impaler proposed piling up a mountain of dirt to reach the command bubble. And weeks before, when Perry had crawled inside the Earth Cruiser, only to discover the thermonuclear warheads still operable, the idea had solidified in his mind. It struck him like a blow to the head that day, and a charge ran through his body like static electricity. There was only one good way to blow open that wall and allow his fellow Nausties inside with enough numbers to overwhelm the garrison. Otherwise, they'd be slaughtered by the thousands. Now it was he alone who would have to make the ultimate sacrifice.

General Hicks walked past Perry, who seemed suddenly very cold and distant. Hicks placed a hand on his shoulder and squeezed gently, as the crowd of warriors around them cheered wildly. Perry stared up the ramp, coolly contemplating the task lying ahead of him. A chill ran through him once again, as a driver brought up yet another battered gray-green electric dump hauler. It was charged up and ready for the ascent. This was the hauler which had the detonators hidden under its payload.

Yes, Suidonji welders had created a rack that held the three detonators in place, just like Perry had requested, and by now he had devised a switch that could activate them as the hauler approached the wall. He could simply flip the switch, leave the vehicle in reverse, and the detonators would begin seeking a target within seconds. That was plenty. Then it would all be over. He'd cautioned Megalocyathus to keep this terrible secret from his comrades.

But the hard truth was this: it did no good. Suidonji welders working on the rack gradually figured it out. Slarts couldn't lie anyway, and with a little probing, those crafty swine pieced it together quickly. That was their nature. It was to be a suicide mission. Even the last fifty drivers who had developed a proficiency in climbing the enormous ramp began to hear about it. Yet it provided no solace to them. They'd all assumed they'd have to draw lots to see who would get to go. Now they were off the hook and it left them with a burning sense of embarrassment that another Naustie would gain the supreme honor of giving his life for their cause.

Previously, no one had speculated on how the choosing would occur. No one really wanted to know either. Finishing the ramp was everyone's main concern. Now they'd learned the truth, and it shamed them. Soon enough, word got out to practically everyone else in the Naustie Army as well including their supreme commander.

The moment General Hicks had been dreading had finally arrived. He smiled awkwardly at Perry and proceeded to prepare for his speech to the Army. By now, there was absolutely nothing he could do. A cold feeling rushed through Hicks' body as he mounted a small platform made from cannibalized mine crusher components. And as he began to address the immense crowd of warriors, his heart seemed to be lodged in his throat. He knew Perry had been planning to drive that tractor all along, and it was killing him to try and speak confidently to his army with this gut-wrenching fear that now possessed him like a ghostly spirit. He struggled to compose himself as the crowd turned to face him.

The general began by addressing the different commanders of the assault units. He bellowed out the names and unit numbers. Every brigade, every battalion, every company, even individual platoons were recognized by the general. The names of the units in that first wave were sounded off by Hicks from memory, as their commanders shouted out acknowledgement. Yet, all the while, Hicks was bravely trying to ignore the fact that his partner was now walking through the crowd over to the last dump hauler – meticulously inspecting the detonator activation switch inside the cab. He tried not to stare for too long.

General Hicks reviewed the order of battle for his audience, which fell hushed as he spoke in a booming, snarling voice that filled most of the canyon. He detailed the order in which the assault would go, so that every being in every single unit knew exactly when they'd be going in. The first wave was a division of shock troops, divided into brigades of about two thousand warriors each. Each brigade was further broken down into battalions of about five hundred warriors.

Enoshi shock troops in one battalion. Earther javelinmen in another, including several platoons armed with EIC's. Zorg slingers carrying sulfur bombs made up yet another battalion. Spleef light infantry comprised the rest. Several of the battalions had a unit of Suidonji heavy infantry armed with shields and makeshift cutlasses.

Of course, everyone knew the battle plan by now, and the commanders in the crowd already knew where they were to position their troops in line. They'd known for days, and even drilled at it, in full view of the Warden's troops above. The only thing almost no one in the crowd knew for sure was – how was Archibald Hicks going to react to his brave adjutant taking the wheel? They soon found out.

Finally, General Hicks called out directly to Perry, who by now was done checking the activation switch. He felt blood rushing to his cheeks as he realized how much longer he had to live. Hicks sensed this. He swallowed hard with rising terror which was something he'd not felt in decades. Perry didn't hesitate though. He was soon starting up the hauler and getting ready to depart. The crowd remained mostly silent in anticipation, with thousands of battle-ready troops encircling the dramatic scene unfolding at the base of the ramp.

"So, Mister Perry. Are you planning on leaving us, my good friend?" cried the General, his voice breaking. Hicks tried to smile confidently and look smart in front of his troops. He'd been dreading this all along and had tried not to dwell upon it. Only in the last hour had he found out what Perry was going to do. For a while, no one had the heart to tell him. A hush fell over the crowd, as word spread among those packed around the base. Hicks' heart was breaking in two inside his chest. He knew there was only one thing left he could do.

Alas, there was no way he could stop his mate from going on that brave and glorious mission. No way in hell that General Hicks could order his best and brightest to simply stand down and let someone else drive that tractor up the ramp, all the way to certain death. Oh yes, if the general commanded it, Perry would have yielded and exited the vehicle. He'd never be insubordinate to a superior officer. But Hicks also knew that Perry could never trust the task of activating the detonators to another. If there were any malfunction, only Perry could trouble-shoot it. Only Perry could be burdened with such a task. They only had one shot to get this right. It had to be perfect.

A murmur ran through the crowd. The noise rose and swelled like that of an ocean lapping up on a beach. The name "PERRY" kept being spoken, then gradually it was being chanted. These would be Perry's final minutes of existence, and as the tears of pride welled in his general's eyes, Perry poked his head out the window of the cab and replied humorously to his commander.

"Yes General, with your permission, Sir." He patted the side door three times and smiled broadly, then added, "You know, I've always wanted to drive one of these things."

The smile on Perry's face was that of a man who'd come to terms with the end of his life and made peace with God. He beamed with pride, the look of a man who had not a single care left in the world. But it was also the look of a man who had made the decision to sacrifice himself willingly, and to do so for the good of his comrades. There was no greater honor. All of these thoughts and emotions seemed to gleam in Perry's eyes, as he threw the vehicle into reverse and began backing up the ramp. The crowd began to cheer even louder, chanting his name rhythmically.

But General Hicks was not finished. He surprised everyone by screaming out in a growling voice that rivaled even the strongest of Eno battle cries. He roared, "WAIT!" And everyone nearby fell silent, turning back toward the general to see what his next command would be. Perry stopped backing up the ramp, and looked out the window, still grinning like a deranged madman. Hicks paused for a moment to blink tears from his eyes; then he yelled out, "Mister Perry! I don't believe you'll be safe without a spotter guiding you. It's a long way up, my—."

Hicks cut short, almost choking on his words. But he soon recovered. Then the general continued in a loud and powerful voice, "If you don't object to my assistance, how about letting your 'ole general ride shotgun?"

Perry paused and tried choking back a pitiful sob. He recovered quickly, then smiled with a playful wink.

A murmur again arose within the crowd, as Perry nodded proudly. Now the full gravity of the situation began to sink in with thousands of beings armed and ready for the final assault. *Good God! General Hicks?* Yes, the General himself was going to join Perry in this mission, joining with him as his spotter for the ride up to the summit. They would be going out together as partners for all eternity, loyal to each other to the very end. Soon, the entire crowd, thousands of

Nausties in all directions, were finally aware of what was happening.

Almost half the crowd could see the whole thing, and those who couldn't see were being told by their neighbors around them. Spleefs hopped up onto the shoulders of Enos. Zorgs climbed up the sides of machinery or nearby stalagmites to watch the growing spectacle. Earthers strained their necks to gaze at this amazing event. This was truly going to be a moment in their planet's history that no one would forget. Their very own commanding general as well as his aide de camp were going to lay down their lives for the good of New Australia. One last heroic act of courage – one that would rival any brave deed anyone else was going to perform that day. This inspired them and prompted thousands of beings from every species to cheer wildly.

Hicks hopped off the platform and strode proudly over to the dump hauler to join his partner in the cab. Warriors stepped aside to let him pass, nodding and bowing their heads. He climbed in, slammed the door shut, reached over the side, and slapped the door three times, signaling to Perry he was ready to go. The cheers swelled louder, then even louder, until it was almost overwhelming.

As General Hicks issued his last orders to his nearest commanders and passed authority back to Architeuthis, he waved to the crowd as Perry slowly backed the hauler up the earthen ramp. Then, out of respect, the whole army, tens of thousands of warriors, were ordered by their commanders to stand in quiet reverence for the brave deed about to unfold. Gradually the entire cavern fell silent once again, with only the eerie sound of the electric hauler serenading them. But it was far more than just a heroic act to Perry and Hicks. It was to be their last five minutes together. In the blink of an eye and with the flick of a switch they'd be gone, right along with a thousand security troops barricaded inside a honey-combed defense network on the other side of that thick glass wall.

Of course, they were quite businesslike to the very end, chattering back and forth as they backed up the ramp. "Good on the right, Mister Perry!" growled Hicks professionally, over the whine of the engine. "Copy that General. Good on the left!" replied Perry quite militarily. They knew they had to go very slowly up the very center of the trail. Slart planners had instructed drivers to follow in the ruts of previous vehicles to avoid causing an avalanche. Five drivers and their spotters had tragically died that way in accidents when they'd veered off course and ended up tumbling down the side to their deaths, especially for the last fifty yards.

When they eventually got close to the edge, Perry yelled over to Hicks, "General, if you please, Sir?" and reached down to flip the switch he'd devised for activating the detonators. Hicks barked out rather formally, "Ah, Mister Perry. Allow me." And with that he grabbed and held up the switch. Perry smiled vaguely at his General then very professionally yelled out, "Thank you General. And goodbye. I'll see you on the other side!"

With that he activated the switch and turned around to listen for the beeping of the detonators. After a seemingly infinite moment, they heard a whining BLEEEEP. Hicks smiled and looked into Perry's eyes for one last second. Perry smiled right back, then turned around and gunned the engine in reverse. Within a mere instant, KABOOM! A deafening explosion rocked the cavern.

The detonators ignited, blowing a massive hole in the side of the terminal. Fully three floors of offices, along with the entire enemy defense network, were instantly vaporized. The crash, the explosion, the sight of so much material, furniture, shards of glass, and body parts falling about was a terrifying sight. Meanwhile, on the cavern floor, soldiers hid under shields – workers ran for cover. And yet, after a few moments of debris falling all around them, those inspired Naustie warriors began cheering wildly once more. The explosives had worked.

All the army needed now was a single command, and with their General now dead, the commanders of the assault units looked back for their spiritual leader, Architeuthis, to give the order. The giant Slartigifijian raised up his left tentacle. Then he pointed to the breach. His words were brave and honest. He said just what needed to be said at such a solemn moment. Architeuthis recognized, just like any being there that day, just how brave the sacrifice had been by both Archibald Hicks and his devoted companion.

Architeuthis spoke. He spoke to the mass of troops with a burbling hum from his neck, indicating true raw emotion which was remarkable for a wise old Slartigifijian. He lifted his head and gurgled out proudly: "*For the honor!*" And with that, all hell broke loose, as troops kept repeating those words over and again, all the way up that long causeway.

"FOR THE HONOR!" they cried. They lurched forward, filing in to enter the path leading up the side of the Earth Cruiser, onto the main part of the incline. They trotted up the earthen causeway in tight formations, many carrying sections of steel planks—all the while chanting, "FOR THE HONOR! FOR THE HONOR! FOR THE HONOR!" The final battle for the control of New Australia had begun. The reign of Warden Ggggaaah was about to come to a very violent and ignominious end.

CHAPTER 8: THE EMPATH

"Good Morning and welcome to the IPN news network, I'm Kallisia Damos," said the news broadcaster on the screen. A swirl of musical notes followed which sounded like typewriters designed to conjure concerned emotions. The wall video monitor had suddenly activated inside eighteen-year-old Felina Toyger's dormitory room, and in a daze, she slowly stirred awake. Very slowly actually.

It had been a long night of partying the night before, and she'd forgotten to turn off her alarm which activated the video monitor designed to help her wake up each morning. Just like an old clock radio, but with a giant 70" screen on the wall opposite her bed. The device came on each morning just in time for Interplanetary News Network's "Morning Update" program.

On screen was a live image of an Enoshi female, fur-covered but humanoid in form, with a predominantly white coat and patches of brown and black mixed in. She had piercing yellow-green eyes, with pupils which formed vertical blacks slit down the center. The rather gorgeous news anchor paused to focus her gaze onto a different camera as the news show music faded out. She now began her broadcast.

"At the top of the news this morning: rioting continues into the twenty-fifth day on Rijel 12, as convicts at New Australia Prison reportedly control most of the planet's interior mining network and service tunnel, as well as the loading bay next to the main terminal, cutting off all access now to the planet's landing facility."

Ms. Damos' expression conveyed sincere concern and anxiety about this tragic event, just like any good news anchorperson on any planet knows how to do. The camera view began to pull back from her face a bit, as a miniaturized screen opened up to the side of her, showing some blurry file photo of the planet. It had the caption *PRISON RIOT* emblazoned in bold letters underneath.

"As reported earlier," she continued, "the Earth Cruiser *The Unity* was captured by rioters in early fighting, and the fate of its crew is still unknown. New Australia Prison Warden Ggggaaah continues to assure officials in recent inter-space communications that the participants have been isolated from the rest of the prison population, and the rebelling convicts have no possible access to the main terminal. In his most recent communication to the media, Warden Ggggaaah issued the following statement."

The miniaturized screen next to Kallisia's face now switched to showing a grainy picture of Warden Ggggaaah himself, in place of the previous image of Rijel 12. Ggggaaah's quoted words were shown on screen. Meanwhile, Kallisia read the Warden's formal statement aloud:

"Though we are deeply saddened by the loss of life and senseless violence, by what has turned out to be a mere handful of incorrigibles, we look forward to suppressing this uprising and returning to normal operations as soon as possible. Our deepest and most heart-felt condolences go out to the families and relatives of those killed in the tragedy thus far. We will strive to end this unpleasantness quickly, and resume business as usual."

Warden Ggggaaah, New Australia Planetary Prison, Rijel 12.

Felina reached for the button on her remote control to turn off the program but couldn't seem to find it. Her milky green eyes were blurry, and her head was pounding from the bender she'd participated in the night before. Way too many mugs of ale, it seemed. The cold reality of the morning after was definitely an unwelcome sensation. She most assuredly didn't want to listen to the news, either. That would only make things worse. She didn't need to be awakened this early in the morning. Not any more, anyway.

As of yesterday, her training as a highly sought-after Empath had come to an end. The elders at the academy where she had been studying for the past two years had unfortunately determined she should be released from the program. And though it was certainly not anything that she did, it was certainly due in part to what she did not do quite well enough, which was to keep her opinions to herself. Enoshi Empaths were highly prized throughout the galaxy for just three very important things: social adaptability, intuitiveness, and instinctive understanding of their mated male's point of view.

Still the news droned on, as Felina continued to groan and slap with her catlike paws at her nightstand trying to find the mute button. Meanwhile, news anchor Kallisia Damos rattled on with her report.

"Recently, as our viewers will recall, New Australia Prison has been the center of bitter controversy, as family advocates have been protesting for years demanding that the prison provide them information on loved ones incarcerated for minimum sentences there. Relatives convicted of crimes who leave for Rijel 12, they contend, are most often never heard from again." The miniaturized screen next to Ms. Damos now disappeared, and the camera view zoomed in slowly on the news anchor's face once more. Her facial expression became even more serious as she continued.

"Warden Ggggaaah and the Interplanetary Authority have been, in the view of many beings in the galaxy, quite less than forthcoming about the true fates of prisoners sent there, and many accuse the Galactic governments of a cover-up. Interplanetary Authority officials continue to deny these claims, pointing out that..."

The screen switched to a blue background with typed words in quotation marks which Ms. Damos read off dispassionately:

"Prisoners completing their sentences at New Australia Planetary Prison are free to return to their homes or travel anywhere they like within the galaxy. Where they choose to go, or whether they choose to re-contact family or relatives, is solely up to the released convict's discretion."

While the screen continued to show this quote, Ms. Damos continued her commentary. "This quote was taken from an official inter-space communication released to the media, but in the opinion of many prison reform advocates, such as Ginga Burseem of the Gava Freedom Party," the camera view suddenly cut to a sound-bite from a recorded interview with a plump, dark brown colored Enoshi female, who was addressing a protest rally. She was irate, to say the least:

"It hints at an effort by Interplanetary officials to disguise the ugly truth. That in reality, prisoners who are sent to Rijel 12 are never meant to come back. That is unjust. It's slavery. And it goes against the very nature of our proud culture. We want answers and we want justice!"

A crowd of protesters standing behind her in the video held up signs and cheered her bold words, as the sound-bite faded then cut short and the view immediately switched back to the lovely broadcast anchor. Kallisia appeared to be moving her eyes from a video monitor off-screen back to the camera, making direct eye contact now. She added with a professional but serious tone, "We will be keeping you informed as to developments on Rijel 12 throughout the day. Stay tuned to Interplanetary News Network for updates."

Felina rolled over onto her back and sat up, rubbing her eyes with the palms of her furry, yet still very humanoid-looking paws. Frustrated, she then slapped the mattress on both sides of her hips, exclaiming "I don't care!" She certainly had her reasons for being annoyed.

Frankly, Felina Toyger had endured a bellyful, and then some, of learning current events and following daily news commentary. It was required of her so that she'd be able to carry on conversations with a potential mate. Then trained to study Galactic affairs, as well as other cultures and customs. This way, they could encounter almost any species of male, and be able to carry on stimulating conversation. It wasn't enough for them to simply be attractive and agreeable. They also needed to be smart enough to converse with members of sophisticated society, and not be an embarrassment to their partner.

That, unfortunately, was Felina's downfall. She learned history, politics, and the social nuances of other planetary cultures quite well, but in conversations she all too often held very strong opinions, which she expressed very clearly and loudly one too many times. It did no good for her instructors to caution or admonish her.

"Yes, Felina," they'd say patiently, "Of course it's unjust. But whether it's fair or not, what matters is what our mate thinks. That's what you're learning here." That sort of thing just didn't fly with a willful Enoshi like Felina.

Meanwhile on the wall video monitor, the network had cut to a commercial. It was an advertisement for a new resort hotel being opened on a former Earth space station located between Enosh and Zorgolong. This facility had once been an intergalactic science and research institute but was recently abandoned after a mysterious outbreak of disease wiped out several hundred scientists living and working there.

Upbeat dance club music suddenly blared from Felina's wall video monitor. It throbbed in Felina's head, reminding her of the send-off party she'd attended with her friends the night before. Felina held her head and moaned pathetically.

"By the gods, where's the damn mute button?" Her eyes were still too cloudy to focus and look around for the controller. For the life of her, she couldn't remember where she'd put it.

The new resort was to be called "Star Fantasy," the sultry male voice announced in heavily Earth-accented Galactic, and it was going to be an intergalactic pleasure palace available "for adults only". The Human narrator then said in a sexy deep voice, "Leave the kids at home. Climb on board and take a little trip. To the new destination of fascination and erotic sensation. Escape tonight to Star Fantasy. Your dream awaits."

Felina had mastered almost every aspect of her training and even excelled compared to others in the program. She was brilliant, quick witted, fit and strong, very athletic, and stunningly attractive. Tiger-striped and perfectly proportioned, she stood about six feet tall which was typical for most grown females. In terms of dexterity, she scored some of the highest marks anyone had seen in many years at her local academy. It was important for her to maintain a physical appearance which was as formidable as her internals, her mind and spirit were equally strong, and gave her the ability to truly understand others. This was one of the most important attributes for becoming an Empath. It's what made them desirable as *gifts* to foreign dignitaries, celebrities, honored nobles, or as rewards for bravery on the battlefield.

The Empath program had begun for Felina when she was 16, but her original discovery as an Enoshi capable of becoming empathic? That came when she was only 12. Early on, Felina demonstrated abilities to sense what others were thinking and feeling, and could react to their desires or needs immediately, just like most any full-grown female could. But her Pride's elders felt she had the basic talents which could be developed much further, given proper training in an academy. Empath training was a very ancient tradition.

The commercial continued, gradually switching from thumping club music to soft, sexy jazz. Now the screen was showing provocative imagery of young female Enoshi, plus female Zorgolongians, Suidonji, Schpleeftii, and even some half-naked female humans posing in tantalizing scenes with each other.

All smiling or casting alluring glances, these assorted females from five different species gave beckoning gestures, mischievous winks, welcoming nods, or puckered their lips invitingly. The Zorgolongians flicked their tongues. The Schpleeftii wriggled their little snouts. Then the human narrator continued in a more salesman-like voice, "Vacation packages starting at only sixty-five hundred Galactic dollars. Yes, there's something for everyone at Star Fantasy. No matter what you desire."

The commercial also showed a few scenes of muscular young Human males, oiled up, and sitting naked around a steaming hot tub. Human male concubines were the latest craze on Enosh, and this was quite ironic given that homosexuality among male Enoshi was nonexistent. However, wealthy male Enoshi who desired something new to experience would occasionally find companionship with young men to be quite fulfilling. Private clubs existed on the planet which catered to this growing fad. Using the Earth term "Bath House", these facilities drew homosexual males by the thousands every year to planet Enosh, as they flocked to the clubs day and night, hoping to meet some rich "Fat Cat", as gay guys from Earth liked to call them.

The Empath Program began thousands of years ago, but originally started as more of a community tradition. It developed over the centuries into something much bigger. Clans would occasionally make war on other clans, and to settle the disagreement, the warring parties would make a peace offering by giving to the other faction one of their more powerful females. This served to integrate the clans and gave the Empaths a positive role as formers and keepers of peace. As the centuries passed, this tradition became more formalized, and as Enoshi civilization advanced through Stone Age into Bronze—Iron

Age into Industrial—Computer Age into Galactic – Empathic females became harbingers of peace and understanding, as well as a means for a clan to demonstrate their power.

Enoshi males were instinctively confrontational by nature, competing with each other for everything, including power, wealth, or for control of harems. Even the most stubborn, unyielding human was no match for the intense personal resolve of the typical Enoshi male. They considered lying or misrepresenting fact to be a terrible disgrace, and when it came to disagreements among males, violence was most often the result, even in modern times.

Subsequently, males were vastly outnumbered on the planet. They simply didn't live very long, compared to their female counterparts. And the more successful a male became in business or from military conquest – the more mates he could afford to have in his harem.

In Enoshi society, sexual relationships were not necessarily monogamous. A desirable female became mated with a successful male based on his ability to support her. And though it was also quite common for a lower class Enoshi to mate with only one female for life, it was also completely acceptable as well as encouraged for a wealthy noble to possess many different females in his household.

That's what attracted homosexual men to the planet. Not only were Enoshi males virile, gigantic, and legendarily tireless lovers, but a wealthy one might simply add a human to his harem, right along with his many female concubines. For a gay man, that could mean a life of opulence and care-free comfort for just as long as the rich feline found him to be desirable.

But dueling and constant confrontation in ancient times also led to the tradition of owing a life debt to the relatives of the slain. Though there was no greater honor in all of Enoshi culture than to die in personal combat, it was also the responsibility of the victor to compensate the family of the male they had killed, at the very least by paying for and arranging the defeated warrior's funeral and elaborate cremation ceremony.

The life debt one paid was predicated upon the victor's position and financial status. Chieftains who were seeking an armistice with rival faction leaders for instance, might simply offer one or several females from their harem to the other leader as a means of securing peace. And as centuries passed, this gesture became common in business, politics, or even inter-galactic relations.

Subsequently, many clans found it wise to develop the empathic tendencies of their more promising female members, and this grew over the millennia into the establishment of academies. The training at these schools was rigorous, and females were brought in at age 16 to begin their tutelage. In this way, every local clan had an ongoing supply of young empathic females who could be valuable partners, as well as important negotiators.

There was only one catch. By age 18, if they were not selected into the negotiator path, Empaths were released from the program. The goal of each academy was to present a trained Empath to a chieftain, who would evaluate her readiness as a negotiator and potential asset for future inter-clan dealings. Those released from the program merely re-entered society and went on with their lives.

Many Empaths who weren't selected for negotiators used their extensive training to become business owners, public servants, or lawyers. Some of them relied heavily on the partnership aspects of their training and went on to either own or work in brothels. Some went on to find partners and led perfectly ordinary family lives. But Felina had dreams, and an ordinary life simply wasn't enough for her.

She had awakened to a new day, having been denied the opportunity she'd been dreaming of for years. She had to come to grips with it. She had to accept this unfortunate setback and find a new path for her life. And she certainly had every reason to believe things would turn out well for her. She was smarter than most. She'd studied not only about the cultures, languages, and customs of every planet's species, but she'd also learned of their physical characteristics and tendencies.

She'd learned anatomy, learned techniques, learned pressure points and erogenous zones for five different species. No matter who she was partnered with, she could anticipate anything her lover might want or need, before he could even speak the words. Basically, just as fast as her partner could think it, Felina could adapt to it.

That's when it occurred to her, hearing that smooth-talking Earthman's voice on the commercial. EARTH! That's where she needed to go. Empaths were insanely popular on Earth. Everyone knew that. She'd heard it long ago when she was very young. Wealthy Earthmen went absolutely crazy for them, and female Enoshi were said to be able to command a luxurious lifestyle in the mega cities of Earth working in the entertainment industry, as they called it there.

On Enosh, there was no equivalent to what humans considered to be prostitution. There was nothing equivalent to a brothel or even a gentleman's cabaret. There were no strippers, either. Enoshi didn't wear clothing. Didn't need it. They were covered in fur from head to toe, and if the climate necessitated it, they simply grew a thicker coat. Their coats protected their underlying hide, and on the female, the fangs were far less pronounced than on a male, so they could do most anything in the bedroom that a human woman could do. Empaths were something that Earthmen had never experienced until just the last few decades. They were a fur-covered fantasy creature come to life. Insatiable, attractive, desirable, intuitive, exotic and instinctive, an Empath could do absolutely anything a man desired, without him needing to describe it.

All that Felina needed was to find a way to raise the money necessary to afford the ticket to get there, plus, maybe a few months' worth of "rent" as Earthers called it. She couldn't just arrive on Earth several months later completely broke. She'd need to make some money – a lot of money actually – before she could make that trip.

But how? Just how could an eighteen-year-old female—only just yesterday released from Empath Academy—come up with the Galactic dollars necessary for a cross-galaxy journey to start a new life? Felina watched the end of the commercial on the video monitor about the new intergalactic pleasure resort called Star Fantasy. They were hiring, it said. Perhaps Felina could find a way to financial success. If she was savvy enough, she could run quite a good business at a place like Star Fantasy. While her primary strengths may take a temporary backseat, it would still require all of her smarts to be able to manage and build career while she was there.

CHAPTER 9: THE END OF WARDEN GGGGAAAH

Though Warden Ggggaaah may have underestimated the rebels, it was due to his own arrogance, more than anything else. It wasn't due to bad information from his subordinates, or poor judgment within his chain of command – wasn't their fault at all. His staff had regularly reported back to him regarding progress being made by the Nausties. What's more, Ggggaaah had always known about technological adaptations prisoners had devised in order to survive down in the mines. Still he was not convinced, and often said so.

"The fools! They're nothing more than mutineers on a pirate ship. I give them another week at best. This uprising will fall to pieces. Too many moving parts and distrust and rivalry to boot. You'll see. Once they panic, once they run out of food that is, they'll kill off the weak while trying to hoard supplies until only a handful are left. Then we can march right in." No matter how his advisors tried warning him, he simply couldn't grasp how serious things had become.

He knew about Slartigifijians being used by crews as engineers to repair and service machinery. He also knew how rebels had used acetylene torches to cut into the walls, ceilings and floors of his food depots. He fully understood that when they'd overrun the service tunnel, the only means of escaping the planet was the Earth Cruiser *The Unity.* Now that ship was in rebel hands. At every stage, right from the initial outbreak of hostilities, his subordinates were keeping Ggggaaah thoroughly informed of the situation.

The capture of the first three guard stations, the securing of the elevators, the clearly sophisticated military organization of rebel forces and the technology they seemed to be using, all of this was reported to the stubborn warden. For that matter, a lot of what the rebels were doing, he could witness first hand from the top of the cavern. But he refused to believe those "dirty convicts" could ever pull it off.

To Ggggaaah, it just didn't make sense that mere prisoners working in a mine could come up with so many solutions, overcome such formidable obstacles, and, for that matter, could unify the prison's rival crews to stage an organized revolt. Ggggaaah kept deluding himself into thinking that the rebellion would come apart once they began to starve, once they began to suffer in the thin air, or when they started to run out of clean drinking water.

Ggggaaah assumed once the final attack began, and the prisoners started taking heavy casualties, that their morale would disintegrate, and they'd scatter like frightened mice. For weeks, he watched them piling up valuable mineral ore. Wondered at first just how crazy they must truly be, thinking they could construct something on such an enormous scale. Then when the ramp was nearly done, he scoffed at the rebels' audacity, ordering the command bubble to ready itself for a counterattack when the ramp got high enough for troops to fire down on them. Technically the counterattack was a disaster for the rebels. They suffered three hundred casualties. But once again, Ggggaaah simply could not appreciate the determination of his enemy. Casualties meant nothing to them.

He had superior firepower, plenty of well-supplied troops, and besides that he believed the Interplanetary Authority would fly to his aid, once their highly profitable mining operation was under threat. Then again, he never expected to seek their help in the first place. He just assumed they'd rush to save him, if it ever came to that.

Yet, every one of his assumptions had failed. When he turned off their electricity, he thought that would stop them. After all, how could they see in the dark, or coordinate a planet-wide rebellion without electric lighting? How could they operate their water filtration systems and replenish their drinkable water supply? When he ordered the guard stations and food depots sealed off, he figured that would stop the rebels too. The guards, he surmised, would fight desperately to hold off their attackers if they knew their lives depended on it. Once the rebels began to starve, he fully believed the revolt would fizzle out.

Instead his guards, in his view at least, betrayed him. They surrendered depot after depot within only a few days. To his dismay, those cowardly post commanders hastily concluded that since they'd been cut off from central command, they might as well seek terms from the enemy. In a matter of days, the Nausties were in control of all food depots, each stocked with supplies they desperately needed to continue the revolt.

Even when rioting, prisoners made it into the service tunnel and began slaughtering security troops—troops armed with advanced weapons and trained at riot control—Ggggaaah refused to order an evacuation. When rebel prisoners slaughtered unarmed mining engineers, then the crew of the Earth Cruiser *Unity*, Ggggaaah showed little foresight and merely ordered the air system cut off to the tunnel and smugly observed, "Sss-see how long they can last with only toxic air to breathe."

And yet, the rebels kept battling on. They built the ramp, they formed into military assault units for the attack, they armed themselves with captured weapons, and then they surprised everyone by blowing a massive hole in the wall of the terminal.

By then, it was far too late to start taking them seriously of course, as they poured through the breach. It was also far too late to request any type of massive rescue effort from Interplanetary Authority. Up to that point, Ggggaaah had been sending reports to his superiors claiming that the prison riot was a "minor uprising" and his forces had it "ninety percent contained." Now, he had to eat his words.

His final few hours in command were spent holed up in his private office at the very top of the main terminal, gazing at the barren planet surface and the striking desert landscape. From his office, he could look out over acres and acres of solar panels, which charged his generators and gave almost infinite electrical power to the main terminal.

Vaguely listening to the fighting going on downstairs, he focused his view on the sky, while his computer sent out automated distress calls to any passing space ships which might land and rescue the beleaguered garrison. Meanwhile, the massacre of his troops, his employees, and his staff was happening right outside his door, as well as throughout the entire headquarters complex, five square miles in size. Watching the sky through tinted windows, wondering what options he had left, he deluded himself into thinking help would soon arrive. None came.

"Where are they?" Ggggaaah wondered aloud. "They must be coming by now. What's taking them so long? They should have been here days ago!" Deep within his soul, he began to get a sinking feeling like he might be fooling himself.

He quickly pushed that traitorous thought aside though, as he glared wistfully at the broiling Rijel sun, shining down on him through heavily tinted glass. He looked away momentarily, squinting and returning his gaze to the endless rows of solar panels arrayed before him. Ggggaaah hissed dolefully when he realized he'd never taken the time to get a good long look at this engineering marvel. "What an incredible feat it must have been constructing all of this," he heard himself saying. It was too late to appreciate such things – he was merely trying to ignore reality.

"Don't they know what's at stake here?" he then ranted. "Don't they realize? Billions and billions of Galactic dollars – a month of production – lost. So much time has been wasted." The insanity within him was clouding his judgment. "Once they get here, once we get back to business, they'll see." He was clinging to the now-absurd notion that things were somehow going to be okay, that his operation would return to normal, and he'd be in charge once again.

Any moment they'll appear in the sky, he tried rationalizing, Interplanetary patrol ships, reinforcements with heavier weaponry and guns blazing. They'll show up and put a stop to this outrage! he thought, placating himself.

Meanwhile, outside the door the sounds of a ferocious firefight could be heard. EIC's were loudly discharging, making their distinctive ratcheting sound, sort of like a toy machine gun only deeper. Zorgs shrieked in pain. Enoshi could be heard roaring. Humans screamed back and forth to each other about whether they had any captured grenades left. An Eno snarled in response telling them no, they wanted Ggggaaah alive. Another Zorg cried out as he was hit by a burst of projectiles. It would all be over soon.

He'd assumed so many things in the past thirty Earth days that never materialized. And as the last elite unit protecting his stronghold was summarily butchered, Ggggaaah became paralyzed with the gnawing confusion of a person who simply can't believe his own fate, who can't believe everything is about to end, and who certainly can't believe it's going to end like it was. Yet his arrogance continued right up until the very end.

When rebels finally burst into his office, he sat and glared at them, coolly holding a ceremonial dagger with one hand while he manipulated the tip with scaly fingers. It almost unnerved the surprised Nausties who captured him. How could he just sit there so calmly amidst the killing and death going on all around? It was like he knew something they didn't, or that he was expecting something to happen that no one else was yet aware of.

"Yield or fight!" was the challenge from the Enoshi warrior who first entered the office. Amazingly, all the Warden did was simply lay the dagger down on the desk and slide it across toward the massive warrior. The now-captured Warden clasped his hands and awaited the beast's next move, with a cold blank look on his face. He finally replied, "I yield."

The Enoshi in that raiding party who'd battled from room to room and made it to his office wondered why he didn't just spring from his chair and fight them. Die honorably. What could Ggggaaah have been anticipating? Was he assuming they'd ransom him to the Interplanetary Authority? Was he still expecting relief to arrive? If so, he was sadly mistaken on both accounts.

Nausties rampaged uncontrollably for days, looting, pillaging, and vandalizing the terminal. There were occasional pockets of resistance, and in a few cases, security troops did make heroic last stands. In the main lobby of the terminal complex, fully a thousand Nausties were mowed down by electrical impulse cannons mounted on balconies. In hundreds of offices and meeting rooms, inside barracks and inside kitchens or warehouses, security troops barricaded themselves and decimated assaulting rebels. But there was no stopping them. Bloodlust and rage, suppressed for so many years, was all being released in one big orgy of violence.

Most non-prisoners attempting to surrender were executed on the spot, but some Nausties went too far. Atrocities were common. With the death of the General, it seemed like no one was in charge anymore, and in the absence of discipline, soldiers of most any army, especially rioting prisoners, can become vicious. That's what was happening here, and whereas central command had been fully recognized prior to Perry's and Hicks' suicide mission, now it was painfully apparent that no one was running the show.

Corpses of slain mine engineers, security troops, and office staff were mutilated and treated in vulgar ways. Certain species were offended by what was done, because in some cultures, there were centuries-old standards for the treatment of the dead. Zorg Nausties noticed humans making gruesome-looking hats out of the skulls of dead enemy Zorgs. This was an affront because in ancient tradition, only a chieftain could ritualistically lop off the head of a slain rival then form a hat out of the top of his skull. A common soldier was not allowed to, and a chieftain would only do so if he personally slew the enemy warlord. Worse, having lived with and among Zorgs for five decades, those humans surely would have known this.

Other acts were deemed culturally offensive to certain species, especially Enoshi who believed that all warriors had a duty to defend themselves to the last breath in combat and should never be expected to yield. If wounded and captured, an Enoshi warrior by custom could, and usually did, request execution to avoid shaming their clan.

Meanwhile Zorgs who captured Schpleefti office staff delighted in torturing them to death and even staged macabre circus-like events where they dragged screaming, terrified, defenseless creatures into a makeshift arena to be slowly burned to death or skinned alive and impaled on stakes. Spleef Nausties were quick to connect this behavior with the repulsive Zorg delicacy of eating infant rodents. Warden Ggggaaah for instance, was reported to have kept a small mouse cage in his office for occasional snacks.

But captured Enoshi security troops faced the ultimate degradation. Some of these poor souls, whenever found alive, would be bound to large tables and shaved from head to toe by cruel Naustie Earthers or Suidonji. They'd then be forced to duel each other to the death with only clubs or daggers in the new arena constructed in the lobby of the main terminal.

The spectacle was disgraceful. It was offensive too. Thousands of Nausties attended these gladiator-style "games," as the Nausties called them. And these offenses ultimately led to former rival crews becoming once again hostile toward each other. Shaving a warrior's fur removed his family breed identity, so when killed in the arena he died in shame. In the afterlife, after his soul left his body and went to *Fukuoka*, as Enoshi called Heaven, he'd not be recognized by his ancestors, and this was a grave insult to the slain warrior, enemy or not.

Warden Ggggaaah was executed for all to see as well, not long after the final battle in the terminal. It occurred about a week after his surrender, and in a fate befitting such a despicable creature, the Nausties dragged the fiend out of the terminal building and onto the center of the retractable cavern roof. There they tied him to a post and left him to die of exposure in the searing heat of the Rijel sun, with temperatures soaring to one hundred fifty degrees Fahrenheit by midday. His scale covered body roasted until it turned white and scaly, blistering and flaking as he suffered.

Thousands watched from inside the safety of the main terminal as he pitifully kept looking to the sky for rescue. He'd gaze upward, searching mournfully, then squint his eyes in the oppressive sunlight, wincing and bowing his head in agony. He groaned and cried out every once in a while, struggling to breathe in the thin air, while painfully baking in the heat. It was a horrifying way to die that many witnessed, and absolutely no one would ever forget. By next morning, after temperatures had plunged into the teens the night before, he appeared to be dead. The Nausties merely left him out there to dry up and disintegrate. No one felt like going out to retrieve his body.

It was the end of an era. An end to not just the life of their tormentor, it was technically the end of the rebellion itself. One big problem had now been eliminated: the Nausties had won their freedom. But with that victory came two new sources of conflict. What's more, both were caused by the elimination of the very system which had once oppressed them, as well as the many deplorable atrocities committed after the victory. Army units were disbanded. Crew leaders hastily rallied their members around them once more. An uncertain future now awaited the victorious rebels of New Australia. Architeuthis called for one last meeting after the close of hostilities.

"Welcome!" bellowed the wise Slart, as he stood at the base of the enormous causeway. He looked up at a sea of fellow Nausties arrayed before him. They were standing all around, on the ramp leading up from the terminal bay platform, packed in tight, fully a thousand, maybe more. Leaders of the many crews that had re-formed after military units had been dissolved. Slarts, Zorgs, Spleefs, Suidonji, Earthers, Enoshi, all were in attendance, along with loyal bodyguards and their most courageous warriors.

"I now declare this planet of New Australia to be ours!" he announced, drawing a swell of cheers from the exhausted throng. Most had only recently left the scene of carnage up in the main terminal. Many had assigned work details for the disposal of dead bodies and severed body parts. These had been hastily piled up outside on the surface and burned. Little care had been taken in differentiating between friend and foe, a detail not overlooked by those who'd taken issue with recent events.

When the cries of triumph and proud oaths slowly began to die down, Architeuthis raised a long tentacle to calm his audience before continuing. He first intended to request a moment of silence for the fallen, beginning with the many warriors who had given their lives in the quest for freedom. No one could do this better than wise old Architeuthis.

"Let us now honor those among our brethren who have made the ultimate sacrifice for our cause," he continued. "Please remain standing and bow your heads my friends, as we recognize our brave heroes."

In that massive loading bay, the giant Slartigifijian's resonant voice could be heard everywhere once the audience of blood-streaked former convicts grew quiet. Architeuthis then listed the many prison crews who had contributed troops to the battle. He spoke the names of each, eliciting triumphant murmurs, growls, grunts, and hisses from the proud throng. He read off names of crews who'd helped in other ways too, including food and supply runs conducted during the campaign. He detailed specific engagements that each had participated in or where Nausties selflessly gave their lives. He ended with the gallant fighters of the Templar Knights, causing many to raise fists in the air as they continued bowing their heads with respect. Then after a moment he recalled the names of two very special individuals.

"We also do honor to the memory of our leader Archibald William Hicks, General of the Army." This led to shouts and valorous roars from Earthers and Enos alike. Zorgs hissed and shrieked. Spleefs jumped and cheered. Suidonji snorted and squealed. Pausing only briefly he continued.

"And to his brave partner. His companion and confidant, to whom we owe our deepest gratitude, Pierre Gaspar L'Orange." announced Architeuthis which caused many to pause when hearing this, looking around at each other in confusion. Architeuthis was, of course, speaking of Hicks' partner, but most in attendance never knew the man's real name. "Perry," he then clarified, and cheers erupted once more.

But the towering creature wasn't done with the ceremony quite yet. No. Caring and compassionate by nature, and even after all that had happened, Architeuthis felt compelled to honor those among the enemy who had died fighting for Warden Ggggaaah, including the thousands of civilians who'd been slaughtered in the ensuing massacre. Despite his noble intentions, this sounded rather odd to those hardened warriors now in attendance. It would turn out to be a terrible mistake.

"Finally, we must honor today those who lost their lives on both sides; not just our own. Security troops, engineers, power plant operators, administrative personnel. All of those who perished in this epic struggle. May the souls of the innocents, as well as those of our former captors, now be at rest." This created quite a stir, and the response from the masses was not at all what he'd expected.

"To hell with those bastards!" screamed an Earther, "They got what they deserved!" Known for their irreverence, one could have expected such biting sarcasm from a human; nevertheless, this still managed to startle even some of his comrades nearby. Yet they reacted with similar attitudes toward their once-invincible foes. One reached over and slapped him on the back, laughing cold-heartedly. Others chuckled gruffly. Architeuthis was mortified. That wasn't the only reaction he got though. It was only the beginning of the upheaval.

"True! Fried them like steaks, we did." laughed a Zorg. His toothy grin drew in several of his fellow warriors to the building tumult. They hissed and snickered at his brashness. Seemed he just had to one-up those grimy humans, and his colleagues couldn't help but appreciate him for his audacity. This exacerbated the situation and Suidonji nearby naturally felt inclined to stir the pot.

"Yeah, skinned 'em alive, some of 'em." a barrel-chested Suidonji called out. Not to be outdone, he wanted to make sure everyone remembered the heartless cruelty of his troops as they rampaged through the main terminal looking for fresh victims to bring to the arena – usually Schpleefti office personnel who'd been hiding under their desks. But then things took a turn for the worse. Not everyone in the crowd was seeing the humor in this, least of which the crews of Schpleeftii in attendance.

"Oh yes! And not only that, Great Leader." retorted one of the Spleef crew leaders who was deeply offended. "Those wretched Scaleys skewered them like meat on a stick. Impaled them on stakes like Shish Kabobs." The little fellow was quite agitated. For a Schpleefti, referring to Zorgs as "Scaleys" was a serious insult, yet to Zorgolongians the term had many connotations, none of them terribly offensive. In fact, the Zorgs only laughed at the angry rodent, which made the crew leader's eyes glow bright red. At that point nearby humans couldn't help but add to the growing viciousness.

"Shaved 'em too!" yelled the first Earther, who'd started the whole embarrassing scene. He then began laughing uproariously, drawing in many of his cohorts and plenty of Zorgs and Suidonji as well. Now it was a free-for-all. Inappropriate comments abounded – some of them audible, some of them not. The response from a band of nearby Enoshi however was both swift and alarming.

"You laugh Earthman? How dare you. HEATHEN! Oh yes, we saw what you and your fellows did in the arena. We saw you removing their fur, those of our brethren whom you captured." His neighbor among the group of giant warrior-cats was more emphatic.

"BLASPHEMER! You know our traditions. How will their ancestors know them when their souls reach Fukuoka?" This only served to provoke the Earthman's ire.

"Brethren?" answered the man, still chuckling but starting to get a suspicious grin on his face. "You call those stinking oppressors *brothers*? Those sons of bitches were fighting' for the other side, asshole! Or in all the commotion did you and your buddies forget who was what? We sure didn't!" His fellow crew members around him only echoed his sarcasm.

"Yeah, flea bait! And it don't matter now do it?" remarked one of them. "They don't got a lick on fur on 'em no more! One looked pretty much the same as the others when I was dragging' their carcasses out to burn 'em! And by the way, didn't see none of your kind helpin' out with the funeral arrangements!" And that's when pandemonium set in.

Fights broke out. Claws were bared. A slash across the face, a dagger brandished, even though no weapons were allowed at this gathering. No one could prevent it from descending into a deadly brawl. Even Archituethis was helpless in stopping it, waving his tentacles frantically and calling for order, but no one paid heed. Angry crew leaders yelled oaths of vengeance toward one another, rallying their escorts around them to fend off attack. Threats of assassination were heard. Smarter ones wisely looked for a hasty exit while others stayed on to jeer at their old foes.

"Brothers! Friends! Please stop this madness!" pleaded Archituethis. Few listened. The triumphs and sacrifices of so many of their comrades suddenly mattered for nothing. Rivalries once dormant were being rekindled in a firestorm of acrimony and resentment. Members of the Schpleeftkorkii crew quickly removed the once-revered spiritual leader from the area. It would be many months before Archituethis would resurface.

Memories of ill-treatment of captured security troops, mining engineers, workers, or office staff inside the arena led to resentments between rival crews. Resentments led to minor skirmishes. Minor skirmishes led to open conflict. Then it got worse.

Now skilled at warfare, and experienced with military organization, many crews which were made up of the same species began to return to their old ways, no longer seeing themselves as fellow Nausties. It was only natural. There was no common enemy anymore. Moreover, there was no one in charge.

Architeuthis was their spiritual leader, not a military commander, and certainly no politician. That meant his job as the inspiration for the rebellion had already been performed. He was no longer needed as the de facto leader of the Nausties. Further no army was necessary. General Hicks was dead, and there was no great urgency to name a successor. Warden Ggggaaah had been defeated. Now nothing remained as a unifying force capable of drawing everyone together.

The mine and the guards, ironically, had been the only source of structure in their previous lives. Without production quotas to determine who got to eat and who might die, there would have been no need for the formation of crews in the first place. Therefore, with the planet under Naustie control and beings competing with each other for resources, crews took on a brand-new role. Members now needed protection from each other. Hoarding supplies after the fall of the prison system became the new mode of survival.

This was the new reality. In the aftermath of their stunning victory, it was time for each to become protective of their own kind. It was all but inevitable, given the barbaric nature of their existence. Crews had always fought for their own survival. Next, they'd fought with the guards for their freedom. The only thing left for them to do was fight each other, for the only two things left on New Australia that had value: food and water.

Fights evolved from the need to reestablish crew territories after the fall of Ggggaaah. Some crews were stronger than others. Some became absorbed into others. Some got wiped out entirely. But as fifty major crews rose to the top and began vying for outright control, the planet began to descend into a devastating civil war.

Amazingly enough, after all they had gone through by uniting to defeat prison authorities, they still fell into the trap of fighting for survival at the expense of their own future. This is precisely what Ggggaaah predicted would happen. Just like mutineers on a pirate ship, they'd eventually succumbed to distrusting one another, and killing off the weak, until only a handful of ragged survivors remained.

The leaders of the bigger, stronger crews knew that only those who controlled the most territory could then vie for ultimate power. Yet, they knew in their hearts it was a zero-sum game. To capture resources meant war with other crews and engaging one crew in battle meant becoming vulnerable to attack from another.

This foolishness went on for many months. It was incredible how quickly things fell apart. The heroism and sacrifice demonstrated by so many now meant nothing, compared with the harsh reality everyone had to accept: that the planet had only a limited amount of food, and no central authority to control distribution. What happened instead was tens of thousands fighting for control. Alliances were formed, then broken. Truces would be established, then violated. Shared Control agreements would be penned by a few warring crews, and a little progress would be made, but with no real means of enforcement, those agreements failed to secure any form of global peace.

Controlling access to food and clean water would soon mean nothing. Even with thousands already dead, there was still only a limited amount left for the remaining population to share. They had to stop immediately and band together once again; otherwise, their entire world would be destroyed.

It almost seemed like it would come to that at one point, with rivals beating each other to a pulp, only to have another crew sweep in to capture the spoils. It was as if they knew better but couldn't come to terms with the inevitable. Starvation drew ever closer with each passing month.

A very similar thing occurred on planet Earth, way back in the twenty-third century. Like with many industrial age civilizations, humans had resorted to burning their planet's fossil fuels to generate power to run their machines. But climate change followed and was exacerbated by carbon dioxide emissions. This sent the planet into decades of violent weather pattern changes, rising sea levels, and gradual extinction of plant and animal species.

Governments at first denied there was a problem, while scientists warned of further disasters to come. The public, for the most part, remained oblivious to the truth, or simply didn't want to believe it. Each generation merely passed the problem on to the next, until finally the results were clear.

Starvation followed years of drought and repeated crop failures. Governments toppled. Nations warred upon each other for control of limited resources, rather than coming together to devise viable solutions. Dictators and tyrants rose and fell. Armies fought, killed, destroyed, and wiped out entire regions. Nothing was accomplished. Just thousands and then millions of deaths, until the few surviving nations of the earth banded together and instituted massive reforms.

Populations were redistributed via forced migration, and families were limited to a single offspring per household to control overpopulation. Massive space stations were developed too, for the production of crops inside floating greenhouses. Even the daily calorie intake of citizens was controlled and dictated by central governing bodies, to avoid overconsumption and conflicts over shortages. Within a few decades, the planet changed considerably, with some coastal cities being abandoned entirely to the rising sea, and populations moving to the interior to reestablish communities.

Now New Australia was going to have to make some tough decisions just like Earth did centuries ago. The first order of business was a general ceasefire.

When the Schpleeftkorkii crew, who'd been protecting Architeuthis all this time, came forward to seek peace with a neighboring Enoshi crew, it created a chain reaction, eventually leading to calls for a global armistice in order to resolve their differences. Everyone was exhausted. There was nothing noble about it. Crew leaders knew very well it would be their own heads on the chopping block if they couldn't feed their members.

A territory map was created using the Warden's old mining network blueprints. These detailed drawings were used to determine borders, and Architeuthis himself came out of hiding to develop a new system of government, where all crews could send representatives to a new Parliament, as he called it. This was to be located inside the main lobby of the old terminal complex.

Ironically, they chose the site of the old arena used by Nausties for entertainment after the capture of the main terminal. Hundreds had been put to death in this place. Yet Architeuthis felt it was important to teach a lesson by reminding his comrades of what they should strive to be, and what they should avoid becoming once again.

But he went one step further, to give all Nausties a new basis for identity. Crews were now to be called Tribes, and the new parliamentary body took on the name of the Tribal Confederation. Not a full democracy, of course, but more of a loose alliance of tribal governments tied together by a common need to survive on a planet that provided no ability to grow crops on its forbidding surface.

This first parliament met night and day for over a month. Each tribal delegation was given its own quarters within the old barracks, and Architeuthis made only one key demand: no weapons of any kind allowed inside. Everyone complied, out of respect for their inspirational leader. What's more, they agreed to be locked inside their rooms at night, so they could all feel safe from one another.

Heated discussions often developed during parliamentary sessions, but a determined Architeuthis presided over every one of them, allowing member delegates to express their ideas freely. Debates were often intense, but no one needed to be reminded just what was at stake. Then, once the basic rules and systems of borders and territories were established, the second order of business became clear: how to bring in new supplies of food for their starving planet.

It was time to get back to basics, as Architeuthis put it. And by that, what he meant was mining. For there was only one obvious way they could get food and resources, and that was to trade for it. Everyone accepted this, for the only things they still had in abundance on New Australia were mineral ore, crystals, and precious gems.

Furthermore, each tribe would have to move to a newly established homeland and put its membership back to work in the mines. That wasn't all. Each of the fifty tribes would also have to send a hundred workers to clear out the massive dirt ramp from the terminal loading bay. *The Anarchy* was now their only means of transportation.

Thus, after all the violence, destruction, and death, after all the devastation and deprivations of global civil war, it turned out that when standing on the brink of disaster, the hardy creatures of New Australia found they could, indeed, halt their decline. It would seem the end of Warden Ggggaaah would not result in the end of New Australia, after all.

Chapter 10: The Star Kitten

"Welcome to Staaaaah Fantaseeeee," announced a low-pitched, disembodied human voice over a loudspeaker inside the cabin. A shuttlecraft from Enosh was now approaching its docking station after a seventeen-hour journey through space. Following a brief pause, the voice continued, "Prepare to disembark and get ready for an experience you'll nevvah evvah want to forget."

Passengers onboard from three different species murmured, chattered, snorted, and growled with delight, including four working class Enoshi males who were arriving for a specially discounted weekend getaway. Star Fantasy was always offering promotional packages like that just to draw in more blue-collar types. These were folks who might never be able to afford a vacation quite like this – not in normal circumstances. In fact, for the typical couple wanting to spice up their marriage, it would have cost half a year's pay just to spend a week there.

In addition to about twenty other beings from various planets, there were also nine or ten Star Fantasy employees on the shuttle. They were heading back to work after having completed their semi-annual two-week shore leave, where they got to go home and visit family and friends. Employees of Star Fantasy lived on-site in crowded dormitories. Many rarely, if ever, went home though, because life on Star Fantasy, it was widely known, was about as fun for the employees as it was for the guests. Management always saw to that. Happy employees meant more satisfied customers, and after all this was a pleasure palace, wasn't it?

Race Middlefield was one of those employees on board. Race was a human, originally from planet Earth. He was excited to be reporting back to work the next day for his job as chef in one of the many fancy restaurants on Star Fantasy. The resort had been open for nearly a year now, and business was booming. Beings from all over the galaxy flocked to the converted space station, which had been turned into an interstellar resort. Most came to escape the drudgery and monotony of their lives – or because they'd won some fantastic prize back on their home planets. Some, just like Race, had come there to start a brand-new life as employees.

Race was ecstatic when he first got the news, and now just twelve months later, as the shuttlecraft pulled into a docking bay at the converted space station, he was ready to resume his duties. Returning from a buying trip back on Enosh to select more exotic species of fish for the enormous aquarium inside his restaurant, he'd again be serving wealthy elite from all over the galaxy, as well as his favorite, daily customer Felina Toyger. Now commonly referred to as "The Star Kitten."

And though he might have imagined at first working for just a year to make enough money to fly back to Earth, within a few months he'd changed his mind. Like many employees of Star Fantasy, he decided instead to stay there for good. It was a fun place to work. Same thing with Felina.

Star Fantasy was like a giant wagon wheel, rotating slowly as it drifted in space, to create artificial gravity. Massive outside, and voluminous inside, the station had once housed over a thousand human scientists plus a few hundred beings from other species. Its cavernous chambers once grew experimental, as well as staple crops on hydroponic farms which yielded produce throughout overlapping growing seasons.

Because of the great distance from Earth, humans had created elaborate facilities for maintaining a lavish lifestyle. They had shopping malls, restaurants, athletic facilities, swimming pools, theatres, and holographic projection centers. Even the sports arenas had concave ceilings which created a three-dimensional image of an Earth-like daytime summer sky. Living facilities for the inhabitants were quite spartan and not much more than a hotel room by Earth standards. But still, this made it quite easy for the new owners to house thousands of visitors in the newly converted resort.

Felina had, by now, been working on Star Fantasy for quite a while. Female Enoshi could work in any section, but they typically stayed in only one area. They were so versatile, that creatures from most any species were thrilled to purchase an hour of their time. Having an attractive humanoid being with cat-like features and an almost uncanny ability to understand a partner's needs was an irresistible opportunity for most anyone, regardless of what planet they were from. But as for Felina, she was the best of the best.

The resort was organized into sections called Planetary Environments. This was a unique concept. The original plan was to create these Environs, as the planners nicknamed them, so that species from different planets could vacation and explore their own private fantasies in a magical world made to replicate places or even historical events from their planet's past. But shortly after opening their doors, management discovered that many species occasionally enjoyed other planetary environs, not just their own.

For Earth's, the creators of the resort chose to create places which no longer existed, except in history books. Global climate change had led to the total immersion of once-famous places like The Bahamas, Miami Beach, Amsterdam, and New York City. Haiti and the Philippines had also vanished under the surface of the ocean long ago, so, a Pacific or Caribbean island-style paradise made sense. But the creators also chose to portray a little slice of Earth history by creating a medieval torture chamber, and a gladiator arena from Ancient Rome, complete with an imperial bath. Muscular, athletic men worked this section, along with petite human females, to create an incredible experience for their numerous visitors.

Then the designers created Environs for other species – like the ones for Zorgolong and Suidonj, among others. Suidonji loved the intricate detail that designers put into their culture's environs, though typically the traditional pigsty only appealed to Suidonji themselves— for obvious reasons.

However, within only a few months, management was amazed to find that the Zorgolong Environs were regularly overbooked; often for weeks in advance. What they couldn't have foreseen was how insanely popular that sector of Star Fantasy would be – to humans no less. Zorgolongians were often hermaphrodites, so to them, gender was unimportant, if not immaterial, to erotic encounters.

To say they were hedonistic would be a gross understatement, even by human standards. They didn't care what you were. Such scenes were both fascinating and inviting to tourists from Earth. The terrariums and steamy jungle sections of the Zorgolong Environs drew human customers in droves, especially Lesbian females whom Zorgs found to be utterly fascinating, as well as delicious. The gift shops of Star Fantasy soon started selling "T-shirts" as humans called them, emblazoned with campy slogans such as "I ♥♥♥ LIZARD TONGUES".

The Enoshi Environs were quite different though. Each chamber was nothing but a large private room with an oval bed in the center and deep shag carpet covering the floor. Enormous clawing posts were in the corners, and the concave walls were made up of full-length video screens. In one corner would be a computer keyboard, where the female, always purported to be an Empath even if she wasn't, could type in a command to put on some video of a beach, a forest, a castle, a school classroom, a garage, a barn, a stadium, a spacious master bedroom, a sailing ship, or even the bridge of a deep space exploration vessel. The Empath would then probe to find out the customer's ultimate fantasy and conjure up imagery which would help achieve that. Then she would service the customer's more intimate needs.

Felina was highly sought-after, and quite well-known by most anyone before they even visited the Enoshi Environs. In bars and restaurants – at party mixers and meet-and-greets – even on advertisements broadcast on other planets, Felina The Star Kitten would often be depicted, either in a live video or in animated form. She was quite literally a celebrity, and she certainly earned that status.

Felina was incredible. Truly she was. Many would say she could have hand-picked her partner or partners if she ever wanted to. But she never did. Whoever was next in line in the lobby, she greeted them as though they were her very first customer of the night. And it didn't matter what they were, what planet they came from, or what they looked like. Felina made them all feel—every being she encountered—like the only creature she'd ever been interested in. Yet she charged no more than any other – didn't need to. "My ultimate reward," she would tell them, "is in seeing your spirits cleansed and renewed." It was other-worldly and highlighted her spiritual strength and training. Humans would return to Earth describing having only a brief five-minute conversation, not even finishing their drinks, and suddenly she was warmly beckoning them to join her back in her private suite.

From that point however, stories varied widely. One-on-one with a male of any species, Felina was both adaptable and engaging. She found out who they truly were inside and what they secretly longed for. No, it didn't matter what they previously had in mind, or for that matter, if they had anything in mind at all. Sure, people did try and fantasize about what they'd like to do before getting alone with her. Many would laugh about it later, when they returned to their home planet. They'd tell their friends about going to Star Fantasy dreaming of some bizarre fantasy they wanted to fulfill: about jungle cats, noble knights, rough-housing bikers, dusty cowboys, wild Indians, policemen, burglars, secret agents, or even some specific act they wanted to try. Yet that was rarely what they experienced once she got them back to her room.

Indeed, when they'd finally get with Felina she'd end up doing something totally different, something which completely surprised them. What mattered to Felina was not just fantasies. Those could be handled elsewhere, and on Star Fantasy there were many different options. No, what Felina sought was what they truly wanted to be as a person. Then, using her special talents and knowledge of every species, she'd relieve the stress and clear the mind of all emotional baggage like regret, apprehension, or self-doubt. She brought the customer to a plane of existence where they were, for several moments, perfect.

It wasn't just what she said either. In fact, she said very little. She simply found a way to get her customer to that place in his mind where the weight of the world was suddenly removed, and the spirit could be freed long enough to see how beautiful they were inside their soul.

This is what gave Felina great personal fulfillment. She was now nineteen years old, and there were a thousand more tomorrows for her. Ten thousand maybe. Yet she didn't have to care about that; her future was limitless. For today, she'd finish her shift, have a scrumptious dinner at her favorite restaurant which was always comped by her friend and head chef, Race Middlefield. Then she'd go back to her private dormitory room to get a well-deserved twelve-hour nap.

Waking up for each new shift was easy. Her soul was at peace. Every coworker and every colleague loved her dearly. Every client appreciated her. In fact, her career ambitions seemed to be headed in the right direction. She was excited to see where she could take things.

CHAPTER 11: SPACE PIRATES

It took quite a while to uncover the former Earth Cruiser The Unity and get the terminal loading bay operational again. But, it was finally done.

In fact, thousands of Enoshi, Spleefs, Zorgs, humans, and Suidonji labored on it for weeks to finally get the ramp cleared out, hauled away, and the area cleaned up. That's what the Tribal Confederation had ordered, and most everyone understood the importance of doing so. Many believed that repairing and getting their captured freighter, dubbed *The Anarchy*, back into space, trading mineral ore and precious gemstones, was the quickest path to replenishing the planet's now dwindling food supply.

Slart planners, once again working for Architeuthis, projected the timeline for the planet's reserves, as well as the time and resources necessary to develop large-scale hydroponic farms capable of feeding the planet. Bottom line was this: in about six months, the population, though vastly reduced from the savage civil war, would starve.

Trading with other planets was the best immediate option for New Australia, or so they said, and the nearest planets were Suidonj and Zorgolong. Between the two, most agreed, Suidonj was the better of the two. The industrial might of that planet consumed far more in the way of iron ore and giant crystals to power their spacecraft – which traded all over the galaxy and were exploring the rest of the universe looking for new planets to colonize. Many in the Confederation, not just Suidonji tribes either, thought this planet would yield great customers. And yet a small minority of Nausties felt seeking trade relations with other planets was a foolish idea, likely disastrous. Solomon Mwanga was one of them.

He was a black African from Earth and still chieftain of the Schpleeftkorkii Tribe. He oversaw the entire operation for restoring the terminal loading bay. He could actually watch the activity from his new office located inside the partially-demolished command bubble overhead. The original structure had most all of its lower floor blown off, as well as part of the second, but Earther construction teams repaired it well enough to support a large office with a conference table. It now had a bank of desks for terminal traffic controllers to once again run the operation below.

Solomon sat in the center at the desk, formerly used by none other than Warden Ggggaaah. His warriors had brought it down from Ggggaaah's now empty office on the top of the terminal dome for him to use. This gesture was in deference to their chieftain's well-known past. Back on Earth, Solomon had once been an African warlord who'd staged a bloody coup d'état in his home country.

The overthrow of the country's regime led to a devastating civil war, which killed tens of thousands of troops, and over a hundred thousand civilians caught up in the conflict. For eighteen tumultuous months, he was the self-proclaimed President of the country, fighting first against republican forces still supporting the ousted former dictator, and then against rebels supported by neighboring rival nations. He desperately held onto power, before finally being deposed, and forced to flee into exile. Captured and tried later in international court for war crimes, he was sentenced to twenty years on Rijel 12. At the time, he was only twenty-five years old.

But that was many years ago. Solomon was a much wiser man now. Wiser and more patient he was, yet cool and calculating, due to his background. Solomon was one of those more realistic souls among the Naustie hierarchy, who disagreed with seeking trade relations with other planets. *Not yet*, is how he saw it. However, as a chieftain and delegate to the Tribal Confederation, Solomon wisely kept his strong opinions suppressed, at least in public.

Meeting with his team of experts before the planned launch of *The Anarchy*, Solomon spoke to his staff of mostly Slarts and a few Earthers. He greeted them calmly, as he always did, with his thick Swahili accent.

"Good day everyone. Are we ready to get this bird back into the air?" Staff members muttered and murmured affirmative replies, which quickly faded. His tone was coldly businesslike, as though he had something very important to discuss – and no time for anecdotal humor. No one would have expected such a thing anyway, certainly not from him.

Solomon, having been installed as "Terminal Chief" by the selection committee at the Tribal Confederation monthly conference, got to hand-pick his staff, and this was far more important than winning over Confederation delegates to his side. He was certainly no politician when it came to things like that. What's more, this gave him a great measure of autonomy in making crucial decisions on his own, without seeking approval from the planet's governing body. Besides, most of those chieftains merely followed the wave of public sentiment when deciding how to vote. That simply wasn't Solomon's style.

Nevertheless, the results spoke for themselves. The terminal machinery, lift mechanisms, and especially the functions of the planet's only space craft were now fully operational. *The Anarchy* was ready to be loaded, and Slart engineers had given it the okay to fly. If nothing else, the Confederation committee had indeed chosen the right man for the job. Solomon and his staff were meticulous and efficient. However, they were also quite intelligent, and to be sure, several of them shared their commander's doubts about sending a trade mission to Suidonj.

Solomon cleared his throat and continued, "Within a few days, as we all know, our facility is about to launch *The Anarchy* back into space. We've readied ourselves for this … spent months repairing, cleaning, and rebuilding. We've considered every potential challenge and setback that we could think of to get this show on the road. I'm proud of all of you." He smiled briefly then quickly returned to glaring at them.

The Slarts fluttered their facial tentacles and hummed with acknowledgment at their boss' compliment, taking Solomon's words at face value, which was their nature. Of course, Slarts couldn't understand human nature and social customs, especially when it came to managers addressing a staff meeting. Human leaders were often times using flowery words and making grandiose statements that didn't convey the full truth of their intentions. The Earthers on his staff murmured obediently as well, but they just knew what was coming. There was no way Solomon was going to say something so sugary and sweet like that—and not follow it up with a "however."

And they were right. Solomon was not the type to lavish subordinates with compliments. He clearly had something else on his mind. Sure enough, Solomon pounded the table lightly with his right fist, and his demeanor changed completely.

"However, we've been making certain assumptions during this process that may or may not come to fruition. We've been naively assuming that Suidonj – or any planet in the galaxy for that matter – will actually trade with us."

Of course, the Earthers on his staff had been thinking this all along, even if the logical Slarts hadn't considered it. Namely: how could they really expect other worlds to trade with New Australia, or even allow a Naustie ship to land in Interplanetary Authority ports?

"We're convicts, after all my friends ... all of us. We're criminals and revolutionaries from six different planets who got sent here to die in the mines. We were cast off... exiled... thrown away... whatever you wish to call it... only to have risen up and overthrown our captors. Despite this our Tribal Confederation has assigned us with sending our planet's only spacecraft to planet Suidonj ... to trade for food." Solomon paused again, leaning back now with his hands gripping the edge of the conference table as he continued.

"Who's to say they don't confiscate our ship and all its holdings?" Solomon pushed back from the table, stood up, and began pacing the office while the Slarts recovered from the shock of his candor. The Earthers grumbled tensely. They, by way of comparison, knew just what he was getting at.

There was quite a long pause while the staff awaited his next words, but Solomon was quite right. From the very start, the Tribal Confederation had been urging a frantic cleanup and repair effort, while all the while portraying that once *The Anarchy* could fly again, New Australia could begin trading with other planets. As if the Interplanetary Authority, or IPA as it was referred to, would truly be willing to let bygones be bygones and forget about the incalculable

loss of revenue, outright rebellion and the overthrow of Security
Forces, the brutal slaughter of mine employees, and of course the
execution of their carefully chosen prison warden.

True, Interplanetary Authority ships never did arrive trying to
recapture Rijel 12, not yet anyway. And when the Warden's staff had
sent desperate messages pleading with passing ships to come evacuate
survivors of the Naustie Revolt, IPA officials had wisely, if not
cowardly, ordered a quarantine, and forbade ships from landing there.

Now Solomon was in charge. He'd been chosen as Terminal
Chief, and in his mind, he could focus his well-qualified staff on the
cold, hard truth they now faced. What Solomon was implying; no,
what he was actually flat-out saying to his staff was this, "If *The
Anarchy* takes off tomorrow to fly to Suidonj, with a load of mineral
ore, it's never coming back. And we all, deep in our hearts, know that
for a fact!" He then smacked his hand on the table top.

"We'll lose our only ship, and the IPA will simply write us off.
They'll let us starve out and die. And that, my friends, is also a fact."
Solomon put extra emphasis on that last part, leaning forward a bit as
he said it. He knew that would get everyone's attention.

The Slarts bristled at his words, fluttering their facial tentacles
with concern. They weren't offended, of course. Honesty and
bluntness were very much a part of their nature. They frankly could
do nothing but tell the truth. The only thing that unsettled them was
Solomon's repeated use of the word: fact. Solomon didn't react to
their rumblings. He knew Slarts had a real problem with anyone
saying something was fact when it hadn't occurred yet; especially if
it hadn't been painstakingly calculated to prove it was irrefutably so,
removing all possible doubt.

Yet the Earthers at the conference table, though they squirmed a
bit in their chairs, knew exactly what Solomon was so clearly
implying. That's really what they loved about their boss. He was
diplomatic and congenial when dealing with the Tribal Confederation
in public, but when he met with them privately, he'd speak
straightforward and soberly. That's what they needed. People were
counting on them. Hell, any Earthman knew: it was perfectly normal
for a governing body to make inflated promises based on vague,
overly-optimistic theories without thoroughly considering potential
obstacles. Earthers knew that, even if Slarts did not.

Besides, governments didn't have to prove they were right, did they? Whoever they placed in charge, or whoever they assigned duties to for carrying out the required tasks, that was the poor bastard who had to answer for it later if he failed. However, Solomon was the kind of person who could handle this level of responsibility. He wouldn't just blindly follow the directives of the Confederation then try and rely on naïve assumptions. That's what made him the right choice for Terminal Chief.

Solomon, after all, had been the one who commanded the highly-lauded Supply Distribution Division during the rebellion. He had been the one who devised the diabolical backup plan where Naustie Spleefs and Zorgs would climb up and down the service ladders of the elevator shafts wearing backpacks filled with water bottles, ammunition, and food rations. If it had come to this, Solomon would have ordered his daring plan to be implemented.

Above everything else, Architeuthis trusted him. That was why Architeuthis went into hiding and accepted his protection during the planetary civil war. That's also why Architeuthis suggested to the Tribal Confederation selection committee that they put Solomon Mwanga in charge as Terminal Chief. Few, if any, objected.

Solomon had said quite enough now. He just needed his staff members to speak up and engage in debate on the matter. A good leader knows how to do that: get his people to talk themselves into it, before issuing orders he already intends for them to carry out.

First, one of the Earthers spoke, a man named Bui Hoang Oh. He was from the Earth region of China, and at one time ran a large Asian organized crime syndicate. Bui leaned back in his chair, unfolding his arms and cocking an eye suspiciously – as he used to do so many times in his previous career as a crime boss. Bui spoke up first, using language that was quite disturbing to his Slart colleagues, but clearly echoed the sentiments of the other Earthers on the staff.

"Right Commander. My colleagues and I have often wondered this. How does the Confederation really expect us to trade with other planets? We're criminals, as you say. They sent us here to die. So now why would they trust us or even talk to us?" Another human, a former mobster from New Chicago named Nicky Ciancio, chimed in next.

"Yeah, boss. The dumbass is right. This is fricking nuts. How the hell do they think we're going to just show up on Suidonj and tell them, 'Hey we got iron ore for sale!' They'll lock up our guys the moment we step off the ship." Bui chuckled. He and Nicky were old friends and the slur didn't bother him in the least, at least not when Nicky said it that is. Anyone else, and they'd have gotten a knife shoved up under their ribs.

Solomon nodded and looked at all the staffers sitting around the conference table. "Most likely yes," he said with an icy glare. He then crossed his arms and waited patiently for more feedback.

One of the Slarts, named Decapodifor, interjected, "But Commander, the Tribal Confederation has ordered us to travel to Suidonj and trade for food. Is that not what we have been working on all this time?"

Solomon remained calm and nodded, saying, "Yes, they did. That's what they ordered us to do." Decapodifor sighed and fluttered his facial tentacles in the way Slarts do when they're flustered.

He clarified, "And so, we're not going to Suidonj. Or are we?" Nicky scoffed at Decapodifor's naiveté, still looking at Solomon with a sly grin.

"What a dumbass. Anyway, I bet the chief's got a better idea already, don't you, Boss?" Solomon's eyes drifted over to Nicky, then back to Decapodifor. The old Slart failed to appreciate Nicky's new term for him. *Dumbass?* he wondered, *What does that mean?* Slartigifijians didn't have asses.

"Maybe," Solomon grinned. Then his face went stony. He slowly stepped back to his chair and sat back down, leaning forward and resting his elbows on the table. He clasped his hands together, and added, "But, we know what our primary task is, and that's to get food for New Australia, isn't that right gentlemen?"

Solomon left that question floating about the room like a nebulous cloud. No one commented further. The Slarts still seemed to be pondering their commander's very direct question. Meanwhile the Earthers sitting next to them nodded and grinned like they were getting the point.

"Our job is not to send off *The Anarchy* into space and never see her return. Our job is to get her back again, loaded with supplies, and if we don't do that, we have failed," added Solomon powerfully. The Earthers among his staff grunted with agreement. Decapodifor was still confused. Nevertheless, he fluttered his facial tentacles again and tried to accept the logic of the Chieftain's comments.

"So, Commander we must disobey Confederation directives in

order to accomplish our task? Is that what you're suggesting?"
Solomon eyed the honorable and intelligent Slartigifijian calmly. It
was vital that his entire staff be totally on board with his thinking –
and yes, he most certainly had a plan in mind all along. The Slarts
had learned quite a lot both from and about humans since they'd been
incarcerated on Rijel 12 and vice versa.

In a Slart's mind, concepts like military deception, financial fraud,
and hollow political promises were impossible to grasp. But what
about results? Now results were something they could understand
completely. Results trumped everything for a Slart. Decapodifor and
the others just needed one more piece of the puzzle to put it all
together – to see how everything fit into place. The greater purpose
had now been stated; the goal had been defined. That's what they
needed to see. The goal was to bring back food, and that's what they'd
been charged with accomplishing.

Several heads began to nod. Solomon then added, "You see,
Decapodifor, it is my responsibility as Terminal Chief to send out *The
Anarchy* and to get her back full of food for our planet to survive.
That's the task I've been put in charge of, and that's what I'm ordering
the crew, that's what I'm ordering all of you, to accomplish." That
was something Slarts could easily understand: responsibility.

In Slartigifijian culture, to take responsibility for something, to
take charge of an operation or to lead an organization to reach a goal,
meant a Slart's personal honor and reputation were at stake. Failing
in accomplishing the task, or failing to protect those you were
responsible for, meant disgrace and ostracism from one's community.
One either achieved his goal or not. There could be no blaming
subordinates or making excuses about unexpected setbacks.

What Solomon was telling them was this: he was taking full
responsibility for the task of bringing food back to New Australia;
therefore, he must succeed or face the consequences. Once he put it
that way, those brainy Slarts had no further compunctions about
defying the Confederation. With that, Solomon relaxed and sat back
in his chair, his hands still clasped much like a man praying to God.

"Now, let me show you what I have in mind," said the big African
as he heaved a deep sigh. The Slarts continued to flutter their facial
tentacles and share glances with each other confirming each other's
adherence. Meanwhile the humans sat forward in their chairs with
looks of keen anticipation.

Long before this day's meeting, Solomon had taken the time and effort to do a little recruiting among the prison population and managed to enlist a crew of former pirates and smugglers. What better place to look than New Australia? In a former prison, those were quite easy to find and plentiful.

His staff in the terminal command center had never known of this. They merely saw him hiring a crew and thought nothing of it. But Solomon wasn't just looking for sailors, crewmen, or former merchants. He wanted bloodthirsty killers who just happened to know how to fly a space ship. His plan was to turn *The Anarchy* into a raider. The tactic Solomon envisioned, he now revealed to his staff, was a very ancient one indeed: the disguised official transmission, or false flag.

"I merely needed to find the right people to carry it out, that's all," as he put it. Solomon knew that *The Anarchy* was once an Earth ship called *The Unity*, and all her transponder codes would be picked up on interspace communications as coming from the freighter and her crew. *The Unity* was once an interstellar merchant vessel, and a long time had passed since her capture. "By now, few will even remember the name," he assured everyone.

Solomon said he figured his first recruit had to be the captain. Based on that crucial choice, the rest would be quite easy, because the captain would know who he really needed onboard to get the job done. "Plus, I needed a good first mate," he went on to tell them, as if he found the right creature for that position, as well.

The next task would be even more ambitious: hiding Enoshi and Earther assault troops within the ship's hold. The basic idea was to lure another ship close enough to dock with *The Anarchy*, then board her and slaughter her crew. Plunder the captured ship for supplies and weapons, use the new ship with its full complement of missiles to slowly build an entire fleet of pirate ships.

He told his staff how he went through twenty candidates before he finally found one rather aged Zorg named Kcsheeech. This older fellow was perfect, but likely too old to be a captain anymore. Nevertheless, he would make for an effective first mate, Solomon surmised. Knowledgeable and experienced, Kcsheeech had once served with Warden Ggggaaah in his wild and unruly pirate days many years ago. But whereas Ggggaaah had gone straight and went on to become a Zorg commander, before retiring from the service to run New Australia Planetary Prison, Kcsheeech had remained a pirate.

Oh, how Kcsheeech resented his former shipmate too. Once the best of friends on board a Zorg marauder, raiding merchant ships all across the galaxy, they parted ways when Ggggaaah's rich family bought his way into Fleet Academy. When Kcsheeech was finally captured several years later during a pitched battle with a Zorg patrol craft, Ggggaaah didn't lift a finger to help him. Kcsheeech, of course, realized that Ggggaaah's family most likely overruled any good intentions his old friend might have had about petitioning the court to pardon him. Still, Ggggaaah had the power to at the very least bring him on as a crewmember – and save him from a life sentence on Rijel 12. He did nothing to help Kcsheeech, and it continued to gnaw at him years later.

Kcsheeech knew quite a lot about pirates and tactics. He told Solomon that pirates in deep space often found it convenient to give out false names and identification signals when making raids, particularly when approaching a space station. Many experienced in attacking outposts preferred to use captured ships for the initial approach so to maintain the element of surprise. Captured ships were rarely used in traditional ship-to-ship actions, however.

"A shooting battle with another ship is far too dangerous," said Kcsheeech in his thick Zorg accent. Solomon could imagine why. "Too many things can go wrong," he assured the muscled African, "and they often will, going toe-to-toe with an enemy vessel."

And the reputed faked distress call? "It rarely works," Kscheeech argued. "Merchants on tight schedules frequently ignore them and simply relay those messages more often than not. Worse, it only serves to attract further investigation by nearby patrol vessels. That can be disastrous. Besides, distress signals will just as likely draw other scalawags seeking to make easy prey of a helpless ship." That's ironically when their concept really began to take shape.

Solomon liked this idea best: lure another pirate vessel to *The Anarchy* and trick them into boarding. Capture their ship and press their crew into service. It could work. An unsuspecting pirate vessel would believe them to be *The Unity* and cruise right up, thinking they were an easy victim.

"But could our warriors hope to overwhelm a crew of seasoned pirates?" asked Solomon. That's what he wanted to know. Kcsheeech only laughed and hissed in that way Zorgs were often known for. "Oh yes-sss, great Chief," he replied. "They're pirates not soldiers. They'll be expecting inexperienced crewmen who've rarely even fired a weapon. I say, go ahead. Let them board, the scum. They'll be completely unprepared for a real fight." Solomon grinned and chuckled. He knew he'd truly found the perfect first mate.

That meant the next task was to pick the right captain. And to accomplish this, Solomon enlisted the help of his star recruit. For Kcsheeech, of course, that was easy. He already knew exactly the right person for the job: Slout Epidyminon. Captain Slout Epidyminon, that is, a Suidonji who he'd befriended during the ramp construction.

Slout was an enormous, rather imposing creature. Most were, for that matter. Suidonji usually stood about six feet tall, but some were even taller. Their haunches were slightly crouched, but the power in their legs was incredible. They had to be strong there too, because their arms were relatively weak by comparison, just like with humans. They walked much like a fat old man, but their heads were enormous, and their bite was deadly in close order combat. A spear and shield or a hand weapon fired at a distance were all they needed to compete effectively in a fire-fight, but close in, they could simply bite off limbs or chomp the neck of an enemy, rendering him helpless.

Years before, Slout had been commander of a Suidonji freighter, which had occasionally dabbled in smuggling before he found himself on the losing side in a war between two rival mobsters. He became the fall guy, and when officials apprehended him and offered him a deal to rat out the rest of the crew leaders, Slout, being the powerful and arrogant type who was accustomed to giving orders and not being bossed around, essentially told the investigators to go screw themselves. Oh, how he regretted it later, when the courts sentenced him to ten years hard labor. But he also knew in the grand scheme of things he was far safer in prison than he was back on planet Suidonj, once those mobsters got hold of him.

Now, after three years on Rijel 12, having slimmed way down and gotten quite lean, Slout was a very intimidating physical specimen. Best of all, he knew all too well how to whip a crew into shape, give commands that sailors would follow without question, and maneuver a spacecraft skillfully.

Solomon told his staff in the command center, "I knew right from the first day that I'd picked the right captain." Slout's barking commands and immense knowledge of the ship's controls, maneuvering capabilities, and hull/speed limitations were impressive. It was like he had never left the bridge of his old freighter. After a few days altering the furniture to fit the big fellow comfortably, the new skipper looked like he felt right at home. Solomon told his staff that on the day they toured the ship; he chuckled to himself and looked down at Kcsheeech, who smiled a toothy smile.

"Yes, good choice, *Keech*," was all that Solomon had said. That unfortunately was the only way he could say the creature's name. Pronouncing Zorg names was next to impossible for the big African. Thus, he took to calling him "Keech" just to save time. Following that, he'd simply exited the command bridge and let Kcsheeech and Slout do their thing. Solomon's rule when it came to delegation was always this: when you find people you can trust with a job, stay the hell out of their way.

And that's how he explained it to his staff of now-acquiescent Slarts and thoroughly pleased humans a few days before launch. The humans smiled, and the Slarts fluttered their facial tentacles. It made sense to them now.

All this time, they'd been working on rehabbing the terminal. All this time preparing the ship to establish trade with planet Suidonj. Now they were amazed to find Solomon had been going around recruiting scalawags and cutthroats to man *The Anarchy* and instead go on a pirate raid. With Solomon's great skill at explaining things and being respectful of his subordinate's cultural practices, he now had their unanimous approval.

Indeed, soon the whole planet would know, and everyone else would gradually start finding out throughout the galaxy: New Australia was soon to be launching its first foray into the blackness of space, and Solomon's humble command center would soon become the secret headquarters of the galaxy's most fearsome new space pirates.

CHAPTER 12: LIFE ON STAR FANTASY

"Good evening, I'm Kallisia Damos and this is the IPN Evening News," said the disembodied voice. It was coming from a video screen in the lounge area next to Race's restaurant on Star Fantasy. Music blared as the famous news anchor pivoted her chair to face a different camera. Then a small window popped up – this time showing a pirate flag attached to a sword superimposed on a picture of some unknown planet.

A small crowd of people sat disinterested, awaiting their names to be called announcing their table was ready. Few were listening as they relaxed around a gigantic fish tank where Race kept his exotic assortment of ocean creatures. Within minutes, many would have their eyes riveted to the broadcast.

"At the top of the news tonight, the galaxy is being rocked by the news of yet another pirate raid on a remote space colony," continued Ms. Damos as the frenetic news show music faded out. Her smiling face had now transformed into a look of deep concern. She paused and then went on reading from the teleprompter.

"Interplanetary officials on Suidonj report that their space colony Frabrak 3 has been raided and looted by the crew of an unknown ship, believed by some to be the former Earth freighter *The Unity*, which was captured by rioting prisoners during the revolt on Rijel 12 two years ago. As our viewers may recall, this riot led to the complete overthrow of prison authority and also the presumed massacre of its entire garrison."

She continued, "Reports of pirate activity have increased dramatically over the past several months, as freighters and even a few passenger ships have been hit by pirate vessels while traveling between planets. Crews and passengers have been brutalized, captured, even murdered. Ships have been plundered, and in many cases disappeared completely from inter-planetary space, never to be heard from again. Presumptions about the fate of these vessels have ranged from pirates scuttling the crafts, to some believing the ships have been pressed into pirate service. Even a few government officials have confided, on condition of anonymity, that pirates may have been building up a fleet of raiders to eventually challenge galactic forces. Officially, Interplanetary Authority denies these theories as mere exaggerations and irresponsible rumors."

Ms. Damos then pivoted her seat once again to look at a different camera, and with a smile introduced a smart young female sitting next to her: another lovely female Enoshi. "With us now is our intrepid field correspondent, Glynda Trexel, who will give us some insight into this ever-expanding story. What can you tell us, Glynda?"

Glynda smiled with the respectful acknowledgment, then she looked right at the camera. It was her moment to shine, she had been waiting her whole career for a break this big. She had covered enough softball stories like missing pets and feel good emotional stories, and she was ready for the bigtime. She eyed the camera with a fire in her eyes.

"Thanks, Kallisia," said Glynda with a bright smile. "Some time ago, it's now been discovered, IPA officials detected an interstellar distress call from a freighter identifying itself as the doomed Earth Cruiser *The Unity*. The transponder code was clearly that of the now infamous ship, and the senders of the message claimed they were its surviving crew now desperately in need of assistance. Patrol ships responded to the area but found no trace or any evidence of debris indicating it might have been damaged."

"Initially the assumption was that pirates might have gotten there first to feast on the supposedly disabled craft, then towed it away to some secret base for repairs. But several weeks after, planet officials on Earth reported yet another missing freighter which had been heading back to Earth from a distant space station in the Zorgolong star system. This ship and all its crew, cargo, and passengers, were never seen nor heard from again."

Glynda now turned in her chair, slowly gesturing toward a gigantic green screen behind her, which now depicted a map of the galaxy with names written in curving letters over the planets Enosh, Zorgolong, and Suidonj. It also had markings on it, indicating the locations of sites where various events had occurred. As Glynda spoke, then gestured or pointed to locations, they would highlight on the map. New ones would appear as she continued with her report.

"Here was the last known location of the ship claiming to be *The Unity*," she said. Glynda then told the known version of what had been transpiring ever since the ship had departed from New Australia. The report was filled with eyewitness accounts and interviews with government officials who spoke anonymously, appearing onscreen with their faces obscured. Theories abounded, wild ones as well as plausible ones. They ranged from beliefs that a pirate alliance had been formed and this had led to their increased aggressiveness, to more bizarre theories that perhaps a brand-new race of beings from a distant star system had invaded the galaxy. Yet she kept on circling back to speculation that Rijel 12 was somehow the origin of this activity. By now, people in the restaurant had begun paying close attention to her report.

"And what of these supposed reappearances of *The Unity*?" she asked rhetorically. "Well those stories have been going around for months. The ship has been reported by witnesses as showing up all over the galaxy. Some witnesses have been credible … some not in the least. But could it really be them—the former rebels of New Australia Planetary Prison?" She then paused and cocked an eyebrow. Glynda clearly seemed to think so. Could the former prisoners have survived and turned their planet into a pirate base? Glynda didn't mince words. With her paw, she touched the green screen behind her in close proximity to the little ball with lighted letters above it saying '*R-12*'.

"Evidence seems to indicate this planet as the origin of all recent raids," she proclaimed, with a lifting of her chin. This drew a noticeable reaction from the patrons of the restaurant – many of whom began worrying about their own safety.

Meanwhile Felina Toyger, The Star Kitten, sat across the restaurant devouring her seafood dinner, a special dish prepared by Race Middlefield. Race always rolled out the red carpet for her – actually coordinated his own schedule so that he could spend the evenings chatting with his favorite gal pal. She was also his star customer, a celebrity who drew lots of attention from Star Fantasy clientele.

Of course, for Felina that attention was no bother at all. She liked her job, loved her customers, and never seemed to be overwhelmed by the trappings of stardom. Beings from every species often recognized her and would come talk to her at the restaurant. She never shooed them away nor brushed them off. It just wasn't her style.

Race was certainly an indirect beneficiary of her generosity. Drawing customers to his restaurant by reserving a private table each night for only Felina to occupy was good for business, and he well knew it. After all, it improved his Employee Grade, which lent him full access to most any attraction, Environ, or venue. Plus, he loved the hunky specimens working over in the Earth Environ at the Roman Gladiator attraction. Most were handsome bodybuilders and all of them were bisexual. Each night, both he and Felina would finish their shifts and spend the evening detailing their exploits of the day, then Race would tell Felina of his naughty plans for the night, thrilling her and humoring her as she'd purr and giggle all the way through dinner.

Theirs was a spectacular friendship. Being that she was an Empath and a very good one at that, yet with an independent streak about a mile wide, Felina was fascinated with a being like Race Middlefield. He was a gay man who had such vastly different desires when it came to companionship, and despite being in his mid-thirties, was still very handsome and active.

Maybe it was more because he had absolutely no physical desire for her in any way shape or form yet loved her deeply as a person. He wanted nothing from her, just enjoyed her company, always interested in every aspect of her life, her feelings, and her desires. No one else ever expressed an interest in things like that before. Felina totally embraced being what she was, of course, but Felina was aware many customers were merely interested in her body. Not Race. He loved her completely like a childhood friend who'd known her all her life, or an older brother in whom she could confide anything and everything. That's what drew her to him.

Race made his way through the restaurant, greeting happy customers and thanking them for dining there that night.   Glad-handing VIP customers who'd been identified to him on the restaurant computer was always a great idea. Passing the lounge area, the video broadcast blaring from the giant screen in the lounge suddenly caught Race's eye, as he noticed the crowd of people now gathering around to watch the news.

They were riveted to the investigative report, which was still being given by Ms. Trexel. At first, he thought folks were just turned on by the pretty Enoshi giving the story, but soon he realized what the topic was, and it got his attention. *Pirates were raiding again. No one was safe.* Race could sense what customers were thinking, fearing for their lives, and certainly for good reason. This could be really, really bad. He approached Felina from behind as she was stuffing another bite of Mahi-mahi into her mouth.

"Well, that's going to be a downer for business, now isn't it?" stated Race as he walked up to her table and sat down across from her. Felina smiled broadly, reacting with pleasant surprise at his arrival. She'd been staring vaguely into the fish tank for some time and didn't know what he was referring to with that comment.

"What's bad, Tomcat?" asked Felina through her mouthful of food. That was her pet name for him. Race sighed. He had just heard Glynda Trexel saying that passenger ships had been targets of pirate raids while en route to different planets. That could spell disaster for Star Fantasy if prospective customers were suddenly afraid to risk interstellar travel.

"Didn't you hear the reporter?" continued Race. "She said pirates are attacking passenger ships now. Might mean fewer customers if it gets out of hand." If he only knew how prophetic those words really were. Felina, by way of comparison, was oblivious to the broadcast, and shrugged her shoulders. She was exhausted anyway. After her nightly chat with Race, she was looking forward to a good long sleep. Nevertheless, that's precisely what had been happening. The Naustie fleet had as of late been turning to raiding passenger vessels for food, supplies, and other more valuable acquisitions.

"So, how was your day, Darling?" asked Race, changing the subject with a smile. Felina grinned but clearly needed to finish chewing her food, so he followed up with details on his plans for the night. The Gladiator Paddock over at Earth Environs was only a five-minute shuttle ride from Race's restaurant. That's where he was heading next.

Race had the employee grade level necessary to get in, and even though other Environs were also accessible to him, he tended to be a creature of habit. Race's employee grade was well-earned because of his restaurant's high profitability. Customer surveys were crucial to this too, so having a celebrity like Felina Toyger showing up each night meant not only numerous visitors, but happy patrons as well. That's what got Race his higher status. Naturally, for other employees this was measured differently.

An employee's grade was earned by job performance and longevity, but it was verified via a chip inserted into the upper arm of each being working there. This chip would send data to Star Fantasy Human Resources verifying body readings such as raised heart rate, prolonged physical exertion, ingestion of fluids, and calorie intake. It measured sleep and health readings too, but mainly this was oriented toward checking up on employees to make sure they were really working and not lounging around inside venues, getting inebriated during work shifts, taking unauthorized food breaks, or toddling off to take a nap.

Body workers comprised a large portion of Star Fantasy employees, and these were evaluated by checking rises in body temperature due to contact with other beings. Imbedded chips communicated information about ingestion of foreign DNA, the presence of sweat from other bodies, or insertions of foreign fluids into their genitalia or rectum. Rises in heart rate, coincidental with these biological indicators would verify the frequency by which they were engaging in sex; therefore, Star Fantasy computers knew and how often each body worker was performing their duties.

Employee grade affected one's pay and access to food and lodging. If all they wanted was to make minimum wage and eat at the employee commissary, sleeping in triple-stacked bunks with three roommates, then mediocrity might be acceptable to them. But why would anyone want to settle for something like that? Employees wanted to be able to enjoy the amazing restaurants and attractions that guests got to experience. And to do that, one had to achieve a higher grade; otherwise, no admission would be granted. For that reason, most workers worked as hard as they could, taking on double shifts, and entertaining more clients. This created a grueling cycle and led to burnout. Burnouts left Star Fantasy with little more than they came with. The ride home was not inexpensive.

The system for customer transactions was just as technically advanced. When a customer purchased a vacation package on Star Fantasy, these included travel and lodging. Some services came right along with it, such as access to the Roman Empire attraction in the Earth Environ or the Jungle Terrariums of the Zorg Environ. Most every package included admission to those popular places. But when customers arrived, they could also upgrade to get access to additional venues or purchase an hour of personal attention with an Empath. Upon arrival, the customer would get their palm scanned, then they could roam the facility freely. Each attraction merely required placing their hand, paw, or hoof over a scanner, and if admission was included in their package, entrance was granted. If not, upgrading was as easy as making the selection on the system's menu.

There was also a point-of-sale function at each venue's entrance where a customer, on some whim of inspiration, could purchase admission. Most of the restaurants worked specifically that way, which was quite shrewd on the part of management. Restaurants were often located right out front of most super-popular attractions and dance clubs, because after an hour or two being naughty, a customer would most likely be famished. And the employees? Well, they just went on to the next client. And the next. And the next.

Bars and saloons were scattered throughout Star Fantasy and numbered in the hundreds, just about as many as there were public bathrooms. Some weren't even bars at all, just little kiosks located along walking paths or right outside shuttle stations. Smiling bartenders were practically everywhere, selling drinks to customers as well as enhancements to keep the party going hour after hour after hour. Liquor sales revenue accounted for a large portion of annual profit, and practically paid for Star Fantasy's labor cost all by itself. Not surprisingly, hard-working bartenders held some of the highest employee grades on the former space station.

Star Fantasy was shaped like a wagon-wheel, with a headquarters and office complex in the very center. Shuttle vehicles traveled back and forth throughout the spokes of the wheel, and employee dormitories were located along those same shuttle routes. Docking stations for spacecraft were located around the outer ring in several locations, so that passenger, as well as supply ships could dock and unload. Often these were very busy operations, as ships would be arriving and departing constantly. Traffic control and maintenance of public order was therefore vital. Not to mention keeping the employees in line. Nothing could hurt business more than a bunch of disgruntled employees organizing to ask for better pay or conditions.

That's why security was everywhere. There were security stations and patrol posts at nearly every corner, in the areas near major venues, and, of course, at docking stations. Each shuttle car moving back and forth throughout the spokes had a driver who was, in reality, a policeman. Of course, the shuttles were operated by computer, and there was certainly no steering, acceleration, or braking necessary. But having a formidable-looking armed guard inside each shuttle was a natural deterrent to mayhem.

In the view of Star Fantasy management, the giant pleasure palace was really more of a floating city, not just an amusement park with a need for uniformed security guards. It had its own power plant and public works. It had cleaning, laundry, supply distribution, water, sewage, electricity, and even its own broadcasting station which advertised throughout all hotel rooms and lobbies about popular attractions. Because of this, from the very beginning, management considered it necessary to have its own police force. It needed one under its own jurisdiction too not under command of the government of Enosh or any other planet.

If they were establishing a gigantic intergalactic resort which was remote and distant from any planet, and if the product they were selling was adult entertainment, and if they had thousands of employees scraping by, then there could be trouble at most any time. Star Fantasy management knew that going in, so they didn't just hire overweight retirees looking to take it easy in their golden years.

Management had them trained in riot control, and even established a position for Police Chief, with his own staff of subordinates and a chain of command all the way down to the lowly beat cop walking through lobbies and hallways. Each patrolman carried an electronic baton which functioned much like an old-fashioned Earth cattle prod. It had settings for lightly shocking an unruly customer and even had a stun setting for incapacitating any miscreant who dared defy the rules.

Police were expected to maintain order. That was their main function. Thus, any disruption or threat of violence was quelled quickly and thoroughly. They prided themselves on that. And why wouldn't they? Most all were Enoshi army veterans who'd finished their mandatory ten-year military service and had come to Star Fantasy to enjoy their middle age. Many others were tough human, Suidonji, or Zorgolongian males who could bear up to the rigorous training. Now they, too, could enjoy the benefits of an employee grade that gave them access to the best venues.

Fearsome and intimidating to begin with, Star Fantasy police, referred to as SFP, loved their jobs, and would pounce on almost any unruly guest for even the slightest infraction. After all, their grade level was based on the number of reported disturbances within their patrol area. Because of that, they'd throw you in the brig for most anything. They didn't hesitate either: if a customer started a fight or quarreled with an employee or another customer, no matter who started it, the SFP would lock you up, refund the cost of your hotel room, and send you back to your home planet on the next available ship. They were just that strict, and they very well could be.

After all, who would a customer or employee complain to? There was no government. There were no courts or judges. Everyone understood that's the way things were. If you came to Star Fantasy, you should be there to have fun. Drink, dance, enjoy yourself then go home. If you were an employee, you should work hard and keep to yourself. But if you got in trouble with the SFP, God help you. No one else would.

CHAPTER 13: THE DAWN OF A NEW WORLD

It had been over two years since the convicts of New Australia Planetary Prison had risen up and overthrown their cruel captors. The initial success of capturing a pirate ship, lured into docking with The Anarchy thinking it was the Earth Cruiser The Unity, led to the beginning of a golden age of piracy for the Nausties.

This role suited them well. Thousands of tough former miners were soon lining up for a chance to join the growing pirate fleet. It eventually numbered ten ships and ranged from small transports all the way up to massive Earth Cruisers, which were fully armed and capable of pouncing on most any vessel of the same size.

After the first victorious battle, in which an unsuspecting pirate ship cruised up to *The Anarchy* answering its fake distress call, the Nausties found themselves well-established in the business of freebooting. Within hours, a brigade of Enoshi and human warriors hidden inside *The Anarchy*'s hold had fought their way onto the vessel to defeat the enemy crew. Captain Slout then recruited the overwhelmed enemy sailors into crewmen. Those who'd survived the brutal combat onboard, that is.

With two fully complemented spacecraft, Slout then turned his attention to searching for new targets. He hastily relocated his squad of raiders to major shipping lanes and waited for new prey. It didn't take long. Within a month they'd seized yet another Earth freighter and plundered it. This ship was loaded to the gills with food, having just left port with fresh produce, pressed sea wafers, and frozen fish. The return to New Australia yielded a full warehouse of food which its people desperately needed and was distributed to a very happy population of Nausties who hadn't seen fresh vegetables and fruits in years.

The Tribal Confederation was thrilled with the haul, and promptly gave Terminal Chief Mwanga carte blanche to continue doing what was clearly working so well. Solomon had assumed correctly. All that tribal leaders cared about were results, and warehouses full of food meant everything to the starving planet. The results were undeniable.

"The Smilodons pledge one hundred new warriors for the Naustie Fleet!" roared the dark gray giant with piercing yellow-gold eyes. It had been a raucous meeting of the Commerce Committee, and Solomon Mwanga had just given his updates on when the fledgling fleet would be departing for its next raid. It was Skarch Chartreux of the Smilodon tribe who was first to speak up after the chief had asked for troop commitments. By now, the mere mention of opportunities to volunteer for missions was being greeted with enthusiastic support.

"More if need be. We'll send all you require, brother!" he added with a snarl. Chartreux and Solomon had a history together. During the Naustie Civil War, they'd squared off numerous times over territory disputes. Even after hostilities ended, they negotiated access to safe passage for Schpleeftkorkii allies migrating to new homelands. Those were some tense days, indeed. Now things were different. Solomon's star was once again rising, and it was wise to support him. Others quickly piled on.

"Make that two hundred from the Lacertilias! Two hundred warriors for the next voyage!" cried Flick, the provocative Zorg chieftain of the Lacertilia Tribe. He attended committee meetings personally and was always trying to one-up his counterpart from the Smilodons. The two tribes had never faced each other in combat, but there'd certainly been a spirited rivalry between Flick and Scratch ever since the creation of the Commerce Committee.

"Let's not give those stinking felines all the glory this time, shall we?" he then stated chidingly. Chartreux eyed him bitterly. This was not the place for quarrels or fisticuffs between delegations, however. Architeuthis was very strict about things like that. Scratch would have to control his temper. His chieftain would have his head on a pike if he got into a fight and thrown out of the meeting. Might as well never go back to his cave.

"Us too!" yelled out Hox, a member of the Suidonji delegation in attendance. His tribe were called the Entelodonts and included veterans who'd rushed up the ramp with the first wave during the Naustie Revolt. "We want in! How many do you need?" he bellowed. "We've got a thousand, all sitting around on their rumps. If we're not making them miners anymore, then I say let's have them go fight!" That sentiment was shared with everyone in the room by now.

"Yeah, we'll do it!" echoed Yersenia, a representative of the Bandicoots. They'd been legendary fighters during the Battle of the Ductworks back when General Hicks had ordered an attack on the prison power plant. "Don't mind a few hundred rats on your ship, do you?" he joked with a wiggle of his nose. This lightened the mood considerably as the whole room broke up with laughter. Skarch Chartreux slapped his thighs with delight. Flick giggled. Even Solomon smiled.

"There's always a place in our ranks for your brave warriors – yes, my friend," replied the big African. "We'll make room for you I'm sure." Putting it that way only made the committee members laugh harder. Schpleeftii were about a third the size of an Eno and wouldn't require much room to fit thousands of them in the hold of an average freighter.

But Solomon wasn't joking. Fitting a hundred Spleefs in the holds of his ships wasn't just practical due to their diminutive size. They moved so quickly, they'd serve as excellent reinforcements after an initial attack by shock troops, plus they were easy to keep organized. Give them an objective and they moved as one combined force. Give them a task and they worked as a team.

Now it would seem everyone was on board. Captain Slout put replacement crews and fresh troops right to work. Warriors could now be armed with captured EIC's for battle, making spears, shields, and daggers no longer necessary. Confederation delegates returned to their tribesmen, ebulliently announcing that their days of glory and riches were only just beginning. The galaxy was going to fear the very mention of their name.

Business was soon booming practically overnight. Slout continued his focus on unescorted freighters in well-traveled shipping lanes for a few months, until he'd built his squadron into a formidable force. This was needed at first, to make sure he could fend off attacks from other pirates competing for prey. Gradually, though, there were no other vessels truly capable of challenging him! Any encounters with these "runts" as he called them, were quickly dispatched. Accomplishing this eventually meant a virtual monopoly on raiding. Slout could then start sending single freighters back to New Australia, laden with food and supplies, while keeping his main fleet out in space looking for fresh targets.

That was only the beginning, however. Next, he turned his attention to remote space colonies, and that's when New Australia's fortunes improved markedly. The galaxy had so many, and Slout knew exactly where to find as well as how to attack them. Kscheeech, his first mate, was a big help to him, because he had direct experience with conducting these types of raids. Besides, the old fellow now had much more to work with than when he was a Zorgolongian pirate. It was far easier to take on a remote outpost when he could unleash a thousand hardened warriors to overwhelm its garrison. Within hours, they could carry off shiploads of food and ammunition, tools and materials, weapons and recruits, before any distress signal could be responded to by patrols.

Frabrak 3 became a perfect target. It was a planet that had been steadily colonized by Suidonj over the years. Lush with vegetation, Frabrak 3 was dotted with islands, ranging from small atolls on up to isolated continents. Most all of these were formed millions of years ago by now-dormant volcanoes. At the summits, rains fell daily, and fresh water would cascade down to valleys below, creating fertile farmland and sometimes giant inland lakes which held millions of fish. Suidonji farmers had cleared the land and began farming the islands there a hundred years ago, yielding produce which was sold at markets throughout the galaxy. This was a fountain of opportunity for the once near-starving souls of New Australia, and the varieties of vegetables, fruits, and fish were outstanding.

Frabrak 3 would go on to become a regular stop for Captain Slout. After each successful raid, local forces would try and reinforce the planet as best they could, but it was no use. When Slout's fleet returned, fully laden with shock troops, replenished units still had no chance. Colonial troops were some of the worst fighters in the galaxy to begin with, so superior numbers and surprise attacks were way more than they could handle. Garrisons fell, settlements were sacked, and recruits signed on to join the pirates of New Australia. Turned out that being a pirate had some appeal to it. Who knew the reasons? A life of adventure, getting away from a spouse or responsibility, limited opportunity, the yoke of boredom? Regardless, recruitment was going swimmingly.

Then they became even more ambitious. Kscheeech knew where most enemy pirate bases might be located, and this was a great advantage to Slout. Kscheeech knew their practices and tactics, so it wasn't long before the captain was directing raids on pirate strongholds.

Intending to destroy their operational capability, Slout would simply time his attack according to enemy movement, knowing when the base was lightly defended by monitoring enemy pirate attacks in space, then following them back to their bases. He'd order the fleet to ambush the enemy craft as she neared her destination and load up the captured vessel with Naustie troops. Afterward, Slout would send an inter-space message back to the base from the captured ship saying they were returning to port. The enemy base would allow the ship to land thinking it was their own craft. Then Naustie warriors would spill out and mercilessly slaughter its defenders, with the rest of the Naustie fleet landing reinforcements to support the attack. Supplies and ammunition, as well as weapons would be hauled on board transport shuttles while the port burned. Once the fleet's freighters were loaded up with plunder, the Nausties would hastily exit.

The big captain and his first mate figured the Nausties could very well dominate the galaxy's entire pirate enterprise within a few more years at the rate they were going. Nevertheless, they wisely continued to avoid any direct confrontation with galactic forces. It was far safer for the Interplanetary Fleet to never detect their movements or the size of their armada, only respond to the scene after they were long gone. The two old friends had a system and it was working out perfectly.

And yet there was more to be asked of them, regardless of what they'd accomplished thus far. Despite all they'd achieved in feeding the planet as well as eliminating rival pirate factions, and despite amassing a fleet of raiders capable of taking on most anything short of the IPF itself, Terminal Chief Mwanga began to envision an even more ambitious goal for New Australia.

Yes, the former African warlord imagined something much grander and more glorious than mere pirate raids and plunder. True, he appreciated the performance of his captain and first mate and even recommended to the Tribal Confederation that an official promotion be given to Slout, making him Commodore of the Naustie Fleet. However, he also saw a future for his planet. Piracy was merely a means to an end. A stepping stone to bigger things. He actually wanted to achieve legitimacy as a recognized independent world within the Interplanetary Authority.

Such a vision was ludicrous at best. True, if they'd tried it when all they had was *The Anarchy*, and no further ability to defend their people, the IPA would have squashed them like an ant. The current pirate culture made more sense for now. The rest of the galaxy didn't want them. Their home planets had discarded them. Now they were making everyone pay and pay dearly. Still, Solomon felt it was time to consider the long term.

Yet to go from criminals, to prisoners, to rebels, to pirates, then seek diplomatic recognition and political sovereignty from the very planets they were warring against? That was completely, or at least practically, impossible. Nevertheless, Solomon envisioned this for his planet. He needed others to grasp it too, and there was only one being on all of New Australia he could seek out for guidance and counsel. One creature he could confide in.

Solomon awakened to yet another glorious morning. This was how he liked to begin his day. The spectacular rise of the Rijel Sun over the horizon was breathtaking, heating and illuminating the landscape, causing shadows to fade, and colors to change rapidly from gray to purple and orange, then tan and brown. It took less than an hour for the process to evolve from near darkness, to twilight, to blistering inferno.

He'd always enjoyed viewing the sunrise as a child back in Africa, but this was indeed something he looked forward to whenever he could make time to see it. He'd never fully appreciated such things as a boy, only remembered the peacefulness and the distinctive smells of the morning: his mother cooking breakfast in their little shack, the crisp morning air, the smell of moisture still lingering from the rains that used to fall every day during the monsoon.

Solomon figured he'd be gone a while. It would take some time to make his way down to see his old friend. He descended the elevator to the base of the loading bay and there he offloaded into an empty chamber, the size of an Olympic sports stadium. Hard to believe it had once been occupied by a freighter only days before, when the last of the Naustie fleet had been outfitted for combat and raised to the surface for launch.

Everything was much quieter now. All the ships had landed and been refitted and restocked then reinforced with fresh troops for their latest raiding mission. One by one, they'd been through their routines, returning to planetary orbit while they awaited departure. Now they were gone, and Solomon could relax for a while. Meanwhile, New Australia would have to soldier on same as before, hoping for their safe return with more food, more supplies, and hopefully more female captives.

He chose to walk this time, which is what he typically did on days like this. Sure, he could commandeer a vehicle and shorten his journey, but he rarely did so. His preference was to avoid bothering those grumpy Suidonji over at the motor pool, choosing instead to catch a ride with a passing transport when possible, or simply make a day of it on foot, making the long hike over to one of the service elevators.

Next would be the interminable wait for a lift to arrive, which would take him all the way down to his intended stop, an extensive communications tunnel left over from the glory days of the Naustie Rebellion. It was now a subterranean trade route of sorts, enabling supply vehicles and the like to travel through the many tribal homelands (Smilodons, Capybara, Templar Knights, Skinks, Dragons, Why-o's) leading to Schpleeftkorkii territory. That's where he was heading, and when he finally got there hours later, he'd spend a day or two at the cave of Architeuthis.

Solomon spoke privately on numerous occasions with his old friend and mentor. Sometimes only Architeuthis could truly appreciate the creative mind he had for planning and devising. Despite being from two vastly different species, there was so much of his younger self Architeuthis could see in Solomon. The two actually had a lot in common, in that Solomon had once been president of a small African nation back on Earth. Similarly, Architeuthis had once been in charge of a Slartigifijian government agency tasked with fighting a terrible plague that eventually wiped out millions on his planet, before a vaccine was developed.

Indeed, the wise old Slart was in those days a young, naïve, and overwhelmed government administrator. In the end, he did finally oversee the development of the vaccine which might stop the spread of the plague, but by then, entire populations of his countrymen had perished. What's more, by the time his scientists were distributing the serum to hospitals proclaiming a scientific breakthrough, it was already quite clear the threat had passed.   Architeuthis was subsequently perceived by his colleagues and the public as having failed. Millions had already succumbed, and the public's mentality turned from desperation to grief for all their loved ones who'd died. That grief eventually led to recriminations over taking so long to develop a vaccine. An inquiry was conducted, and heads were sure to roll.

Architeuthis was discharged and eventually, as a result of an official investigation, he was banished to Rijel 12. Disgraced and humiliated, Architeuthis at first saw himself as having allowed millions to suffer, while his staff labored tirelessly to try and save the planet. But the banishment only made him more determined than ever to seek fairness. His scientists really did develop the vaccine that would have saved his species from extinction – if the plague hadn't run its course already. His banishment was, in his mind, merely his own government looking for someone to blame, and it truly was unjust. The plague did all the killing, after all. Not him.

To Architeuthis, Solomon's past was nearly identical. As a rebel leader, he'd overthrown a brutal dictator, and when he could no longer hold onto power, he had to flee the capital. In the end, he got fingered for causing the events that led to tribal violence and the massacre of innocent people. They just needed a scapegoat – someone to take responsibility for the many civilian deaths. Tribal death squads committed those atrocities, not Solomon, but World Court judges "had to find someone to swing for it," as Solomon once put it. Solomon was the most recognizable figurehead who could be indicted in an effort to satisfy worldwide outrage.

Therefore, they were both once high-profile figures on their home planets, who'd done what they thought was right at the time for their people or their country—and by failing they'd found themselves sent here, to this barren planet to die.

Solomon eventually arrived at the cave of his old friend, after many hours traveling across once-hostile territories to his destination. No one bothered him. Most recognized him by now at tribal checkpoints. Border guards simply waved him through. There wasn't much going on these days, deep within the planet's old mining network. Sentries would typically see only an occasional supply transport – might be days in between before they'd see another. He stood at the entrance to the cave only momentarily before walking in. Seeing who it was, Architeuthis greeted him warmly.

"My friend. Welcome. Come sit with me," beckoned the aging Slartigifijian. He'd been meditating on a pallet of seaweed brought to him as a gift only weeks earlier. Each morning, Architeuthis would wet the leaves to keep them from drying out, then enjoy a peaceful day resting upon them. This day was like most others for the semi-retired leader. His only visitors were usually members of the tribe, but that was rare. Most Schpleeftkorkii had since moved on and taken jobs near the surface. Only a thousand or so still lived there.

"What can I do for you today? Is something troubling you, my boy?" asked Architeuthis. The big Terminal Chief didn't answer immediately. There was a lot on his mind, and he wasn't sure quite where to begin. The long journey down to see the great leader had given him time to think, but he still didn't know where to start. Solomon took a few minutes to arrange a pallet to sit on made of straw mats – a luxury only a few years ago but now commonly used by Nausties still living in the caves below.

"Plenty," he finally replied, sighing as he sat down. He first wanted to update Architeuthis on the latest developments back at Terminal Command. His old friend listened patiently, but it really wasn't necessary. Architeuthis knew his brilliant protégé hadn't made this trip just to tell him news of recent raids and what goods were being brought back. Such information didn't interest him in the least. Solomon detected this, then slowly trailed off.

"But that's not all I wanted to talk to you about," he said. The old Slartigifijian's eyes widened. He gestured with one of his tentacles for his guest to elaborate. Chief Mwanga heaved another sigh and cracked a tired smile. "Old friend, I don't know much about your planet's history, but on mine, robbers and thieves sometimes become princes and kings," he went on to say, pausing to let that statement marinate in the mind of his mentor. Architeuthis certainly knew a little about Earth history by now and began to nod patiently. Solomon continued.

"And if I may be so bold, I must say we've turned our brave little planet into a global pirate base. A damn good one at that, I might add. However, I'd like to accomplish more. I feel there's so much we could do with what we have here." Despite the exhausting journey, Solomon's eyes burned bright when he said this.

"Oh?" responded the aging Slartigifijian. "There is something greater you'd like to achieve for us? Is that what has prompted your visit today?" To this, Solomon nodded matter-of-factly as Architeuthis folded his tentacles over his lap. "Then by all means tell me." The Terminal Chief cleared his throat of the dust he'd accumulated in his mouth that morning, preparing to answer.

"The future I see for New Australia is to make us a respected member of the Interplanetary Authority," continued Solomon. "I envision a day when a delegation from our planet is able to attend the Galactic Convention as a member planet within the alliance, equal to all others."

Architeuthis was intrigued. As of now New Australia's recognized independence was only a myth in their own minds. A reality only because the IPA had no official knowledge of their existence. As far as he knew, they considered Rijel 12 to be a quarantined planet. Publicly, the government claimed that the last of the planet's population had starved to death when food ran out.

Architeuthis remained silent, gazing at Solomon with his enormous eyes and patiently listening. Solomon added, "I foresee the day when we negotiate trade agreements and vote on Galactic policy. That's what I want to accomplish. Unfortunately, we have such a long way to go. And yet, I believe this can be achieved."

Architeuthis fluttered his facial tentacles. It was always so fascinating, listening to the big African. Solomon was one of those rare individuals who had the vision to see things as they needed to be, as well as the will to make them so. This is what set him apart from others. Architeuthis took a moment to collect his thoughts; then replied.

"Oh yes my friend," he began, "I know of your history. Humans, that is. Genghis Khan, Napoleon Bonaparte, Tamerlane, Attila the Hun, they all came from humble beginnings or dubious pasts, yet seized power and tried gaining legitimacy through world conquest. Perhaps this is what you see as our future?"

Solomon interjected, "Ah, but you see my friend. I don't intend to conquer. I don't even intend to seize power. What I am talking about is New Australia gaining political autonomy, an independent planet which can be respected and negotiated with."

Of course, Solomon already had a clear idea of what that would entail. First of all, the planet had to become self-sufficient and economically sustainable. Had to be able to feed itself, then had to be able to defend its citizens. To do that required wealth. Wealth would pay for the weapons and the ships and the highly trained military with which New Australia could protect its political interests. Wealth would pay for the supplies and materials to build a true civilization underground, beneath the Rijel sun's oppressive rays, and safe from the devastating weather patterns on the surface.

True, Solomon could see why Architeuthis was drawing comparisons to the way the Mongols and the Huns rose from obscurity as nomads to become hordes of rampaging warriors which threatened to overrun Europe. But those two examples didn't quite match what New Australia needed to become. To Solomon, their foray into piracy was not a dead end. It had an endgame. It was required now, but in time, the planets in the galaxy would inevitably want to trade with New Australia. They had to, really. The almost infinite mineral resources of the planet were vital to the galactic economy, and on New Australia, these could be mined and sold cheaply.

The mines would therefore need to be reopened, Solomon knew. Perhaps not immediately, of course; for now, the tribes were enjoying a Renaissance in the advancement of their warrior cultures, delighting in the new market economy developing within their territories. Tribes were evolving from a violent gang culture into sophisticated, almost feudal societies. Because of the variety of goods brought in, a lively mercantile system was evolving. These were things he certainly didn't need to remind Architeuthis of.

The great leader knew precisely where Solomon needed to focus his efforts next. Establishing a brave new society on Rijel 12 was the first order of business. A society born from oppression that valued freedom and fairness above all else. A society that appreciated hard work and sacrifice for the greater good. There had been so many examples of both that Nausties would never run out of stories of greatness to tell their young. And there was the problem. In order to forge a new society, they needed families. Strong, stable units that would bring new Nausties into the world, teach them, love them, nurture them, and reinforce their core values. The one thing missing the from the equation was females. If New Australia were to become a true society, it needed to find a way to bolster the number of women. This was simply a fact.

It was true that there were women on New Australia already. When a ship was overtaken by the Naustie pirates or after a raid a few brave and adventurous women would opt to the join up. However, this was the exception rather than the rule. For every twenty recruits the only one or two of them would be female. Given this, their numbers on New Australia were meager. As it stood, there was one female for every three hundred males; this was just not going to work. Further, human women were most common. They represented eighty five percent of the female population while Enoshi females made up a paltry one percent. Ships returning never seemed to have females from the Enoshi home planet. Enoshi merchant vessels never had female crewmembers, and besides Slout routinely avoided them. It was far too dangerous doing battle with their sailors in close order combat. The best colonies for raiding, for instance Frabrak 3, were run by Suidonji. Freighters typically had only Zorgs and Humans. And Spleef females? They could be found just about anywhere. But, Enoshi females just didn't seem to travel much.

The women of New Australia had already proved invaluable. They brought a new perspective, intelligence, compassion, and, typically, a more measured approach to matters. Even the Templar Knights sought out women to join their tribe. While avowed homosexuals, not interested in females for reproductive purposes, they counted on their women for their counsel and eye for aesthetics. The Templars had created one of the most vibrant villages on New Australia; a purposeful yet beautiful space that was envied by all.

But, the heart of the problem remained. If they were to build a new society based on family units and new generations of Nausties, they needed more females, and more from the other races to boot. But how could they go about recruiting more? They were already raiding as many ships as they could. Something had to done. But what? Then one day, the returning *Anarchy* docked in his loading terminal, and Solomon got to meet with his trusted friend Kscheeech, as well as Captain Slout. Over a mug or two of ale, which had been plundered from a captured Earth freighter, they sat in Solomon's command center and chatted privately. Technically, it was a debriefing, but in reality, Solomon was interested in hearing about their adventures. Their stories were always so fascinating.

"I've enjoyed hearing your reports today, Gentlemen. You've impressed everyone with how adept you've been at finding resources for our planet, while at the same time keeping our location secret. I'm deeply grateful to both of you," said Solomon. He slurred his words a bit from the effects of the ale. Hadn't consumed alcohol since leaving Earth – wasn't much of a drinker to begin with.

"However," said Solomon, now measuring his words. He knew he was getting tipsy and needed to be careful how he worded his next question. "However, in the matter of female recruits," he began again, then hastily put the back of his hand up to his mouth trying to cover up a belch. "I've been amazed at how bringing female Earthers, Zorgs, Suidonji, and Spleefs back to our planet has had such an impact. It's worked out rather well. Gentlemen, we need more of them. For New Australia to grow and flourish, we must find a way to get more females to join us. Especially Enoshi, we have very few."

Kscheeech and Slout looked at each other, then back at Solomon grinning. Slout snorted and grunted humorously while letting Kscheeech field the boss's question. He could already anticipate the answer, but this was clearly Kscheeech's bailiwick.

"Boss, if you want more female recruits I believe we already have a place in mind where we can acquire exactly what you're seeking," he stated slyly. "Have you ever heard of a place called *S-ssstar Fantasy*?" Solomon reacted with that kind of inebriated humor one typically gets from that first glass of beer following a long period of sobriety. Then his eyes widened.

"It's called what?" he laughed. Slout grunted again, regaining his composure. It suddenly occurred to him this was a very serious matter they were discussing. Chief Mwanga was rarely the type to find humor in any situation, let alone laugh at a joke. He set down his beer on the conference table and leaned forward in his chair to speak.

"Star Fantasy, Commander," repeated the salty captain. "It's a converted space station now functioning as a galactic resort. Enormous place. Very near planet Enosh I might add. Thousands of females, sir. Every species, you name it." Then Kscheeech jumped in with, "Yes-sss, let us tell you more, shall we?"

"One assault on this floating pleasure palace," Kscheeech assured him, "And New Australia could triple or even quadruple its female population. They have Enoshi females too." That's all the Terminal Chief needed to hear. New Australia would invade Star Fantasy. With the blessing of Architeuthis, preparations began. The dream of a new society was now within their reach.

CHAPTER 14: THE VOYAGE

The voyage to Star Fantasy would take about three weeks. However, they asked Solomon to give them up to three months to return from carrying out the mission. "Things could get dicey," Slout warned him, as they boarded their ship and prepared to launch. Then, with *The Anarchy* joining the fleet in orbit around New Australia, they set out for their goal, many light years away.

Now, one week into the voyage, Kscheeech found himself in his quarters contemplating the daunting task assigned to him. Alone with his thoughts, he typed out a battle plan on a handheld touch screen with his long claws. The general idea, per his discussions with Terminal Chief Solomon Mwanga, was to take off from New Australia and travel through deep space undetected. Stay out of well-traveled trade routes, finally appearing in major shipping lanes in about two weeks. That, of course, was the easy part. Ten ships, including *The* Anarchy, were outfitted for battle, each of them loaded with a brigade of assault troops. Two additional cargo ships traveled with the fleet but would be held in reserve and remain outside of Interplanetary Fleet patrol zones.

If the attack were to be a failure and the IPF showed up ready to do battle, then the Naustie pirate fleet was to break off the attack and head for New Australia. Each ship would take different routes home to confuse any pursuers. That had been Slout's suggestion. If the attack were a success, the two reserve ships were to be called in to dock and extract prisoners. Each could hold over three thousand recruits, which was ambitious.

The Anarchy was now the flagship of the Naustie fleet, and Slout had been made Admiral. But Slout was still just an old ship's captain at heart; good at commanding and delegating the rest to subordinates. Kscheeech, however, was a sharp-minded assistant who helped his Admiral with quick decision-making and the avoidance of dangerous situations. That's what Slout liked best about him. Pirates throughout history understood they could only stay alive as long as they avoided direct confrontation with naval fleets.

For this mission, each of the eight assault ships in the fleet had been stripped of most all their cargo to make room for troops. A full brigade was packed into each while leaving room enough for them to train and maintain battle-readiness. Things might be a little more difficult this time, Kscheeech suspected.   This attack would be occurring in space, not on some tropical planet surface like Frabrak 3. This presented a quandary.

Kscheeech took a break from typing and watched a recorded broadcast from the IPN network on his monitor. These had been stored in the ship's computer for Kscheeech to study during the voyage. There was a lot he could learn from them: news broadcasts about pirates, reports about distant colonies that made for good targets, etc. He even had recordings from the *Star Fantasy Channel*, which transmitted direct from the converted space station. From this channel, Kscheeech was able to download shows that he could watch over and over again in order to research his target. It was like a general being able to watch a documentary about a fortress he was about to attack… in advance of the attack.

His favorite was a program called "Your Safety on Star Fantasy." It had maps, diagrams of the station, animated cutaways showing locations of police stations, patrol routes, shuttle vehicle security and emergency call stations, response procedures for "disruptions of the peace." It even had a map of the police headquarters. It gave Kscheeech the idea for his attack and he planned it out to the most minor detail after the broadcast ended. For the next hour, the ideas flowed.

Land with a newly captured freighter under a false flag. Secure the dock with shock troops. Fan out to capture nearby stations and land additional craft. Pretty simple really; only Kscheeech wanted to swing for the fences this time. He knew Solomon was counting on him. Travel on shuttles to police headquarters, then to other sections of Star Fantasy. Eliminate all resistance. Capture police headquarters. Accomplish complete takeover by day two. Land additional freighters for the extraction of the prisoners. Load recruits and plunder. Head for home.

Kscheeech figured they could use the space station's own shuttle system to transport captured females out to waiting Naustie freighters and in a matter of hours pile them in, then get the hell out of there before IPF patrol ships arrived. He eventually fell asleep on his bed dreaming of the mission as images swirled in his head about the big haul they were about to make. He needed to rest up. In six hours, he was to meet with his superior officer to present his plan.

The next day, Admiral Slout read through the report on the bridge of *The* Anarchy, looking up occasionally to gaze at his trusty First Mate. The Admiral snorted a few times with apprehension. This was incredibly dangerous, and he wondered how the generals would react to it. Kscheeech could understand his Admiral's hesitation. This was certainly ambitious, to say the least. Nevertheless, in his mind they needed to seize the entire facility, not just a section of it. Slout was impressed with his boldness.

"So, you really want to capture the whole space station?" asked the Admiral, with a look of concern. "That's a tall order, my friend. Are you sure we have the necessary firepower? Do we have enough troops to secure the place? I mean these are Enoshi we're talking about here. They're not just going to let us waltz in and take over; not without a fight, that is. We've talked about this before, haven't we? It's the first time we've gone up against them since the rebellion." Slout was keenly aware of what it would be like taking on a fortress defended by those big monsters. Attacking a Zorg-held pirate base or facing off against Suidonji colonial troops on Frabrak 3 was one thing. Kscheeech was adamant though.

"But Admiral, don't you see? A small attack would be pointless. When Star Fantasy Police respond, they'll be arriving in force. I have no doubt of that. And if there is to be a battle, our troops will be pinned down with no chance to focus on rounding up captured workers. At least until local security forces are eliminated. Therefore, why not an all-out attack which eliminates the threat entirely before trying to take on recruits?"

Slout wasn't so sure. He gave a big snort and muttered to Kscheeech, "Like I said, old friend this is a tall order, going up against Enoshi. They'll fight tooth and nail. I know how those bastards are." The Admiral was still more of a fan of hitting quick, grabbing loot, rounding up a few captives, then getting out fast. That had always been their system and it had worked very well for them. And as for Star Fantasy? There were five main Environs, each with three hundred police on duty. Plus, there were fifty to a hundred cops patrolling each of the docking stations and maybe another one hundred working the shuttle routes. That could mean three thousand police to have to fight for control of the space station!

And besides that, what about the deluge of people clogging the walkways and enjoying the many venues and attractions? Indeed, this could be a very, very difficult task. Star Fantasy had the capacity for up to ten thousand guests at any given time. He gave in eventually however; yielding to his first mate's assurances that they had the necessary manpower to pull it off. "We have more than enough troops, Admiral. Let's hit them hard and fast. Swallow them up in one big gulp," urged Kscheeech. Slout chuckled at the clever metaphor.

"Very well then, let's see what the generals say at our meeting in a few days," he replied. "I've always trusted your judgment old friend." And that was that. Kscheeech thanked the Admiral and returned to his post.

Later that week, Admiral Slout held his staff meeting with the different brigade commanders via a ship-to-ship short range channel. In deep space this signal was too weak to be detected by the Interplanetary Fleet, but it was sufficient for nearby ships to be able to communicate with each other. Eventually those signals would bounce off something in space and end up on some IPF computer appearing as nothing but gibberish. But this static-laden garble could be triangulated back to its origin within a few days of its original transmission, and the IPF might know something was coming their way. That's why they had to be extra careful.

For the meeting they sat in the ship's conference room. There they watched a giant video monitor which showed an animated map of Star

Fantasy. This map was actually a fifteen-second video which Kscheeech had excerpted from a commercial advertisement about luxury vacation packages on the Star Fantasy Channel. He'd recorded it onto a loop which played out over and over again while Slout conducted the call.

When he spoke it converted into code for transmission. Then his words would appear on screens inside the conference rooms of all nine other craft now hurtling through space. When they replied or asked questions, he'd see pop-up boxes along the side of his video display and be able to move his laser pointer to select a box and address their question verbally. The computer would again translate his answers into code and transmit it to everyone.

"And what about Star Fantasy sending out a distress call?" one of generals asked.

"That should be no problem," Kscheeech replied to him promptly. Seems he had a little something up his sleeve when it came to that potentiality.

Slarts back on New Australia had recently developed a jamming device using captured components from Earth freighters. The device flooded the IPF with fake distress calls and pointless inter-space banter which made it difficult to discern between what was real and what was fake. This would buy them time before authorities triangulated the origin of the message and responded with a patrol squadron. It would take several days to calculate this and respond to the scene in force, according to estimates.

Kscheeech predicted that it would take two days to capture the entire facility, but if they eliminated all police units quickly, they could have a fully secured space station filled with people to sort through and take whichever ones they wanted. Tactical planning was to be delegated to the brigadier generals themselves, he added. And that's when the arguments came popping up onscreen. Before he had even opened the floor for questions, they were already chiming in.

"Too bold," the first one said. "Too risky" another one of them complained. A third stated, "This is too much." And the fourth? He simply replied, "This is crazy!" Kscheeech hissed out a little chuckle at that last reaction – had to suppress his laughter for fear of being detected by the computer. But the drawback, one of the generals pointed out, was a valid one indeed. "In space you can't make mistakes. We have to land, dock, deploy troops, and capture additional docking stations. Then we've got to eliminate trained riot police, drive toward some headquarters at the very middle of the wagon wheel. And you want us to secure the command complex at the center of the space station? No, this is too much."

The whole meeting turned into a fiasco after that, with Brigadier Generals lighting up the screen with rebuttals and objections. They even argued with themselves and hurled insults at each other. Slout finally had to stop the meeting just to let things cool down. He clicked on the pause meeting button on the ship's computer screen, and soon a very large typed message came across the video display at the center, saying MEETING RECESSED FOR 15 MINUTES.

The screen froze, as pop-up messages continued to be displayed with comments like, "It'll get my men killed," and "How the hell are we going to get this accomplished in a day – fighting the whole way across it?"

It was very good point. Just one pitched battle inside that shuttle transport tube or near the employee dormitories, and a whole brigade could be pinned down for hours. Kscheeech sighed, sat back, and thought about it for a little while. General Xonos seated down at the end of the conference table chuckled to himself, muttering incoherently. Slout heard him and snorted humorously as well. Neither spoke. They knew to leave Kscheeech alone with his thoughts. He'd come up with something. And it didn't take long either.

Kscheeech glanced up suddenly at the screen, then he began staring at the section called "Enoshi Environ." He remembered a video he'd watched earlier during the journey; a saved program about a rather special creature, a female named Felina Toyger. She was "an Empath," it said: "mysteriously talented beings who can anticipate thoughts." Of course, he'd never actually met one, but Kscheeech remembered them from his earlier days as a pirate. Virtually impossible to acquire, they were usually consorts to wealthy businessmen, noblemen, conquering Chieftains, superstar athletes. Suddenly it gave Kscheeech an idea. It glowed like a light bulb in his reptilian brain. He looked over at Slout and Xonos sitting down the table and grinned.

Kscheeech looked at the map again. There was a docking station right near the Enoshi Environ and the Roman Empire venue was a mere half mile from it. They'd only need to capture one more station after the false flag got the first freighter safely docked. They could form a bridgehead to block police reinforcements from one direction; while advancing toward the Earth Environ in the other. One brigade could pull off the whole operation, but if a second warship landed after that initial dock was secured, that would put over two thousand battle-ready warriors on Star Fantasy at the same time. All the police could do then would be to contain the attack in those two sectors.

Kscheeech told Admiral Slout of his thoughts. "Captain, I believe I have a solution," he began, pointing up at the screen. "If I were to limit the attack to say, two docking stations. Let's say the one near the Enoshi Environ, then attack toward the Earth Environ from that bridgehead, how would that sound?" Slout nodded in silence, waiting for Kscheeech to finish. "If we did that, we could secure the area and seal off access. Fend off any form of counterattack until we have control. My guess is they'll merely try and isolate us in those two sections in hopes of protecting the remaining guests at the resort.

Slout commented, "That's what procedure would dictate, wouldn't it?" He immediately saw his first mate's logic. "They're cops after all. They'll treat it like a riot, because that's what they are trained to do. Losses of territory won't concern them. Losses of customers will mean everything. The only real disaster would be for the entire station to fall, and everyone be taken hostage. That would ruin business and customers would be terrified of ever going back there. Yes, I see your point. All they'll want is for us to get what we came for and leave. They'll be glad to see us go."

General Xonos agreed. Slout reopened the transmission channel and awaited all the angry generals to sign back in to the meeting. Once they did, he briefed them on Kscheeech's plan.

Replies started popping up along the side of the broadcast screen. Most were affirmative. Kscheeech sat back in his chair and kept on detailing his revisions to the plan: two ships landing. Two brigades deployed. Secure areas and capture prisoners. Load prisoners and leave. No takeover of the entire facility. No pitched battle with determined defenders fighting for their lives on an isolated space station.

He needed to be a good salesman, and this was certainly not in his nature. Slout winced about the security breach but he let it slide. In a few days the IPF would pick up this transmission and wonder what the hell was going on out there! By the time this meeting concluded, all seven were clearly on board.

"We have been charged with this mission because our fellow Nausties felt they could trust us with the task. Now the future of our planet rests squarely on our shoulders. Let our troops fight bravely and swiftly to bring this mission to a successful conclusion. Good luck to all of you. Over and out."

As the screen flashed a message stating in bold letters, END TRANSMISSION, Admiral Slout looked back down the table at his clever old friend Kscheeech and nodded with approval. General Xonos growled with delight as well. He'd done it. Kscheeech had sold the generals on a battle plan to raid Star Fantasy. And with just a little bit of luck, nothing would be able to stop them; certainly not the Star Fantasy Police.

CHAPTER 15: ATTACK ON STAR FANTASY

"Deep Space. That's an ironic term isn't it?" asked Slout. "All of it's bloody deep," he then added with a smirk. Some of the crew working nearby heard him but the Admiral's words sank in with only a few. A couple of them snickered however most didn't respond. They'd been on patrol now for several days, looking for any unsuspecting freighter traveling through the area, and the boredom had taken its toll.

Slout was standing on the bridge of the Naustie flagship looking up at a massive video display spread across one entire wall of the command deck. It showed exterior views of space, with one large image in the center and four smaller images showing starboard and portside views as well as rearward and below. He'd been staring at the screens for hours, just like he'd already done for days on end.

Of course, ship's computers did all the work of detecting approaching craft, but it gave a ship's captain comfort in knowing he could see around the outside of his ship. It's just that he didn't need to. The crew took care of reporting to him regarding nearby ships or calculating distances to destinations. Perhaps it was only force of habit or that it made him feel like he was actually doing something.

They'd been cruising slowly back and forth across commonly used shipping routes leading between planets and space colonies, hoping to catch a lone vessel they could raid and use for landing on Star Fantasy. There they would employ the old "false flag" trick used by pirates for centuries. It had been this same search for days, and the crews were getting antsy.

But, Kscheeech was right. If Star Fantasy detected a fleet of ships approaching and no explanation as to why, they'd send a distress call and within days IPF forces would be chasing the Naustie fleet all over the galaxy. Many would never make it home. New Australia might even be identified as the source of all recent raids, and authorities could soon be directing an attack on their home base. No, this was much better: sneak in under a false flag just to get the first brigade safely landed. Once there, they could scramble any communications coming from the area.

Nevertheless, the waiting was aggravating. Slout knew his people were getting agitated. Something needed to break the monotony. Yet they had to remain at their posts for 12 hours at a time, on high alert for any passing craft. That had always been procedure. The hours ground on and on. They jetted back and forth across a three-hundred-thousand mile expanse of space, turning around every few hours and repeating the process as Slout and his crew waited. And waited some more.

Then finally, in the silence, with thirty crewmembers on the ship's bridge, nothing left to shoot the breeze about, it finally happened. A notification lit up on the display panel in front of the navigation officer, a Suidonji named Frilbriliram. He startled to attention, having drifted off in a mindless daydream about wallowing around in the cool mud. Only a minute before, he'd been counting down the last two hours of his duty shift, looking forward to a game of cards or a pint of ale at the officer's club. Not anymore. Now he and five others monitoring the control panel were springing into action.

"Admiral, sir!" snorted Frilbriliram who went by the nickname Brilly. Slout instantly reacted, knowing instinctively what this meant and what Brilly was referring to. Coolly he commanded in a gruff but calm voice, "Main screen, Mr. Brilly, please."

Within a few seconds, the screen showed a magnified image of a small cruiser, growing like a little white dot, nearing *The Anarchy,* maybe twenty thousand miles off the port side of the Naustie flagship. This was just what they'd been waiting for. With a nod of his big head, Slout ordered Brilly to transmit the message they'd been waiting to send whenever they finally found a good target:

"Hailing Earth craft with course bearing Alpha-Zulu-Tango, niner-eight-three-six, Enoshi system. Request passage for civilian passengers returning to Enosh wishing to attend funeral for family patriarch. Price negotiable. Request docking. Over."

Such a message was sure to get attention, Kscheeech figured. Everyone in the galaxy knew the strict Enoshi tradition of attending a family member's funeral, especially when the eldest male of the tribe passed away. A patriarch commanded deepest respect among the males within the family. Not attending his funeral meant shame and embarrassment; no matter where one was on the planet or even within the galaxy, when receiving word of the death of their family elder they had to drop everything and travel home for the ceremony. No exceptions!

What's more, an Enoshi would pay anything and do anything to get home in time. Therefore, this meant a wonderful opportunity for the Earth craft approaching them. Who knows? Fifty or even a hundred Enoshi traveling home together? Oh, they'd pay every penny they had just to get back to Enosh. The Earthers could charge anything they wanted, and they'd fork it over with no hesitation. The captain on that ship would have known that. His crew would as well. And it worked! Within five minutes a message came in on Brilly's computer saying, "*Acknowledged. Requesting number of passengers to accommodate. Over.*"

Slout snickered when Brilly read off the message. The Earthers were buying it. And why wouldn't they anyway? The Earth craft would have scanned *The Anarchy* by now and found that it had very little cargo and over 1500 life forms on board. This must be a large freighter full of rich passengers! If the ship required 600 to operate the craft, up to 900 of them could be Enos trying to get back home for their Patriarch's funeral. The Earther captain could make a fortune!

Brilly observed, "They're probably guessing we've carried the poor bastards this far … picked them up somewhere out in space … and now we want to get on with our voyage, eh Admiral?" Slout only smiled and nodded, looking down at Brilly, whom he'd known since he first arrived on New Australia.

"Or maybe they figure we want to stop at Star Fantasy for shore leave and dump them onto another freighter heading toward Enosh. That's probably it right there," replied the Admiral with a snort. He could only chuckle at the genius of his first mate. Crewmen nearby laughed right along with him. Once again, he had to hand it to Kscheeech. So many years as a pirate before being sentenced to New Australia, he sure knew what he was doing. Greed. Lust. Compassion for someone's apparent distress. There were just so many ways to fool an unsuspecting victim.

"Steady as she goes, Mr. Brilly," added the big admiral. The young ensign gladly complied. "Battle stations. Tell General Xonos to ready the troops." Brilly happily relayed the message over the ship's intercom.

Within an hour, the Earth ship approached and via interspace communication channels a deal was struck for taking on five hundred and forty-six Enoshi in exchange for a quarter ton of precious gemstones *"from the family treasury."* The captain of the earth freighter must have been licking his chops by now. Meanwhile, the entire exchange of messages was being listened to by the rest of the Naustie pirate fleet waiting in silence thousands of miles away.

The two ships docked so that their holding bays could be opened and allow movement between. As agreed, crewmembers from *The Anarchy* were first to drive in an electric hauler loaded up with diamonds, rubies, and sapphires from New Australia. The gems were packaged in cloth sacks as if they'd been gathered together from family fortunes. It all looked completely legitimate to the gullible Earthmen.

Looked just like they'd imagined it would too until warriors walking slowly behind the vehicle a few minutes later suddenly lunged forward and slaughtered the terrified humans. The rest of the brigade followed and swept through the craft killing or capturing the entire crew of over five hundred Earthers. The entire battle lasted less than twenty minutes.

The Earth freighter never got off a distress call. *The Anarchy's* assault brigade, under General Xonos, knew exactly where to go and how to get to the command bridge before any attempt could be made. The captain had been one of the first killed, as he'd foolishly gone down to the cargo bay to greet the "mourners" in person. After he'd fallen, the rest of the ship's crew were unable to mount any form of resistance.

Thus, within two hours the Earth freighter, named ironically *The Chengshi* (Chinese for *honesty*), was cleaned out of all dead bodies.

A new crew was installed to run *The Chengshi*; then in no time, the hold was filled with General Xonos' brigade and it was off to Star Fantasy. *The Anarchy* stayed behind to watch out for any following ships.

Finally, in an effort to signal the rest of the Naustie fleet, the newly captured *Chengshi* sent an interspace communication across public channels hailing Star Fantasy space station. This was yet another of Kscheeech's clever ideas. The other pirate ships would intercept this message, and based on its content, would know when it was time to begin their journey to the space station. No other ship to ship communication would be attempted. It was far too dangerous. They'd already heard *The Anarchy's* message which was intended to lure the Earth ship to dock with it. Hearing nothing else, they could only assume the ambush had worked. Up to now they'd been listening for a distress call indicating that *The Anarchy* had found a ship to engage. But there'd been none. Instead, they got even better news! It was clearly their fellow Nausties hailing Star Fantasy using the captured ship's communication system.

Chengshi, with its new owners at the controls and Kscheeech taking personal command, sent the following message, "Hailing Star Fantasy space station. Hailing Star Fantasy space station. Request docking for Earth freighter Chengshi. Arriving in seventeen hours. One thousand five hundred passengers and crew for vacation and shore leave. Please acknowledge with available port information and terms for docking. Over."

To everyone's delight a Star Fantasy communications officer replied only fifteen minutes later. "Acknowledged. Earth ship Chengshi. Transponder code confirmed. Stand-by for docking information. Welcome to Star Fantasy. Over." So far so good – everything was going to plan. Everyone in the fleet knew what to do next.

"Well, I guess that's it then, eh, Admiral?" asked Ensign Brilly with a sly grin. He sat back in his chair and swiveled to face his superior. "Nothing more for us to do now but wait, right?" The big Admiral nodded with a snort. "That's right, Ensign. Keech will take it from here. The rest of the fleet has bound to have heard all of that. Looks like we've pulled it off." He then glared at Brilly. "You know what to do now, don't you?" he asked. Brilly spun 'round to his work station to program a new heading.

For the next seventeen hours, the newly captured *Chengshi* travelled on to Star Fantasy with its hold filled with General Xonos and his assault brigade. They knew when they approached the station that Star Fantasy sensors would verify the number of beings on board, as their biological heat readings would indicate the ship indeed had about fifteen hundred creatures inside. In reality it was a brigade of about twelve hundred bloodthirsty pirates and a skeleton crew of two hundred and twenty manning the controls.

Meanwhile *The Anarchy* and the remaining fleet were cruising through space, several thousand miles back, waiting for any communication between *Chengshi* and Star Fantasy customs authorities announcing they were clear to offload passengers. That would be enough to signal the attack. And once the message was received, the rest of the fleet was to appear right in time to dock at any newly captured ports on Star Fantasy to further the assault and reinforce where necessary. As it would turn out, the Nausties would end up being rather glad they brought along such a large force! There were many more surprises in store for them.

"Welcome to Star Fantasy, Captain," said the kindly voice. "You said your name was *Keek*, was it?" Kscheeech hesitated momentarily before acknowledging with a "Mmmm-hmmm." He'd worried about this the whole seventeen-hour trip –sounding like a Zorg when he was posing as captain of an Earth passenger ship. "Very good then," she continued, oblivious to his accent. "Well, my name is Meerah and I'll be assisting you with docking procedures today. I hope your journey was uneventful. Any trouble getting here?"

A still image of the port authority officer appeared on-screen. Kscheeech was astounded. It was a female! Not an Empath, no, but actually an aging Enoshi who'd been employed by Star Fantasy to greet landing space craft in a feminine-sounding voice so to make visiting crewmen and their captains feel at ease. It made sense; nevertheless, the crusty old pirate was taken by surprise. "No," he answered, trying to avoid sounding like a Zorg, "No trouble getting here."

Her voice was soothing and warm. "Good, we've got plenty of room for your passengers and crew, Captain Keek," said Meerah. "You know, frankly we haven't seen ships coming from Earth for several weeks now. Those awful rumors about space pirates, you know? Reporters on the news scaring everyone. Must've frightened them off. That's my theory anyway."

Kscheeech chuckled. "Sssss-send us some porters to handle our luggage." he hissed, then hesitated for a moment. *Whoops*, he thought. He almost gave away his Zorg accent again, and feared Meerah might detect he was not human. He corrected himself quickly. "I'm sure my crew and passengers will want to head straight for the Enoshi Environ; grab the first available Empath they can find. It's been a long voyage, Officer, uh, what did you say your name was?"

She laughed, "Oh just call me Meerah. Everyone else does around here. No need to be formal, Captain Keek."

Kscheeech knew that all Meerah could see on her end was just a camera view of the ship as it was docking and hear the audio of his voice, so he tried to suppress his accent best he could before continuing, "Alright then, Meerah. You can just call me *Keek*."

Meanwhile, as the access tunnel was linking itself to the *Chengshi's* cargo bay, General Xonos' brigade were standing at the ready, snarling with anticipation. They'd waited patiently while Kscheeech and his crew steered the ship into its moorings; and when they heard the access tunnel linking to the cargo bay, they braced themselves to burst through the doorway. A big thud was followed by some motorized sounds which indicated a vacuum seal was being created. Soon the door would open. "Get ready, brothers," growled their commander.

The brigade was made up of five companies of troops. Three companies of warriors from the Smilodon tribe formed the brunt of it. These units would fan out quickly and gun down defenders. Then there were two artillery companies of humans, further broken down into fire teams of five to ten men, which operated large-sized Electrical Impulse Cannon's. These units would carry the components of these cumbersome weapons out to a secured position and assemble them. Once done, they could spray the enemy with fifty caliber projectiles and obliterate most enemy defenses.

When the door finally opened, General Xonos roared like a tiger. "Go! Fan out brothers! Shoot anything that moves!" It was a ferocious surge that caught the poor customs staff completely off guard. The Nausties then swept through the port facility with ease and began fanning out in both directions to secure additional ports. Meanwhile Xonos took two companies of infantry and one artillery company; a force of about nine hundred troops and headed toward the nearby Enoshi Environ. His other two companies moved out toward the Earth Environ to secure the next port for reinforcements to arrive. For the first sixty minutes, things went smoothly.

Reports coming back to Kscheeech were positive, at least initially. Nausties blasted away in every direction as they entered large lobby areas, mowing down anyone foolish enough to resist. Beings of all types fled in every direction or wisely fell to the floor and lay completely still while the battle raged.

Going from chamber to chamber the Xonos' troops forced workers and guests into secured areas and closed them off from the lobby. Male noncombatants were either ignored or simply knocked to the ground while the Nausties snuffed out any remaining resistance.

Indeed, Star Fantasy Police were quite overwhelmed in those first sixty minutes due to the sheer ferocity of the attack. But, as the battle wore on, they solidified their positions with reinforcements and the tables began to turn. Suddenly, the police force was counterattacking and regaining lost ground. The hunter was gradually becoming the prey! Before long, those three companies under command of General Xonos found themselves trapped.

"General! We're surrounded!" screamed Corporal Martinez. He'd survived not only the attack on terminal headquarters during the Naustie Revolt, but the vicious civil war following. Now was the first time he'd gone up against trained soldiers and he was panicking. "We got bullets coming in from all directions, sir! We got to get the hell out of here!" Even his police training back in New Los Angeles was failing him. SF Police were pinning them down with direct fire and all the while moving about to slowly tighten the noose. He feared they'd be overrun.

"Nonsense, Corporal!" he cried. "Hold your position! Return their fire! If they want a fight, then let's give it to them!" Xonos hadn't seen real combat in many years, not since he was an army officer back on his home planet. It excited him. Meanwhile, other Enoshi nearby echoed his resolve. Dying in battle, for them at least, was the greatest honor possible. "We'll fight, General! Let them come!" cried one. Corporal Martinez found inspiration in their zeal for battle.

"Alright then!" responded Martinez. "You. Private Slocum! Cover that balcony up there. I'll move around and try to take them out with a grenade. You got me?" The frightened soldier nodded, bravely raising up on one knee to blast the enemy while his comrade moved into position. Within seconds he was dead, shot through the face with a burst of projectiles. Martinez was soon pinned down once more behind the body of a dead policeman. He could feel bullets hitting into the mangled carcass as he curled up in a ball.

"Slocum?" he screamed. No answer. Projectiles continued to bounce off the tiles around him and into the body of the dead cop. He cried out for help once more. "Peters? Ibrahim? Anyone? God dammit I need cover fire!"

Unbeknownst to the Nausties, Star Fantasy Police had an arsenal of hand-held EIC's. The SFP suddenly turned into fiercely determined defenders who methodically regrouped to fight the now surprised and under-supplied pirates. As they re-formed and armed themselves with EIC's from a nearby station, they opened fire with merciless intensity.

General Xonos and his three companies took appalling casualties. The enemy threw up barricades using anything they could find, even half-naked bodies of guests, and mowed down the invaders caught out in the open. No one had warned General Xonos that the SFP carried anything more than night-sticks with a cattle prod on the end. Now he was realizing the awful truth. The invasion was turning into a disaster.

While they were pinned down by murderous enemy fire, enormous security doors descended several hundred yards behind them shutting off the whole section from the docking station. All Xonos could hope for was that Zorg messengers would notify Kscheeech in time and hopefully he'd have some way of rescuing them. If not, his seven hundred or so remaining troops might be slaughtered.

Meanwhile, the other two companies, who'd journeyed in the other direction toward the Earth Environ hadn't fared much better. They'd secured the port there but soon found themselves in a similar predicament. The Nausties were able to take and hold the docking facility and eject the vessel at berth there so that an additional Naustie ship, *The Warthog*, was able to land and offload fresh troops. However, by then the SFP had shut off the area by closing thirty-foot security doors on either side of the port. This squeezed the nearly four hundred Nausties into a pocket about one mile wide, with the port they now held as their only means of escape. Word got out immediately.

"Admiral, sir!" bellowed the young ensign. "Our troops! They're being massacred. We've got to do something!" He'd been intercepting transmissions between police units fighting the Nausties, and many were reporting progress. *"Enemy is contained and pinned down near Enoshi Empath Chambers. Counter-attack successful. Enemy is retreating into food court area and cut off from escape."*

Slout was furious. In an angry snarl, he commanded his crew in the engineering area to arm their warheads and prepare to fire. He could see no other alternative. If the Chief of Police on Star Fantasy wanted an all-out battle, then he was about to get one. The Admiral hastily mounted a response.

First, Slout ordered his crew to fire neutron torpedoes at the command center in the middle of the space station. The blasts would open it up like a can opener and obliterate those who occupied the top levels. It was risky; but Star Fantasy leadership needed to be removed from the field of battle. It was only logical, and now Slout was regretting not pushing for an all-out takeover of the space station like Kscheeech had originally proposed! It was too late for that now. He angrily clipped off orders to his subordinates to commence firing. Minutes later he watched as the center of Star Fantasy exploded before his eyes. No one could have survived.

Meanwhile, Slout ordered his crew to stand by with thermonuclear warheads just in case the attack had to be scrubbed. If that happened, the Admiral knew what he'd have to do and that was destroy the entire station including all his troops still trapped on Star Fantasy right along with it. If they were going to have to make a run for it; Slout knew he must leave little evidence behind of who was responsible for the attack. For another two agonizing hours, Slout weighed that option, while he awaited news from below.

Slowly, the Nausties' situation began to improve. Kscheeech exited *The Chengshi* and set up a new headquarters in the terminal port command pod so he could take command of the operation to save the beleaguered units. With him, he brought teams of Suidonji from his own ship's crew to venture out with acetylene cutting torches to slice open a passageway through the security barriers. This allowed Xonos' troops to get resupplied and rally for an eventual counterattack. Swiftly, he then ordered *The Chengshi* to depart so that another ship, *The Varanus*, could dock and unload reinforcements. Thus, when fresh troops from *The Varanus* landed and *The Warthog* landed with the Templar Knights brigade at the captured Earth Environ passenger port, the situation finally started to turn around.

Of course, up until then Xonos had proudly held on, promising his troops reinforcements and brashly admonishing them to be brave. "No retreat!" he screamed repeatedly. "Hold your ground! Hold your ground until help arrives!" His courage was outstanding, given the circumstances. He was holding on by a thread; but he knew his troops were not about to break. Morale was not the problem; ammunition was really what he required. Now, the resupplying of his troops meant the trapped pirates could apply murderous return fire, and slowly the tide began to turn. The enemy was gradually driven from their defense line when reinforcements arrived.

Kscheeech, for his part, stayed in the port command pod, directing the operation and remaining visible, while reports came in constantly and messages were sent up to the front lines. The Star Fantasy command center had been demolished with neutron torpedoes by then, so the disruption meant police units in the field had to make decisions on their own. Not knowing exactly what to do, nor when they'd be reinforced, the defenders were soon withdrawing from the Enoshi Environ en masse.

Same thing was occurring in the Earth Environ. With the arrival of General Vlad and the Templar Knights brigade, the police's defensive lines began to crumble. Soon, General Vlad's forces were pouring through, and those workers who'd been trapped in that section were soon being rounded up. Victory was finally achieved.

As the last of the SFP were being rooted out, Vlad and about fifty of his best men suddenly found themselves standing right in the middle of the enormous holographic imagery deck made to look like a Roman gladiator arena. It had been used as a sanctuary for noncombatants while the SF Police had formed a defensive barricade. Vlad and his men stared in amazement at the scene now arrayed before them: nearly five hundred scantily-clad Earthmen and women, crowded into the middle of a simulated Roman coliseum. It was like they'd stepped onto a movie set!

Some were customers. Many more were male body workers, dressed in gladiator costumes or skimpy togas. Some wore nothing at all. Most of them were bodybuilders with oiled skin – muscles rippling and bulging. They were clean and gorgeous, one and all. The Impaler didn't know quite how to react to such a sight.

"*BO zheh moy*!" exclaimed Vlad in his native Russian. He quickly took charge of the situation. "Greetings everyone," bellowed Vlad. "I hope you'll pardon the interruption to tonight's performance. We are the pirates of New Australia and lucky for you, we are accepting new members. Anyone interested?" The timing of the raid couldn't have been better. Employee resentment at their treatment was at all-time high. Why not throw in with the pirates? Not surprisingly, more than half the employees raised their hands including one pristine young man with boyish features and a carefully-crafted physique. The hairless, tattooed general looked down at him with a smile while the young man attempted to appear brave while clearly fearing the worst. "And as for you, my handsome friend," he said with an evil chuckle, "You can call me Vlad."

CHAPTER 16: THE STARFISH

During the battle, Felina and Race had wisely scurried out of the way of danger and quickly found a place to hide inside the kitchen of the Starfish Restaurant. When fighting began, the two were just sitting down to a peaceful dinner together after Race had finished his shift. He'd been relaxing in a comfortable chair when the shooting started.

There were a hundred chairs just like it throughout his restaurant, in various colors. The decor depicted an ocean world theme. Soft pastels like lavender, teal, blue-gray, baby blue, seaweed green, and pale pink dazzled the eyes, along with decorations and art that replicated sea vegetation. The interior was dimly lit, with table lamps made to look like over-sized glowing pearls inside a splayed-open oyster; soft track lighting running along the tops of the walls.

The restaurant's seating was oriented around a massive fish tank that held thousands of gallons of sea water and was large enough for crews to work inside of it to clean and scrub the interior. It was oval shaped and extended to the ceiling. Customers could sit around it and wave at half-naked swimmers, scrubbing and scraping the sides of the tank, while the walls of the restaurant showed holographic images of marine life. The combination of this imagery made customers feel like they were seated at the bottom of a magical sea while they dined.

But the ambiance was violently disrupted as explosions rocked the food court outside.

"Did you hear that?" asked Felina, "And why are all those people running?" Before long, the terrified screams from out in the food court combined with bodies falling dead in the street made Race spring into action.

"Holy shit, we've got to get out of here!" Race yelled. He grabbed Felina's wrist and dragged her away from the table as she spit out her mouthful of food. Seeing the chaos going on outside his window, Race put things together fast.

This must really be them, he thought, *those space pirates I've been hearing about in the news!* Now they had finally come to Star Fantasy. But why? Then it dawned on him. Star Fantasy had around five thousand employees and over half of them were female. Was this a raid or a recruiting exercise?

Race was barely 5'10". Felina normally towered over him at 6'1". But in his desperation to protect his friend, he yanked her away from that table as if she were a rag doll. He acted instinctively. If there was to be shooting going on, Race knew the windows of his restaurant would surely be the next thing to go. Problem was, there was no available escape from the restaurant itself. There was no back alley to flee to. They were on a space station! He quickly weighed his options.

At first Race pulled Felina under a large table inside a private booth and they hid there for several minutes. Many customers and staff had done the same thing, hoping to be protected from flying glass. But Race could hear what was going on outside and whoever the attackers were, they seemed to be rounding up prisoners! He looked back at his friend Felina, who was curled up next to him.

"If they're here for recruits, they'll surely want you, Felina! You're famous!" he yelled over the cacophony of noise. He knew he needed to find a better hiding place for them to be safe, and he needed to hurry. It wasn't long before things got even nastier.

When SFP responded to the scene and opened fire on the raiders their projectiles pierced the glass of the restaurant windows and began ricocheting off the giant fish tank. Customers and wait-staff cried out in fear. Not Race however. Something else had caught his attention. He winced when he saw bullets leaving pock marks and divots in the thick glass.

"Not good!" he exclaimed. He just knew that humongous aquarium was eventually going to shatter and flood the restaurant with twenty-five thousand gallons of sea water. He needed to get Felina out of there, but where to hide in a restaurant? They couldn't go outside. They'd be shot to pieces! Race thought for a few moments then looked over at Felina. Race yelled to Felina over the din.

"Come with me!" Felina nodded and they both crawled out from under the table.

Race knew where they could be safe. They both crouched and scurried toward the kitchen, barely rising above tabletops as projectiles pinged off of artwork, table tops and chair backs. Soon they reached the kitchen and Race held the door open.

"Good job," he breathed. "Now let's get into one of the pantries and hide until this is over." That's when they noticed kitchen staff members were already piling into the freezer or into food pantries and broom closets, leaving no room for more. Race sighed as he looked around for other options.

"Where are we going to hide?" Race looked around for a moment and thought of a potential solution. "Just follow me. I got an idea!" he yelled.

Outside the screaming and yelling could still be heard. Bullets continued to fly into the restaurant, smashing lamps and ricocheting off the aquarium. Race knew it was eventually going to crack and break. Race led Felina over to a massive stainless-steel prep table with shiny sliding door cabinets underneath. It was the only thing left he could think of.

These cabinets were filled with serving trays, chafing dishes, burners, racks, and other serving equipment for when the restaurant catered events over at the Earth Environ. Rex slid the doors open and motioned to Felina to help him throw everything out on the floor so they could crawl in.

It would have to suffice. True, it would be a tight squeeze, but Race needed to make Felina disappear. If it worked, the pirates would see nothing but a royal mess and that would make sense after the kitchen staff would have fled in panic. At least he hoped it would fool them. It was their only option.

Race and Felina crawled in, bumping heads, elbows, and knees. They grimaced and grunted while struggling to secure themselves inside as Race carefully moved the sliding door closed from the inside.

He left it open just a small crack to let in air; then they sighed with relief, hoping to wait out the attack.

He had judged correctly, for it was just about that time they could hear folks out in the restaurant screaming that the aquarium was about to burst! Screams of wounded and dying soon filled the room as the ensuing hail of projectiles finished cracking open the enormous fish tank. With a terrifying, thundering crash of glass, a torrent of seawater gushed through the restaurant. Race held Felina tight throughout the ordeal.

Not long after that, Naustie troops from General Xonos' brigade made Starfish into their headquarters and moved inside to create a fortified position. The smell of fish likely drew them in. They ransacked the interior looking for any females they could find then rampaged through the kitchen grabbing food and opening up closets or storerooms. "Join us or head outside. It's your call!" shouted the pirates.

The searching went on for quite a while longer in the kitchen, as the pirates yanked open refrigerators, freezers and pantries to find more petrified kitchen staff cowering inside. Again, they heard, "Join or us or take your chances outside." Race figured any moment they'd throw open the cabinet door and drag them out. He braced himself for the inevitable.

Eventually though, the pirates left. They moved back into the restaurant to work on setting up a defensive position from which to fight off an SFP counterattack. Race sighed with relief. For now, they were safe. But then he noticed something else.

He could hear them outside the kitchen door commenting about how they were getting low on ammunition. Also, he could hear them struggling to move out all the dead and dying marine life from the shattered aquarium. Race could hear Earthers among them too, rushing in and assembling equipment. Most spoke to each other in Galactic, but occasionally Race could hear them cursing in old Earth languages like English and Spanish. He hadn't heard Earth profanity in years. It immediately got his attention.

"Shit!" exclaimed one of them. "I'm low, man. Itsuko, you got another cartridge?" A voice replied in a heavy Japanese accent, "*Nai jigoku!* I'm almost out too, Kyle. What the fuck are we gonna do now?" Race could only hope they'd soon retreat, and SF Police would carry the day. "Corporal, we're running out of bullets goddammit!

Tell the General! We got our nuts in a vice, man. Them cops are going to run us over pretty soon!" However, the man he was speaking to couldn't be heard over the din of battle.

Somehow, the pirates out in the restaurant fought on. The next two hours were a harrowing experience, as several waves of Star Fantasy Police assaulted their position. The pirates fought desperately as police sprayed the restaurant with bullets almost incessantly. Yet they were repulsed several times, until the battle seemed to descend into an ominous stalemate. Felina could soon hear police off in the distance yelling obscenities and insults; jeering at their counterparts, trying to provoke them. Cooler heads prevailed though, and the pirates stayed put, hurling back vicious retorts at their tormentors and occasionally doing even worse.

Then finally after about two hours, Felina could hear the pirates chattering back and forth about reinforcements. That's when one very strong voice spoke up above everyone else's and admonished them to hold their positions. It was General Xonos himself, though she couldn't have known that yet. He was telling them to be patient while ammunition was being ferried up to them. She whispered the translation to Race and he sighed with frustration. More pirates were on the way, it seemed. "Shit," he muttered. If the police withdrew, just how would they get out of this mess? Nevertheless, Race and Felina huddled in their cramped hiding place, uncomfortable, but still glad to be alive. All things considered, their situation could be a lot worse.

Pirate reinforcements could be heard arriving outside, and with fresh ammunition, the raiders began firing back with a vengeance. The mood of the pirates outside in the restaurant turned from desperation to renewed confidence as more voices and more troops could be heard moving about both within the restaurant and even outside in the food court. When the pirates in the restaurant left their positions to go assault the SF Police barricades in the distance, the place finally began to quiet down.

Race carefully slid the cabinet door open a few inches and barely made a sound. But even that small crack let in the foul stench of dying marine life which had been expelled from their happy home. Then he gasped and held his breath, for as he looked out, he found himself face to face with a bloody corpse looking right back at him! It was one of his cooks. He'd been shot through the face and the entire back of his head was blown out. He rolled back toward Felina and said, "Um, this way is blocked. Let's see what's on the other side."

The cabinet had sliding doors on the either side too, so Race knew they could get out that way, but he once again hesitated when he heard some more movement going on outside in the restaurant. Then he heard a voice. An Earthman, one of the pirates, was speaking about all the females recruits. It was deeply accented English, like Race hadn't heard since the last time he'd seen an Earth movie about gangsters.

"Fricking weird, man. Chicks are *crazy* looking! Have you seen them?" said the first pirate, laughing derisively. Race could hear the man sliding a chair out to sit, and the sound of his EIC being dropped onto a table as if the fellow were taking a break. He was clearly not alone.

"Yeah, I sure have. Five hundred joined us so far," replied a second gruff voice with a Southern twang. "Maybe more out there, General says. There's got to be more around here." Race realized they were talking about Enoshi bodyworkers and empaths.

"Second thought," he whispered soothingly, "let's just stay here a while longer. Make sure it's all clear before we make a break for it okay?" Felina sighed, "Sounds like a plan."

Meanwhile back in the command pod at the Enoshi Environ passenger port, Kscheeech was getting reports of smashing successes in that sector. Suidonji had already cut open a large hole in the security door and let in reinforcements, who brought badly needed ammunition. Things were looking better and better. The SFP were being driven back. Fresh units of Nausties were overwhelming their barricades, messengers said. Wounded and dead were being retrieved. Recruits now numbered nearly nine hundred from assorted species. This was great news.

Kscheeech was profoundly relieved. General Xonos had managed to stave off disaster and keep the enemy at bay against incredible odds. Now he could round up prisoners and get everyone the hell out of there. He also heard that Earthers had cut open the security wall separating the Earth Environ, and messengers reporting on their situation returned with similar news. General Vlad had secured the entire Earth Environ and taken on several hundred more recruits.

But what of Felina, the famous Star Kitten? Kscheeech pondered whether she might very well be among the new recruits in the Enoshi sector, and that presented a quandary for him, as he looked down upon the dead body of Meerah, the customs officer who'd been so kind to him earlier. Could he recognize Felina in a crowd? While surviving Nausties began boarding a freighter for the trip home, Kscheeech put one of his best officers in charge and set out to look for her. Was the famous Star Kitten even alive? Could she have lived through the firefight? Or was she captured already?

Arriving at a large gathering of new recruits watched over carefully by his own troops, Kscheeech saw an amazing site: hundreds of wondrous creatures. They were beautiful. And there was something else he noticed.

In a way, it almost seemed like they were ... *singing*! Could that be right? Was this some ancient ritual, to mourn the death of fallen comrades? Were they singing some traditional hymn? Kscheeech walked up to them and stared as he approached. Mesmerized, he almost tripped over a dead body and some debris on the ground.

Suidonji were all around going through the battle site, scooping up weapons off dead cops, tossing them into bins and carrying them back to the docking station. Others came along and scooped up bodies of fallen Nausties and returned them to the ship. The wounded were being hauled off for a quick evacuation. But Kscheeech wanted to be on that ship as well with his most important new recruit: Felina Toyger. He searched in vain through the masses.

Everyone was busy working. Only those assigned to managing the recruits stood by or walked slowly around the group. They were armed, sure, but the pirates' appearances were far more terrifying than their guns. Even if they'd been armed with butter knives, not one of the recruits would have considered a change of heart.

Kscheeech debated how to handle this. These recruits needed to come along on their own. Solomon's plan wouldn't work if they started forcing recruits to join them. So, he simply said, "Greetings, new members of New Australia. We welcome you with open arms. We offer you freedom and a chance to make a difference. Nothing more. Those of you who wish to depart and remain here may do so now. Those who wish to join us, remain."

He was pleasantly surprised when only a handful gathered themselves and walked off into the station. He addressed those who remained, "Welcome. Please remain here until our operation has concluded. You'll be assigned to a ship and a crew. Await further instructions. That is all." The newest members of New Australia looked at Kscheeech and nodded and began chatting amongst themselves.

He couldn't understand a word, and for that matter, wasn't really sure if they were saying anything at all. He then looked around and saw a large billboard overhead that had an electrified screen showing scenes of the Star Kitten herself, waving back subtly and glaring alluringly. He recognized her face immediately as the animated image showed Felina the Star Kitten holding up a finger to her lips as if to say "shhhhh," then winked seductively. The five-second video was on a loop and continued to play over and over again while a banner repeatedly scrolled across urging customers to *"Make reservations with an Empath tonight."* It gave him an idea!

He walked up to a giant Enoshi female and stood for a moment with his hands on his hips. *Hmmm, what to say to these creatures*, he wondered. At first, he stammered out, "Um, excuse me." She just looked at him. He pointed up to the flashing billboard overhead and yelled, "WHERE IS FELINA???" She looked up at the sign and looked right back at Kscheeech, "You don't have to yell. She usually hangs out at Starfish at this time of night. You might find her there. If there is anything left of it."

Starfish was the name of the restaurant she always went to for dinner after work. Kscheeech remembered learning that from talking with Meerah earlier that day. If she'd gone to that restaurant after work, she'd probably been trapped there during the battle. He now knew precisely where to search for her. With a spring in his step, he walked briskly down the street to what was once one of the fanciest restaurants on all of Star Fantasy. Within a few hundred yards, he'd found it.

Here it was, the famous Starfish restaurant. But oh, what a woeful state of affairs met his gaze when he arrived! A shot-up sign dangled from the entrance, secured on only one side. It once displayed a big yellow-gold star with a pink cartoon fish winking back, including long eyelashes and luscious red lips. Now it was riddled with bullet holes. Kscheeech sighed. It depressed him to see the destruction the battle had caused. In a way, he longed to see what it had once appeared like, before projectiles had ripped the place to shreds. It was far too late for that, though. His cold reptile blood ran a bit colder when he saw the devastation. *How could anyone have survived?* he wondered. The feelings of dread got even worse when he walked through the doorway.

Bodies were everywhere. The carnage was appalling. Some of the dead were piled up on top of barricades to create shields against enemy fire. Their bodies had been pulverized and mangled. The interior had been shot to hell, too. The giant aquarium had been obliterated, and dead or dying sea creatures were strewn across the floor. It smelled disgusting and looked horrific. Could Felina have been inside when all this occurred? If so, how could she have lived through it?

Kscheeech made his way through the bodies and debris back to the kitchen. It was silent now inside the restaurant. He carefully slipped around a sand shark that lay on the floor motionless, its beady eyes seeming to be staring right back at him. He winced when he stepped on a spiny sea urchin, though his big feet didn't puncture. He stepped lightly through puddles of sea water mixed with algae and blood. And yet, his innate senses kept on telling him there was still someone hiding somewhere in the place. He could feel it in his gut. He crept carefully into the kitchen, moving slowly and quietly like he was stalking prey.

More bodies. A dead human male crumpled in the corner. Yet another human was lying in the doorway of a walk-in pantry. Inside the walk-in freezer there were two or three young Suidonji that Kscheeech could see, all face down and clearly dead. He stepped slowly and gently through puddles of sea water which had dribbled in from the burst aquarium. It smelled like a fish market; actually, more like an abandoned fish market at the end of a long hot summer day back home on Zorgolong. Sensing she was near, Kscheeech picked up a large chef's knife from a cutting board in the center of the very large kitchen. He walked carefully between the food prep area and the stainless-steel industrial stoves until he found yet another body.

This dead human corpse was so grotesque it even made Kscheeech, old hardened space pirate that he was, shrink back with disgust. The nose of the man was obliterated, the eyes and mouth still wide open, aghast with horror, as though the victim had been pleading for his life when he was shot. The entire back of his head was gone, and brains were oozing out of his shattered skull. Kscheeech actually felt a bit nauseous at the gory sight. But then the old Zorg noticed a slightly open cabinet door.

Could this be large enough for someone to be hiding inside? he wondered. It sure looked like it. What's more, no one would have thought to look there! In their haste, the pirates apparently opened closets and pantries and walk-in freezers. They wouldn't have bothered to check cabinets, certainly not a sliding-door cabinet underneath a kitchen counter. Kscheeech looked around the kitchen floor; and grinned evilly. Chafing dishes and pans were strewn everywhere, clearly taken from somewhere and dumped out on the floor. *But why? Only one reason for it*, thought Kscheeech. A cabinet had to have been emptied, and in a very big hurry.

He nodded and snickered. She was probably still in there hiding, likely had been all along right under everyone's noses. Kscheeech gripped his chef knife and nimbly hopped from the floor onto the stainless-steel table top. It made a huge *CLANK* from his big feet when landing upon it, and someone inside let out a stifled yelp. "Ah…, there you are, my dear," snarled Kscheeech in a low menacing voice. Rustling could be heard in the cabinet below him.

He knelt and crouched on the table, peering carefully over the edge so that his long snout was near the cracked-open sliding door, and as he did so, he could see his reflection in the polished steel stove door across from him. Inside, he could see movement and shining eyes glaring out at him. He muttered slowly, "Well, well. Hello, Felina. I've been looking for you."

CHAPTER 17: A NEW RECRUIT

Felina slowly crawled out of her hiding place, hobbled and sore from being curled up inside for so long. Following her was Race. She just glared at Kscheeech as if expecting him to say something. The awkward moment stretched on. Finally, Kscheeech broke the silence. "Join us?" he asked.

She looked Kscheeech square in the eye and said, "Not a very good sales pitch. But, very well. I'm due for a new adventure. This place is tiresome. Your timing is spot on. But he's coming with us too. He's my best friend. His name is Race. He's a chef and a darn good one. He goes where I go, and that's not negotiable." Kscheeech was flabbergasted. *Is she serious*, he wondered? How audacious of her, giving demands to a ferocious Zorg brandishing a knife. She should have been petrified. He glared back at her for a moment, heaving an indignant sigh. "What?" he exclaimed.

But Felina just continued to glare at him, and it wasn't long before he found himself accepting her demand. In fact, it was after only a few seconds of staring into her eyes that he remarkably gave in. Maybe it was her imposing size. Maybe it was her stunning beauty. Whatever it was, he wasn't sure. Somehow, she seemed to have some magical effect on him.

"Very well then," he hissed in frustration. "If that is what you require, so be it." He then proceeded to march his two recruits back to the docking station. The odd-looking pair followed with no further argument.

As he sat in the command pod, now cleared of dead bodies, he got to know the famous Enoshi and her Earther friend quite well. From that point on, during the course of an hour conversing with Felina, Kscheeech became enthralled. She had lots of questions for the paunchy Zorg. Her male companion did as well. They chatted tentatively at first, keeping the conversation superficial, but they became emboldened as time passed.

"So, space pirates, eh?" asked Felina, "sounds thrilling. Where are we going next?"

Kscheeech was not taken aback by her bluntness, just amazed with her candor. She was just so easy to talk to. He found it impossible not to express himself honestly with her, no matter what she asked.

So, Kscheeech told her everything. The prison, The Naustie Rebellion, the Civil War which followed, the threat of food shortages, and finally the decision to become pirates. She didn't appear to judge answers given. She merely wanted to understand him; that's all. And in time, as *The Chengshi* was finishing preparations and taking on passengers, Kscheeech answered every question she posed to him.

"So, you're taking us back to your planet, New Australia? And it was once a prison. Now you're trying to establish yourselves as a legitimate planetary government to join the IPF?" asked Felina. Kscheeech nodded and smiled, tongue flicking the air. He then expanded on his answer. "Yes, my dear. We were all sentenced to prison terms on the planet. It was once called Rijel 12, you see. But we rose up and overthrew our captors." He paused to let it sink in.

"So, you were all criminals?" she clarified. Kscheeech chuckled, "Oh yes. All of us. Every planet in the galaxy sent us there for breaking the law in one way or another. Some deserved to be there, I'm not going to lie. Me, I was a pirate, captured many years ago and sent there to die. By the way, I would include myself among those who got what was coming to them." He then grinned sheepishly.

"And how is it that you propose to legitimize yourselves? Raiding Star Fantasy isn't going to make you any friends in the galaxy. How did your mission today help you achieve your goals?"

"Our mission?" asked Kscheeech folding his little arms. "Well, you see my dear, our mission today was to recruit females to bring back to our planet. We don't have very many, because the prison only had male inmates. So, we don't have much in the way of families on New Australia." Saying that he smiled broadly, adding, "And my personal goal today was to find you." Felina leaned back in her chair looking perplexed.

"Why?" she asked.

"Because if we are going to build a new society and negotiate our place at the table with IPF, we need the best Empath we can find. That's you." Kscheeech replied

Kscheeech felt a warm rush of adrenalin go through his body, like his mind was being relieved of some tremendous burden. Just the whisper of her mental touch did something wondrous to his soul. His mouth dropped open, without him consciously noticing it. *Great Goddess of the Sea,* he thought. It was like she had read and absorbed everything about who he really was deep inside, both good and bad. And now she was about to reach right into his heart with her words.

She leaned forward to grasp both of his claws. Felina looked into his tiny eyes for a moment. By the time she finally spoke, Kscheeech was already mesmerized.

She said in a soft voice, "I understand, Captain. You were all desperate for a better life, so you rebelled against your cruel masters. You killed them, and in that you felt justified. You captured the planet from them. Then it became your home. But you still needed food to survive and there was no one to go to for help. So, you became pirates. That was the choice you made."

Kscheeech nodded like he had been hypnotized. His body floated like a leaf descending from a tree in autumn. He felt nothing but her touch. He saw nothing but her beautiful gray-green eyes. Blood flowed through him like a rushing stream, which he could practically feel pumping within his little body. But alas, she had even more to say.

"You came from violence. Lived with violence. Survived violence. And then used it to further your existence," she added in a voice barely more audible than a whisper. "And now your warriors want to experience comfort and joy. They desire happiness and community and acceptance, the things that bring fulfillment, the things that every intelligent creature wants." Kscheeech was so relaxed and intoxicated by the feelings he experienced being near

Felina, that the words he responded with were mere mutterings which he doubted she could hear.

Felina reached up and caressed the scaly fellow's face with the back of her left paw while she continued to hold his claws in her right. She replied to him, "Yes. The only life you know. That is, until you learn a better way, a better life for you and for everyone. That's what you desire, deep in your heart." She gently placed her paw on his chest, right over his now thumping heart.

The captain startled at first, then bowed his head and sighed deeply. Tears welled in his eyes, something that hadn't happened since he was a hatchling. He then leaned into Felina's paw as it gently touched his skin. *Yes, what she says is true!* he thought. Like Solomon, Kscheeech shared the vision of a better life for his fellow Nausties and a peaceful co-existence within the galaxy. He lived for the day when he could quit being a pirate and settle down to enjoy the twilight years of his life. And yet she knew this! He could see it in her eyes! She knew! Wave upon wave of memories flooded through his mind in a mere instant.

Years ago, he'd seen his good friend Ggggaaah abandon him to the authorities and allow him to be exiled to Rijel 12. For years, he seethed with hatred for his former compatriot, and lived off that hatred coursing through his veins. It kept him alive. It kept him sharp and alert, working down in those infernal mines, hardened his heart to the pain and suffering around him and drove him to survive. But when Ggggaaah was captured and executed by his fellow inmates, something changed in Kscheeech. An odd peace descended over his soul.

Kscheeech found he had no one left to hate anymore. He had no reason to be angry either, or to seek the demise of another being. He found friends among the brethren within his crew, and during the rebellion he befriended Slout, who later became his Captain onboard *The Anarchy*. The killing and the raiding? It was a necessary evil. He ordered it done because that was his duty. And he did all those things because his comrades needed him to. They relied on him. Kscheeech found no joy nor any morbid fascination with it. A means to an end, that's all it was. And someday, hopefully, it wouldn't be necessary.

Felina was right. And she had deduced all of that by merely grasping his claws and sensing his deepest feelings. She truly was just as amazing as he'd imagined. Even more so! For the first time in many years, he wept.

"Yes-sss," said Kscheeech raising up and taking a deep breath. "A better life," he added, "for everyone." Felina smiled and leaned in further to kiss the end of his nose. Then she grasped and squeezed his claws with both of her paws one more time and released them. The session was now complete, and upon her release, it seemed the blood was flowing normally within his body again. Yet it felt like he was still under her spell. He recovered himself a bit more and sat back with a bright smile, his body feeling like he'd just had a refreshing twenty-minute nap.

Afterward, they all three got up to go get on board *The Chengshi*. It was about time to load the last of the supplies and get the crew to their stations. New recruits and seasoned crewmembers were ready for their commander to give the order to disembark. Yet soon everyone was amazed to see a rather odd-looking threesome scurrying onboard, with Kscheeech their Captain and a very tall, very gorgeous Enoshi chattering back and forth.

CHAPTER 18: THE VOYAGES HOME

The Voyage of *The Varanus*

The Varanus was the first of the Naustie ships to high-tail it home. Seeing no Star Fleet presence as of yet, her commander steered toward New Australia at full power, careening through deep space and hoping to dock back at the main terminal in just over two weeks. They had good reason to hurry.

"Set a course for home, Mr. Groink," instructed the Captain of the ship, a Zorg who went by the name Blink since his real name was impossible to pronounce. "Full speed ahead. Program the most direct route possible into the computer. No stopping either, Ensign. Not for anything. If you receive a distress call, ignore it. No exceptions!" The recently-promoted First Officer snorted in response.

"Aye, Captain. No exceptions," he replied. The young Suidonji knew exactly what to do. And he knew why. Time was of the essence.

The hold of *The Varanus* had by then been converted into a massive field hospital. Her cargo was made up of surviving troops, including General Xonos himself, from the near-debacle back at Enoshi Environ. The General had been severely wounded in the battle and his condition was critical. Medics on board *The Varanus* did their best to try and dig out the projectiles from his body. He was a hero because of his leadership back on Star Fantasy. Somehow, they needed to save him.

"Very well, then," said Captain Blink. "You may take the helm now, my chubby friend. I'll go check on things below." Groink acknowledged with a nod, turning back to his control panel to continue his search for enemy craft. The fighting on the station had been costly and time consuming! Plenty long enough for a nearby patrol to arrive and pounce on them. Still, he worried for Xonos and the others suffering and dying below decks. *If only we had Slarts with us,* he thought to himself. *They'd know how to save the general.*

Of course, they'd make do with what they had available. A hundred or so Empaths were sent with *The Varanus* to be nurses for the wounded. They were like healing angels right from the start, soothing and comforting the troops. It really made a difference. Not all were going to make it, that was apparent. Several would die and have to be removed to a make-shift morgue set up in the cargo bay. Almost all of the dead were Enoshi, so by tradition they were to be given a military funeral when they returned, honoring them for falling in battle. It was a rather somber sight which greeted Captain Blink when he got there.

"How's the general doing?" asked Captain Blink. He whispered when he spoke, so as not to disturb the sleeping patient. Meanwhile a nurse acknowledged him with a sad look. He shook his head.

"We're doing all we can, Captain," he replied. "He's stable for now. We got all the fragments out of him. All we could find, anyway. Now all we can do is hope." Blink nodded.

"Then that's what we'll do, I suppose. Thank you, and well done," was all he could think of to say. He could only imagine the reaction from the Smilodon Tribe if Xonos died before they could get him home. Then again, maybe it wouldn't be so bad, all things considered.

Death in combat was the greatest of all fates for an Enoshi. It was the foundation of their warrior culture. It's what drove millions of males every year to seek military service. Glory in battle was only fleeting, after all. Life was otherwise meaningless to them. But to die fighting? That meant eternal honor in the afterlife.

All Enoshi grew up believing that those who'd been slain in combat would be permitted to enter *Fukuoka*, which was their word for heaven. No matter what their moral failures in life might have been, if they died in battle, their sins would somehow be forgiven. Best of all, they'd be allowed to join their ancestors in the Great Hall of Warriors. There they could spend the rest of eternity drinking ale made from sacred herbs, singing and feasting, all the while awaiting the rest of their clan to join them at the table.

What's more, for the very bravest of warriors, there was the additional possibility of reincarnation, or at least the Enoshi equivalent. This was because the descendants of brave heroes regularly paid homage to their ancestors. When called upon for intervention, it was said that an ancestor's spirit might actually enter the body of the warrior who'd summoned him and live within him until a task or quest was complete. Such beliefs encouraged bravery in battle that was unsurpassed among other species. Captain Blink watched as the nurses moved about quietly, tending to the wounded and dying.

• • •

The Voyage of *The Chengshi*

The Chengshi was the last of the three ships to leave the station. It departed right after *The Warthog* disembarked from the Human Environ docking station. Captain Kscheeech assumed command and took his place onboard.

The appalling conditions of the mess hall threw the Race Middlefield into a conniption fit when he saw how food was being prepared and stored. The tables, the counters, even the prep tables were downright filthy. Race couldn't believe people would eat there. This simply would not do. He marched right up to the command bridge and requested an audience with the Captain.

"Step aside please, Private," he impatiently stated, to the sentry guarding the command bridge, "this is a matter of public safety." The big Suidonji smirked. "Public safety, eh? Well wait here then, Human." The guard turned to announce to the captain that he had a visitor. Ksceeech agreed to receive him.

"Captain, sir. Our kitchen, the galley I mean, is disgusting." exclaimed the former chef. "It's downright unacceptable, especially the lack of proper care for and handling of raw meat. It's a health hazard. I mean, I can't believe we're not sick already!" Kscheeech waited for him to take a breath, as nearby crewmen giggled. After listening to Race's tirade about the cleanliness and sanitation of the serving areas, he knew just what to do.

"Well then, I'm putting you in charge," he calmly said. "Consider yourself promoted. There's no more capable creature onboard that I can think of. Go fix it, my friend. The job's yours, if you want it."

Race gaped in surprise, wondering if he'd heard him correctly. Could he really do that? Barge into that disaster area down in the ship's galley and take over? *Well, heck yes*, he thought. *I ran one of the best restaurants on the station for the past two years, didn't I?* He sighed and smiled awkwardly. "Sure! I mean, yes, captain, thank you. I'll get right on it!" And with that, Race was back in the restaurant business.

That very day Race took over as kitchen manager, and did he ever put those poor kitchen staff through hell! But they came through for him, all those Spleefs and Suidonji working there. Race whipped them into shape within hours, and by the time of the next evening's meal, the crew and their recruits were eating delicious cuisine. It was served buffet style, with servers wearing clean white aprons, spooning out aromatic concoctions that both titillated the senses and satisfied the tummy. Running that kitchen consumed almost all of Race's time from then on.

Kscheeech, by way of comparison, spent his days running the ship from the command bridge. His task was different than that of *The Varanus* however. *The Chengshi* was to serve as a decoy to distract any potential pursuers while *The Varanus* jetted toward home with the wounded. He was to zigzag back and forth, swizzling as he called it, while he cruised about a day behind the lead ship. This would enable him to confuse any Star Fleet vessel which might be tracking him. Meanwhile, his friendship with Felina continued to grow.

Kscheeech enjoyed being around Felina, watching her absorb information like a sponge. She made every day more joyful and fulfilling. She listened intently and did not appear to judge. Crewmembers told her everything: about the ship, their private lives, their pasts, and even their deepest desires. Her presence improved the morale of the crew more and more with each passing day; not the least of which the captain himself.

Kscheeech took time to make sure Felina knew everything about New Australia, leaving out very little, including graphic details about life there: what they went through to survive, and eventually gain their freedom. The ramp, the final assault, the takeover of the main terminal, the depravity inside the arena, the execution of Warden

Ggggaaah, the degeneration into civil war; he told her far more than he should have. But why shouldn't he? It was time she knew it all. She was going to make a difference on New Australia, he hoped.

• • •

The Voyage of *The Anarchy*

Meanwhile back onboard the flag ship of the Naustie fleet, Kscheeech's old friend Admiral Slout had fresh concerns of his own. After seeing the rest of the fleet departing and having just intercepted inter-space communications indicating something was coming their way, the Naustie flagship took off on what was intended to be a wild goose chase. Only in this case, *The Anarchy* was the goose being chased. Admiral Slout had good reason for delaying their departure until *The Chengshi* had long since left the area.

The rest of the fleet had loyally waited in the distance for ships docking on the station to disembark and head home. They'd been listening to local communications traffic from and between the Police units and determined that most were withdrawing or retreating. This was how they knew whether the attack had been successful. Joyful at the early indications of victory, they'd stayed put in case the Interplanetary Fleet showed up. However, once the remainder of the fleet saw *The Varanus* departing the station and heading toward New Australia, all bets were off. They scattered in every direction possible.

But not *The Anarchy*. Admiral Slout's crew had been monitoring transmissions coming from far away across the galaxy; as the hours passed, it became clear that an entire squadron was now heading toward them, speeding toward the beleaguered station. This was bad news, especially for the one creature solely responsible for the safety of the Naustie Fleet. The mood on the command deck quickly changed from elation over the victory to apprehension and fear.

Typically, an IPF squadron consisted of a battleship, two fighter carriers, and a few destroyers. At times some cruisers, supply ships, etc., would be included in the formation. But the Nausties had nothing like that. Made up solely of converted freighters, their small ships would be no match for the Interplanetary Fleet. A squadron might include up to ten warships sometimes; seven typically, with the battleship being the mobile central headquarters, commanded by a Fleet Admiral.

Battleships were too powerful to be defeated by anything besides another battleship. They were the size of a skyscraper. On top of that, several destroyers escorted a battleship along its flanks to fend off any attackers. This wasn't really necessary because even without escorts, a battleship could deal with most anything in space besides a large asteroid.

A squadron typically included fighter carriers which could launch a hundred short range craft to be used in attacking any enemy ships. They could be used in devastating a planet's surface installations and defensive positions, enabling cruisers to land and deploy assault troops. IPF fighter pilots were the elite of the elite, and matchless in close fighter combat. In surface battles, they were quite deadly too, capable of bombing vital industries or disrupting access to natural resources.

Slout knew exactly what was going to happen if he didn't act. That squadron had been assembled for one purpose and one purpose only: to track down this pirate fleet all the way to its base and eliminate it. *But how was a force this large assembled and outfitted for combat so quickly?* he wondered. *How could they have been ready so fast and deployed in less than two days?* Better question was, could IPF have been tracking the Nausties through deep space and detecting their communications between ships? *If so, how?*

Reality was, unbeknownst to the Admiral, intercepted ship-to-ship exchanges between *The Chengshi* and *The Anarchy* two days before had raised suspicion. Foremost, transponder readings for the second craft didn't make sense. The ship hailing *The Chengshi* didn't come up on Interplanetary Authority registry anymore, and officials on Enosh had no knowledge of any noble family patriarch recently passing away on their planet. Ironically, despite all Naustie efforts to scramble their messages and plan their attack so carefully, IPF already knew something was amiss, and had begun mustering this squadron days before. Now it all started to make sense to him. They'd been waiting for this attack all along. The Nausties had finally taken one chance too many.

Hell, they had no intention of saving the station, it never crossed their minds, the bastards, Slout figured. And why would they? They wouldn't give two shits about a galactic brothel, no matter how many distress calls they got. If anything, the doomed former space station was a decoy to draw the pirates into a trap; a lure to identify where the pirates were heading afterward, just so IPF could eventually follow them to their base. The Admiral could feel his blood run cold when it suddenly hit him how clever his enemy had been.

True, the Nausties' avoidance of using inter-space communication channels and maintaining radio silence meant that IPF's task was more complicated. But the command center of a fleet battleship housed banks of computers, with a hundred assorted crewmembers monitoring information. This meant they could triangulate the origin of most any electronic communication within space – even announcements from inside their vessels. A battleship could track a fleeing enemy for hundreds of thousands of miles through space. Once their tracking devices locked on to an enemy ship, they could follow it infinitely. They merely needed to program the ship's computers to pursue it, then wait patiently until their prey tried to land somewhere.

A battleship could do such things, and the only reason a full squadron hadn't been deployed yet was due to bureaucratic red tape on the part of the Interplanetary Authority. Such a massive undertaking was difficult for the different planets to commit to, and the resources necessary to mobilize such a force were expensive. Furthermore, it was time consuming. It had been several months in the making: organizing the fleet, outfitting it, manning its crews, and choosing a commander. The increase in raids over the past year and the resulting public outcry had pressured officials within the various planetary governments to finally take action.

Slout knew a force was heading their way which could wipe them out; or worse track them back to New Australia if they tried to escape. And even though the plan for the raid had always been to take separate routes home in the aftermath of the battle, this now meant one very cold hard truth that Admiral Slout grasped.

One ship would have to end up being tracked down and, in all likelihood, destroyed, no matter how hard they tried to confuse their pursuers. No matter how clever they were, once a battleship had identified at least one Naustie ship and tracked it, that ship was doomed. Admiral Slout knew what he had to do. His ship, *The Anarchy*, the flagship of the Naustie Fleet, would have to serve as bait. *The Anarchy* would have to be the fox, hunted by a pack of angry bloodhounds. It was the only way. Someone would have to be sacrificed and, just like any brave commander, he couldn't leave such a task to others. Only Admiral Slout knew how to navigate through the galaxy and lead that squadron on an endless chase. He was the most skilled commander in the Naustie Fleet, by far. Even Kscheeech lacked the sort of experience Slout had. Oh, Kscheeech might have been quite clever in sniffing out an ambush. He knew when it was time to bug out. But this was different. Once detected by a battleship, only Slout knew how to keep his pursuers busy for months, if not longer.

And so that's exactly what he did. He first steered *The Anarchy* directly toward them, waiting to hear inter-space chatter indicating they'd indeed been identified. Once accomplished, Slout then turned his ship in the opposite direction of New Australia and sped away at top speed. His attitude up on the command bridge was now one of cool determination, yet he was witty and humorous throughout.

"Well, my friends, now that they've seen us, let's give 'em a real chase, shall we?" he joked with his crewmembers sitting nearby. His men laughed and gave a few affirmative grunts, though many still wondered what the Admiral was really up to. Only a few fully comprehended the mess Slout had purposely gotten them into. "Mr. Brilly, I'll take the helm now," he then said, as he programmed in a new heading. Next, he ordered his communications officer to open up the ship's intercom system, so he could make an announcement to the crew. Brilly hesitated for a moment, baffled, thinking that if they did wouldn't enemy sensors be able to intercept the message?

"Um, with all due respect Admiral," he argued nervously, "with the Interplanetary Fleet this close to us, they could bloody well hear us fart if they listened hard enough. Do you think that's a good idea?"

Slout glared at him for a second or two until Brilly began to understand the true purpose. Brilly's eyes widened then he gave a knowing nod. He scrambled to open up the ship's internal communication system for the Admiral's announcement: "Now hear this. Now hear this. This is the admiral speaking. We're setting a course for Earth. I repeat. We're setting a course for Earth. All departments shall prepare for deep space conditions and rationing of supplies. That is all."

Slout knew they'd scramble to pursue him. His was the first ship identified and the enemy Admiral would never break up the squadron to pursue other leads. That was against protocol. Meanwhile he only had about three hundred left of his original crew. He had enough food and water to supply an entire brigade for two months in space. They were going to be in space for a very, very long time.

"Thank you, Mr. Brilly," said Slout after he'd finished the announcement. He then sat back in his custom-fitted chair. "You know, Ensign? I must say I look forward to testing my knowledge of the galaxy and matching wits with a real Fleet Admiral for once." Ensign Frilbriliram glanced back at his commander and smiled loyally. He'd always looked up to Slout. And now, every day that their commander eluded danger and kept them alive, that was a victory in and of itself. A victory for their brethren back on New Australia as well. It made his heart swell with pride.

It would end gallantly, most likely in a giant deadly fireball once IPF caught up to them. Yet that suited Slout just fine. An honorable death for him and his crew with the safety of his home planet assured. He felt young and vibrant, defiant once again. Just like when he'd been a smuggler back in his youth.

• • •

The Voyage of *The Warthog*

The Warthog took off from Star Fantasy with over one hundred seventy-five male and three hundred female recruits from the Human Environ. Counting the crew and the remaining Templar Knights brigade, the ship carried about twenty-one hundred beings from four different species. It was a very crowded ship. And, with the equivalent of a warehouse-full of liquor, there was very little room to spare. Cases of liquor were opened and soon the party in the troop section of the ship was in full swing.

Vlad made the gorgeous young man he'd met during the raid his personal consort. No one objected. Phillip was his name and, at first, he was quite terrified of the tattooed, scarred-up general. But after about a week, the two became quite cozy together. Before long, it looked like Phillip was enjoying the arrangement. And why not? Vlad was a very powerful and influential man.

Vlad had a plan for the journey home. One that might serve to throw the IPF off their trail and get him and his crew some much needed rest and relaxation, or R&R, as he called it. He was going to suggest to the captain of *The Warthog* that they take a "little detour" on the way home. It was not long after they disembarked that the captain of *The Warthog* received a special visitor on the command bridge. It was Vladimir. And he reeked of liquor.

"My friend, may I suggest an alternative," began Vladimir. Captain Razorback snorted and nodded with a polite if not slightly annoyed grin. True, the captain was a bit miffed at the intrusion, but he figured the general was far too powerful to defy, drunk or not. Razorback didn't protest, even if the man's breath smelled of vodka. Vlad was always such a charmer, especially when he wanted something.

"Sure General, what's on your mind?" replied the frazzled commander. It had been a trying day so far.

His real name was Razzelbrach, but during the Naustie Rebellion he'd distinguished himself in battle and been given the nickname Razorback by his human counterparts. Now he was Captain Razorback, and he was more than a bit perturbed. Rumors had been going around that Interplanetary Fleet had responded in force to the raid and might at this very moment be tracking them. For the past hour, he'd been conducting damage control with panicked subordinates. The mood on the bridge was tense. Nevertheless, he made time for the inebriated Russian.

Vyebyvatsya was standing shoulder to shoulder with his consort Phillip. Leaning on his bronzed trophy, Vlad managed to bow and tilt his head slightly in deference to the commander of the ship. The Impaler then boldly straightened up and explained his idea.

"Why go straight home?" he queried, then paused a moment to let the rhetorical question sink in before continuing. Vlad grinned slyly, revealing his graying teeth. The rest of the crew sat in silence, wondering what he was about to propose. "You see, Captain, IPF will be hunting far and wide for us, for the whole Naustie fleet. Everywhere. Anywhere. If we go home, they'll follow us no matter which route we take. And if they follow us home they'll obliterate us. Have you considered that?" Razorback grunted, worrying how his junior officers on the bridge were reacting to this. Vlad merely raised his eyebrows and gestured gently. Smooth as ever, he continued.

"On the other hand, what if we were to just disappear, so to speak? What if we hide somewhere for a while?" Captain Razorback crossed his short arms and listened while General Vlad elaborated.

"What say we don't go back to New Australia? Not yet anyway. Nine other ships are heading there. Any one of them could be tailed by the authorities. This is far too dangerous." He'd heard the same rumors by now that IPF was tracking them. A few officers nearby muttered in agreement, making the captain start to feel like the general was onto something. "Instead, may I suggest, we head to a safer harbor? Like, say, Frabrak 3? We've been going there repeatedly over the past two years. The entire planet is full of islands. Few are inhabited. Only a portion of the planet is said to have been explored. If we found, say, a deserted island, far from other settlements, we could disappear for weeks, even a full month before heading back. Maybe even get a good tan in the process, eh?" This the general added with a humorous shrug. Razorback grinned and nodded, clarifying the details. It was the first good idea he'd heard all day.

Razorback thought it over. This was indeed a brilliant idea. Ironically, he'd thought of something very similar only hours before when he imagined the deadly race ahead of them. What's more, even if they'd eluded Star Fleet patrol ships, who's to say Star Fleet might track another ship heading back? What then, a pitched battle while defending their home base? Razorback feared that more than anything.

So, the two commanders agreed: dropping out of sight for a while made sense, just like bank robbers after pulling off a big heist. Let things settle down a bit. Therefore, that's precisely what they decided to do with *The Warthog*. A slight change in course, then in a few days they could be cruising into orbit around Frabrak 3, avoiding detection by Suidonji surface units. They'd merely find a large island, on the stormy side of the planet which was sparsely populated, with a nice valley they could secretly land in. Set up shop and wait.

"Set a course for Frabrak 3," ordered the captain.

"Roger that, sir," replied his first officer. He then hastily typed in the coordinates as General Vlad grinned and chuckled merrily.

"I'm liking your idea, General," said Razorback. "Let's give it a try. I know just where we can hide this time of year."

All islands on Frabrak 3 were created by volcanic activity. In fact, scientists believed that the planet, five million years before, had shifted its dipole magnetic field and engulfed much of its surface in a fiery holocaust that eradicated all surface life. Not surprisingly, earthquakes and tidal waves were still quite common. Hurricanes could, and did, wipe out colonial outposts from time to time. Captain Razorback knew this as well as any Suidonji. He also knew the importance of finding just the right location where they could go disappear.

The Warthog was roughly the size of a three-story office building. So, when they finally decided on an island a few days later after orbiting the planet, Razorback's crew calculated they'd found the perfect spot to hide out for a few weeks – at least until hurricane season. It had everything they were looking for in a vacation destination as Captain Razorback snorted humorously when they made orbit.

The island had a giant mountain in the very center, which spiraled upward into the clouds. At the top of the mountain, which was a ten-thousand year-old dormant volcano, it rained nearly every day and fresh water ran down in cascading waterfalls which irrigated a large valley filled with ponds, lakes, and streams. *The Warthog* fit nicely. Turned out, colonists had tried farming the island many years before and their original plantation was still there, now in ruins. Long abandoned to the jungle, the plantation house was gutted and overgrown with vines and vegetation, but the fields were still void of trees. Thus, *The Warthog* was able to plop down on relatively flat terrain and open its massive cargo bay doors with ease.

As the ramp descended and eventually settled down onto the grassy island surface, over a thousand Nausties and their exhausted prisoners looked out onto a world few of them had ever seen. It was nearing dusk at the time, and for many, their senses were quite overwhelmed. The smell of sea air, the odors of the jungle, and the glare of natural sunlight were quite breathtaking for those who'd been cooped up on spaceships. Many had never even seen a sun setting before – some had grown up on space stations and had never seen a real sun! More than a few wept with joy at the sheer beauty of the scene unfolding, as they gazed into the evening sunlight and the towering mountain above them.

"Well, how's this for a hideout, General?" asked the big Suidonji with a grin. Vlad was impressed. "Yes, perfect. This will do nicely, Captain," he said with a laugh, "Very nicely indeed! Looks like no one's been here for a while." That's when a strange smell caught his attention.

Suidonji colonists and their workers were long gone by now. But in their absence, the plantation seemed to have been taken over by new owners! A breed of giant birds roamed the island and when *The Warthog* landed, it had incinerated thirteen of the strange beasts grazing on the site of the old plantation fields. Roasting carcasses were strewn about beneath the propulsion jets of the large spacecraft, and everyone soon took notice of the smell of burning feathers.

Captain Razorback looked at the smoldering corpses and remarked, "Not too bright, are they?" Vlad chuckled. Apparently, the birds, which stood in some cases nearly five feet tall, had stared at the sky mesmerized until the descending craft's engines had roasted them alive.

Meanwhile off in the distance Razorback could hear the rest of the flock gobbling confusedly. A pack of about fifteen caught his eye in a nearby clearing. Ugly creatures they were, all of them. He threw up his hands to try and scare them off, but they only glared back at him. "I don't believe our hosts are very pleased with us landing on their feeding grounds, eh General?" he snorted. Again, the General laughed. At least from far away, the gigantic birds seemed harmless.

Next morning the recruits and troops, as well as half the crew and marines, got to enjoy some well-earned shore leave. They headed straight for the beach. The remainder of the crew, mostly Suidonji and Zorgs, stayed behind. Captain Razorback endeavored to keep a small staff onboard the craft at all times, which quickly converted into a commissary handing out food and tools. Eventually their task became more or less managing the distribution of liquor however. Vlad immediately instructed his troops to go enjoy the island to the fullest. But to the staff remaining he privately clarified this order.

"One bottle per person per week. No more than that, please," he told them, winking. "Alcohol you see, may take a long time to kill a man, but it's always much quicker than one thinks. Trust me on that. I'm a Russian!" Then he gave that trademark grin that everyone had come to recognize by now, eyes squinting, and face cocked to one side.

Fully fifteen-hundred made their way toward the beach that day. It was the first time many had ever seen one. The first time they'd ever dangled their toes in the sea, frolicked in the frothy waves of ocean surf, or felt sunlight on their bare skin. Many got tanned, sunburned, and in some cases very sick after only a single day, but no one complained. They simply passed out in the shade and awakened later to do it all over again.

In the mornings it rained for over an hour. They built huts out of leaves and twigs and bamboo which they gathered from the forest around them. Earthers made canoes out of large trees using hand-axes and toured the coastline for miles in both directions. Then, as always, the Nausties formed into factions.

An island society gradually developed over the weeks, based on nothing more than a live- and-let-live philosophy. They formed communities, settled disputes among themselves, formed parties to go hunt or gather food, and shared everything equally in a communal society that valued free expression and especially free love. Beach life became like a student's first semester away at college, experimenting with the independence and pitfalls of living with no real supervision. Then at night it turned into something more like Spring Break! Everyone wanted to experience something new or seemed much more open to new things than before.

The Enoshi became amazingly popular with both the female and male recruits from Star Fantasy. In fact, when they set up their lodge just inside the tree line. They worked for days constructing it. It started off as a giant canopy that kept the morning rain off of them then lava rocks were stacked up around it to keep out critters. Some of the women enjoyed the company of the Enoshi while others found them to be far too rough. But one by one they stopped by to experience a night with the burly fellows just to see what they'd been missing.

Vlad built himself a nice hut and spent most of his waking hours enjoying his new partner Phillip, along with a bottle of vodka of course. They made the occasional appearance at local parties. Otherwise he slumbered in his bed, sending Phillip out for breakfast each morning while the general lay in a hammock made from vines and thick jungle leaves. Unbeknownst to him, whenever Vlad would pass out drunk, Phillip would sneak over to the Enoshi lodge. Luckily, no one dared speak of the young man's exploits.

Meanwhile, there were those giant birds which roamed the island. They looked much like cassowaries from the island of New Guinea and were easy to catch. Within a few nights, almost every campfire was roasting one on a spit, or folks would enjoy their eggs for breakfast in the morning with fresh fruit. The birds had faced no natural predators since the colonists had left, so it was easy to kill them at close range with daggers strapped to bamboo-like poles. One hen could easily feed twenty people in an evening.

Trees had fruits much like mangos and avocados. Pineapples, coconuts, even miniature bananas grew there too and tasted quite delicious. Berries from bushes could be picked in the morning to make for a decent breakfast while searching for bird eggs and that proved to be rather simple. All one had to do was find a nest that had been left behind by a mother hen who had moved off to get water. Hunters learned to grab two, then run like hell. If seen doing it, those angry hens often gave chase and then things could turn out badly. Their beaks could slice through flesh and break bones easily. It actually happened to early-morning egg hunters a number of times.

Rains came right before dawn every morning, replenishing reservoirs the Nausties created using large tree leaves and some strategically placed empty liquor bottles. When arranged correctly, bottles would refill every day with fresh drinking water. It was nice living there. Many dreaded leaving the place.

In time though, Captain Razorback determined it was high time they left. There'd been no sign of Interplanetary Fleet nor any interspace communications showing up on *The Warthog's* computers. Nothing to indicate anything was going on nearby. No patrols hunting for pirates were being spoken of on official IPA channels. It seemed there was no reason to hide out there any longer. It was time to head on home. On top of that, ship indicators were detecting a massive storm system brewing, and absolutely no one wanted to be caught on that island in the event of a hurricane, least of all the ship's commander.

Just like the previous colonists who'd struggled to make a living there, the Nausties were going to have to flee the coming storm or face the consequences. Once the fields flooded, they'd have a devil of a time firing their propulsion jets which were designed to lift the enormous craft into orbit. In the end, only the big birds would continue to reign over their island paradise. Only they could endure the ravages of a hurricane, like they'd done for thousands of years. The Nausties by way of comparison, despite all their ingenuity and technology, were ill-prepared for such a debacle. Razorback traveled out to Vlad's private hut and awoke him one morning with the news.

"General, if you please ... my apologies for disturbing you, but a storm is brewing. Our sensors are detecting a front moving in and we can't risk it another day, I'm afraid. This is hurricane territory, as you may recall." He then sat down on the floor of the hut and rested his tired legs from the mile-long hike out to the beach. Phillip set out a tray of freshly-gathered fruit for their guest. Razorback thanked him then continued.

"We'd better get the troops and crew on board and get off this planet before it's too late. I've no ambitions of becoming a submarine commander. Another night on this island and we may find ourselves in a bit of a pickle." Vlad rolled out of his hammock and rubbed his head, chuckling groggily. He'd been anticipating this for days.

"Yes, I guess all good things must come to an end eventually, Captain," he replied. "We knew this would happen." He reached over and grabbed an open bottle then guzzled down half of it, causing the captain to shake his head with a grunt.

"It's only rainwater that Phillip brought me this morning," he laughed. Razorback snorted humorously. Vlad gave that famous smile of his; then wiped off his mouth with the back of his hand. "I'll order my men and the recruits onboard immediately," he then added professionally. Razorback nodded.

"Yes General, thank you," said the Captain, "we leave at dusk by the way. Eighteen hundred hours on the dot. Have your people loaded up and ready to go. Tell them we're heading home."

CHAPTER 19: THE ORDER OF HEROIC MERIT

Back on New Australia, there were exciting changes taking place. Big plans were made and approved, in anticipation of their warriors' triumphant return with hundreds, perhaps thousands, of new recruits.

Slart planners and scientists had been working the past month designing a brand-new domed farming facility which would span across the desert. When completed, it would cover a five square mile area, just like the old main terminal which had been converted mostly to indoor farming. Solomon liked the idea, but just like his mentor Architeuthis would have done, he pushed for a more realistic assessment of the planet's needs. He had his staff calculate projections for food consumption over the next five years, the next ten, and even the next twenty. With all this data he and his staff concluded what needed to be done. Before approaching the Tribal Confederation with his ideas at their next meeting, he wanted cold hard data.

"Alright, Gentlemen," began the big African as he opened his morning staff meeting. "Let's get to it. What do you have for me?" Dofleini, as always, had the numbers. He raised a tentacle to be allowed to speak first as the former warlord braced himself for the answer.

"Farm production will need to quintuple for New Australia to ever gain self-sufficiency, Chief Mwonga," he flatly stated. "Even with this new facility we're designing, sir, we still have a long way to go, I'm afraid. We'll need five times our current output just to feed our population." No one doubted his accuracy.

Solomon sighed and rolled his eyes. As usual, the best thing about Slarts was also the very thing that annoyed humans about them. They were smart, no question about that. The problem was that they were too honest. "Quintuple? Even after we build this monstrosity we've designed? Good God," he muttered. Dofleini only nodded calmly. He'd done his job, had no qualms about summarizing the results, whether it was good news or not. That's the way Slarts went about things. He shook his head with dismay. Nevertheless, those were the facts.

"Very well then, I'll address this at the next Tribal meeting. Thanks, Dofleini." Solomon then moved on with the next order of business. "And how are we coming with the new surface repair facility? Any news on when we can break ground?" Solomon glanced over toward Decapodifor, who'd headed up the design team for a new building which could house ships on the surface while other vessels could access the loading bay. This had been a problem in the past, with ships occupying the loading bay for days on end, while others had to land on the planet surface and await their turn to offload. This new facility was to be a massive three-sided building with an ingenious sloping roof to ward off sand storms. It was going to have a gigantic roll-up door which sealed workers and spacecraft inside to work throughout the night and make terminal operations far more efficient. Decapodifor glanced at a small electronic notepad he'd used to draw it up.

"Whenever you're ready, sir," he replied. "Mind you, same as with the new farming center, construction will be extremely difficult for this project. Workers will have to operate at night, wearing protective clothing and breather suits to erect the basic structure. We have plenty left over from the previous owners, so we can begin digging the foundation immediately. We have all we need for that, by the way, excavation equipment, etcetera, and once we have materials to construct footings, we'll be able to attach walls to it. As indicated, we have much of the machinery we need already. A month for the foundation, two months for the framing."

Solomon then directed him to create a list of what he needed their ships to acquire. Within months, he knew things would be taking shape up on the surface. "Nicely done, Decapodifor," he said, sitting back in his chair. "Thank you. I'll inform Admiral Slout of our requirements when he returns. Good work, Gentlemen. That is all."

At the next meeting of the Tribal Confederation, Solomon motioned for the creation of not just one, but eventually five domed solar farms. All would be accessed via the service tunnel network below the surface. All would be in dimensions of about five square miles in size. This, he knew, might not go over well with some in attendance. He anticipated there'd be spirited debate once Architeuthis opened the floor. However, attitudes were slowly changing. Tribal leaders were beginning to embrace a more ambitious future for New Australia.

To each delegation, Solomon's staff passed out electronic notepads with drawings of the new proposed facilities, along with detailed descriptions of their amenities and specifications. Then he surprised everyone in attendance by having Decapodifor himself describe the designs. Barely five feet tall, he timidly stood before the audience of fifty chieftains and their staff as they perused his artist renderings. It was only the second time a Slart had addressed the assembly.

"Massive shutters will cover the glassed-in roof as you can see," he began, "so that in the event of a sandstorm, the facility can seal tightly and endure the ravages of the wind. My associates and I have designed the concept, as well as the mechanism, for operating them from inside. Basically, these solar farms will be giant reinforced greenhouses, but with a few key differences. There'll be dormitory facilities attached to them to house laborers, and the fields inside will be hydrated via a pipe and hose system which will pump water from our planet's aquifers below into a reservoir located inside each new building." Solomon could detect a few murmurs from the crowd as the little creature directed them to move on to the next screen.

"Now, as you can see, the entire facility will be airtight. Fresh air will be pumped in from an oxygen generation plant constructed for each location. These plants will make their own oxygen—from water—by a process called electrolysis." He then endeavored to explain how this would work.

"Electric current generated from solar panels on the roof will pass through water from one positively-charged electrode called an anode to another negatively-charged electrode called a cathode. A small concentration of salt in the water will conduct electricity. In the process, water will split into hydrogen and oxygen gases. Hydrogen will be pumped out of the airtight facility and expelled through hoses, while the oxygen will be circulated inside. Crops growing inside will complement this process of course, by giving off their own oxygen as a natural byproduct." The murmuring now rose even louder. At that point Solomon figured it was time to try and close the deal.

"The latest population estimates on New Australia are at about 84,312 beings from six different species," said Solomon. "And that number is soon to be growing. Already Schpleefti tribes are reporting pregnancies in their homelands, and with hopefully thousands more females being brought back to the planet from our latest raid, New Australia should begin looking to the future in terms of population growth."

He concluded, "Food, as we all know, is what has always been both a problem on New Australia as well as a solution to keeping the peace. Food is what drove us to fight for our freedom, and now food is once again the key to our self-sufficiency as a people. Therefore, I submit that we must see to the future of our planet. See to the future of generations to come." Architeuthis had heard plenty. He moved quickly for a vote on the issue.

"All those in favor of the proposal, say AYE!" bellowed the towering Slart. He sensed that it would carry without further debate and he was right. The Tribal Confederation approved the measure easily, with only a few dissenting votes. This was a vote that had to do with much more than just food. Most certainly, New Australia should begin preparing for the needs of an advanced society, a true civilization. Others could see it now, just like Solomon did, that a rich new culture was developing. A society enhanced by its own diversity. One that could not only survive but actually prosper and grow. New Australia, given a few generations to evolve, could become a microcosm of the galaxy itself. Even the hardened souls within the more warlike tribal delegations could see it.

Of course, this would mean no more piracy, and some were diametrically opposed to that. To attain a level of civilization like this would mean raiding must cease. Eventually, this part of Naustie culture would have to evolve. Many had already begun to accept that as fact, and not just Slarts like Architeuthis. It was time for New Australia to move forward from its violent past.

The first of the ships finally returned, about forty days after she had left New Australia. However, it was *The Varanus*, not *The Anarchy,* which showed up first. This ship carried the survivors of General Xonos' brigade. The dramatic arrival of this now battered force caused quite a stir. Everyone was concerned when seeing this first ship make port with so many dead and wounded on board. Luckily General Xonos had survived. In fact, once he got out of surgery, where Slart physicians removed another fist-full of projectile fragments, he became instrumental in bolstering morale for the mission by describing the bravery with which his warriors had fought. Plenty on board who'd survived the near-catastrophe had told the stories, but when Xonos confirmed their accuracy, it filled everyone with a sense of pride.

The bodies of those killed during combat were transported out onto the surface of New Australia a few hundred yards from the main terminal. A giant pit was dug, about ten feet deep using a huge earthmover. Then at dusk, when the heat of the day was waning, nearly ten thousand Nausties rode out from the main terminal on mining vehicles wearing hoods to protect themselves from the wind, or walked alongside, to the funeral site. Even the short distance was exhausting because of the thin oxygen, but the Nausties did their best to join in with the elaborate Enoshi ritual of singing repeatedly the names of the slain.

Because there was no particular order or organization to this practice, the spontaneous wailing and moaning and crying out of the names of the heroic dead rattled on and on for quite some time, even after the pit was set alight and the bodies cremated. All those who'd fought with or knew the deceased were to sing his name—that was the tradition. However, in the thin air, it was difficult, so during this mass burial, the thousands of warriors, farmers, and miners in attendance joined right in, creating a truly remarkable experience for those who'd attended. It brought everyone together. It reminded them of who they were as a people and the great sacrifices that were made for the benefit of all Nausties.

The dead were lauded as heroes, permanently enshrined in Naustie folklore as gallant warriors whose souls could now join their ancestors in Fukuoka. The stories of their heroism would be told and retold hundreds of times over the decades. Grandchildren of the grandchildren of those standing around that funeral pyre that night would hear of their deeds. However, the survivors of the battle, especially those who'd been severely wounded like Xonos, would still have to endure the pain of recovery, not to mention longing for the glory they'd missed by living through the battle instead of dying heroically. Something needed to be done for them as well, most everyone agreed.

A week after Xonos came out of surgery he was able to visit the next meeting of the Tribal Confederation as a delegate. To a standing ovation, Xonos entered the converted arena on crutches, along with seventy-three of his troops who'd been singled out for extraordinary bravery. Some were in worse shape than Xonos, missing arms, eyes, or legs. But to their delight, a new citation for bravery had been created by the Tribal Confederation called the "Order of Heroic Merit." Xonos presented each of the warriors with a scroll that commemorated their heroism, and each stood with him before the Assembly while he detailed their deeds.

It was a proud day in New Australia's history. These first seventy-three recipients were later given a medal to wear around their necks, something permanent and enduring. A diamond was attached to a silver pendant with the words, "Order of Heroic Merit" etched around the rim. Carvings made of the newly developed symbol for the independent planet of New Australia also adorned the top. Architeuthis himself was said to have come up with the idea for it, and miners selected the diamonds from the mines below. It was quite beautiful, and the new symbol created for this medal would later become part of the planet's new banner: a crimson red flag with a crossed miner's pick-ax and spear superimposed over a partially-clinched fist with claws.

Meanwhile, more ships arrived, including *The Chengshi*. Its complement of recruits was three times that of *The Varanus* and most all of them were Enoshi. Indeed, two hundred and sixty-seven were Enoshi. The rest were a mix of humans, Zorgolongians, and Suidonji. But the Enoshi females were the real prize, and Captain Kscheeech was proud to inform Terminal Chief Mwonga that *The Warthog* was also on the way back with hundreds more. He met privately with the terminal boss in his big office up in the command bubble shortly after arriving. To his dismay, Solomon was less than pleased with the results.

"A thousand female recruits? That's all that we got total?" he asked. "I must say Keech, that's not even half of what I was looking for out of this operation. Are you sure that's all?"

Kscheeech was hard-pressed for a good answer to that question, given what had happened. "But I'm sure you've been informed of what happened when we tried securing the place, Chief." he then said. "It turned into a fiasco rather quickly. We couldn't have expected that level of resistance from the SFP. We were lucky, my friend. Very lucky things didn't turn out far worse."

Solomon groaned and rolled his eyes worriedly. Kscheeech reached into a sack of plunder he'd brought along for the meeting and pulled out a bottle of scotch whiskey. He offered it to Solomon for a nice jolt to get his mind cleared.

"Don't worry yourself though, my friend," said Kscheeech. "I'm sure we weren't followed. I'd have detected it by now. Besides, we should be happy with what we accomplished. Rest assured we followed all procedures regarding radio silence during the raid and cleaned up the evidence of our presence quite thoroughly. The IPF will never know who was behind this. I promise." He then opened the bottle with his claws. "How about enjoying a glass or two with me to celebrate, huh?" he asked. Solomon happily agreed.

Frankly he loved the idea of a shot of whiskey right about then. Remembering his past and the humiliation of trial and banishment in his youth had left his mouth as dry as a desert. Those memories still haunted him, even after all these years, and right now a drink sounded fantastic. "You read my mind, Captain," he replied.

Kscheeech pulled out two oversized shot glasses that were humorously shaped like female breasts. They had STAR FANTASY in hot pink letters embossed over the top of each breast. He then poured them both a dram. Solomon snickered boyishly, then grabbed one of the hilarious glasses and joyously swallowed it down. Kscheeech slowly sipped his own while Solomon winced from the alcohol burning his throat. It had been years since he'd drunk whiskey, but he recovered nevertheless and gestured with the now empty 'boob glass' for another. Kscheeech laughingly poured him another.

"But that's not all I brought back from Star Fantasy," he then said, grinning. "I brought someone very special with me. Someone that can help us achieve our goals and then some. May I introduce you?" To this Solomon raised an eyebrow. The alcohol was already hitting him hard.

"Oh really?" he asked suspiciously. Kscheeech hissed humorously in response.

"Yes, my friend. Allow me to go fetch her for you." He got up and walked over to the door of Solomon's command center office to open it. Solomon sat in his desk chair confusedly sipping his scotch, watching the funny little Zorg saunter over to the office entrance.

"Her? Wait. What? Who is she?" he slurred. In response, Kscheeech snickered.

"I'd like to introduce you to someone very special." He then pulled open the door of Solomon's conference room. "Would you come in, Felina?" he said to someone outside, and after a few moments, Solomon could hear someone in the hallway standing up from the floor and walking toward the doorway.

To be fair, Solomon had most certainly hoped Kscheeech had brought back much more than just a bottle of scotch with two shot glasses shaped like a lady's breasts!

As soon as Felina walked into his office, Solomon was understood. It was Felina Toyger. The most famous Empath in the galaxy. This was amazing! How had he done it? An Empath of Felina's magnitude could shave years off their timetable! He stood up from his desk chair and absent-mindedly downed the rest of his scotch.

Felina smiled. Kscheeech smiled too. Solomon gaped in amazement, then a contented smile broke across his dark brown face. "Well, I bet you two have a lot to discuss," he said as he slowly backed up, turned, and left.

CHAPTER 20: CHASING *THE ANARCHY*

The other ships in the pirate fleet made their way home to New Australia via various routes. Some even did some additional raiding on the way home, which only aided in further confusing the Interplanetary Authority as to just how many pirates there actually were out there.

The Basilisk for instance, was a captured former Zorgolongian patrol ship that had recently been lured into docking with what it thought was a disabled freighter. Naustie pirates had captured it and scuttled their craft in favor of the quicker, better-armed vessel only ten months earlier.

Zorgolongian patrol ships carried a crew of one hundred sixteen, plus room for a few hundred troops when at full capacity. Therefore, *The Basilisk* would have made an excellent reinforcement craft for the attack on Star Fantasy if it had been called in for support. However, the arrivals of *The Warthog* and *Varanus* ended up supplying plenty of muscle to tip the balance in favor of a Naustie victory. *The Basilisk* never saw any action during the epic battle. The captain knew his crew members were still spoiling for a fight. Therefore, when it crossed paths with a civilian ship on the trip home, the Captain decided to let his crew have a little fun. Their victim of choice was an old Zorgolongian freighter.

Slow-moving, carrying lots of passengers and food, it was an easy target. They overtook it and sent a message for the freighter to surrender or be fired upon. The helpless freighter, knowing it was outgunned, surrendered without any further argument and allowed *The Basilisk* to dock with it. Naustie warriors then rushed on board and took it over in a matter of minutes. Eventually they captured twenty-five crew members, plus fifty-seven passengers who'd been traveling onboard. They were given an ultimatum: either join the pirates or be jettisoned into space to die. Naturally all of them readily agreed to join the pirates.

The freighter they captured was not scuttled like it should have been, because the captain believed he could man it with enough of his own crew and some of the new recruits. This was also a mistake. It was loaded with food in its cargo hold and the captain of *The Basilisk* wanted to bring all of it back to New Australia to trade. This would be challenging, given the size and complexity of the much bigger freighter, but the skipper felt they could get it home under the command of his trusted first mate, a Zorg just like himself.

Then the unthinkable occurred. After only a few weeks traveling near the Zorgolong star system, the previously trustworthy first officer turned on his own captain and tried taking the big freighter back to Zorgolong! Theories abounded later, as to how it might have happened but somehow the group of Zorg recruits had staged a successful mutiny of some kind, forcing the first mate, or convincing him, to betray his own crew.

No one ever found out what happened on that command deck, but some would later speculate that he'd fallen under the influence of one of his shipmates. Maybe it was that. Maybe the first mate really did decide to try and go back to Zorgolong after so many years away from his home. Regardless of motive though, the captain of *The Basilisk* had simply no choice but to give chase and destroy the vessel, killing not only his former first officer but all on board.

Within a day, *The Basilisk* had caught up to the captured Zorg freighter and obliterated it. There were no survivors, and little left as far as evidence or remnants of the destroyed ship. Body parts floating in space and a few ship components were all that remained. It was a sad day for everyone on board. Many mourned the loss of not only their fellow crew members but much worse the denigration of their self-image. Naustie Pirates had always seen themselves as something of an elite. The mere notion of a Naustie turning on his fellow crewmen was incomprehensible. This betrayal was quite unsettling to the remaining pirates. It was a long, sad flight back home to New Australia.

Quite similarly, the flight of the Naustie flagship *Anarchy* was fraught with danger as well as the ongoing threat of mutiny. Admiral Slout, however, was anticipating it.

"Report, please, Mr. Brilly. Any news on the crew?" asked Slout. Ensign Frilbriliram had been keeping tabs on his cohorts as of late – knocking back pints of ale at the pub after his duty shifts and listening in on their conversations. Most were longing for a return to New Australia someday, a return that would never happen most likely, and Brilly didn't have the heart to tell them. Still, the worry lingered in his mind that they'd slowly figure out that their current mission was a one-way trip at best. He was reporting on this to his commander during a private meeting inside Slout's quarters.

"Nothing new, Admiral. The usual banter. Zorgs from Engineering section are starting to piece things together, it sounds like. I'd keep a close eye out for them, sir. Suidonji aren't catching on quite yet. All they talk about is how happy they are to have those females we kept from *The Chengshi*. Seems to be solving their problems more or less … that and having plenty of ale to drink … for now anyway. Earthers still don't have a clue, I'd wager – but you never know with their kind." Slout understood completely.

Yes, he knew it would eventually sink in with his crewmen, that this would likely end in disaster. And no matter how brave they'd all been thus far, time would surely test their loyalty. He was sure of that. Question was, when would they begin to organize? When would they make their move, once resentments grew as to the reality of their circumstances? Or would they accept their fate and trust their skipper to keep them alive for another day, another month, maybe longer? That was also a vague possibility.

"I see," replied Slout. "And I agree with you regarding those Humans. Never know what's going on in those scheming minds of theirs. One speaks up, another agrees. Soon they're trying a take-over. Get a few beers in 'em and you never know what's going to happen." He then snorted nervously. True, he was quite lucky to have Brilly with his cheery demeanor, working for him behind the scenes when he was off duty. That said, the kindly Brilly couldn't be everywhere at once. "Fine job, Ensign. That will be all," he said. Frilbriliram saluted and exited his cabin.

He took measures to make sure his crewmembers weren't tempted to rebel. That staved off insurrection for a time. First, he changed the crew and its assignments, switching things around just to keep crew members from spending too much time with the same colleagues. Avoid giving them time to hatch a plot. He shortened duty shifts as well, to give crew members more time to relax. That gave them more opportunities to spend time with the female recruits, which they took full advantage of every chance they got.

Meanwhile for the next month, the IPF chased *The Anarchy* through space at top speed. Slout made it as difficult on them as he possibly could. This was crucial, for no matter what the enemy Admiral may have suspected about the origin of the pirate fleet, Slout knew his counterpart would err on the side of caution and tail this one vessel until it tried to return to base. That was likely the enemy Admiral's orders; and if it had been Slout, that's exactly what he would have done. Just follow at a comfortable distance and track them all the way to their secret hideout.

Slout was playing a very dangerous game though. The crew were already wavering. It was apparent in the questions they asked, and in the way they seemed to be expecting much longer explanations whenever Slout would clip off a reasonable but far too brief answer. There was no real destination, only a very violent end in store once authorities caught up to them. Nevertheless, he was up to the task of prolonging his pursuer's frustrations for several months at the least.

Slout directed *The Anarchy* to fly toward Earth for two weeks. Then he suddenly ordered that they change course to a brand-new heading before getting too close to Earth's solar system. This erratic move befuddled the enemy commander, causing him to form all new theories as to where the pirates were ultimately heading. However, it technically made sense for them to do so, because on their present course they might run into hair-triggered Earther patrol ships. Captains of those vessels had a nasty habit of acting like overzealous border patrolmen: obliterating anything that looked suspicious and asking questions later.

"Let's stay away from those cowboys and yahoos, shall we Mr. Brilly?" bellowed Slout when he ordered the new course. "We don't need any trouble from their kind. Set a course for the Kapteyn Star System." Brilly complied.

"Roger that, Admiral," he responded, as he dutifully typed in the coordinates. By then he'd learned to stop asking questions.

Besides, if he had he wouldn't have liked the answer. *The Anarchy's* next tactic was to head toward a planet called Kapteyn-B, about thirteen light years from Earth. This planet had been colonized by Humans years before and had but a few habitable areas along the coasts. The surface was solid, and there was water on the planet, but most colonies existed beneath its oceans, where men and women farmed plankton and harvested sea creatures for food. The only buildings were shipping ports located next to gigantic food processing plants. There the Admiral planned on merely dropping down near one of the Kapteyn-B ports and unloading all the recruits from *The Chengshi*.

The recruits were now becoming a liability. Slout feared they'd be a problem once food stocks started running low. He knew what he had to do. After another month in space, and with the IPF still tailing them several million miles away, they finally reached the Kapteyn star system.

"Find us a good spot, Mr. Brilly," ordered the Admiral, as they reached Planet B, "Not too close to civilization though. Let's not make 'em roll out the red carpet for us, understand?" Ensign Frilbriliram certainly did.

"Aye, aye," he replied, then programmed into the computer a good landing area that would accommodate the big ship. That was the tricky part. Meanwhile the planet was already hailing them on the main video screen, inquiring as to their intentions.

"You can ignore that, Ensign," interjected the big Admiral. "We won't be there long. No need to trouble our hosts."

The Anarchy plunged through the milky atmosphere and set down on a barren, muddy plain. They were easily three miles from any known port facility but that's as close as Slout would dare go. The planet's oxygen was barely breathable, but again Slout had little choice. The recruits would have to do their best to slog through the foul muggy air to safety. The crew was sad to see them go, but Slout knew they'd have to face facts. *The Anarchy* did not have enough food to keep feeding them for several more months in space. For that matter, it was also a moral issue.

Slout knew if he kept those poor recruits on board, they'd perish right along with everyone else when IPF ships finally caught up to them. He couldn't bear the thought of that. So, Slout and his crew watched them trudge away through the mud with absolutely no idea if they'd make it to the safety of the seaport miles away. Many would fall victim to swamps or quicksand. He waved goodbye and watched them stagger off, wincing at the bright sunlight and gasping in the thick air. He could do nothing more for them. It was time to get back on board.

It was risky, sure. They'd used up three precious hours already and those were three hours that Star Fleet could use in closing the gap. But Slout knew what he was doing. Those humans he'd recruited off *The Chengshi*, they had no idea who the pirates were nor where they came from. That said, most everyone in the galaxy had been suspecting all along that pirates were operating from a base on Rijel 12. The average human, Zorgolongian, Schpleefti, Suidonji, Slart, or Enoshi watching news broadcasts on their home planets had been seeing reports about pirate attacks for over a year, along with all the speculation as to where the attacks were coming from. They knew what reporters were implying: governments didn't want to acknowledge it because it was too controversial. They didn't want to admit it because they'd indirectly caused this in the first place. New Australia Planetary Prison had been an embarrassment for the IPA, and now this embarrassment was sending out pirate ships to raid galactic vessels.

And no, the Interplanetary Authority wasn't going to spend taxpayer money just to send an invasion force to New Australia. They'd have a hell of a time landing there, even if they did. What's more, if there really were hostiles living below the surface; the IPA wasn't about to try and go underground to find and kill them. That could be disastrous. Frankly, they wanted to forget all about the fifty-year mistake they'd made in creating a global prison where planets could simply discard their criminals and undesirables. That's why it was far safer to simply track the pirates back to their base and destroy it.

To that end, the admiral on that massive battleship chasing *The Anarchy*, had but one major task: follow this pirate ship as long as necessary. If it turned out that the ship tried to fly to Rijel 12, then Star Fleet would have the proof it needed to warrant an attack. That certainly made things easier for the enemy admiral. He only needed to bide his time. In a few months, they'd have to land somewhere for supplies, and when they did, his squadron would finally have them. Yet on the battleship command deck, there was still confusion. Who exactly was this that they were following? Which ship was it exactly?

"Admiral, sir, we keep getting readings and they don't make sense," said the young Ensign, a human from the Earth province of Southern Asia. He'd been tracking the transponder signature of the pirate ship and it was confusing him. Was it, could it be, *The Unity*?

"Explain, Ensign," growled the admiral, a Suidonji just like Slout only far less trimmed down and muscular from years living on New Australia.

"Well, sir, eliminating all other possibilities I'd have to say it's that long-lost ship from several years ago. You remember I'm sure. The ship that was overrun by rioting prisoners on Rijel 12, the crew reportedly lost and never heard from again?" To this the Admiral snorted with delight.

"*The Unity*? Are you certain?" he asked with a snarl.

"Yes, sir. I'm positive. It's a match," replied the young intelligence officer. The enemy admiral reacted by sending the fellow right back to his station.

"Then keep track of her, Ensign. Don't leave your post for anything, not until she reappears onscreen. If we lose her, I'll have your head on a platter. Understand?" The young officer saluted in response.

"Aye-aye, Admiral," he said, then hastily returned to his computer. There was no way he'd fail his commander; not with the technology he had at his disposal.

Sure enough, as the squadron neared Kapteyn-B, they picked up the trail of the fleeing pirates once more. The admiral and his staff merely assumed they were trying to land and take on supplies, but when the mysterious ship took off again they figured the pirates had changed their minds and fled before the IPF could catch up to them. Could this swampy, inhospitable planet actually be the pirate's secret base?

For an hour, the battleship's command deck was in a frenzy, scanning the surface to detect all known structures like food processing factories and ship docking stations. Nothing. Everything checked out with Star Fleet records. Kapteyn-B was certainly not the home of some clandestine pirate headquarters.

However, during the time the squadron first detected the pirates leaving orbit, they were dangerously close to *The Anarchy*, just a few hundred thousand miles away. This was the lucky break they needed because they were able to generate a hull reading for the craft. This was much more defining than a transponder signature.

Now there was no doubt. She was a dead ringer for *The Unity*. Only a battleship's sensors could be this thorough, and the Star Fleet Admiral believed he finally had what he was looking for. He now had proof that it had been former convicts from New Australia Planetary Prison all along. Everyone in the galaxy would accept the undeniable truth: that rebel prisoners from Rijel 12 had not only survived their uprising but were the very same space pirates who had been pillaging and terrorizing the galaxy!

The enemy admiral sat back in his chair and issued his next command. "Lock on target. Steady as she goes, Mr. Helmsman." Then he grabbed at his crotch to adjust himself. A look of evil satisfaction now showed on his huge face. "Run away, little chicken," he chuckled. "Run-run as fast as you can. It won't be very much longer. We've got you now."

CHAPTER 21: FELINA ON NEW AUSTRALIA

Folks back on New Australia knew absolutely nothing about what was going on with The Anarchy. Time passed without any indication as to her fate. However, within a few months after the raid on Star Fantasy, the planet was happy to receive the triumphant return of yet another proud member of their fleet, The Warthog. The Captain and her crew arrived at a joyous reception as hundreds of beautifully tanned females as well as some spectacular, glistening young men stepped off the ship into the terminal loading bay. Vlad the Impaler brought out Phillip and proceeded to officially offload the new recruits from the former space station.

Solomon later met with and debriefed both Captain Razorback and General Vyebyvatsya. They told him of their exit from Star Fantasy, and their decision to avoid Star Fleet by hiding out on Frabrak 3 rather than risking detection by flying home. Solomon was satisfied with their decision. He couldn't blame them one bit for wanting to avoid a headlong race back to New Australia being chased by a patrol ship. That would have been a disaster. He accepted their explanations without further argument. However, neither of them had the foggiest idea what might have happened to Admiral Slout and *The Anarchy*.

"When was the last time you saw her?" asked Solomon. "Was she still in the vicinity of the space station?" Razorback could only shrug his shoulders. No communication between ships was ever allowed during raids. Commanders were never to send messages back and forth for fear they'd be recorded and their transponder codes logged into IPF computers.

"No idea, Chief," he replied. "We only knew what we had to do, and that was to get the hell out of there, right General?" Vlad nodded in support of his Captain. "It is a mystery, yes," he commented dryly. "One which will unfortunately have to remain unsolved. At least for the time being. We had our orders and that was to get home any way we could."

As half a year passed by and things slowly returned to normal, there was still no sign of *The Anarchy*. No one heard anything about what fate had befallen her. Not a blip; not even a peep. Nothing detected by Naustie vessels monitoring inter-space communications. IPN News broadcasts which Naustie ship captains could pick up while in route to the Suidonji star system revealed nothing. The shocking story about the attack on Star Fantasy also faded from the news. Something must have happened, but the network was either not reporting on it or was unaware of the outcome. It sounded more and more like there'd been a cover-up.

Therefore, sensing the whole thing had blown over, regardless of what had really happened to *The Anarchy*, the Tribal Confederation authorized Solomon to send out more missions. But this time things were different. There was to be no more raiding, and sure enough, within a few months, trade had been established with black market ports located on distant Suidonji colonies. Not only that, but Zorgolongian freighters were found who would take on mineral deposits, gemstones, and giant crystals in exchange for food. Trade was done secretively by maintaining the necessary discretion to keep New Australia's identity concealed. Kscheeech spearheaded several such missions while in command of the fleet's new flagship, *The Chengshi*.

"Having spent the past few years acquiring knowledge of the galaxy's clandestine trading centers," he told Solomon, "I've boiled it down to a handful that I feel are safe to trade with." That's how he explained it initially. The two met frequently in the days leading up to his departure for Frabrak 3. "Many are the same old ports I visited as a pirate, years before. Some are new. But you see, Boss, all are technically under the jurisdiction of the Suidonji government. That's why we have to be careful. They're colonial ports which can operate far from the watchful eye of authorities. Nevertheless, our ships must move in fast, do their business, and then get out. It's merely a matter of knowing who we can do business with. Don't worry. It won't be difficult to find corruptible souls who won't ask too many questions, not if the price is good."

That was enough to convince the terminal chief. Soon Naustie ships began hauling away tons of mineral ore and crystals, filling their holds with payloads instead of brigades of bloodthirsty pirates. And there was also one more big change to be applied in their approach to establishing trade relations. Solomon and his team of advisors had one more bright suggestion for future missions.

Empaths now accompanied the crews and aided in the negotiations. They turned out to be very shrewd businesspeople. Black market traders loved working with them. Very little in the way of haggling and there was rarely any drama. It was like they were born to do it.

Empaths were brilliant negotiators. They merely stated how much in minerals or gems they had to trade, and what food or supplies they needed. It worked wonderfully. Suidonji and Zorgs flew the crafts. Enoshi Marines continued to remain hidden on board in case of any attempt by port authorities to seize their vessels. Meanwhile, Empaths gradually took over the business end of things, while ship captains did what they always did, avoiding detection by IPF patrols.

"Welcome back, Keech!" exclaimed Solomon. Kscheeech had just returned from a trading mission and was delighted to report on his latest acquisitions. The chief was sitting up in his office watching *The Chengshi* being unloaded, when the little fellow walked in, fresh from his latest venture. By now, things were rapidly changing out on the surface next to the main terminal. In the six months since the Star Fantasy raid, not only was the new service garage completed, but construction had begun on the first of five solar domed farms. That's precisely why he was so thrilled to check in with his superior.

"Great news, boss," he hissed excitedly. "We were right. Construction materials were easy to come by this time around. Those colonies out on Frabrak 3 are perfect for finding what we need, just like we thought. Pre-fabricated building components, steel beams, concrete, they have everything we needed. Just look, will you?"

Solomon peered down into the terminal bay one more time to see what he was referring to.

"It's all different out there now. You'd hardly believe it. Six months with no pirate attacks and things are booming. Mostly, it's modular housing and partially constructed building sections that have to be connected together on site, but we can make them work for our projects I 'm sure. Everything comes factory-direct from Suidonji. Whole warehouses full of them. I could have filled three ships if we'd had more time." Solomon liked what he was hearing.

"Excellent," said Solomon, "And what about tinted glass for the roof on the new dome; any word on that?" Kscheeech was confident as always, only not as specific with his answer.

"Right. That's on my list, I promise. Not so easy to find out there and not so inexpensive either. Not like walls, beams, and concrete, I'm afraid. However, if it can be bought, it can be got. I wouldn't worry. A source will reveal itself soon enough, once I've established a chain of traders that is. Once I figure out how to keep our identity concealed well enough that the factory has no idea where their product is going, assuming they care, which they probably don't." Solomon chuckled. He had little reason to doubt Captain Kscheeech was right on that assumption.

Upon seeing things were moving along smoothly, Slart engineers started planning for the layout of the farms, and the proposed crops to be planted. Soil would need to be engineered; therefore, Spleef tribes took over the not-so-appealing task of gathering manure and other organic waste throughout the planet. They scooped it into dump haulers and drove all over the planet like legions of garbage men. It was a dirty job. Waste had been collected over the years in caves then buried with sand and dirt. Now these dung heaps were to be excavated and the decomposed material processed into fertile soil.

Spleefs made for a perfect solution to this task. They didn't seem to be bothered by it in the least. On the contrary, their work crews had no problem moving this pungent natural resource up to the surface to be processed. Soil production became a monopoly for Schpleeti chieftains. To the Spleefs, this task was no less honorable than farming or mining. They relished their new title as Soil Production Engineers. Their tribes grew rich and powerful.

Solomon was pleased with how things were coming together. He and Felina had spent months planning and preparing. They selected

Decapodifor to oversee construction and allowed him to choose his
own staff as well as supervisors to run the worksite. Felina and
Solomon had become inseparable.   While Empaths were now
negotiating on behalf of New Australia with their new trading
partners, the important negotiations were going on right on Rijel 12.
Any Felina had taken to it immediately.

"Are we going out to the job site today?" asked Felina. She
dreaded putting on that ridiculous breather suit again. They were
designed originally for Suidonji and fit her like over-sized coveralls.
Even with her height they were baggy and cumbersome.
Nevertheless, they were a requirement. Each suit was fitted with an
acrylic helmet which protected the head and possessed its own oxygen
system so one could breathe better on the surface.

"Yes, I believe we will. Are you up for it?" asked Solomon. He'd
awakened that morning to find her curled up next to him in bed. Up
until then he hadn't put much thought into what he was going to do
that day. "I have no other pressing matters to attend to. Let's make a
trip out there this morning, you and me. If you can stand the heat
again, that is." She nodded as she rested her head onto his chest. Now
she was regretting asking him. *Another day out in that broiling sun?*
she sighed. But there was no way she'd refuse.

Construction workers were delighted when they drove up in their
surface rover. It always resulted in a pleasant conversation and a
much-needed break. Workers gathered around to enjoy a cool drink
or a snack they'd bring out in the bed of their vehicle. In their baggy
suits the two looked hilarious.   Crews could recognize them
immediately. Their presence never failed to lift spirits and increase
morale.

Work was grueling in the surface heat even with breather suits on.
Solomon and Felina couldn't imagine what it what be like to work out
there day in and day out. The suits made their bodies feel like they
were in a sauna. Any prolonged exertion would cause them to
overheat. But they went out to visit the work crews every few days or
so without fail. The workers came to count on it.

"Well, alright then," she said, stroking Solomon's chest with her
paw, "I guess it has been a couple days since we checked in on them.
They probably miss seeing us by now, don't you think?" Solomon
chuckled. If anything, those tough construction workers were missing
Felina, not him. That's what made her so irresistibly delightful. Her

effervescent smile, her kind demeanor. "Oh yes, my dear," he replied. "I'm sure they do. We should get going before it gets much hotter outside. When we get back I've got some more people I want you to meet."

The chief and Felina were seen everywhere on the planet, not just job sites. They visited tribes within the planet interior as well, arranging diplomatic missions to go meet with the different chieftains, their warriors, and their farmers. Solomon wanted Felina to see everything; wanted her to know everyone.

The Inshallah tribe were quite intriguing to Felina. She'd never experienced such a thing. Muslims all, they were found kneeling in prayer when they arrived later that evening. As for Solomon, he'd seen Muslims as a youth back in Africa. But Felina had a lot of questions to ask of them in order to try and understand their customs.

The tribal elders patiently answered her questions. They were proud of their little society, as well as their abstinence from imbibing alcohol or committing sinful acts. They were proud of their piety, and grateful for all of God's blessings. Felina listened patiently as they showed her around. She later sat with them on straw mats and talked, absorbed their words, and most of all heard the deep meanings behind what they said. She summarized for them what she she'd learned.

"So, you believe God delivered you here to not only purify yourselves with penance for your sins, but he also gave you the opportunity to seek peace within your souls. You've become godlier in the process, and you demonstrate your piety and respect for him by abstaining from liquor and sex. I think that's beautiful." An audience had gathered around her by then in the main cave where they conducted their religious ceremonies. Many of them started murmuring excitedly. The tribal elders nodded politely in response.

"Yes, Felina. That is exactly what we believe," smiled their chieftain, an old man from the Earth province of North America who now called himself Abd Al Hammid. "We call it At-Tawba, which means repentance. It's in our Qur'an, Sura sixty-six, verse eight: 'O ye who believe. Turn to Allah with sincere repentance, in the hope that your Lord will remove from you your ills and admit you to gardens, beneath which rivers flow.' You see, Allah loves those who turn to him, those who purify themselves." The old man then chuckled and added, "But I like how you said it too, Felina."

Solomon was amazed by her. Yet he suspected they'd only

scratched the surface of her true potential.

Not all of their diplomatic tours were a pleasant experience for Felina though. Some tribes were downright barbaric in their treatment of females. In some instances, they were not allowed to participate in tribal governance. They were merely there to breed and tend to domestic matters. This was unacceptable.

In one case, she encountered a warlord from the Bandicoots, who'd dueled with and killed another Schpleefti in an attempt to seize his property. However, the property taken after the deadly duel included twenty females from three different species. The perpetrator of this injustice was a frightening looking specimen named Muroid. Regardless, Felina decided to take action. One night, she and Solomon dined with Muroid in his private cave. This was his palace and as his guest, Felina was expected to act accordingly. After a bountiful meal and with the warriors of his tribe in attendance, Felina spoke up.

"So much you have achieved. So much that you have to be proud of, Muroid," she began. "Your warriors are some of the finest on New Australia. Gallant and fearless during the rebellion." Proud murmuring arose from the audience of tribesmen sitting around the cave. "The hardest of workers. Valued in the industry of soil production. Diligent and dedicated too, toiling tirelessly on farms nearby us that feed your tribe. Yes, you control a vast estate down here and your generosity toward your subjects is deeply admired by all." The massive Spleef smiled proudly at her words. He'd become accustomed to receiving compliments as of late.

"However," she said, "you have the opportunity to show your greatness in so many other ways, my lord." Muroid continued to smile, only now he blinked his red eyes with confusion. He was intrigued. Meanwhile, the room gradually fell silent in anticipation of what she'd say next. Felina's reputation preceded her, and her charming demeanor put him at ease. "If I may elaborate," she began again after a pause. The Spleef nodded, sniffing the air curiously.

"Your females, my lord. You have taken these beings and reduced them to livestock. Yet they are so much more valuable to you if treated as equals. Equal to all other subjects whom you now reign over. Strong they are, oh yes. Smart they are, too. And when this strength and intelligence are combined, then they, too, will become loyal subjects who will love and respect you as their wise leader."

Felina smiled calmly. She waited for the words to sink in before proceeding. Muroid was quick with a response.

"And do they not respect me? Is this what you're implying? Do they not fear me?" snarled the big Spleef. "Must I bend to them in order to gain their loyalty?" he asked defiantly. The other warriors in the cave grumbled derisively. A few even chuckled. Felina answered without skipping a beat.

"No, my lord. Even better. Give them equality. Protect and respect them as equal members of your tribe. It's what all intelligent beings desire: to be valued and to be needed, to participate in the tribe fully, to be safe and without worry." Felina revealed little change in her soothing voice, but a growing intensity now shown in her eyes. Murmurs continued to rise among his agitated warriors as she reached out and grasped his tiny pink fingers with her paws, leaning closer as she spoke.

"You alone, among all Schpleeftii, you alone will be admired if you do this. It's the next step in the achievement of your greatness, my lord, a greatness which you and all enlightened rulers truly desire. To be recognized throughout New Australia for your wisdom. You have power, but you desire even more. I see that in you. You desire respect among all Nausties, just like your fellow Spleefs are gaining every day with their amazing contributions to this planet's future."

An even bigger swell of murmuring temporarily distracted her host. Muroid recognized that his beautiful guest had somehow struck a chord with their audience. Besides that, she was correct. Spleefs were gaining respect among other species on New Australia due to their diligence in producing soil for New Australia's farms. He merely needed to look over at the knowing smile on Solomon's face for a few seconds to make the connection. But to be enlightened like Chief Mwonga, that was the next step for him to take in his rise to power. My God, she might be right. He could elevate his females to full tribal membership. The whole planet would soon know of it, too. He imagined the fame he would enjoy.

Then Felina released the creature's claws and sat back on her stool, folding her paws carefully over her lap. What she said next shocked everyone. "Warden Ggggaaah was a fiend. Solomon has told me all about him," she stated. Muroid's warriors gasped at the mere mention of the name. Memories of oppression at the hands of Zorg prison guards swirled in their minds: torture, abuse, even murder. Chief Mwonga wondered if she'd finally gone too far!

"It was said that he kept tiny cages of mice on his desk for snacks," she went on to say. "When he was hungry, he merely pulled out a helpless mouse and devoured it whole."

Muroid's eyes widened with moral outrage. He too gasped, shifting his weight on his stool, clearly unsettled due to the image this conjured. Such an implied comparison with the reprehensible former Warden was something that would have struck home with any Spleef. What's more, upper class Zorgolongians had always been known to raise lower order mice for harvesting as food back on Zorgolong, and the practice was reviled by all Schpleeftii everywhere. It unbalanced him.

"Schpleeftii" growled Muroid with a fiery glare, "are not Zorg!" He raised his snout proudly. "And Muroid is not Ggggaaah!" Felina remained calm as the entire cave erupted in supportive retorts. "NO! NO!" they shouted. Solomon winced and sighed, muttering to himself, "Oh God, she's done it now." But Felina knew exactly the point she was trying to make and continued without hesitation.

"No, you are not. You are Muroid. Lord Muroid. Great and powerful among all Schpleeftii everywhere. Great among your fellow chieftains. And with that greatness, now must come *vision*. A vision of your tribe's potential. Wise leaders have this. That's precisely what I see in you too, Mighty One, and you alone can show how mighty you truly are. Give your females equal say in the tribe. Demonstrate to the world the bounty of your generosity."

The Spleef sighed and smiled, visibly relieved. No, she wasn't comparing him to Ggggaaah. She was differentiating him from the tyrant, one who'd abused the powerless. He saw it now. He knew what he needed to do to demonstrate his wisdom as a leader. He must follow her advice and treat the females in his care as equals. Give them rights of participation and equality so that everyone everywhere would hear of his magnanimity. He beamed confidently, taking in a long prideful breath of air like some soldier receiving a decoration for bravery. She leaned forward and grasped his little pink claws once again.

"Solomon and I thank you for your hospitality and value our new friendship with you. Whatever you decide, we are proud to be your loyal ally." Then she shocked everyone once more by giving the customary Schpleefti greeting of placing her nose up to his snout and sniffing his breath. Such a custom was never seen performed except by other Schpleeftis, and it impressed all in attendance. Even Solomon was taken aback. Yet this was something from Felina's training as an Empath years before. She understood customs from every known species in the galaxy. Schpleeftii as well.

Muroid was startled at first but his eyes widened with joyous surprise at the polite gesture. Spleefs were not accustomed to being shown sincere courtesy from other creatures on New Australia, or anywhere in the galaxy for that matter. This was something very new to them. She'd honored him greatly, and right in front of his own people.

Muroid smiled, and grasped Felina's paws tightly, then leaned in to sniff her breath, which was the customary reply. He sniffed three times just to demonstrate his courage, then pulled back to proclaim boldly, "Yes! Muroid. That I am." He smiled and gestured to his warriors to calm themselves. Felina smiled right back at him. She knew the furry little fellow was trying to impress his tribesmen by getting dangerously close to the fangs of a cat! Muroid then stood up and addressed his audience. "It shall be done," he proclaimed. And so it was.

"You go out and tell them, Great Chief," he then said. "Tell them what we've accomplished here." Solomon nodded in agreement.

"Gladly, my friend," he replied, "I will speak of your deeds wherever I go."

Solomon was in love, and an even bolder gesture on his part was now in order. A *personal* gesture, that is. He knew just what he could do next to inspire radical change among other Naustie tribesmen, and that would be to publicly declare Felina to be his wife.

However, he also wanted it known throughout the planet that he'd done so. That's why he chose to propose to her right in the middle of the Tribal Confederation Assembly later that month. This bold act would send the message to all Nausties that females were expected be treated with respect, as equals, and that marriage was the way to express it. This would change everything. Families would be started, and offspring would be raised according to each tribe's customs. New Australia would have a new generation of heirs to carry on the traditions of their free and independent planet.

Once this was set into motion, the whole culture of the planet would be altered. Thus, a ritual would have to be performed. And the rules and format would need to be devised right there in the Tribal Confederation Assembly, setting legal precedent for thousands more to follow.

A wedding needed to be planned: one that would show beings on the planet how a male would commit to something other than just himself or his tribe. When Solomon stood to be recognized before the Assembly later that month, he used his customary five-minute speaking time to turn to his delegation and ask that Felina step forward. He dropped to one knee and took her paw saying, "My darling Felina, will you marry me?"

Hundreds looked on with elated surprise and anticipation. When Felina said, "Yes!", the council erupted in cheers. Vlad the Impaler and his Templar Knights delegation stood and clapped, while Vlad's male companion Phillip smiled with delight. The Inshallah tribe soon chimed in with whoops of joy. Suidoni, Slarts, Enoshi, Spleefs, and Zorgs joined right in with them.

CHAPTER 22: THE WEDDING

First came the planning, then came the arrangements; like many weddings, it grew into an event so grandiose that any notion of a simple ceremony soon faded. What evolved instead was an extravaganza that couldn't accommodate everyone underground. There simply wasn't a location large enough.

"You realize how big this is going to be, don't you?" observed Solomon. He and Felina were enjoying a few minutes alone after dinner, discussing a venue for their growing guest list. "The only possible site I can think of is the new solar farm. It's nearing completion, and when it's finished it could easily seat thousands." To Felina that sounded reasonable enough. What's more, because it could be protected from the forbidding climate of New Australia, beings from every tribe could sit through the ceremony comfortably. Manufactured air could be pumped into the facility from its new oxygen generation plant attached to the building, and by performing the ceremony right after sunrise, the temperature inside would be quite tolerable.

"That sounds perfect," she replied.

"Now, as to the setup a dais can be constructed, just so everyone can see us," he went on to say, "and since there is no official religion here, we have no need for a priest or a church. We simply create a ritual, with a procession and music and some wise words recognizing our bonds of matrimony. I know just who we need for that."

Architeuthis was the obvious choice to perform the ceremony. As the spiritual leader of the planet, only he could stand before the throng of guests and declare this union official. To be sure, when asked he was delighted! And when requested by his old friend Solomon to do so, he worked tirelessly to devise a ceremony which would both impress, as well as set a precedent for hundreds of such weddings to follow. There'd be many more.

"Invitations must be sent out." explained Solomon. "The occasion will warrant inviting all tribal Chieftains and their entourages." They sent out easily a hundred invitations, not on paper but in person, via messengers who traveled throughout the planet and met with each chieftain in person to present it.

Covered in fur from head to toe, Enoshi didn't wear clothes, but the humans suggested a gown be worn by the bride. Felina liked the idea. Blooming plant buds were to be woven into her mane, and a vail was made using pieces from old costumes worn by the handful of Star Fantasy women who still possessed their medieval dresses and Roman togas. It made for a colorful array, and Felina agreed it was a dazzling outfit. Her bridal gown had a train that extended several feet behind her, and when she walked up the aisle to the dais constructed at the front of the assembly, it would trail behind her to a team of attendants who held the ends and marched slowly behind.

Solomon was to be adorned in a dapper tuxedo crafted from material collected by Felina's staff of attendants, and it was tailored to fit his muscular frame. Choosing white as the base color, they created a jacket and pants that made him truly stand out. Then a scarf and tie were crafted using a rainbow of colors that matched Felina's dress, which was really more of a cape that fastened across the top of her chest with a silver chain. This gown framed her tiger-striped fur and would make her an incredible sight to behold come wedding day.

Thousands made their way to the elevator leading up to the new domed solar farm. They started out early, hours before dawn most of them, heading up from their subterranean homelands to the old service tunnel and tried catching a ride on an empty dump hauler. Practically every tribe sent even more than their invitations allotted, but it mattered little.

Race had been living with a tribe called the Jaguarondi. There, he had extensive duties as personal chef to their chieftain, but he also had a staff of ten other young men who worked directly under his supervision. When it came time for the wedding, his services were graciously donated by the leader of the Jaguarondi to serve as caterer. For days leading up to the ceremony, he'd gathered foods from all over New Australia and devised a multicultural menu that would be acceptable to everyone. He also had Suidonji erect partitions to shield the cooking area from view. It was a hectic morning for Race the day of the wedding, the type of environment in which he excelled, but by the time of the ceremony, he was finally able to stand outside the partition wall to watch Felina come up the aisle. Wiping his hands with a dish towel, already soaked in sweat from the heat, he mopped his brow and subtly dabbed tears of joy.

For his best man, Solomon had chosen his good friend Kscheeech, which surprised no one. To Solomon, this was the least he could do to honor his loyal ship captain, and for that matter, the creature most responsible for this happy occasion. Solomon went further by selecting twenty groomsmen: staff from his command terminal mostly, plus a few trusted warriors from his tribe the Schpleeftkorkii. Meanwhile, Felina had nearly sixty maids of honor.

There was one conspicuous absence that day: Admiral Slout and his crew from *The Anarchy*. It had been so long since the ship's disappearance. Those in attendance were pleased to see Solomon's kind gesture of leaving one open spot between his groomsmen to signify Slout's absence. Also, a chair was left unoccupied at the front of the audience draped in black ribbons with a crimson Naustie flag folded and placed in the middle. Laid over the top of it was a newly minted *Order of Heroic Merit*.

After all the preparation, after all the hard work from hundreds of staff and volunteers, Solomon and Felina came down the aisle. Felina's gown's train was carried behind her, and the march up to the platform where Architeuthis stood took several minutes. The audience stood and watched. Many wept. Everyone smiled and beamed with satisfaction. Music and singing accompanied their slow journey until finally they reached the front. Then Architeuthis motioned politely for everyone to be seated.

"Thank you for coming," he began in a booming voice which echoed throughout the enormous building. The spiritual leader spoke in his usual deeply resonant tone as though he were addressing not just dignitaries and nobility, but indeed the whole planet itself. He knew his words would be recorded for use in ceremonies just like this for years to come.

"Brave creatures of New Australia. Honored guests. Welcome to everyone here today. Nausties, proud citizens we are, one and all. We stand here today as warriors. Defenders and champions of freedom and this great planet!" This drew a round of enthusiastic applause from the audience.

"We are also farmers, engineers, and miners," he said, pausing after each title or function to let the crowd react. The audience murmured approval after each recognized role within Naustie society. "We are Suidonji, Schpleeftii, Zorgolongians, Enoshi, Slartigifijians, and humans." After each name, the crowd murmured even louder, as groups once identified reacted with pride.

"We are both male and female!" he then proclaimed. He spoke this in a raised tone and when females were recognized, a vast swirl of applause erupted from the audience, prompting Archituethis to have to pause for a minute until the cacophony of cheering settled down. It was as if each cheer had to top the previous one. A crescendo of noise exploded throughout the cavernous arena. It took a while for things to calm down.

"Yet, we are all proprietors of this free and independent world," Architeuthis then added as the eruption gradually dissipated. When everyone had simmered down, he fluttered his facial tentacles at the reaction he'd gotten. Then he went on with his speech.

"We have come together in this beautiful setting to witness the joining of two of our own kind in the bonds of marriage. Nausties just like all of us, they stand before us today, committed in their devotion to one another. They come before us to declare their union and their vows of marriage. They come before us today to profess lifelong devotion to each other until death finally parts them."

Architeuthis paused. He lowered his voice then kindly said, "Would you like to read any personal vows of your own choosing to each other?" Solomon spoke up first.

"Yes, Architeuthis. I'll speak." However instead of facing Felina, he turned to face the massive audience. The sun was just starting to peak over the horizon outside, illuminating the interior with an orange and magenta-colored glow. He looked down at his feet collecting his thoughts for a moment then raised his face, glancing about at the sea of people.

"Good morning everyone and thank you for coming," he began, his voice clearly audible above the huge blowers circulating fresh air into the facility. "Before I speak my vows, I wish to make a confession to all of you about who I truly am, and what brought me to this moment of great happiness today," he said. The audience fell silent. Few had ever seen a real wedding before and no one knew quite what to expect.

"When I was a young man, I thought like a child," Solomon continued. "I spoke as a child and acted as a child, because that's all I was deep inside my soul. Exceptional in some ways, some would say, average in most others, to tell you the truth." Solomon grinned sheepishly, which elicited a few snickers from among his groomsmen at this feeble attempt at modesty.

"My ambitions might have been that of an adult, and my moral fortitude was certainly that of several men, but my heart was filled with blind courage and naive confidence. I gained a reputation for bravery as I grew older. I gained wealth, and not surprisingly friends aplenty. Men followed me ... even made me their leader. I eventually had all I'd once dreamed of as a boy and much more. Yet my soul remained empty. No god could fill this void within me. My pride prevented it, and eventually my distrust for others made me a cynical creature, who I could only assume had been forsaken when my life was later turned upside down."

Solomon looked out into the crowd and glanced for a brief moment at his friends from the Inshallah tribe who'd made the long journey up to the surface. They nodded proudly at seeing how much Solomon had learned, how much he'd gleaned from his time visiting with them. Here was a man, powerful and respected among others throughout the planet, humbling himself before Almighty God and his people.

"It was only me against the world," he then explained. "It was only I who believed in myself and therefore, I trusted in no one but me. I was born with ability and strength. I saw that I had wisdom and intelligence to become a powerful leader someday. Yet this ambition was never fully realized. And when I was exiled to this planet to die, as many of us were, I finally looked to the Lord. It was only then that I sought Him out." Solomon then bowed his head in shame for a moment, raising one hand and an index finger toward the brightening sky above him. After heaving a big sigh, he raised his head once again and looked out bravely at his audience.

"Yes, I looked to God. But not as a solution to my despair did I finally choose to seek His guidance; not even for protection from the threats to my safety. Instead, I looked to Him to take pity on me as a poor sinner, and mercifully allow my life to end. That is what I, in my arrogance, prayed to Him for. I begged the Almighty to let me die."

With that, he gave a long pause and sighed deeply once more, bowing his head before an audience made up of thousands of the bravest and mightiest warriors he'd ever known. Eyes welled up with tears. Heads nodded in shared remorse for their own past transgressions. Many others sat in awe at Solomon's candor. Humans, Suidonji, even some Enoshi, Spleefs, Zorgs, began to weep. The emotions were already quite high, but even with all the expectations previously held of an inspiring occasion, no one anticipated something quite like this.

Solomon was only getting started. He continued proudly, "But God did not allow me to end my life, nor did he allow me to have my life ended for me. I lived on, tortured over my painful past and haunted by regret. I toiled, along with many of you, in the mines. I served, along with many of you, in the rebellion. I fought, with some of you, for the survival of my tribe. And when it was over, I helped see to it this planet lived on. Still, my heart was a desert."

"Then one day, the Lord allowed my suffering to come to an end. I emerged from the icy cold prison which was previously my soul. God so loved me that he sent this beautiful creature to help guide New Australia and to be my companion." The crowd began to murmur with delight, as the message became clearer. Solomon turned his head toward Felina and reached toward her with his hand. She grasped it lovingly in her paws.

"Felina, you have healed my soul and changed me into the man I was supposed to be, the man I should have sought to be all along." Then he turned completely toward her, grasping both of her paws in his hands, adding "I will devote the rest of my life to you my darling, my wife." She glowed with happiness, as the inside of the building grew brighter from the rising sun.

With the conclusion of Solomon's vows, it was now Felina's turn.

She smiled then turned to face the huge audience as Solomon had done. She knew her voice would be difficult to hear above the sobbing, sniffling, murmuring throng, but Architeuthis gave a calming gesture with his tentacles that alerted the crowd to quiet down to let the bride speak. Boldly, she lifted her face to raise her voice loud enough to be heard.

"When I was very young," she began, "the local elders recognized me as having empathic abilities, abilities beyond that of an average Enoshi and perhaps those strong enough to gain admittance to the local academy. Years passed, and the dream came true, the dream of many, and to the greatest honor imaginable for my clan, I was selected."

At this, hundreds of Enoshi females in the audience burst into applause.

"Like any Enoshi, I was filled with joy. My family was delighted, and the local patriarch even held celebrations in my honor. I was the happiest I'd ever been up to that point in my life. A world of possibilities now seemed available to me. Would I negotiate peace treaties between species? Would I marry a titan of industry and serve as his consort? Would I help heal ailing souls? All of these fantasies filled my sleep. Yet, I was destined to be denied. No such fantasy came true, not for me."

She paused to let the message sink in. They all needed to know. She needed them to understand part of the reason she was here. She had not become the Star Kitten because she was great or exceptional. Anyone can be exceptional, even for a brief moment in their life. No, she needed them to understand she was a *failure*, and that was why she was standing before them that day, now a fellow citizen of New Australia.

No, Felina was no better nor any worse than any Enoshi who'd ever lived and certainly no greater than anyone else in that crowd. Failure and disappointment had put her on Star Fantasy. And failing to meet the rigorous standards of the Empath academy had led to her denial of being assigned a mate.

"I eventually reached the maximum age limit," she continued, "which meant being released from the program. My young heart was broken," she added, then closed her eyes tightly in a look of regretful sadness.

"And so, I came to be an entertainer," she continued with an awkward smile. "Just like thousands who ended up on Star Fantasy. A new existence offered itself to me, and I embraced it. Maybe it could lead to more. I had abilities and skills that I could use to better the lives of customers I came in contact with. I could relieve their loneliness and the dullness of their existence. The Star Kitten, they called me. And so, I went to work every night, proud of what I could do, yet yearning for more. A chance to make a real difference." The reality of this dark confession struck home with many in the audience. Felina again paused, looking about with compassion for what likely hundreds in attendance that day had felt and dreaded in much the same way.

" I accepted this as my fate and strove to make the best of it." After a pause, she smiled saying, "And yet I was wrong. I was wrong all along, don't you see? And thankfully too. I was quite mistaken."

She laughed unabashedly, in that disarming cackle which had charmed thousands already over the years. It was contagious too, leading to some relieved chuckles from the sobbing and emotionally riveted audience. As laughter rippled throughout the building, she raised her voice a little higher, saying "Oh yes, fate had quite another surprise in store for me, when a very odd looking but surprisingly gentle Zorgolongian burst into my life and delivered me to this strange new world, where I was finally able to meet this wonderful man standing next to me." Kscheeech grinned and nodded proudly at being recognized by Felina, while the crowd cooed with delight.

"Yes, a man, an Earther," clarified Felina. "Powerful, beautiful, and spectacular. Ironically just what I'd been trained for." She then turned to face Solomon once again. "And with you, my darling, I have finally found the love and happiness I've dreamed of ever since I was young."

Above the joyful chuckles and giggles, one laughing voice could be heard above all the rest. It was Kscheeech, dressed in his robe and wearing a laurel of flower blossoms like all the other groomsmen were adorned with. If anyone else might have been overcome with pride that day, it could not have been more greatly felt than by her loyal friend and supporter. His hissing snarl echoed throughout the vast chamber above everyone else in the crowd and only died down when she turned to acknowledge him with a respectful nod. He returned it, still laughing and glowing with pride.

Felina concluded, "So I commit myself to you Solomon, my

partner and companion, for all the rest of our days on this, my new home planet, New Australia." At this, cheers and applause erupted, filling the gigantic building with a thunderous roar. It was a cheer for the collective satisfaction of seeing a couple clearly in love, and yet also an acknowledgment of what Felina was implying every being on New Australia could be. The applause and cheers now grew into a cacophony of noise that echoed and seemed to build upon itself. The happy couple hugged each other lovingly. Then they remained entwined while they waited for the crowd to calm down.

It took quite a while, but they were in no hurry. The applause rose up a few more times as many in the crowd just wanted the moment to last and seemed to want the celebration to keep on going! But finally, the arena became silent, as the crowd got it all out of their system and folks turned about to hush each other and let the ceremony finish. Tears were wiped away, sniffles and sobs were stifled. Bodies hugged each other warmly. Felina's words were unforgettable. Solomon's were too. After a long patient wait, Architeuthis spoke to each of them directly, but again with the same booming voice which enabled everyone in the crowd to hear without so much as straining their ears.

"Solomon Mwonga, do you of your own free will, take this female, Felina Toyger, as your lawfully wedded wife and companion. To love, honor, and protect her, forsaking all others? To stand by and defend her, at the risk of even your own life, as long as you both shall live?"

Solomon stepped back and, from his love's embrace, holding her paws, thereby establishing the tradition that would become performed countless times in thousands of wedding ceremonies to come. Grasping both of her paws, he exclaimed in a bellowing voice, "I shall!" In response, Felina gave out a joyous Enoshi roar, which humored the crowd and even elicited some laughter. Then Architeuthis turned to Felina who continued to face her man but cocked an eye toward the aging Slart.

"And now, Felina Toyger, do you of your own free will take this male, Solomon Mwonga, as your husband and lifelong companion? Will you love, honor, and protect him, forsaking all others? Will you stand by him and defend him, even as might require the sacrifice of your own life? And will you do so for as long as you both shall live?" Smiling broadly, Felina replied delightedly, "I will!"

"Therefore," concluded Architeuthis, "by the powers vested in me

by the Tribal Confederation of the independent planet of New
Australia, I now pronounce you husband and wife!"

CHAPTER 23: FIVE YEARS PASS

Over the next five years, Rijel 12 prospered. The marriage of Solomon and Felina brought the dawn of a new era. The former warlords and pirates of Rijel 12 settled down and started families. Work on creating a future for the children of New Australia continued in earnest. The domes were completed, and what was once a barren rock became a home. One could say that Rijel 12 had become civilized. Meanwhile, however, things had been developing quite differently on a planet far, far away that few Nausties thought of anymore.

"Good evening and welcome to Galaxy Watch, IPN's weekly news magazine. I'm Guy Stevens," began the reporter. "Thanks for joining us." The well-dressed Earthman was seated looking at the camera, next to a table with two empty guest chairs. The set was made to look like a small conference room inside a corporate office building and included a large window behind him which looked out over the lights of New York City. A century or so after moving inland to what was once Jersey City, New Jersey, The Big Apple had once again risen to become the news capital of the Province of North America. It was the perfect location to host the show.

"First off," he said as the intro music faded, "we'll begin by discussing the ongoing drama surrounding planet Rijel 12, which has reemerged as a hot topic as of late. Reports have been coming in for the past five years ever since coughing, wheezing former passengers from a ship called *The Chengshi* staggered into one of our bases out on Planet B in the Kapteyn star system. They claimed to have trudged through miles of choking swamps and barren wastelands to make it to safety. Once recovered, they told tales of their brief time as space pirates." Guy then formed a concerned expression on his face.

"*The Chengshi*, they said, had been their original ship; when their Captain had been duped into halting their voyage to take on passengers posing as Enoshi nobles making their way back for a funeral, they claimed they were instead overwhelmed by brutal pirates."

The view onscreen now turned to file footage of the return of the former captives to Earth. Images of the women, arriving from Kapteyn B months after their ordeal, showed them waving happily and rushing out from the air terminal landing pod to be reunited with their families. Next came footage of the many survivors being interviewed by the press and holding news conferences.

"Several of these survivors even hired publicists and went on the video talk show circuit. One or two, then several, tried writing a book, and eventually at least three different versions did get published, based directly on events that unfolded on board. One version in particular, was an intergalactic bestseller, published in three languages and also made into a movie, simply called "Recruit," which was a box office smash."

"It made for scintillating viewing, that was for sure," commented Guy Stevens, "but even more significantly, the controversy has since played into the hands of political conservatives who have been actively campaigning for tougher policies regarding Earth's relations with the Interplanetary Authority." That certainly was an understatement.

Accusations of ineptitude and malaise had occurred ever since the return of the former captives. Editorials pointed fingers at government officials or at the government itself. No one wanted to be the next target. Investigative reporters were all too keen to point out the conspiracy; and found many expert witnesses and highly placed officials who they could bring on to verify or at least allude to an ongoing cover-up in regard to pirate bases and raids. Unnamed official sources were commonly cited, and when they ran out of those, there was always a retired IPF officer or an eager politician willing to weigh in on the issue. Action needed to be taken! Everyone seemed to agree. And like what so often happens, people took sides based on political agendas.

First there was the Earth military complex: not just the generals and their yes-men, but the entire industry of mega corporations feeding materials, machinery, supplies, and weapons to the military. They were the first to champion the cause. Vengeance for the nearly one hundred pirate raids, and justice on behalf of the victims who'd died or suffered the degradations of captivity: that was what they demanded. Many upstanding citizens supported this as well. Guy Stevens continued with his report as the movie clip faded and the camera view returned to the studio.

"The military has been clamoring for a mission to Rijel 12 ever since the devastating raid on Star Fantasy five years ago." He was now leaning back in his chair, elbows perched on the armrests, his hands clasped in front of him. "Back then a pursuing Interplanetary Fleet squadron reported they'd detected the infamous freighter *Unity*, and of all credible sources, nothing tops a battleship's computers – not unless the ship landed in the middle of Nebraska and surrendered to authorities. The IPF did eventually break off the pursuit, but only because *The Unity* headed into deep space and the commander chose to cut his losses. Frankly, the chase became pointless. Wherever the pirates were from, if they kept traveling that far from civilization, they'd perish in uncharted space. Meanwhile, it was noted that the IPF officially ruled out the raiders being from another galaxy. They were not unknown aliens."

No, there was no way the IPF was going to risk having a battleship flotilla following a ghost ship into infinite space and vanishing forever. This was too valuable of an attack force. And by the time the fleet returned to Earth's solar system, it didn't matter anyway. The story had already leaked out about the released captives on Kapteyn B. Their harrowing stories of abuse were plenty enough to confirm that the perpetrators of the Star Fantasy raid were from known species. And where could they have come from? Someone knew the truth. Someone somewhere high up in the Interplanetary Authority knew who they really were. Unfortunately, no one in the government was talking.

"And the former captives? What do they believe?" continued the host, as the camera view pulled back to show the conference table. "Most have no idea, but some have been more than happy to speculate about their observations." He then turned to face two women now seated across from him.

"With us tonight we have a couple of survivors that our viewers may recall being in the news a few years ago. Well, I'll spare you any questions about what life was like onboard," said Guy Stevens. "We don't need to go over all of that again, I'm sure. But what I believe our viewers are most curious about these days is who you might believe these people were. Any thoughts on that? The pirates themselves – where were they from?" Darlene only shook her head and rolled her eyes.

"Same as we told everybody back then. No idea," she replied, "The government folks asked us the same thing. But I'm telling you, they never said who they were." Guy nodded in response.

"I see," he commented. But he pressed further nevertheless. After all, he wouldn't be doing his job if he didn't try and get more information from his guests. People needed to know. Besides that, the network was counting on him.

"Yet you stated, if I may point out, that you remember one of the pirates was named Slout. And you said they called him Admiral on occasion. Isn't that correct?" To this both ladies responded affirmatively. "Now of course Slout is a common name back on Suidonj. I admit that. However, was there anything else you can remember about him or what was said to him that might shed some light on their origin? Where they came from, I mean? Is there anything else you can remember? Anything else they called one another, a title, perhaps?"

"Not really," replied June. "Other than *nasties* – I heard them say that once or twice. Might've been *nah-stees*, actually." Guy Stevens raised his eyebrows. *Nausties?* he wondered. What could that possibly mean? Was it a nickname, or could it indicate a place the pirates came from? Their host could only speculate at that point. And he wasn't the only one who wanted to solve that lingering mystery, not just the military but others just as powerful.

For example, there were also the ultra-conservative "firebrands," as they were often referred to in the media. These folks quickly glommed onto public outrage and the sudden surge in militarism, by urging Earth to mobilize and raid Rijel 12. Not all were so irrational, of course. Cooler heads among them speculated that Interplanetary Authority wanted to bury the issue by simply letting the pirates kill themselves off over time or be eliminated in skirmishes with IPF forces. This theory made sense with a lot of people, but it did little to quell the growing bitterness over Interplanetary Authority's hesitancy to act.

And then there were the families of prisoners still unaccounted for. This group often found its way into the media over the years, and when no further attacks occurred after the Star Fantasy raid, they wildly speculated that IPA had the excuse it needed to sweep it all under the carpet and hope the pirates had disappeared or otherwise perished. Of course, this group had been lied to and given the brush-off so many times over the decades, they were no longer willing to listen to any official explanation, no matter how logically put to them. In their minds, their loved ones were still alive somewhere, and the government needed to go find them. Never mind that in reality most reports indicated human raiders had been seen on many of the raids including Star Fantasy. It did no good trying to convince them their once-incarcerated relatives might well have turned pirate right along with the other rebelling convicts from New Australia Planetary Prison. They simply wouldn't hear of it.

So that now put three main political lobbies, three major factions with financial clout or at least strong public sentiment, in league with each other. The military wanted to act because of the raid. The ultra-conservatives wanted revenge. The families of long-missing relatives sent to prison there wanted justice. If the IPA wasn't going to do something about it, then Earth needed to take matters into its own hands.

But the biggest issue was the effect all this was having on the Earth's economy. A worldwide recession had gripped the planet for some time now, due in large part to competition from economic rivals Suidonj and Zorgolong. These two planets were enjoying a wave of prosperity as of late, offering manufactured goods for better prices throughout the galaxy. Suddenly Earth-made products were overpriced and uncompetitive. This led to an economic decline as intergalactic corporations began laying off workers especially in the mining industry.

When the rebellion on Rijel 12 shut off supply to tons of cheap

mineral ore, platinum, and perovskite crystals, Earth's economy
nearly crashed.   Fortunately, the big mining companies hastily
developed new sites for those resources on places such as the Earth's
moon or the asteroid belt between Mars and Jupiter. Within a few
years, the economy stabilized. Thousands of men and women found
jobs in the booming new industry, which was supplying not only
Earth, but eventually most of the galaxy. People went from working
meaningless, dead-end service economy jobs to becoming highly-paid
mining personnel or contractors. Millions on public assistance were
able to return to work.   The quality of life on Earth improved
dramatically.

But it ground to a halt when regular customers like Suidonj and
Zorgolong stopped buying, Enosh and Schpleefti as well.   Earth's
economy took a tumble this time that many analysts feared would take
years to recover from. People were out of work once more. The good
times working class Earthers had enjoyed for so long were now a thing
of the past.

Yet mysteriously enough Suidonj and Zorgolong seemed to be
expanding. If just didn't add up – unless those planets had identified
a new, cheaper source for raw materials.   On Earth the gradual
disillusionment with the IPA and its malaise in dealing with pirates,
smugglers, and clandestine markets had evolved into bitterness and
distrust.   Firebrands campaigned for earth's secession from the
planetary union. Eventually, a brand new development would offer
an even better opportunity for all these factions to try and push for
drastic change, because it was soon going to be Earth's turn to host
the Galactic Convention.

The Galactic Convention occurred every 4.3 Earth years, so when
it fell in the month of March according to Earth calendars, a choice
for its location had to be determined that would be hospitable for
creatures visiting from other planets. Several cities were considered,
eliminating those which would be forbiddingly cold for species like
Zorgolongians and Slartigifijians. Also, the location would have to
be a city that was capable of hosting such a massive event. Cities like
New Orleans and Miami were long gone by now, submerged hundreds
of feet below the sea. Europe would still be in the throes of winter.
Las Vegas was a possibility. But Southern California was finally
chosen, and preparations were made as well as choosing an Earth
delegation that would properly represent Earth's economic interests.

This started a wave of political maneuvering that captivated the public and the ever-opportunistic media for months beforehand. Delegates from other planets arrived at Earth space ports, finding themselves besieged by reporters pestering them for comments regarding the throngs of protesters outside. These protesters had traveled from all over the planet to camp outside the convention site located in what was called "New Los Angeles." The original city had been destroyed by an earthquake a century before and had been rebuilt several miles inland.

It soon became a mecca for unemployed families to travel to from around the world. Conservative political action groups gladly bankrolled their journeys by funding "charities" to support their cause. The city swelled in population for weeks prior to the opening of the convention, so by the time foreign delegations arrived, thousands and thousands of these bitterly angry men and women were rolling out of their thermal sleeping bags each morning to stage protests, sing songs, and join in with the growing tumult. Each day they gobbled up free food provided by "volunteers" then followed the crowds to the daily rallies or demonstrations. Bands played. Speakers representing various causes stirred them up. It was quite a scene, and oh yes, the press had a field day. Reporters and camera crews were literally everywhere every day filming and capturing emotional sound bites for the 24-hour news machine.

"All we're asking for is justice!" screamed the man with the bullhorn. "We want the truth!" he cried, eliciting cheers from the masses assembled before him. "It's time for our government to do something!"

Families of convicts long since unaccounted for in the mines of Rijel 12 stood next to relatives of those taken or killed in pirate raids. Unemployed miners who'd been out of work for over a year gladly joined them. Here they all were, tens of thousands of protesters, calling for action, even if the irony of that odd alliance didn't seem to occur to anyone else at the time.

Other species in the galaxy were quite amused with Earthers and their strange arrogance. After all, to Enoshi, Suidonji, Schpleeftii, Slartigifijians, and Zorgolongians the matter seemed to have already resolved itself. The pirate threat had disappeared. Jobs in the mining industry had dried up, yes, yet humans thought their betters should do something about it.

"The people demand answers! The planet demands action!" screamed the protester wearing a hard hat and armed with a megaphone. The cameras recorded it all, and the news stations splashed video monitors all over the galaxy with images of chanting, wailing, singing, and crying humans thrusting their fists into the air. It was great entertainment!

When the Galactic Convention finally convened, the hot issue brought forward early on by the Earth delegation was the clandestine trading of energy crystals, precious gemstones, silver, platinum, and other mineral ores, and most importantly the issue of Rijel 12 being the source. If this planet truly was the origin, as well as a base for pirate raids, then a military mission to investigate the planet was long overdue. And, that's what Earth's delegation proposed. They also demanded sending armed reconnaissance using IPF forces to find out first hand if this was indeed the deadly pirate base everyone had imagined. Debate against the proposal was swift and furious.

"Non-sssense!" hissed the Zorgolongian delegation leader. "This is nothing but Earth imperialism." And he was right. Earth had once tried solving its energy needs by turning an entire planet into a working mine using prison labor. "Now," chuckled the Zorgolongian delegation leader, a grotesque-looking Zorg named Vraaak, "these same greedy Earthmen want us to use IPF's power to rescue their economy. From what? A little bit of competition from the mines of Rijel 12? Ha! This is the same planet, mind you, that they sought our help in conquering so many years ago! Or has anyone forgotten?"

This brought a surge of retorts from the Earth delegation, realizing now that the Zorgolongian delegate had just indicated having a complete knowledge of Rijel 12 as the true source of these cheap raw materials. The hundred or so Zorgolongians in the delegation laughed derisively, which only made it worse, and some of the Suidonji delegation laughed right along with them. Now it was all out in the open, and the gloves were about to come off! Meanwhile the Enoshi were not the slightest bit amused. Amidst the hissing laughter and snorting giggles, their delegation leader rose from his chair.

"It's so very convenient isn't it?" yelled the elder feline. "My counterpart from Zorgolong knows very well how his own planet benefits from cheap black-market energy crystals. Yet he has the audacity to taunt our honorable hosts with this!" The Zorgolongians hissed their resentment, while the Suidonji delegates chuckled a little more subtly. True, Suidonji traders were getting discounted energy crystals and mineral ore too, but it was always so entertaining to watch Zorgs and Enos squabble with each other.

That being said, it could get dangerous! These two species had once warred upon each other for decades, resulting in the deaths of millions, but that had been long, long ago. The resentments still lingered between the two species. However, both sides had years before realized the futility of interplanetary warfare.

The war between Zorgolong and Enosh began with minor skirmishes in space between ships trying to colonize planets. The two species found each other distasteful right from the start, and the arrogance of Enoshi regarding their reputation for honor and integrity ran immediately counter to the Zorgolongians' tendencies for dishonesty and shifty negotiating practices. Conflict was bound to result. Zorgs considered Enos to be stupid and barbaric while Enoshi underestimated Zorgolongian tenacity. Both sides were completely wrong about each other, and neither had any idea how terribly long and bloody the conflict would be when they finally declared war.

Enoshi ground forces were the best in the galaxy at the time but capturing large amounts of territory accomplished little. Zorgs would simply isolate forward units occupying captured cities and obliterate them with nuclear missiles—incinerating their own fellow Zorgolongians still trapped in those areas. Enos would retaliate by fanning out and slaughtering entire populations of civilians in reprisal, destroying farms and factories and infrastructure in the process. Zorg fleets would counter by flying to Enosh and leveling entire cities with nuclear attacks, only to be overwhelmed and obliterated by patrol squadrons before they could escape to the relative safety of their own star system.

There was no victory to be achieved; only more massacres as momentum shifted back and forth between the warring powers. Total war was accomplishing nothing for either side other than the destruction of their societies and decimation of entire generations. Peace negotiations were all but impossible. There was too much bitterness between the two species. Enoshi would never trust the Zorgolongians to live up to any treaty, and Zorgolongians considered Enoshi to be nothing more than snarling morons who deserved to be deceived. For years it went on like that, until both sides were exhausted.

It was only then, after years of devastating war, that the Slartigifijians stepped in to broker a peace accord and all other planets joined them in creating the original Interplanetary Authority which had maintained peace in the galaxy for many years since. The lesson had been learned, back then anyway, that war accomplishes nothing but loss of life and destruction. No one really wins, and only the dead will ever see an end to the suffering that it brings.

The Slartigifijians finally weighed in with their opinion on the Earth proposal as well, once the sniping and bickering between Enos and Zorgs subsided. The delegation chairman from Slartigifij, a feeble old administrator named Pharynx, argued against armed intervention, especially if on behalf of Earth mining companies.

"Such an effort would be both unnecessary and unrewarding," he said. "This lesson has already been learned. An economic solution to the problem is in order, not a military one."

In the arguments between the Enoshi and Zorg delegations, it had become clear that the Zorgolongian economy was benefiting from the supply of minerals and energy crystals via the black market. This had driven down the prices of these resources, prices which had been maintained at a lofty level by Earth mining companies attempting to control them after the fall of New Australia Planetary Prison. This benefited their bottom line. However, it also taxed other planets' economies. But that was a trivial matter, at least in Pharynx's view. There was a bigger issue to be addressed.

"As an alliance of intelligent species, we all know we committed a terrible wrong many years ago. Our ancestors did this, back when we opened the prison on Rijel 12. Now we reap what we have sowed. Why are we so befuddled by the dilemma we face today? There is no doubt that the survivors of that rebellion at New Australia Planetary Prison nine years ago have found a way to live and devised a way to prosper, despite the challenges they must have faced. That said, the raids have all but stopped. Pirate bases all over the galaxy have been wiped out. Interplanetary Fleet patrols have been responsible for some of these, yes. Yet evidence has shown that many more have been destroyed by other parties. The pirate alliance that we once feared never materialized."

This led to a long dull rumble from the crowd, as tempers cooled and angry delegates began to settle down and take their seats. The Earth delegation though, was all ears and listening anxiously to every word the old fellow spoke. His calm soothing voice was deep and resonant, but anxiety was growing. Just what was he implying by all this? Was he about to state a rationale for leaving the suspected pirate base unmolested? Was he proposing to forgive the Star Fantasy raid, and leave things well enough alone on Rijel 12? This might have been the more logical path in the long run, but there was no way it would settle with all those angry protesters outside. They were most assuredly listening in on the proceedings. The session was being broadcast throughout the galaxy. Outside tens of thousands were watching it on giant video screens. Pharynx then turned toward the Earth delegation and spoke directly toward them.

"Let us not add to our already shameful past, by invading this planet now and warring upon those who we once discarded—those who we once sent there to die," he said resolutely. This caused a stir among the Earth delegation who began bristling at the inference that indeed they should shoulder the blame for the travesty that had occurred with the creation of a prison for violent criminals, only to have it turn into a dumping ground for every planet in the galaxy. True, Earth may have exploited the opportunity to rid itself of political dissidents and undesirables, but every planet shared in this practice. Why should Earth bear this guilt?

"Our esteemed colleagues from Earth," he continued, this time addressing the entire assembly, "we all understand what they're seeking. And they're correct in assuming that the source of all black-market supply is coming from there. But let us face facts, shall we?" He then took in a deep breath of air to raise his voice loudly and confidently. "They want to attack Rijel 12 and recapture it for themselves solving their own economic problems through military aggression. That's all this is about, nothing more."

Retorts could be heard from within the Earth delegation. Indignation began to rise from their section while Enoshi sat staring blankly at them and Zorgolongians hissed with delight at the spotlight being cast upon their economic rival. Suidonji and Schpleefti delegates grinned slyly as well. It was now Earth delegation's turn to squirm.

"This is the wrong path for us," Pharynx added. "It will lead to, well, let me say it will bring even more shame and sorrow to the Interplanetary Authority. War is never the answer, as we've learned so well over the centuries. We as a galaxy cannot and should not support this type of aggression."

Earth delegates reacted furiously to Pharynx's words. They grumbled and catcalled, griped and shouted angrily. And of course, they made sure whenever possible to be seen on camera doing so. But it galvanized them, making them more resolute. The delegation suddenly came together as one. Maybe, just maybe, secession was an option after all. Earth knew it stood alone in its determination to solve the galaxy's pirate problem, even if that threat no longer seemed to exist.

At that point, the Earth delegation didn't even need to wait for the vote and several delegates began urging one another to stage a walk-out if indeed the measure failed to pass. When Earth's resolution for an "Armed mission to Rijel 12 to investigate illicit business activities including operations of piracy, smuggling, or clandestine trade" was put for a vote, Earth delegation prepared itself to exit the meeting hall arm-in-arm, chanting "RI-JEL TWELVE, RI-JEL TWELVE." The tension in the assembly hall, as well as outside in that sea of protesters, was nearing its boiling point.

The convention chairman, who was from the Earth Province of India, read off the votes with a sternness that clearly gave away his bias on the issue. "The votes have been cast for the resolution from Earth to send an armed mission to Rijel 12," he began with a thick Hindi accent. "The resolution has failed to pass by a vote of five to one." He then smacked his gavel down several times to finalize the matter and braced himself for the reaction.

Five to one. No one needed more clarification than that. Earth stood alone on the matter. If any action were to be taken, Earth would be doing it alone. Many Earth delegates stood up to march out of the meeting hall in protest, but the brave little convention chairman admonished them to sit back down.

"Sit down please, gentlemen!" he bellowed repeatedly over a storm of retorts from angry Earth men and jeering hisses coming from delighted Zorgolongians. He smacked his gavel repeatedly to get their attention. Surprised at his courage, most complied without any more drama; however, outside the convention, the news was not taken so well.

Riot police in full battle gear armed with EIC's containing rubber bullets and capable of launching tear gas canisters up to one hundred yards, moved in to quell the enraged crowd. The rioting that ensued was soon suppressed, but it surely made for great ratings for all the media outlets who enthusiastically filmed altercations between police and protesters. The whole galaxy was watching too. They saw it on the news back on Enosh, Schpleefti, Slartigifij, Zorgolong, and Suidonj. They saw it on IPN broadcasts out on remote colonies days later, and everyone on these planets wondered: just what would happen next?

On Earth, the message from this was abundantly clear. Once again, when faced with the need for bold action in regard to a threat, Interplanetary Authority proved, in the minds of most Earthers, its own ineptness. Earth now remained the sole planet with the gumption to act. Patriotism reached its zenith, as the media fed the frenzy and many Earthers abandoned all common sense regarding the oft-forgotten realities of making war on intelligent beings fully capable of defending themselves. Within a month, the Earth's Global Assembly voted overwhelmingly to mobilize its forces for a mission to Rijel 12. From that day forward, humans as a species began preparing for war.

CHAPTER 24: EARTH INVADES

An all-out attack on Rijel 12 was a much taller order than folks made it out to be. First off, Earth's forces were woefully unprepared for such a campaign. To conquer an enemy hidden below ground inside caves? Ground troops from Earth were trained at surface battle tactics, mainly city fighting and riot control. What's more there had been no large-scale armed conflict on Earth in nearly a century, never anything more than minor flair-ups in Africa or the Middle East. That's what concerned the Global Security Administration's chairman when he called together the heads of the planet's military branches. They gathered to meet in Brussels during the summer following the Galactic Convention.

"Alright Gentlemen, what do you have for me?" asked Bastien Calamine. He'd been head of the GSA for several years and had never faced a challenge quite like this before. "Can we pull this off with what we've got? If not, what do we need to make this happen? My people are taking a lot of heat right now from those damned Assembly members who over-promised and left us holding the bag. Needless to say, all eyes are upon us. Let's start with what we have to work with so far. Karl, how about you?" He was addressing Karl von Spee, general of the army and supreme commander of Earth's ground forces.

"Well, we have airmobile infantry for starters, sir," replied the general, a large, barrel-chested man whose ancestry was German, but he'd lived all over the world. "Probably the most technologically advanced in the galaxy I'd say. But to be honest, airmobile really know only one thing well and that's securing real estate, maybe boarding an enemy craft to engage and eliminate its crew, that's about it. They're elite. They can fight at night, using infrared guidance systems. They've got heat detectors that'll warn them of enemy presence nearby. Short range radio communications can be transmitted into their helmets, and a soldier can transmit to others in his unit via a microphone located on the side of his helmet. But the issue we're going to run into is getting enough breathable air so they can function in that harsh climate. I've heard it's like an inferno there." His observations were duly noted by Chairman Calamine who was listening intently while an assistant feverishly typed suggestions to him on his electronic notepad. He acknowledged his general's concerns.

"I see. Then we need to devise a full-faced helmet and a body suit to keep fresh oxygen trapped inside. Is that what you're saying?" he asked.

"That's right," replied General von Spee. "Seal 'em up completely. Keep them cooled and hydrated with fresh air from a small oxygen tank built into their field pack. Make them impervious to extreme temperatures for extended periods of time. I figure if they can breathe and if they can see in the dark and if they can keep their bodies protected from the heat, then yeah, they'll find their way through those caverns and caves." It seemed simple enough. They certainly knew what they needed to succeed.

Thus, the Earth military set itself to preparing for invasion and after nearly a year, the mission to Rijel 12 was finally ready to commence. A fleet that included ten warships and troop transports containing ten thousand airmobile infantry was soon speeding across the galaxy. It departed with great fanfare. The press broadcast live updates as the planet cheered them on. Many expected little in the way of resistance even if the inhabitants could mount a decent defense. That debate had consumed the news media for months and it only continued after the fleet departed Earth's orbit.

"Let's face it," some said, "they're only former convicts and lowly pirates, right?" That seemed like a legitimate argument and many shared in this sentiment.

"How can they stand up to the most advanced troops in the galaxy?" other commentators would opine. "They wouldn't dare go toe to toe with that IPF battle fleet after the raid on Star Fantasy, so they obviously knew better than taking on trained military units with superior firepower, didn't they?" And that was also a fair assessment. Airmobile infantry could and would mow them down. That's what Karl von Spee and his generals assured Chairman Calamine, and that's what most soldiers wanted to believe. Of course, they wouldn't have been the first to publicly underestimate their enemy, bolstering their troops with confidence before sending them into combat. Based on what they thought they knew about the place they were heading, they had every reason to believe it would be a very simple operation.

"And what of the Enoshi?" queried certain members of the media. "Won't they want a piece of the action?" Not in the least as it would turn out. Surprisingly these warlike creatures chose to sit this one out. Not as greedy, they'd weighed the cost of a campaign versus the potential of getting a share in the spoils. Earth would have gladly given them a minor stake in the mine just for aiding in the campaign. Nevertheless, the planet elders chose to keep the troops at home.

"But why?" asked reporters, "Enoshi are the most warlike of all beings? How could they miss out on a chance like this?" It was certainly a valid question.

"Could it be because of the whipping they suffered on Star Fantasy?" some wondered. Possibly. Most SFP units were made up of military veterans, it was widely known. Many talk show wags would argue this as the true reason for their passing up the chance to join the campaign.

"The former space station was a well-defended facility with a garrison of seasoned troops. Whoever was behind that pirate raid really had their shit together," said one well-known political conservative. "Those pirates really did a number on that space station," he also stated, "and I'd wager that the defeat of its security forces was a humiliation many in the military simply could not fathom." Guy Stevens summed it up nicely on his weekly news magazine *Galaxy Watch*.

"One would think vengeance would appeal to them," he said during one of his broadcasts. "One would think that a chance to square that account would be in order. But not so; the Enoshi Planetary Council has chosen to uphold the decision of the delegation returning from Earth, and when military leaders were rattling their sabers for a chance to join the mission to Rijel 12. What we're hearing is their elders have been standing their ground, waving them off."

That was true, actually. "Let the Earthmen handle their own problems," they admonished their nobles. "Should they call upon us for assistance, we will surely respond to their aid," they said, "but for now let us respect the vote of the Galactic Convention." That's all it took to quell the clans still spoiling for a fight. No one ever questioned the rulings of the planet's elders – never. And with that, Enosh bowed out of the conflict.

Suidonj and Zorgolong did the same. Schpleefti as well. To them, Slartigifijian Delegation Chairman Pharynx was right all along. Officially, Earth had every right to deal with Rijel 12 as it wished, because the planet had once been its outpost. But what Earth was intending to do would only compound the mistakes they'd made by sending all their undesirables to New Australia Planetary Prison. And what had been the result of incarcerating brutal hardened criminals with disgraced intellectuals and educated political dissidents? As wise Pharynx had put it during his speech to the convention, "We have all reaped what we have sown."

And that begged the question: was Earth about to learn yet another harsh lesson? Were Earth forces going to trample an inferior foe or were they about to enter a death trap, a quagmire from which they could not escape once fully engaged?

As the Earth fleet approached New Australia, news reporters followed their every move, detailing battle plans, strategies, tactics, and military objectives for the campaign even before the fleet reached orbit. For weeks the press reported on their progress. It made for great entertainment on the nightly news! The government's approval ratings soared back home. Politicians who'd supported the war rode the waves of popularity to reelection. Folks anticipated a swift victory.

However, this information was also broadcast throughout the galaxy. In other words, everyone in the galaxy saw it, and New Australia knew all about what was coming their way a full month before their guests' arrival. Indeed, on New Australia they knew how many and how soon the Earth fleet would arrive. Solomon and Felina put Kscheeech in charge of the Naustie merchant fleet and just as everyone anticipated, they put Vlad the Impaler in charge of Naustie ground forces. As the arrival of the invaders fast approached, the Terminal Chief and his two commanders met daily to discuss the planet's survival.

"First task is simple," said Solomon, trying to calm his worried commanders. News of the upcoming attack had initially come as a shock to New Australia. Mobilization quickly followed though. For Solomon it was something he'd hoped would never happen; yet in his heart he feared that it would come one day or another. He was from Earth, and knew what his species was capable of, especially when money was at stake. However, as always, he had a plan.

"We must assign the fleet to hover around New Australia until the enemy are near enough to detect our space craft. Then we must disperse in every direction, is that clear?" Felina's strategy was for the enemy to see them scatter, thus creating the illusion that their base had been abandoned. Perhaps lure the Earthers into landing on the surface thinking they'd be unopposed.

"Once we've beaten off the attack, assuming we can, then you may return and evacuate survivors," Solomon added. Kscheeech nodded in agreement. Next Solomon instructed his general on what he had in mind for the ground war: to establish ambushes for the enemy and cause as many casualties as possible.

"Now, as for your part General, we will not win this war by defeating the invader in one or even several great battles. Our opponent is far too strong and well-equipped for that." Solomon's idea was to engage the enemy throughout the planet and slowly attrition their forces until supplies and reinforcements were exhausted.

"Let them land, let them destroy our surface facilities," explained Felina, "and let them drive deep into our caverns and caves. Mount a defense wherever possible yes, but never linger too long if things seem hopeless, just retreat deeper and deeper into the planet. Make them suffer terribly for the ground they gain. Arm everyone capable of wielding a weapon, and make the invader pay dearly for each village they capture. Meanwhile, keep the army moving. Never let yourself get trapped. Understood?"

Vlad got the message. What's more he fully agreed. Defending an entire planet against an invader whom he could dodge and elude then pounce on whenever the enemy was vulnerable made perfect sense. Because he had numbers on his side, technology mattered very little. The darkness of the mine shafts and tunnels was his biggest advantage. "Understood," he responded. "I'll wait until the proper time to make my stand."

It wouldn't take long to find out if their strategy would work. Earth forces did finally arrive, and as the merchant fleet followed orders and scattered in all directions, Nausties everywhere braced themselves for the initial bombardment.

When it came, it was terrible and devastating, lasting for days and days, as torpedoes leveled anything standing. The solar domed farm went up in a huge fireball as did the old main terminal. The new hangar was blown sky high as well. Earth ship commanders let them have it, destroying anything their sensors could detect on the surface.

They fired surface-penetrating missiles into the loading bay too. These "bunker busters" broke through the canopy and obliterated the enormous elevator which lifted ships up to the surface for launching into outer space. The resulting explosions killed hundreds of Nausties positioning themselves for the expected ground assault. It was a real eye-opener for the surprised defenders. As a result of this disaster, Vlad pulled his army out of the region and placed them throughout the spider web-like service tunnel network hoping to draw Earth ground troops into ambushes.

However, their visitors from across the galaxy seemed to be in no big hurry. The landings just never seemed to come. Earth space craft instead circled the planet and used sensors to detect any life forms below the surface. Their missiles proved to be able to penetrate hundreds of feet before detonating, and each time one exploded, hundreds more Nausties would be vaporized. Eventually the surviving army and thousands of terrified refugees fled ever deeper below the planet surface.

To the invaders up in orbit and especially those flying around the planet from a few thousand feet, it must have appeared like nothing could live there after a week of this devastation. From the air, the planet was beginning to look much like the Earth's moon— pockmarked with craters the size of cities. Worse, the bombardment obliterated seven Naustie homelands which had located near or within the service tunnel years before. Thousands died and there was nothing anyone could do but simply flee within the planet core.

But the consumption of time during the bombardment did give

Vlad and his war council an opportunity of sorts. It gave them time to prepare. If the Earthers intended to land and try burrowing through the core to hunt down its occupants, then it was merely a matter of predicting their paths of attack. Set ambushes along the way. Draw them further down. Let them establish forward bases and dig in, then counterattack. To that end, Vlad armed everyone he could in an effort to slow down the enemy. Technicians, miners, farmers, all were given a weapon, and all were shown how to fight. Stealth and surprise would be the key, but so would overwhelming numbers.

"They will come soon enough," said General Vlad to tribe after tribe. "and when they do, you must hide, comrades. You must conceal yourselves in the darkness. Then you must pounce on the invader like angry hornets. Kill them before they kill you. Show them no mercy. They will offer none in return, I promise you. We must fight for our own survival or there will be nothing left when they're done!" The only question was whether they could outlast the enemy onslaught once it began.

That said, Vlad did still have forty thousand warriors under his direct command. He had Solomon, who had moved his command center deep underground in anticipation of the ground attack; and of course, he had the remarkable Felina traveling constantly throughout the planet, rallying terrified Nausties or securing new living facilities for the now growing number of refugees. Felina became an incredible motivator.

"The Earthmen are coming my friends!" she warned them in speech after speech, "and we shall fight them until they're defeated! You see, only when we have won this war … only when we have driven them from our planet … only then will we have won our independence. Fight them anyway you can brothers and sisters, and never yield. They came a long way from Earth to kill us. Let's make them regret their arrogance!" Many heeded the call. Many others set to work supporting the war effort in other ways.

First off was the production of breather units. These included a small air tube connected to a mouth piece. The other end connected to a device which converted water to oxygen by separating out hydrogen, leaving breathable air to inhale. Electrical current passed through a small tank of water strapped to the back. It was a crude system, but it was light, it worked, and it was very easy to mass-produce. It was certainly durable enough for miners to use during an average work shift—so it could handle the rigors of combat. A factory was set up for creating hundreds of these a day—way down deep inside the planet—and it soon employed over a thousand new workers from among the refugees.

Next came weapons, and many of these were quite ingenious. Nausties knew that airmobile infantry from Earth would be armed with Electrical Impulse Cannons that could spray .30 caliber projectiles in quick bursts. They had enough rounds in their cartridges for an extended firefight, so the best solution was to hit their flanks with incendiaries, or perhaps draw them into tunnels and detonate explosives to cause cave-ins.

Clay pots were sufficient for this in burning faces or hands but also in disrupting their breathing systems. Enemy airmobile troops would likely carry oxygen tanks, and these could be ruptured causing mayhem among packs of attacking soldiers. But there were even more surprises in store for the invaders.

Darts made of pig iron could be fired at the enemy by using a crossbow mechanism created originally during the Naustie Civil War years before. Slart engineers standardized this concept and developed factories to mass produce them. These were excellent for ambushes and anyone could operate them for at least one salvo before fleeing the battle and running to safety. That being said, Earth troops had absolutely no intention of facing roaming bands of crazed warriors with nothing but lightly armed infantry. Seems they'd brought along a rather nasty surprise of their own.

Finally, it came time for the ground attack and the sky filled with space craft. But as troop carriers set down upon the planet surface, large shoe box-shaped craft planted down several hundred yards away from them. These ships were three times the size of troop transports, and when their ionic wind thrusters began contacting the desert surface from one hundred feet in the air; they stirred up a cloud of dust the size of a football stadium. Once landed and the dust began to settle, their enormous cargo bays opened and from inside rolled out monstrous tunneling vehicles that had been donated by mining companies and altered for combat.

These gigantic machines had a massive drill bit that protruded twenty feet from the front of the vehicle. Each was mounted onto a chassis with enormous tracks to move it about instead of wheels, so it was capable of burrowing through tunnel cave-ins, or even creating new tunnels to try and encircle a well-entrenched defender. What's more, each of these fifty steel monsters had been altered to include a troop carriage on top which contained units of twenty to thirty-five soldiers, protected inside a climate-controlled reinforced steel cabin.

These tunnel tanks stood about thirty feet high at their tallest point. Attacking the front was all but impossible. All the Nausties would see coming at them was a spinning metal drill. Attacking the sides was suicidal too as the crew of fifteen to twenty operated fifty caliber guns which could spray projectiles in several directions. The rear was nothing but a wall of thick steel which could be opened to create a ramp for troops to spill out and perform mop-operations. What's more, the roof of the craft was solid metal and the electric engines were safely located underneath, just inside the reinforced belly of the craft. No defense could withstand them, and no amount of bravery could endure a fire-fight with one. From the moment they faced one of these steel giants in combat, Naustie troops could see they were totally outmatched.

And that wasn't all. General von Spee and his staff entered the war with a good amount of intelligence about New Australia's interior. The entire network was designed and built by Earth mining engineers. They knew the original layout of the planet's underground system of tunnels, elevator shafts, and caverns. These plans were shown to General von Spee and most tank operators had at least a rudimentary knowledge of the mine network. They carried a map of it inside their command bridge.

"We should be able to operate below the surface for months if need be," General von Spee boasted to his staff. And in the view of most at Fleet Command, it was only a matter of time before they'd achieve absolute victory. "Forward units are to eliminate resistance and then to exterminate all living creatures they can find," he went on to say. "No one is to be spared. If it breathes, we kill it." Those were his orders – and they came from the very top. Meanwhile, supply channels were established to keep forward units well-supplied and constantly moving. The onslaught needed to be just as constant as it was brutal.

In the first week of the ground campaign Earth troops moved virtually unopposed through a hellish wasteland in the areas near the service tunnel. Dead bodies lay everywhere. Naustie army units simply had no solution for the tunnel tanks and wherever they went the army retreated, telling every villager in their path to flee to unoccupied territory. The previous strategy of forcing the enemy to capture tribal homeland after tribal homeland in exhaustive engagements was clearly no longer feasible. Airmobile troops simply spilled out the back of those metal beasts and rampaged through villages destroying everything. Naustie civilians caught within these areas were executed on site and hiding out inside burrows or dugouts did them no good either. Earther troops with infrared sensors could detect body heat and see life forms hiding behind rock formations. Tanks would drive through whatever they were hiding behind, and mercilessly roll right over them.

Casualties for Earth forces were comparatively light. By the end of the second week, it seemed everything was going General von Spee's way. Setting ambushes rarely worked, except to kill four or five Earthers at the cost of twenty or even a hundred Nausties. Vlad and his army could only retreat further below and try to survive another day. What's more, the fifty tunnel tanks were able to fan out and spread destruction in multiple directions, leaving Vlad at a loss as to exactly where to counterattack them. They needed a better plan and fast otherwise things were going to get desperate. Clearly the tunnel tanks were moving in patterns that indicated they were trying to drive the Naustie Army to a point within the core of the planet where the columns could converge for one last battle and annihilate them. The only question was where.

"The patterns of their movement," Decapodifor told Solomon, "are forming a sort of spiral. Look." He gestured toward a large map of the New Australia mine network as Solomon nodded and observed. The old Slart then pointed to several points on the map where battle sites had been marked, making a swirling motion as he moved downward. "Imagine a marble rolling around the inside of a funnel. The marble moves slowly around the outside of the cone at first, then speeds up as it reaches the base. See?" Felina wasn't in need of a clever metaphor this time however. What it looked like to her was the enemy were simply hunting the Naustie Army, attempting to trap and destroy it near the bottom of the mine. A cold chill ran through her body as she began to sense the inevitable.

But then reports came back one day about an enemy tank which by accident penetrated a volcanic vent shaft. The shaft ran from the molten core up to a dormant volcano. This natural anomaly within the planet's interior had been discovered by miners only within the past few years so Earth mining engineers from years before could never have mapped it. Naturally, the release of noxious gas from the vent quickly cleared out the cavern of Earth troops who feared for their lives! But what intrigued Solomon and his staff was just how did the Earth men not notice the increase in heat as they drove closer?

As the surviving enemy tanks retreated, they created a cave-in which sealed off the shaft. Naustie Army units, when they retook the neighboring village a few days later, discovered this had happened and found where the lead tank had accidentally smashed through the wall of the volcanic vent and plunged thousands of feet into the molten core of the planet. Everyone celebrated the minor victory. A tank had finally been destroyed.

Yet Solomon still had to pose the question: "Just how could they not know they were getting close to a volcano? The heat in that tunnel would have been unbearable to any Earthman, unbearable to all of us!" He looked around at Felina and their staff as they met inside the command cave.

"Was it because of those climate-controlled suits they're wearing?" he asked. Decapodifor thought about it for a moment. Solomon had raised a good point. Naustie miners working near this area typically wore protective clothing at all times, and the heat was so stifling they had to take breaks every hour to cool off. However, these invaders somehow didn't detect the sudden increase in temperature before they'd inadvertently caused their own deaths.

"That is the only plausible explanation," he replied to Felina.

But that only piqued Solomon's curiosity. He couldn't resist asking the next, even more provocative question. "Gentlemen, just what would have happened if this had occurred, say, deeper and closer to the planet core? And what if it had not been a tank, but an explosive charge? Could it have caused an eruption?"

CHAPTER 25: HELL CRACKS OPEN

"Could a volcanic explosion be caused by our own efforts? Could it cause a chain reaction?" asked Solomon. This drew several blank looks, but Felina was nodding.

A Slart among his staff who could fielded the question, a slightly-built creature named Skyles who once lived among the Why-O's. He'd recently joined the planning staff after several years re-developing the planet's mining operation however, it was known he had an affinity for volcanology. As a younger Slartigifijian, he'd studied geology which made him immensely valuable as a prisoner working in the mines, but his greatest passion by far was the study of volcanos. Skyles eagerly responded.

"If you want to try causing a volcano to erupt, you'll need to do a few things beforehand, Chief Mwonga." All eyes were soon fixed upon the normally shy fellow. Felina gestured for him to continue. It was about time to find out if the odd-looking creature was a good addition to the team.

"First you must find a volcano that is already showing signs of magma instability," he then said. "This might be high levels of volcanic gases, shallow earthquakes, or deformation of the volcanic shaft. Basically, you want something primed to go." Solomon could see why the Why-O's tribe recommended him. Sounded like he knew his stuff!

"We have one such magma chamber about ten miles below the surface and it's located right underneath one of our tribal territories. May I show you?" he asked. Solomon nodded emphatically.

"Yes, please do," he said. He then watched as the diminutive Slart rose up from the floor and proceeded across the cave to a bare wall.

Skyles took out a grease pencil that miners often used and drew a diagram of New Australia. He drew a big circle and detailed the interior of it, showing the location of where they were in relation to the magma chamber. He also marked where the lands of one tribe were located nearby. A volcanic vent did indeed lead right past or next to this massive cavern where miners had been digging out industrial diamonds for the past several years. While he drew the enormous picture on a smoothed off section, he continued to educate Solomon and the others on how a volcanic eruption can be triggered.

"You need to figure out a way to release the lithostatic pressure that's keeping the cork on the bottle. This must be done so that bubbles can form. Think of a bottle of champagne. When sealed inside the bottle, the liquid is dormant. As we know, once the cap is released, the carbon inside the liquid tries to escape violently. Thus, if we were to set up enough explosives to remove this cap, then this could create instability in the magma below." Solomon was beginning to believe it might be feasible.

"Ah, so then it can be done with explosives?" he asked, thinking it was now merely a matter of collecting enough materials to detonate over the top of the magma chamber and release the deadly forces below. But that was not all they'd have to do unfortunately.

"Not exactly, Chief," replied the little Slart. He was shorter than the others currently working for Solomon and his face was more elongated – as if he were a different race of Slartigifijian. "To set off an eruption, we would then need to figure out how to get a lot of water into the magma chamber rather quickly and rather suddenly." As Skyles envisioned it the eruption could be triggered much like the Indonesian volcano Krakatoa which erupted on Earth back in 1883.

"It could work very similarly to a disaster which occurred on your planet nearly a thousand years ago. There was once an island there called Krakatau. You know of this event?" he asked. Solomon vaguely remembered the name. A series of massive explosions destroyed most of the island, as he recalled. He'd once read about it during middle school: equivalent of two hundred megatons of TNT – about thirteen hundred times the yield of the atomic bomb dropped on Hiroshima during World War II. One hundred sixty-five villages and towns were destroyed and at least thirty-six thousand people died, with many thousands more injured.

"Yes, I'm familiar with it," he replied.

"Well you see, in this case a series of earthquakes led to the rushing of sea water into opened volcanic vents, and the resulting instability led to a series of explosions, which at one point occurred every ten minutes over a two-day period. That, I believe, is how it could be done," explained Skyles. "Millions of tons of water flowing into an already unstable magma chamber."

"You see, dropping a bomb into a volcano doesn't address the pressure issue, because the explosion couldn't possibly remove enough of the overlying rocks to release lithostatic pressure. Drilling into a volcano won't work either. That would be like trying to bleed a giant blothar to death with a single needle prick. Not enough pressure would be released to really make a difference." Now it made sense. That's why the Earthmen in the rest of the column behind the doomed tunnel tank did not perish in a volcanic holocaust.

Skyles then paused again and waited patiently for all this science to sink in with Solomon. Out of respect, he waited for his commander to ask any clarifying questions. Seeing none, he continued. "Here's how I think we can do it." Solomon smiled with relief. He had sensed all along that the odd-looking Slart knew just how to cause a volcanic eruption and this was now his moment to shine.

The little fellow went on to detail his proposal to Solomon and the rest of the team. Reactions were mixed; but as much as Solomon could understand, it was clear that the planet had everything necessary to cause a massive eruption. The only challenge, as Skyles cautioned his commander, was the issue of time. Could the triggers be put into place at just the right time—and cause an eruption at just the right moment—when Earth forces were massed in a confined area and most vulnerable? An even better question was whether the rest of the planet could survive the succeeding explosions which would consume thousands of miles of tunnels and shafts!

Luckily for the planning team it was up to their commanders to decide if they should proceed. Felina and Solomon didn't hesitate.

They listened to Skyles explain his plan and when the presentation concluded, Felina simply said, "Very good. Makes sense to me." Solomon met her gaze, nodded, and said, "Let's do it." After the meeting, Naustie Central Command sprang into action.

Orders were issued, and tasks were delegated. Felina went out and organized units of tunneling crews, taking some Suidonji battle units out of the front lines to begin digging. The soldiers were not told why, but each day they'd be given diagrams and told the direction and distance they were to cut. Teams worked in shifts around the clock, rotating in fresh crewmen to keep up the pace. No, they were never told why they were creating all these new tunnels, but they were told this: "You'll have to hurry!" Earther tunnel tanks were progressing rapidly toward them from many different sections of the mine.

The plan was complicated but nevertheless ingenious: construct a system of channels for the volcanic vents to reach subterranean glacial ice. These glaciers were located throughout the planet and on top of them were subterranean aquifers that held millions of gallons of water. The heat from the volcanic vents would melt the ice and drain glacier water down into the magma chamber below. The water would then create instability and cause pressure to build just like sea water did at Krakatoa. Eventually, once the magma chamber reached an acceptable level of agitation, charges could be placed underneath the cavern floor located above this massive chamber and detonated.

The resulting blast would release the pressure and likely cause an eruption which would send lava shooting up tunnels and shafts and incinerating everything in its path. It was dangerous, yes, but Solomon and Felina believed it would work. They would calculate all probabilities for success and take into consideration potential threats to the rest of the planet. More specifically they would calculate acceptable losses to the Naustie population, but that was something Solomon and Felina didn't like to think about.

Such an approach to the planet's defense did, indeed, have its drawbacks. The team warned them that once unleashed, the lava flow was bound to go wherever it pleased. It might very well wipe out enemy units, yes, but it would also devastate much of the planet in the process – and that was only if they created an eruption large enough. There was nothing they could do to control it once it began. The calculations showed that several areas within Rijel 12 would be obliterated no matter what happened. This meant large portions of

Nausties would need to be relocated.

Felina visited the areas which would be devastated by the resulting cataclysm. She pleaded with some of the more stubborn chieftains to evacuate their homelands and move further away from the enemy to safer locations below. She traveled everywhere, giving speeches to terrified villagers and demoralized warriors.

"The tanks are coming my friends. Leave your homes so that our army may fight the invader. A new homeland awaits you elsewhere, but for now you must leave."

To each village she'd give that speech and each time it was argued vehemently. Schpleefti tribes working near the planet core were adamant about staying and fighting. Enoshi tribes who'd been isolated down there for decades protested as well. And they had a point. Had not General Vladimir already visited weeks before telling them to stand their ground and fight? It was actually an Enoshi tribal chieftain who posed this argument best. After she spoke to his tribe gathered in the center of their cavern, Chief Razor of the Cave Lions climbed up on a huge stalagmite and addressed the crowd.

" Felina tells us leave this place and abandon homes. She tells us not stay and fight. Army going to kill Earther soldier with fiery lava." He glanced over at Felina and nodded his head out of respect. Then he continued.

"So be it. We trust Felina and so we shall do as she bids. However, Cave Lion know that lava has no master." He put his hands on his hips and thrust out his chest defiantly, inhaling before he continued.

"Lava take commands from no one," he then said. "Does what it wills. Lava go wherever it wishes. Explosion, Felina says, will kill the invader. And I, Razor, Chieftain of the Cave Lion, agree. But lava will surely kill Naustie too." He pointed out at the crowd, then concluded, "Earther troops will die, yes, but I believe so will all of us!"

The crowd jeered at Felina as she stood on a platform of steel plating erected over a group of stalagmites. The cavern was the size of an auditorium. Though relatively young as a tribe, having been established only within the past thirty years, the Cave Lions were extremely loyal to their lands and considered the volcano beneath them to be sacred. For three decades they'd been scratching out an existence mining industrial diamond. The cavern was located right next to a volcanic fissure that bubbled up hot mineral water into a large spring. They'd carved out caves to live in during the past few years, and recently begun having children. Mewing babies could be heard back in their caves, while a thousand of them stood voicing their disdain.

"This is a disgrace!" some said. "If we are going to die, then let us do so in battle with the enemy. That would be more honorable! Let us fight!" Felina, the negotiator, cool and calm as ever, merely nodded patiently and waited for the uproar to subside.

"Yes, brave and mighty Chief Razor," she replied. "I wish for you and your tribe to follow me out of this cavern and abandon your homes. For when the tunnelers have burrowed under to allow charges to be placed beneath our feet, when the blasts create a gash in this floor below us, the effect could very well be global holocaust. A dangerous force that, once unleashed, wipes out all life on New Australia." She paused for the crowd to absorb this. There was no use telling them everything was going to be okay when she had no real assurances to give them.

"However, I must tell you that wise Slartigifijians have calculated that the seams created from this detonation will explode gases and lava upward through the shafts occupied by our enemy. If successful, fire will race through those shafts, back to the planet surface, wiping out those coming to kill us."

Felina then paused for a moment. Her audience was almost completely silent, and in a sense, they seemed to be hanging on her very words, anticipating her next sentence with great anxiety. If she could just say the right thing, they'd follow her out of that cavern. But what could she say? Perhaps she was asking too much of them, such proud beings intending to die gloriously rather than flee before the enemy. That's when it occurred to her. They revered the volcano underneath them as though it were a god. A smile grew across Felina's face. The words formed in her mind and on her lips without her even measuring what she said. She was merely channeling what she felt from her audience and speaking instinctively.

"Therefore, I say let the planet decide if we live or die!" she blurted out, then paused to give herself a chance to think about what she'd just said and consider whether it even made sense. Suddenly she started nodding enthusiastically.

"Yes! That's what we need to do. If we are, as a people, to inherit this planet, then let the planet choose us. Or if the sacred volcano wishes instead for us to join our ancestors in Fukuoka, at the great table in the hall of warriors, then so be it! Let us all die with honor, if that shall be our fate!"

Murmurs began arising from the crowd. Shouts rang out too. She was making sense! The crowd started nodding in agreement, with even a few raising their paws to show their support. Felina continued, sensing she was winning them over.

"If we are wrong my friends, and the planet intends to kill us all, then let it be so! Because...." The crowd now began cheering as she raised her voice even higher, "because if we are to possess this planet, if that was ever our right to do so, then I believe this planet shall choose us!"

She then paused to let her audience finish the thought process. They could see it now. The volcano below them, once released, would determine who was to live or die, and who was to possess New Australia once and for all. Only the volcano could determine if they were indeed worthy.

Razor interjected, "Yes Felina! We must let the volcano decide whether we live or whether we join our ancestors at the great table!"

The crowd rumbled with excitement. Felina had convinced them. She called out one last time to them, saying "Thank you Chief Razor, and now those of you who wish to, pack up your belongings and your families! We leave tonight!" In a wave of cheers the entire tribe did just that. Finally, the last of the endangered areas had been evacuated.

By now, Skyles's plan seemed to be coming to fruition. The vent tunnels had been dug, which routed intense heat to one of New Australia's largest subterranean glaciers. Crews worked in the stifling heat to the point of exhaustion, but the result was that in only a few weeks water was trickling, then gushing down into the magma chamber below. The ongoing rush of water was leading to a rise in the magma readings. The steady increase in bubbling indicated to him that things were progressing toward a major eruption. It just needed one last trigger to set the whole thing off.

In the meantime, however, the Naustie Army was taking a terrible beating at the hands of Earth forces. Naustie battle strategy had by now degenerated into retreating and leading pursuing Earth forces down tunnels which had been bored-out underneath. Explosive charges would be placed in a large section of the tunnel floor then detonated when enemy columns passed over. This would take out the lead tank and in the ensuing chaos bands of screaming Nausties would storm the cave-in site to massacre confused troops. Occasionally it worked, and a hundred Earthers would be eliminated. Other times it was a dismal failure, leading to a couple hundred Nausties killed.

The good news was that engineering units attached to the Naustie army were getting smarter about setting directional charges that worked in clearing out hollow sections of rock. This would prove to be crucial, because Skyles had already estimated the necessary number of explosives to create a blast large enough. As he kept telling Solomon, "Remember, Commander. We're not exploding the magma itself, we're blowing up a large section of rock above it just like we are uncorking a bottle of champagne." Meanwhile, as miners tunneled under, then honeycombed the cavern floor with directional charges, the Naustie Army was slowly disintegrating. With the draining off of their best mining engineers, setting ambushes without explosives was gradually becoming suicidal.

At first, Vlad ordered his soldiers to tunnel out the back of existing caves to conceal themselves. In larger caves he'd sometimes hide platoons of Enoshi or elite Templar Knights units as well. Tunnel tanks rarely followed into existing caves because of the belief this was a waste of time and energy. Instead, Earther infantry would burst into caves spraying the interior with EIC's or toss in phosphorous grenades to incinerate anyone still hiding inside. However, once the Nausties had tunneled some ways back inside these caves, this was ineffective. Earthers found that if they didn't invest a platoon or at least a fire team of soldiers to explore the cave for additional "rat holes" as they called them, then in a few hours, a squad or even an entire company of crazed warriors might emerge. That's when things would get ugly, because Nausties were deadly killers.

Because of this tactic, the Earth offensive was slowed to a snail's pace as Naustie death squads wiped out hundreds of Earther troops and disrupted supply lines. It was effective, but it could only work for a while in slowing down the tank columns. Frankly, Vlad was running out of elite fighting units capable of executing these attacks. And besides, once the enemy got wise to the tactic, Earth forces were better prepared for them. At that point, Naustie casualties were no longer acceptable. The losses were too great to keep on fighting this way.

The net result was that it caused a concentration of Earth forces.

To that end, Vlad's tactics were successful because getting the enemy army into a confined area was the ideal scenario. "A decent eruption might just wipe out half their forces in a matter of minutes," predicted Skyles. The images it conjured in Solomon's mind were both thrilling and terrifying. At times, he'd imagine the planet spitting up torrents of molten lava killing thousands of enemy soldiers. Then at night he'd have nightmares of their entire world exploding, devastating all life, killing everyone including his wife and daughter. Felina could see it in her husband, and she worried for him. He wasn't getting much sleep anymore.

"Solomon," she said to him finally, "You need to rest. Come to bed and let me relax you." He could only bow his head in shame. He couldn't bring himself to tell her just how terrified he was deep in his heart. It was all in their hands now: they'd either save New Australia or destroy every living thing. They had no way of knowing exactly which was going to happen. She sensed his thoughts and sought to comfort him. Choosing her words carefully she continued.

"You know of course, don't you? It has only ever been you," she said to him. This intrigued him, and he looked up at her as she spoke. "Don't you see? Only you could have led our people this far. And only you can save them now. All of us who love and respect you, we'll perform our duty. We'll carry out our orders. It's because we believe in you. It's because you have become the great leader you always wanted to be. It's what you longed for all your life, isn't it, to lead your people to freedom?" It certainly was. It had been his lifelong dream. "Now you've become that man you always dreamed of being. And I love you, Solomon," she said. "I love you with all my heart." To this, he sighed deeply and embraced his loving wife. He then wept quietly in her arms for a while.

However, the couple was soon interrupted and this time not by yet another messenger bringing dire news from the front. It was none other than their adopted daughter, who burst into the cave demanding attention. She was five years old now, and when she wanted Daddy's attention, she was certainly going to get it! Solomon adored her and didn't mind the interruption one bit. They had named her Estrella.

Originally, when Feathers brought the beautiful baby girl to Felina begging her to care for it, Felina agreed without hesitation. But when she asked the big man what the baby's name was, he said he hadn't thought of one yet. She asked him what he might name her, and to that he also fumbled for a reply. "Well Señora, I believe I would name her after my mother … Melody Estrella Esperanza Milagros Carolina Macarena." Felina struggled momentarily to repeat the name back to him.

"Melody … wait, what was the rest?" she asked. Feathers chuckled a bit then patiently repeated it. "Yes, Señora. Melody Estrella Esperanza Milagros Carolina Macarena. That was my mother's name." Felina tried several times until she had it memorized, then she finally asked, "So, what did you call your mom?" Feathers' eyes moistened as he began remembering his dear sweet mother. She was long gone by now, as he was already quite old when he was sent to prison.

"Ah, I called her Ma-má!" In the large cave where everyone stood standing, there were about twenty other people from the Michoacano tribe. They all laughed at the tattooed giant's reply. Then Solomon clarified, "No, my friend, my wife means what name did she go by?" Feathers gasped in realization, then smiled broadly.

"Estrella, everyone liked to call her Estrella." With his accent, it sounded like he was saying "Eh-stray-uh," so Felina practiced pronouncing it over and over until she could match his pronunciation. Soon the whole cave was chanting it right along with her in soothing voices while the baby cooed and yawned. Solomon then sent out for a wet nurse to feed the baby, while Feathers smiled down at the child one last time. The child bonded with Felina immediately as she held it in her furry arms.

"Hey, you know what, Señora?" whispered Feathers. "I think I know what you should call her. You should call her bebé Estrella!"

In Spanish that meant "star," and the name stuck. Felina had been the Star Kitten, and now she had a daughter they could call Star Baby.

When Estrella walked into the family cave only to find "Da-da" crying, she immediately began to console him. "Did Dada get an owie?" she asked.

Felina said, "Yes, Daddy has an owie. He needs a kiss." Estrella cooed, then embraced her father's muscular arm, kissing and smooching toward his cheek which he lowered down to her.

"All better now, all better," she then said, clearly believing in her five-year-old mind that she'd miraculously cured her father of all his troubles in one simple gesture of affection. She was quite right of course! The beautiful little girl with pudgy cheeks and jet-black hair, olive skin and dark eyes, was the most wonderful thing in his life, besides his lovely Felina. For just a brief moment, the burden of the world was lifted from his shoulders.

Besides, he could take comfort in knowing that they would be far, far away from the blast when it finally occurred. Using the old dump hauler with a drill attached to the front, the one used as a decoy during the rebellion years before, Solomon assigned a team of Suidonji to drill a new escape tunnel for the refugees. Felina and Estrella would be going with them too. They'd be miles from the blast site when the charges were detonated.

The Naustie Army was in headlong retreat by now, and the Earth Army was only days – at most, a week -- away from closing in on them. That's why the very next day, Solomon was adamant that the refugees, his wife and daughter included, immediately depart down the newly-dug escape tunnel. The sooner they left the better.

Breathing devices were given out so they could endure the march. Acetylene lamps were fixed to headbands, or to the front of vehicles for lighting their path in the darkness. A small escort of troops was assigned to guard them on their journey, and when the throng of raggedy survivors gathered in a large cavern where the last of the Naustie army was camped, it was a tearful farewell to be sure. To many, this seemed like it might very well be the end of New Australia as well.

Thousands of family members hugged, kissed goodbye and made tearful promises to reunite someday with their husbands left behind to make one last stand against the invaders. It just had to be a lie, everyone sensed it, but no one wanted to let on in front of the children. This was going to be the last gasp of the rebellion, and if they lost here, if the volcano eruption didn't work and Earth troopers extinguished the last of Naustie resistance, then the only hope Solomon and everyone else had was that the enemy would turn back toward the surface believing the planet was finally secure.

Meanwhile, the miners were to cause a cave-in, sealing them off permanently from the disaster about to happen behind. Then they were to move in a switchback pattern up to the surface, using existing tunnels occasionally but most of all avoiding detection by Earth forces. If they indeed ever made it to the surface, they had orders to try and hail any Naustie merchant ships patrolling the airspace looking for survivors.

But that didn't seem very likely anymore. By this point, Kscheeech and his fleet were scattered throughout the galaxy, hearing every day about Earther military units driving steadily and meeting dwindling resistance from pirate forces. IPN broadcasts were not government-controlled. If that's what they were having reported to them from Earth commanders, then it must be true. With immense dread, Kscheeech and the other ship captains listened in on the hourly news updates. For days the news had been very bad. Earth troopers wearing helmets with lamps to light their way in the dark were being interviewed by frontline journalists.

"We've cornered the last of the enemy," one said, "probably about twenty thousand of them by our latest estimates, in a defensive position about a mile below us." Later yet another young officer, speaking to an embedded reporter assigned to his unit described it like this: "Our scouts are reporting we have one more cavern to clear and barring any more ambushes; we may be able to eliminate this last defensive position within a week or so. We'll use this cavern here as a staging area."

Little did that officer know, but his brigade was parking its tanks and setting up camp right on top of the very cavern that the Nausties were about to detonate. However, to the crew onboard *The Chengshi*, it seemed like it was all over but the shouting. Maybe a week, and their home planet would be finished. A few more days of reports like this followed while they awaited the news they'd been fearing all along: that Earth forces were victorious, and all resistance had been eliminated.

Yet that news never came. Something else happened instead. Something incredible yet horrifying. It was so extraordinary that for hours news broadcasters were at a loss as to how to describe it. Was it a natural disaster or was it something else? On *The Chengshi*, Kscheeech sat at his command station watching the broadcast, with nearly a hundred crewmen crammed onto the bridge. No one knew what had really happened. The reporter on television was certainly just as baffled.

"Good evening, I'm Glynda Trexel, and this is the IPN News," said the Enoshi journalist. "Breaking news tonight from the renegade planet Rijel 12, as imbedded reporters on the ground with Earth forces have been sending desperate messages from the surface telling us, at least in one communication, '*hell itself has cracked wide open*.'" The pupils in her yellow-green eyes dilated as she spoke.

"Volcanic eruptions from the center of the planet have engulfed thousands of Earth troops, with nearly two thousand already reported dead, and another three thousand missing or unaccounted for at this time." She turned her head to change to a different camera view as a screen behind her began to show live video feed straight from the planet surface. The scene was so awe-inspiring that the whole bridge of *The Chengshi* erupted in gasps and shocked surprise. "Great Goddess of the Sea!" hissed Kscheeech.

Glynda Trexel was now standing in front of the screen. Behind her were live broadcasts of lava erupting from craters all over the surface of Rijel 12. The planet looked like its entire core was vomiting up fiery death from below. Kscheeech muttered to himself, "Poor bastards," as the diabolical scene unfolded.

Glynda continued her broadcast, adding, "The death and destruction have been horrendous, spelling the apparent end of the Earth invasion. Transports and medical evacuation units have been frantically pulling mangled and badly burned bodies from the chaos. New eruptions seem to be occurring almost every hour, pinning down rescue units and thwarting relief efforts. According to sources within the military command structure, currently in orbit around Rijel 12, this is no longer an armed reconnaissance mission. It is now a search for survivors."

CHAPTER 26: THE SEARCH FOR SURVIVORS

Weeks passed, and the nearly fifteen thousand refugees slowly made their way to the surface. They trudged along through miles and miles of tunnels, with teams working ahead of them clearing out passageways to access large caverns long-abandoned during the war. Sometimes they'd break into areas which had yet to have been explored by the invaders. Sometimes they'd find reservoir tanks filled with safe drinking water. Sometimes they'd even find food. But still they marched on, rarely resting for more than a day.

The exploding magma had certainly done its job, blasting out most every tunnel leading into that last big chamber vacated by the Cave Lion tribe. When the floor of that cavern disintegrated in a horrendous blast, fully a thousand enemy troops and fifteen tunnel tanks with their crews were incinerated instantly. The rushing glacier water set off a massive eruption a few hours later, which penetrated through miles of tunnels and elevator shafts, creating a geyser up to the surface and spitting up tons of molten lava. Thousands more Earthers trapped in those tunnels or elevator shafts were either killed or horribly burned.

The explosions compounded themselves, too, because other underground aquifers were subsequently released to cascade into opened volcanic vents, creating even more eruptions. The debacle continued throughout a full day and halfway into the next, as evacuation teams searched in vain for survivors or extracted whatever mangled bodies they could find. Within a week, the first of the Earth transport ships had left for home and within another week, the whole mission was scrubbed. New Australia was saved.

Unfortunately for the refugees, they really didn't know whether it mattered anymore. What if Earth had already won the war? And how would they find out if that's what had happened? On the surface it was chaos, and on the other side of the planet's interior, it was likely nothing but death and destruction. If they only knew about the miraculous victory and the success of Skyles's eruption.

They just kept on tunneling and walking, tunneling some more then walking several miles further. Felina did her best to keep them motivated. They'd rest for part of a day while tunnelers cleared a path for them, then they'd struggle to their feet a few hours later to do it all over again. Progressing slowly, they climbed higher and higher, moving steadily toward the surface, where they would most assuredly face an unknown future.

Three long weeks had passed since their departure from the cavern below. Then one day, scouts came back to report that they'd broken into the service tunnel. "Thank the gods!" exclaimed Felina to the Spleef scouts reporting in. "You mean we finally made it? Thank you!" She then grew stern. "And what about food warehouses? Did you find any? You know we have a lot of hungry folks." The Spleefs informed her that they had found the remnants of a food warehouse, but it had been demolished by Earth missiles. "Can't we catch a break?" Felina exclaimed. Nevertheless, she thanked the loyal scouts and told them to get some rest. They'd need it in the days ahead.

Felina knew, now that they'd found the service tunnel, it was only a matter of locating supplies. She sent out patrols in both directions looking for a storehouse still intact, while the rest of the ragged refugees marched into the partially lit service tunnel to make camp and finally get a much-needed break. Patrols searched far and wide, hoping to hit the jackpot, then within a week or so, they found one that had not been destroyed. This discovery ended up yielding several days' rations for the now starving refugees. However, one thing they never found, even after another full week of scouting, was enemy troops. There were none to be seen. Not anywhere.

They'd traveled for miles through the service tunnel, and one unit even made it all the way back to the remains of the terminal loading bay. The Earthmen were gone. All of them were gone, and the evidence of their hasty exit was apparent.

Hospital pods, modular buildings that had been transported to the surface and connected to form a vast medical complex, stood abandoned near troop transport landing sites and inside some of them were found the telltale remnants of meatball surgery. Human body parts were left behind which had been amputated from injured soldiers. Burn units had been established to quickly treat wounded who'd been carried up to the surface. It was a horrifying sight and the smell of death and burnt flesh still lingered inside the abandoned facility which had beds for nearly a thousand patients, plus doctor's quarters, nurse's stations, bathrooms, showers, and triage centers. Yet it was all vacant.

The miracle had indeed happened. Felina, her eyes wide with excitement and her chest swelling with pride, addressed the refugees that evening with the news. "Earthers are gone!" she exclaimed to the crowd. "The war is over. New Australia is ours!" she then cheered.

Felina and her daughter rejoiced with the others. Her husband and all those gallant heroes below, they'd somehow pulled it off. Naustie refugees celebrated joyously when the news was announced. Everyone heaved a sigh of relief. For all these weeks, they'd been slogging it out day after day not knowing their fate, and for that matter, even now they weren't completely sure. But when word got around about what scouts came back describing, the refugees began to accept that at the very least the most dangerous of their problems was gone. The invaders had given up and gone home. The only remaining task was to try and find the Naustie merchant fleet.

"Any volunteers wishing to participate in a scouting mission are to go with an armed escort up to the surface," Felina announced. Of course, she was the first to volunteer. "The trip will take several days. When we get there, we'll look for friendly ships and them if possible." She then assured them, "Don't worry, the fleet will be there. They promised they'd return for us."

Many were skeptical about going, but Felina didn't hesitate. These were Solomon's orders to Kscheeech and she believed he'd return. She and Estrella quickly joined up with a squad of Spleefs, and also several brave Enoshi for the mission. Many of the refugees were hesitant. What if the spacecraft landing there turned out to be an enemy vessel coming back to pick up more enemy troops? A few of the refugees riding with Felina posed the same question. However, the Spleef scout leading the squad merely wiggled his nose and replied dryly, "Well, if they don't try to kill us, then we'll know they must be Nausties. How about that?"

Felina chuckled. She appreciated the simple logic and it was absolutely the right answer. They'd have to risk it if they were going to be rescued. And yes, they'd have to go up during the day, no matter how hot it was.

Riding in the back of stinking dump haulers once used by Spleefs to haul compost, they took off for the terminal loading bay. They sped along the smoothed-out highway of the service tunnel, dodging debris and destroyed vehicles as they cruised along, slowed only by patches of pitch darkness through which they lit their way using acetylene lamps. Not only that, but occasionally they'd travel through a massive crater created by a missile attack, and this exposed them to the brutal Rijel sun. When they came across these areas, they had to zigzag through rubble-strewn surfaces. This slowed them to a crawl at times, making the journey all the more difficult.

In a few days, they finally reached their objective. That's when they saw the horrible scene everyone had been talking about. The stories about carnage and destruction didn't begin to do it justice. It was even more incredible seeing it in person. It was like a scene from a tortured dream of hell. Everywhere was the smell of death. There were noxious fumes coming from the cooling lava expelled from the bowels of the planet. Bombed-out buildings on the surface were splayed open like giant whale carcasses that had been picked clean by scavengers.

Felina kept her daughter close by her side. The Spleefs warned her there were things a little girl shouldn't see out there. So she had one of the other Enoshi watch Estrella for her while she toured the abandoned enemy campsite with a small band of scouts. She covered herself in a hooded robe made out of a nearby tarpaulin.

After exploring the scene of devastation and death for several hours in the afternoon heat, Felina finally began to succumb to the intense Rijel sun as her feet were beginning to burn on the scorching sand. She had ten Spleefs with her and they were not doing much better, so they decided to bolt for shade where they could regroup and devise a plan for signaling Naustie ships after the sun set.

Suddenly they heard the roar of a space craft entering the planet's atmosphere. It scattered the Spleefs like mice but Felina stood still. She merely pulled her robe tighter, shielded her eyes, and looked up at the sky.

As the craft approached the ruined wreckage which had once been the main terminal, Felina tried to ascertain if it was friend or foe. Could this be the Naustie fleet come back to rescue them? Or was it another enemy craft, returning for survivors? Felina stood and waited. The craft was getting closer and closer to her. If it was the enemy, it would do her no good to run and hide, and wherever she ran to, it might bring missiles down upon her that would kill all her friends and her daughter. So instead she remained still, shading her eyes with her paw.

Within a few minutes the craft was landing. By now, she figured they had to have seen her. She was standing in the middle of what had once been the assembly hall for the Tribal Confederation. The Earthers had demolished an entire corner of it and there were no walls standing within a hundred yards of her. They couldn't miss her. Felina stood bravely and gazed at the large craft as it landed in the desert sand and kicked up a vast cloud of dust. She shielded her face, as the thrusters whined and moaned to an eventual stop. Then there was a long silent pause, as Felina could hear her comrades off in the distance begging and pleading with her.

"Get down Felina! Get down!" they yelled to her. "Please hide! Please! We don't know who they are!" Felina ignored them however. Instead she raised up her paw in a gesture of greeting.

But this friendly gesture was greeted only by a massive *kah-thunk* and a release of air as the cargo bay door of the craft opened and a large loading ramp ever so slowly descended to the ground. Felina tensed with anticipation, but still she did not move. She stood there like a proud oak tree and waited. The billowing dust cloud obscured who was about to exit the craft, but after a few moments Felina could make out a large group of silhouettes through the haze. When the ramp finally rested onto the ground with a metallic clunking sound, the occupants of the craft came walking out. Felina's heart beat in her chest like a kettle drum.

When they got about two hundred yards away, Felina could count about fifty creatures walking toward her. Felina sucked air from her breather unit with anxious anticipation. The creatures coming toward were clearly Zorgs! Could it be the crew of *The Chengshi*? She tried not to get her hopes up.

But then Felina began to make out one little figure in the middle. It was a Zorg with a noticeable paunch around his mid-section, a creature she'd recognize anywhere. It just had to be him. She shed her fears and started walking toward them. She started waving again. They paused. Then she stopped too. Then one of them waved back. They recognized her. Suddenly the whole group started waving; and several of them began running toward her.

It was the crew of the *Chengshi*. And in the middle, waddling toward her as briskly as he could, was Kscheeech himself. As the Zorgs celebrated around her, shaking and squeezing her paws, jumping about in celebration, the admiral came up to her and affectionately threw his scaly arms around her waist. Felina bent over and hugged his huge head. Kscheeech was breathless with excitement.

"Great Goddess of the Sea! Felina? Felina! My dear, am I glad to see you!" he hissed with relief. Felina chuckled and cackled joyfully while the other Zorgs hopped up and down around her. She replied, "We're so glad to see you too, Keech! We're glad to see all of you!" Kscheeech looked up at her with a broad toothy smile that gradually faded into a slightly concerned look.

"Just how many of you made it out?" he asked. Felina lowered her voice and replied, "About fifteen thousand." Everyone in the group heard her. She could hear them murmuring and repeating the number to each other, while she took another long drag of oxygen from her breather unit. Chattering amongst themselves, the mostly Zorg crew passed the word along. Out of nearly one hundred thousand Nausties on the planet before the invasion only a handful had apparently made it out alive. However, Felina was only thinking he meant how many were in her group of refugees. She didn't mean the refugees were the only survivors.

The rest of Felina's scout team along with Estrella had by now come out to join Felina and their rescuers. They joyfully scurried inside the ship to get out of the withering heat and get some water to drink. Kscheeech also ordered a meal to be prepared for them. He and Felina sat together and talked privately about what had happened the past few months, while Estrella played with the crew.

"Actually, we returned to New Australia within a week or so of hearing that the commanding general had scrubbed the mission and Earth forces were heading home," explained Kscheeech. "Every afternoon since, we've been landing on the surface near the Terminal Loading Bay waiting for survivors. I'd send surface rovers out to scour the area including over by the new solar domed farm." This had gone on for many days while they waited for signs of life, he went on to say. Each evening they'd explore the old Terminal and the wreckage of the Loading Bay as well. Then, when the area got too dark and too cold to function effectively, they'd return to their ship and continue orbiting the planet.

"I've got to tell you, many among the crew urged me to abandon the task when they saw the level of destruction everywhere. I considered heeding their suggestions at times, especially when it had been weeks since the Earthers abandoned their base and none of you appeared. But Solomon gave me orders to come back looking so that's what we did, night after night."

Kscheeech went on to tell Felina what he thought she didn't already know. He told her about the final battle, the massive explosion reported in the news, the subsequent eruption, and finally the horrific fireballs exploding up the shafts and tunnels of New Australia which wiped out over half the enemy army. It was a horrifying scene on the news and his crew had watched it all unfold onscreen.

"It seemed to members of the press like we perhaps decided to blow ourselves up right along with our enemies using mining charges. This triggered a volcanic eruption, their experts were telling us. They thought it must have been accidental," said Kscheeech, "but they weren't sure. Just what did happen?"

That's when Felina realized that Kscheeech, the media, and best of all the Earther commanders had it all wrong. The whole galaxy must have thought… oh my God, could it be? Felina smiled broadly then she laughed. She laughed long and hard too, until she finally had to cover her mouth with her paw. This completely unnerved Kscheeech.

"Felina, what is it? What's so funny?" asked Kscheeech with a confused smile. Felina had suddenly realized that the press had made the mistaken assumption that the entire planet's population, all the Naustie army and most of the Earth Army right along with it, had perished.

"By the gods, Kscheeech! Don't you realize what this means? The galaxy thinks we're all dead!" she said, still snorting and cackling. "If they think we're dead then... well... do you see what this means for us? They're not coming back, Kscheeech! Ever!"

Kscheeech thought about it for a moment. She was right. The Earth army had left. And they thought the planet was uninhabitable now. Mining companies would never try and come back to mine here. Kscheeech could picture the political fallout back on Earth from suffering a military disaster at the hands of barbaric pirates. It would mean an overwhelming backlash toward the same hawkish conservatives who'd urged this doomed mission. The public would turn against them. No, the Earthers would not be back. Not ever.

He hissed with delight at the thought of this for a few brief moments, nodding and chuckling right along with Felina. Then an even darker thought slowly came over him. True, the Earthers were never coming back, but was Felina implying they were going to stay? So far, Kscheeech only knew of the fifteen thousand survivors and no one else. It appeared that the Naustie army had perished in the eruption. He understood what Felina was saying. But what would it matter if everyone in the galaxy thought every soul on the planet was killed? With hardly any people left, what was the use? How could they expect to rebuild the planet with only this handful of refugees and less than two thousand crewmen from the whole Naustie merchant fleet combined?

With a dismissive grin he said, "Well, that's all well and good, my dear. But we need to get the rest of the fleet down here to evacuate what's left of us." He bowed his head and blinked his eyes respectfully as he continued. "And we must honor the dead now that our brave warriors have sacrificed their lives so that we might live on." That's where Felina corrected him.

"Oh no, Kscheeech, they're not dead old friend. They're still down there. The army is still down there in the mines. We just have to go back in and find them." Kscheeech looked at her long and hard like she was insane. As Estrella came over to jump up into her lap, Felina explained to Kscheeech what happened.

"The detonation of explosions was designed to occur so that it blew the Earthers up the mine shafts and tunnels from where they came. Our army was well protected at least a mile away from the magma chamber. Walled off behind cave-ins so that the eruption would not harm them. In fact, the army is likely trying to tunnel out right now as we speak."

Kscheeech looked at her sadly. She couldn't believe what she'd just said. Or if she did, she must not understand physics. Nothing could have survived devastation like this. He thought long and hard about explaining to her just how unlikely a rescue could be, but he couldn't bring himself to do it.

"Well, if you think they're down there, then we'd better go and find them," he said. He couldn't imagine being able to tunnel down through simmering lava, just to find what was going to be nothing more than twenty thousand dead bodies. Even if Felina was right and they'd survived the blast, they couldn't have endured the noxious gases emitted from the volcano. Even if they survived the gases, they'd have run out of air by now and suffocated. If they had breather units they could live for a while, sure. However, how would they have enough food to eat and how would they ration it? They'd have no way of knowing if the refugees ever made it to the surface. What's more they didn't even know that the Earther army had withdrawn.

Above everything else, even if Kscheeech, the refugees, and the crews from all the Naustie fleet started digging and reopening tunnels immediately, it could be up to another month before they reached any Naustie warriors. Surely, they'd all be dead by then.

However, Kscheeech had underestimated Felina and the refugees. They had survived together in the bloody war with Earth. So much death around them every day, yet they'd lived through it together and grown far stronger than Kscheeech could have imagined.

It only took five more days for the rest of the refugees to arrive at the wreckage of the Terminal Loading Bay. When they saw what had happened to their planet, many were heartbroken. Kscheeech saw their reactions and initially prepared his crew to take on passengers for evacuation, as was the original plan. However, many more were downright furious. No way in hell were they going to give up; exhausted or not, the Nausties were going to stay. No, there'd be no evacuation to Frabrak 3 for a new life. Nor was anyone considering going back home to their original planets. This was their home.

Kscheeech realized it was no use suggesting that they abandon Rijel 12. Instead he ordered his crew to bring out food and fresh water. Then he ordered his own officers to help clean out the hospital facilities and barracks left behind by the enemy. "These can be used for temporary housing," he said. His officers rolled their eyes and smirked then flew into action before Kscheeech could say another word about it.

These buildings left behind by the invaders were air-conditioned and powered by solar energy panels, so they could run indefinitely on the planet surface. Kscheeech knew living arrangements would be quite crowded, but it was still a vast improvement over living in the dark tunnels below the surface the last few weeks. The Earthers had even left behind fresh water tanks to provide facilities with running water. Finally, Kscheeech ordered his communications officer to send a short-range message to the remaining fleet up in orbit around New Australia. It simply said, "Evacuation cancelled. Clear to land. We're staying."

The decision was made. They would set tunneling teams to work burrowing down into the bowels of New Australia. They'd start immediately, using any equipment they could find. Kscheeech didn't argue any further about the futility of this. Frankly, they were all so determined! Besides, even if they found one family member alive, they'd have considered it a moral victory. Felina stood in the middle of a crowd that first day work began and addressed the brave tunnelers.

"Citizens of New Australia, we know what's at stake here. We have soldiers, fathers, brothers, and friends down there, and they need our help. It is up to us. Let's make them proud!" And to that, the assembled crowd cheered with delight.

Everyone found a way to pitch in. Farmers joined support teams which kept the tunnelers fed and hydrated. Zorg crewmembers from the ships joined in as well, aiding Spleef detection teams as they opened up pockets of caves and caverns searching for survivors. Enoshi joined teams of rock handlers who would ferry out small stones whenever Spleefs smelled a body. There were cave-ins everywhere. Areas were unrecognizable at times, even to those who were from those regions. Sometimes it looked like they were boring into hell itself to try and rescue their loved ones. Body after body would be recovered. Usually it would be an Earther soldier which would promptly be discarded. Often it was just parts of bodies. But occasionally a Naustie body would be found and everyone would fall silent out of respect.

It was grueling work, and crews worked night and day, rotating in as often as possible. But it was so exhausting – and demoralizing. So many bodies. So much death. They'd do whatever it took. They'd do it to find their loved ones. They'd do it for Felina, who was right there alongside them working every day in the dust until her fur was so filthy she was unrecognizable. But most of all, they'd do it for themselves and their stubborn pride.

Besides, even if they did get tired and discouraged, even if they worked all day just to find nothing more than a pile of dead Earther bodies, they'd soldier on anyway. It was the Naustie way.

Even the thought that they might never find the army or Solomon and his staff, even the thought that they might find them dead, they wouldn't stop. They believed they were alive. Hope was all they had, and as long as there were more tunnels and caverns to search, they kept on believing. Unfortunately, the searches typically yielded nothing. Occasionally there'd be a cavern they could open up, hoping in vain that the Naustie army had tunneled up this far. But alas, they'd find no one alive. No matter, though. They just went right back to work and kept tunneling deeper into the mine network, through cave-in after cave-in.

Then one day it happened. Tunneling units were interrupted from their drilling by Spleefs who ran up to their vehicles waving madly. They smelled something. They turned off their vehicles and waited for several minutes while detection units ambled over rocks and debris to sniff the rubble. They listened too. Humans working in the unit also came forward to listen through the pile of rocks to hear any noises coming from the other side. That's when a human miner yelled out, "Oh my Gods! Here!!!" A crowd descended upon the area, and with wildly waving hands and arms, the woman hissed at them to keep quiet. A faint scratching sound was heard. It was coming from the other side!

Within a few hours, Zorg crewmen, Enoshi, and humans working with bare hands and claws, carefully dug and ferried away stone after stone, then bucket after bucket of dirt, until they punched a hole through the top of a thirty-foot-high cave-in. Miraculously all their toil had finally paid off. On the other side were thousands of emaciated and dehydrated warriors. The Naustie army had finally been found!

After this big success, word spread all the way back to headquarters inside *The Chengshi*. Survivors were being brought to the surface! The celebration began in earnest. Cheers and screams. Crying and singing. Kscheeech himself flung his breather unit with excitement and roared with pride like some prehistoric dinosaur. They'd actually done it! They'd found the lost troops. On *The Chengshi*, *Warthog*, and other ships now landed on the surface, hospitals were created inside loading bays, and canopies were constructed to protect the wounded troops as they were brought up from below.

A massive elevator system had by now been constructed using wenches and pulleys which lifted platforms full of warriors to the surface, then lowered fresh supplies and reinforcements for teams below. It was a long trek back up to the surface, but the thrill of rescuing someone's husband or father was motivation enough to keep thousands of hard-working volunteers ready and willing to get the job done.

And there was even more good news. There were still more Nausties further down below in the mines. Estrella, with her mother in tow, darted through the crowds of grateful warriors awaiting evacuation from the caved-in tunnel. The sweet little girl asked warrior after warrior, "Have you seen Dada? Did you see him?" And warrior after warrior would gently assure her, "Yes. Your father is back there," then gesture for her to look further down the tunnel. Felina would of course follow up with each and clarify, "Just how much further down, brother?"

Felina found out that Solomon and his team had joined another small unit of troops and made their way through an access tunnel to detonate the charges. They'd planned on fleeing to a safe place before the detonation. Felina came upon a big Enoshi who was terribly wounded but alert.

"You should be proud," the field commander stated solemnly to Felina, "it was an honorable mission." He was from the Cave Lions who remembered her vividly. He spoke in a low voice, right up next to her face, and safely out of earshot from Estrella, who was carrying around a canteen half full of water and greeting soldiers. Felina's heart sank. His words made it sound like it might have been a suicide mission. However, one of the warrior's badly injured Human comrades nearby quickly interjected with more useful information.

"The detonation did not set off the eruption immediately. He had time to get out." Other warriors lying on the ground nearby agreed with him. They confirmed that the eruption within the magma chamber developed some time after the blast and it did not explode violently until much later.

"How much later? How long do you think they might have had?" she asked the Human, who was gashed and scarred from God knows how many battles but also burned horribly along his arms and both of his legs. She doubted he'd live very long with injuries like that, not unless he got to a surgeon immediately. The man rolled his eyes and gasped in reaction to some shooting pain that was sending his body into waves of agony.

"Plenty. He had a detonation team with him which set timers on the charges. Plus, they had their escape route all planned out. Even had that Slart named Skyles with him who knows so damn much about volcanoes."

The injured man suddenly winced again with pain. His comrade next to him gently offered him Estrella's canteen, but he waved him off. The brave fellow knew there was no use wasting water, he knew he was dying anyway. Felina didn't need to trouble the poor man any further. She bent down, kissed his forehead and placed her paw on his shoulder. Then she stroked his cheek and purred softly. The man faded into unconsciousness.

Felina knew in her heart Solomon would plan everything down to the finest detail. His placement of the explosives was designed to destroy only the cavern floor. He and Skyles must have set the charges to explode within twenty or thirty minutes. This would have enabled them to get at least several miles away if they were using a mine vehicle, possibly more. And if the eruption had not occurred until several hours later then Solomon and his staff could have been walled off safely long before it went off. Besides, knowing Slarts, they must have provisioned their protective hiding place quite well to try and live through the debacle for as long as the eruptions lasted.

As the Human warrior breathed his last breath and his fellow soldiers looked on sadly, Felina stood up and thanked them for their information, wiping tears from her eyes with the back of her paw. Then she turned to her daughter with a motherly smile. She'd found out all she needed to know.

For the next several days, Felina and a team of Suidonji tunnelers with Spleef detection units traveled deeper and deeper into the devastated mine. More troops were found as they descended, and steaming lava flows had to be avoided constantly. Eventually, hundreds more warriors were discovered, passed out exhausted from their breathers running out of water to operate or nursing battle wounds. Vlad the Impaler was found too. But he was in woefully bad shape and had to be evacuated immediately. His troops insisted that he go first, even those who were more seriously injured. He'd led them to victory, and best of all he'd kept many of them alive to see this day. To these guardians of the planet's defense Vlad was truly their hero. Still the search for Solomon continued.

Another grueling week passed and the chances of finding Solomon's team alive were getting slimmer and slimmer. A question was raised: why would they have stayed put in the first place? Solomon wouldn't have waited for a rescue effort, would he? Then again, he would never have abandoned his team either. Solomon would have tried to escape and take his team with him. But which direction would they go? How would they get out? Once that question was answered, the rest was beginning to become clear. It was soon agreed: Solomon and his team would have tried exiting the mine the same way the refugees went. And they likely traveled that direction for as far as they possibly could before their water and food would have run out.

With the rest of the surviving Naustie army rescued or accounted for, Felina turned the team's attention to finding the route which her fellow refugees had used to escape the planet. It took little time to retrace it. For another agonizingly long day they travelled, knowing in their hearts this must be the way Solomon and his team had gone. Yet they dreaded what they might find. It had taken so long.

And then, after several frustrating hours, they found them. Bodies slumped over rocks. Bodies lying face-down on the floor of the cave. Bodies seated with their backs against the wall. There were Slarts among them and some had clearly been dead for days, including the great Architeuthis. He'd passed out and never reawakened. A Human was found, the former Chinese mobster Bui Hoang Oh who worked on Solomon's team. Spleefs went to work on him immediately trying to resuscitate him. Then they found the body of Skyles. He'd collapsed when he'd run out of oxygen, it looked like. His and everyone's water tanks were dry, and their breather units had very little moisture left in them. It looked like they'd all had one last meal together then camped in this spot while they drifted off to sleep and slowly suffocated.

The Slarts died off first, then when Bui Hoang also passed out, someone from the group tried to drive out on his own. Spleefs in Felina's unit noticed the tracks, and everyone not tending to the few survivors hopped into one of the dump haulers and began speeding down the tunnel. "It's him. It's got to be Solomon!" she cried as she and Estrella got in, and sure enough, in another couple hours they found him, unconscious in the driver's seat, slumped over the wheel, head resting on his arms. Nevertheless, he was alive.

Springing into action, Felina and the rest of the team pulled Solomon's large body out of his drill hauler and laid him on the tunnel floor. Felina stood by frozen in terror while Spleefs went to work on him. She wanted to cry out, wanted to weep, but she didn't want to startle her child. She didn't know how to pray like Solomon often did, so she just muttered to herself what she thought Solomon would say:

"God, please give me back my husband," she said. "Please him see his daughter again." Amazingly, with all her talents and skills at sensing and feeling and communicating with other intelligent creatures, this was all she could think of to say. But it was enough. Estrella came running up to her and embraced her legs, saying "Dada?" You find Dada!" Before Felina could answer, the little girl looked over to see her father lying on the tunnel floor being administered oxygen from a spare breather. A cloth soaked with water was being applied to his dried out and cracked lips. Her father's body was now grayish white from tunneling through the repeated cave-ins and from all the tremors which tumbled dirt and debris onto his tunnel vehicle.

Estrella dropped to her knees and knelt right beside him, as Spleefs worked on reviving him. Suddenly, he coughed. Felina let out a gasp of excitement. Estrella was tickled with delight. "Dada! You awake! You okay?" Slowly the tough old former warlord began to gain consciousness. His thoughts went from embracing death to suddenly realizing that the lamps flashing in his face from workers all around him meant that he'd been rescued. It felt like he was in a dream where he was hearing his lovely daughter's voice. But the sensations he felt in his body: thirst, pain, and the burning in his lungs, could only mean one thing. He was alive, and this was his daughter Estrella, now patting his chest gently and caressing his cheek.

Solomon coughed one more time, nearly hacking up a lung, before lying back down on a rolled-up shirt that had been placed to make a pillow for him. His eyes slowly adjusted to the light around him, and suddenly there, with his beautiful wife's silhouette looming in the background, he saw his baby girl. He smiled feebly and gazed upon her adorable face.

She'd never doubted they'd find him of course. Never for a moment. And now she was here with him. He was going to be okay. He'd live to watch her grow up someday. Solomon's eyes danced with delight. He could hear Felina sobbing with joy. She knelt down on the other side of him and the family embraced once again, just like they'd done so many times before.

With a raspy voice, Solomon uttered feebly, "You found me, Estrella. Good girl." He coughed again, this time sounding like he was finally hydrating. "Daddy is so proud of you," he added, still coughing and choking. When he recovered himself more, he forced out the words, "Perhaps we should start calling you... Scout."

Thank you for reading Rijel 12: The Rise of New Australia. We hope you enjoyed it. If you did, please leave a review on Amazon. It only takes a minute and makes a huge difference. We really appreciate it! King is working hard on the next book in the series. Want to know when it's ready? Do you like free stuff, early access to new releases, deals, discounts, exclusives, and giveaways? Join our awesome mailing list today!

https://www.chandrapress.com/newsletter

— *The Chandra Press Team*

chandra

www.ingramcontent.com/pod-product-compliance
Lightning Source LLC
Chambersburg PA
CBHW031657170626
46808CB00005B/1499